IMMORTAL

Finn knew he shouldn't, but the pull was as strong as that of the moon on the earth's tides. Suddenly he was desperate for her warmth. Literally and figuratively.

Just one kiss, he told himself as he leaned toward her. To satisfy his curiosity.

As his lips met hers, she sighed, her breath mingling with his. Her lips were soft and pliable, the scent of her perfume utterly intoxicating.

Fin couldn't stop at one. His first kiss tested the waters. On the second, he waded in. She tasted as good as she smelled and his fingertips found her slender neck as he deepened the kiss.

This time she moaned, first rising on her knees on the bench, then climbing into his lap. She wrapped her arms around his neck and curled her body around his. He kissed the side of her mouth, trying to catch his breath. His lips, of their own accord, slid downward, over her jawline to the slender length of her neck . . .

Books by V. K. Forrest

ETERNAL

UNDYING

IMMORTAL

RAVENOUS

Published by Kensington Publishing Corporation

IMMORTAL

V. K. FORREST

ZEBRA BOOKS
KENSINGTON PUBLISHING CORP.
http://www.kensingtonbooks.com

ZEBRA BOOKS are published by

Kensington Publishing Corp.
119 West 40th Street
New York, NY 10018

All Kensington titles, imprints, and distributed lines are available at special quantity discounts for bulk purchases for sales promotion, premiums, fund-raising, educational, or institutional use.

Special book excerpts or customized printings can also be created to fit specific needs. For details, write or phone the office of the Kensington Special Sales Manager: Attn.: Special Sales Department. Kensington Publishing Corp., 119 West 40th Street, New York, NY 10018. Phone: 1-800-221-2647.

Zebra and the Z logo Reg. U.S. Pat. & TM Off.

ISBN-13: 978-0-8217-8101-2
ISBN-10: 0-8217-8101-4

First Kensington Books Trade Paperback Printing: December 2009
First Zebra Books Mass-Market Paperback Printing: September 2011

10 9 8 7 6 5 4 3 2 1

Printed in the United States of America

Chapter 1

"How was Florence?" Fia stood directly in front of Fin, pushed his hands aside, and grasped his thin, navy blue tie. "Let me do this before you hurt yourself."

"Florence was . . ." He shrugged, letting his hands fall obediently to his sides. He was roughly sixteen hundred years old and still taking orders from his big sister. "It was Italy: motorbikes, nice leather, sexy women, superb pistachio gelato." He had to speak loud enough to be heard over the sound of the *SpongeBob SquarePants* cartoon blasting from the living room. The tiny cottage he and his brother had rented for the summer was already feeling too small.

"Much trouble?" She looked into the green eyes that mirrored her own as her fingers deftly manipulated the fabric.

Fin exhaled, surprised he was nervous about his first day on the job. Especially since he didn't even want the damned job. "Assignment went fine. We're tracking this guy who belongs to an organization here in the

U.S. called *The Brotherhood*. It's like a serial killer club." He laughed but without humor. "Bunch of freaks."

"And we're not?" she teased.

He grimaced. "Guy was on *vacation*. I saw him stalk three different middle-aged women in four days, just from my chair at a café on the palazzo."

Fia looked down at her handiwork as she slid the knot snugly beneath his light blue collar. "I have no doubt in your abilities to fact-find. You're the best. I'm talking about the visions."

Fin pushed her hands away, suddenly having had enough of his sister's fussing. "They're bad." He touched the knot of the tie and drew his hand downward over the fabric. The memories were still so fresh in his mind, he didn't have to close his eyes to see the blood slick on the stone tiles of the town square. "You sure it's straight?"

"You look great." She stepped back and smiled. Then her gaze flickered to his again. "You should see Dr Kettleman about the visions."

"A shrink? I don't think so." He picked the hairbrush up off the sink and drew it through his still-damp dark hair. "I'll be fine."

She stepped back, giving him room. "But you said they were starting to affect your work."

He tried not to think about the decapitated heads rolling through the rivers of blood. "They're only bad when I dematerialize."

She crossed her arms over her chest, her facial expression one of annoyance, impatience, and worry all rolled into one big-sister grimace. "And that's not affecting your work? Every time you dematerialize you fall into some kind of karmic bloodbath and you're saying that's good for *business?*"

"They'll subside. They always do. They're always worse just before and after I make a trip to Italy. You know that." The visions had plagued him intermittently since the incident in the sixteenth century, but they seemed more vivid this trip. More real. He didn't know why.

He glanced in the mirror over the sink in the tiny bathroom. He looked too young to be a cop. His youthful appearance was an advantage when traveling abroad for the sept. It was easy to make people believe he was a college student, but he had warned the chief of police that this was a bad idea. Fin was going to take a load of crap on the boardwalk. He just knew it. "I have to go. Thanks for stopping by." He stepped around her into the hall and had to squeeze between the wall and a stack of cardboard boxes to reach the living room. "You going to do something about the rest of the boxes?" he shouted to Regan, who lay stretched out on the plaid couch they'd picked up at Goodwill.

Remote in hand, his identical twin stared at the TV atop a cardboard box marked *sheets & blankets* in black Sharpie. On the screen, SpongeBob was flipping Krabby Patties as he argued with his pet snail. Loudly.

"Regan!" Fin barked.

Remaining prone, Regan glanced at Fin. He looked him up and down. "Nice outfit."

Ignoring his brother's jibe, Fin stepped in front of the TV, shut it off, and turned around.

"Hey!" Regan clicked the remote control in his hand, but Fin was blocking the transmission to the TV. It didn't come on. "I haven't seen this episode."

"I asked if you were going to get those boxes unpacked and out of the hall, but I guess the TV was too loud for you to hear me."

"I'll take care of it. Now, can you move? Patrick's having a crisis."

"Patrick?"

"SpongeBob's best friend," Regan explained.

"And a job? How's looking for a job going?"

"Jezus," Regan groaned, sitting up. Barefoot, he wore boxers and a T-shirt. It was three o'clock in the afternoon. "I'm still in a delicate state here. Fee, help me out." He gestured to their sister with the remote. "I'm just out of rehab. Can you explain to my brother how difficult the transition back into the world can be after ninety days of detox?"

"Two hundred and thirty, give or take," she said dryly. "If you count the other time and a half you were there in the last year." She walked toward the front door. "Fin, you want a lift to the station?"

Fin stood in front of his siblings in the uncomfortable uniform, wishing he was anywhere but here. At this moment, even the palazzo in Florence, with its rolling, decapitated heads of children, seemed a better alternative. "I'm only doing this out of duty to the sept." He glared at Regan. "And to my family. I'm doing it because I was asked, not because I want to."

"Maybe you'll get some kind of award at the end of the summer from the Council. You know, for finding lost dogs and toting beach bags to cars for tourists." Regan got up off the couch, tossing the remote on the indentation in a cushion. "You going to the grocery store? There's nothing good to eat around here." He headed for the kitchen.

Fia held open the front door. "Come on, Fin. You'll be late."

Reluctantly, he followed her onto the porch.

"You know, this is a good thing you're doing here," she told him.

"Babysitting my brother for the summer when I should be on assignment making the world a safer place?"

"Helping Uncle Sean fill the summer vacancy on the force, and keeping an eye on Regan. I really do think he's going to stay clean this time. He just needs some family support."

Fin followed her down the porch steps. "You could take a leave of absence from the Bureau and keep an eye on him." He halted on the sidewalk and pointed to the shiny shield on his uniform. "In fact, you could have *this* badge. You know I'm not cop material, Fee. But *you* are."

She reached out and straightened his tie one last time. "Sorry. The family took a vote. You won fair and square. You were appointed Regan's keeper for the summer."

"And where was I during this vote?"

She walked toward her car, parked on the street. "Um . . . Brussels, I think." She smiled, giving a smart-alecky salute. "Have a good first day at work."

"You know, I haven't been able to stand you since you and Arlan hooked up," he called after her as she climbed into her car. "You're way too damned happy!"

Fin's radio crackled in his ear and he groaned. Four hours on the job and he had walked at least ten miles.

He had carried two beach umbrellas to a car, pushed a wheelchair and its octogenarian occupant in a red bikini out of the sand, chased down a runaway shih tzu on a pink leash, and shown a teenager how to shut off the car alarm in her new Mustang. Twice. That was the sum total of his police work. No kidnappings. No assaults. No armed robberies. The only citizen complaint he had fielded concerned the portion of fries a retired woman on a fixed income got for her four dollars and seventy-five cents these days.

"BP-5," the static voice popped in Fin's ear. "Come in."

He tapped the mic on his shoulder. "BP-5. Go ahead." Why he was beach patrol five, he didn't know. As of right now, he was the *only* Clare Point beach patrol officer. Didn't he at least get to be #1? And he was barely a policeman; he didn't even carry a gun, just a billy club, a small can of Mace, and a bad temper that flared more often than he cared to admit.

"BP-5, report of a possible F-5 in progress First Ocean Block. Hilly's Five-and-Dime."

"Proceeding to Hilly's Five-and-Dime," Fin said into the radio.

"You're supposed to say *copy that*," the dispatcher corrected.

"Sorry, Mrs. McGill. I told you I wasn't good at this," Fin explained into the radio as he turned south. The boardwalk that ran along the Delaware shore was only three blocks long, so no matter where he was, everything was close. "And I don't intend to get good at it," he added testily.

"Copy that, BP-5. We really appreciate your help," the sixty-year-old woman said. "Stop by tomorrow for homemade snickerdoodles before you head out on patrol."

Fin couldn't resist a grin. "Copy *that*. BP-5 out." Careful not to draw any attention to himself, he wove his way around families with strollers, bare-backed teenaged boys carrying skateboards on their shoulders, and couples walking hand in hand. He walked fast, and with purpose, but doubted it would occur to anyone he passed that his destination was a possible robbery in progress. It was a nice evening on the boardwalk and locals as well as visitors were out enjoying it; the sky was clear, a cool breeze coming off the water. Despite the humidity, the temperature hung at a refreshing eighty-one degrees, according to the giant red thermometer at the Italian ice stand.

As Fin approached the five-and-dime owned by Mr. and Mrs. Hill, he noted no unusual activity under the blue and white awning that ran the length of the old brick building. Patrons were entering and exiting through the glass doors, a wind chime jingling over their heads. There was chatter and laughter. If there was a robbery taking place inside the store, it was an unobtrusive one.

Fin stepped inside the door and a blast of cold air from an air-conditioning vent decorated with red, white, and blue streamers hit him in the face. The chimes overhead signaled his arrival. Inside the doorway he hesitated, making a careful observation of the store. Nothing appeared or sounded out of place. Brightly colored beach chairs, sand pails, and rafts hung from the ceiling and there were long rows of shelving displaying various sundries of the summer beach trade. In business since 1910, the old building smelled of suntan lotion, mildew, and a piece of Americana that was fading fast.

"'Bout time you got here," Mrs. Hill called from behind the counter. She was ringing up two sand pails, a plastic shovel, and a romance novel for a customer whose neon sunburn clashed with her bright orange dress. "Guess we'd be dead if they had handguns. You know, handguns ought to be outlawed. That'll be twelve forty, ma'am." She began to drop the items into a plastic bag.

"I came as soon as I got the call, Mrs. Hill," he said respectfully, not bothering to point out that she could not die from a gunshot wound. Or any wound, for that matter. His gaze drifting, Fin took note of teenagers, two boys and two girls, standing at the end of the counter. Mr. Hill appeared to be detaining them. All the kids were locals. All men and women Fin and Mr. and Mrs. Hill had known since the fifth century. The bandits?

The teens didn't look much like bandits. Or vampires, for that matter. The girls were his niece Kaleigh, the resident would-be wisewoman, and her best friend Katy. The young men the girls were dating, Rob Hill and Pete Cahall, stood beside them. Rob stared at his big feet. Pete seemed to be scrutinizing a Scooby-Doo raft hanging overhead.

Fin approached the huddle, thinking to himself that if other small American towns had only these kinds of criminals, the world would certainly be a safer place. "What seems to be the problem, Hilly?" Everyone called Mr. Hill "Hilly" though he didn't know why. They had all once been Kahills but after their arrival in the New World from Ireland in the seventeenth century, many had taken on new surnames so as to not draw suspicion from humans. Fin found it amusing that most families had not strayed far from the sept's original name.

Kaleigh, in red pigtails and a teeny tiny tank top, crossed her arms over her chest and presented a bored teenager's posture. *The guilty party for sure.* Fin adored Kaleigh, but the girl was a pain in the ass every time she became a teenager again.

Before Mr. Hill could speak, Mrs. Hill came from behind the counter. "Have a good day. Come again!" she called after the customer in the orange dress. "What's the problem? I'll tell you what the problem is." She turned to Fin, inflating and deflating her cheeks like a puffer fish Fin had seen at the Baltimore Aquarium. "These kids are thieves and they should be arrested!"

"I told you we didn't *steal* anything," Kaleigh protested emphatically.

Fin just happened to catch a glimpse of a smirk on Pete's face. Oh, yeah. Something was going on.

"Little liars. Lying ought to be outlawed. Handguns and liars," Mrs. Hill proclaimed.

Fin spread his legs slightly, taking an authoritative stance to balance out Kaleigh's surly one. "Could you tell me what happened, Hilly? And you keep quiet, Kaleigh," he warned.

The man with a stubby crown of white hair barely got his mouth open before his wife cut in. "I'll tell you what happened! Those kids stole a pack of bubble gum. Pink Double Bubble. The king-sized pack. Seventy-nine cents," she declared righteously. "They owe me seventy-nine cents and they ought to go to jail. The girl for stealing it. The others for not turning her in." She pointed an accusing finger with an artificial nail on it like a talon.

Fin shifted his gaze to his niece, deciding that there wasn't a chance in hell Mrs. Hill was going to let Hilly speak in her presence. She hadn't in at least a century. "Kaleigh?"

"We didn't steal the stupid gum." She held both hands up, palms out.

"Liar! The gum was there on the counter when I looked down at the register to make change for your drinks. Then the gum was gone."

"You can look if you want." Kaleigh shrugged her slender, suntanned shoulders. "Rob, show Uncle Fin, I'm sorry, *Officer Kahill,* the bag."

Rob, a pleasant, shy young man, reluctantly stepped forward and opened the white plastic bag. Fin peered into it: two cans of Coke, a Mountain Dew, and a water.

"Well, of course they wouldn't put it in the bag!" Mrs. Hill's cheeks began to puff again. "Check their persons. I'm pressing charges, I swear I am. Teenagers shouldn't be allowed inside stores. It should be against the law! No one under eighteen inside stores."

"Want to pat me down, Uncle Fin?" Kaleigh turned around and placed her hands on the counter, spreading her feet.

Pete ran over to the counter and copied her pose. "You should pat me down too, Officer Kahill," he said, excitement in his voice. "Just like on *Cops.*"

Katy began to hum the theme song from the TV show. "Bad boys, bad boys, whatcha gonna do?" the teen sang dramatically under her breath. "Whatcha gonna do when they come for you?"

Fin shot Katy a look that silenced her and then turned back to Kaleigh, obviously the ringleader. She always was. He waited.

"You can search us all if you want. Maybe you

should search everyone in the store." Kaleigh glanced over her shoulder at a young Asian man with a baby in a backpack. He pretended to read a suntan lotion bottle.

The young father glanced at the teens spread-eagled at the counter and then Fin in his uniform, and made a hasty dash for the door, leaving the lotion behind.

"Enough with the drama, Kaleigh," Fin snapped. He'd had just about enough of the kids and this job. He was disappointed in his niece. It was hard to believe that this smug young woman had stood up in front of the entire General Council the previous week and made several well-thought-out suggestions on how the sept could aid recently reborn members adjust to American culture. One day she was an integral part of the governing body of the sept, the next day a would-be hooligan.

Fin glanced at his wrist watch. He was off at eleven. He wondered if he could make it another two and a half hours. "Get over here, Kaleigh," he ordered, indicating the spot beside him.

Recognizing that he meant business, she hurried over.

Fin held out his hand for the gum.

"I don't have it. We didn't steal it," Kaleigh insisted.

Fin looked at her sternly.

She exhaled. "Fine. We were just having a little fun. It's there." She pointed toward the ceiling.

Fin squinted. "Where?"

"On the green raft," she said, as if he was an idiot.

His gaze settled on a green and white striped raft just to the left of the cash register and hanging a good eight feet over it.

Mr. and Mrs. Hill stared at the pink pack of gum

resting on the edge of the raft. "Liars!" she accused. "I only looked away for a second."

Fin lowered his gaze until he met Kaleigh's. He waited again.

After a moment Kaleigh exhaled and reached up and tweaked her own nose.

She was trying to tell Fin something, but he had no idea what. "Kaleigh . . ."

"You know," she said meaningfully. This time she wiggled her nose without the aid of her fingers. "Like on *Bewitched*."

"We've been watching the reruns on Nick at Nite," Katy explained to the boys. "I like the first Darrin better, but Kaleigh thinks the second one is way hotter."

Fin looked at Katy and then back at Kaleigh. Then, what the teen was talking about finally dawned on him. The 1960s TV sitcom *Bewitched*. In the show, Samantha was a witch and wielded her magic with a twitch of her nose. "You're not supposed to be using powers in public and you know it," he chastised, lowering his voice.

A human male in swim trunks, rubber flip-flops, and white cream smeared on his nose walked up to the cash register. Everyone turned to look at him, fearing he had overheard them, but he was preoccupied, busy stacking cans of five-for-five-dollars potato chips on the counter. Mrs. Hill hustled over to check him out.

Fin turned back to Kaleigh again. "And since when are you telekinetic?" he whispered.

She shrugged. "Comes and goes, like most of my powers. I was practicing." She looked up at the raft overhead. "It worked." She smiled, then looked at Fin again and the smile faded. "Sorry," she whispered.

"It's Mr. Hill you should be apologizing to." He indicated the stout man, who was at that moment far more interested in a human female in a bikini at the cold drink case than he was in the *misplaced* pack of gum.

"Um, I'm really sorry, Mr. Hill," Kaleigh said, tucking her hands behind her back, looking angelic. "It was rude of me to play that joke on you and Mrs. Hill. But I never intended to steal the gum. I swear it. I just wanted to see if I could do it. I'm supposed to be developing my powers—for the good of the sept, of course."

Katy sniggered.

Mr. Hill was still watching the purple polka-dotted bikini. The woman leaned over to grab a drink out of the case, presenting her shapely bottom to Mr. Hill.

Fin cleared his throat. "Get the gum down, Kaleigh, and then get out of here."

She nodded vigorously and glanced up at the gum.

The other teens and Fin looked up. Hilly continued to analyze the scenic view at the cold drink case.

Kaleigh scrunched up her pretty face in concentration.

The gum didn't move.

Kaleigh exhaled loudly. "Come on, come on," she whispered under her breath.

The pink king-sized pack of bubble gum stubbornly held its position.

"You got it up there," Katy murmured. "Why can't you get it down?"

"I don't know." It was practically a wail. "Stop looking at it. You're making me nervous!"

Fin waited another moment and then, feeling sorry for the kid who was now obviously becoming embarrassed, he moved to her side. "You just move it or did you dematerialize it and then put it back together on the raft?"

"Dematerialized it," she whispered, now close to tears.

"Nice," he whispered. "That's a lot harder to do."

She looked up at him, sneaking a quick smile.

Fin smirked at her and then glanced up. All he had to do was see the gum in his mind on the raft, then on the shelf below the counter. It disappeared instantly from the raft, as if it was never there.

"There you go. Enjoy your chips," Mrs. Hill told the customer who had no idea what was going on nearby.

Fin walked over to the register. "The gum has been returned to its place, Mrs. Hill. I'll escort these young ladies and gentlemen out of your establishment. Have a good evening."

"That's it? You're not going to arrest them?" she called after him as he ushered the kids under the air-conditioning vent and out the door. He was so intent on getting away from Mrs. Hill that he didn't see the woman in front of him until he nearly collided with her.

"Excuse me," Fin said, startled, reaching out to be sure he hadn't knocked her off balance.

"Scusilo," she murmured, not sounding at all offended.

The teens bolted as Fin glanced up and saw the face of a dark-haired angel.

Chapter 2

"*No, lo scusa,*" Fin responded in Italian. It came out unconsciously; he had a thing for languages. He spoke thirteen fluently, including two dead languages. Then in English he said, "I'm sorry. I was keeping an eye on those kids." His fingertips lingered on the HF's arm a little longer than necessary. *Careful,* his subconscious reminded him. Human females were strictly off-limits to male vampires.

The glass door behind him closed, taking with it the last breath of cool air, and he was once again enveloped in the possibilities of the hot, humid night.

"No, I was the one not paying attention." Her voice was light with amusement. Warm with sexual overtone.

He met her gaze. Human or not, she was an astonishing beauty. Late thirties, he guessed. Mediterranean olive skin. Pale pink lipstick on plump, sensuous lips. Big, dark eyes fringed in black lashes. He sensed he knew this woman, but how?

She was not an American. He could tell even though

her English was impeccable. European women, in particular, had a certain air about their speech patterns. Americans sometimes took the tone for snooty. Fin had always seen it simply as a refinement in speech cultivated over thousands of years. Americans sometimes forgot just how young their culture was.

"Officer Kahill," she said, smiling.

And for an instant, as she took him in, Fin knew what women suffered through every day of their lives; a feeling of being objectified, of being totally consumed. He enjoyed his moment of *suffering* immensely before offering his hand. "Fin Kahill."

"Officer Kahill, a pleasure to meet you. Elena Ruffino." Her handshake was firm, but feminine. He caught the faint scent of her cologne on the night breeze; it was pungent, almost feral. And utterly intoxicating.

"I'm not really a cop." He withdrew his hand, touching the shiny new badge on his uniform, trying not to think about the hot, sweet blood that pulsed through her veins. Of course, the more he tried not to think about her blood, the harder it became. "Actually—" he stumbled. "Actually, I am, but—" He fell silent before he made a complete ass of himself. "Long story," he finished, stepping back to open the door to the store for her. The wind chimes overhead this time sounded different, as if majestically proclaiming her arrival.

Other women on the boardwalk were dressed in casual beachwear; cut-off denim shorts, tank tops, flip-flops. Their faces were sunburned, their hair pulled in sloppy knots on top of their heads. Elena wore a pale yellow dress that skimmed sun-bronzed knees, and strappy sandals. She was a gleaming sand dollar on a beach of dirty, chipped ark, sea pen, and clam shells.

She walked past him, into the store, leaving a trail of her scent behind her. *"Grazie."*

"Siente benvenuto." Fin watched her enter, musing how out of place she looked in the artificial fluorescent light with the colored rafts and buckets hanging over her head. What was an Italian woman of her caliber doing in Clare Point? Despite her fashionable clothing and the hip designer bag on her shoulder, she didn't even seem of this century. He let the door close and walked out from under the store's blue and white striped awning, forcibly pushing the thought of her out of his mind. He gazed south, then north.

As in nearby and far more popular Rehoboth Beach, wooden benches lined the boardwalk, ocean side. With the setting of the sun, the street lamps had automatically come on and now glowed high overhead, casting circles of white light on the worn floorboards. He could still smell the cotton candy, the roasted peanuts, and the suntan lotion, but also the more timeless scents of the darkness and the incoming tide and the elements they carried, both good and evil.

Two benches north, he spotted his gang of gum-dematerializing juvenile delinquents talking to one of the town's oldest occupants. Victor Simpson was a retired fishing boat captain who had a face like a wizened apple and a disposition to match it. Victor was one of the few members of the sept who had not been cursed by God, but by a Kahill. He had once been human, a nineteenth century ship's captain, but had been turned into a vampire by one of their own. An unfortunate incident and one strictly prohibited. So, despite his disagreeable nature, everyone in town had a soft spot in their hearts for Victor.

Fin walked up to the teens surrounding the old man. "These kids bothering you?" he joked.

"Sure as hell are," Victor grumbled, scratching his scruffy chin. The man had no sense of humor. "I was scared for my life."

"We just asked you if you had change for a dollar," Katy scoffed. "Sheesh, old man."

"Go on with you." Victor shooed the teens and they scattered like seagulls.

"Later, Uncle Fin." Kaleigh waved as she walked away. "Thanks!"

"Go home," Fin called after them, trying to sound threatening. "All of you. And I better not see you again tonight or your parents will be picking you up at the station."

"We're going to the arcade. We'll be in by curfew. I swear," the girl promised.

Fin rested his hands on the wide belt of his uniform pants. He watched the kids go, his thoughts drifting back to the Italian woman. *Elena.* He liked the taste of her name on his tongue. He made himself return his attention to Victor. "They weren't really bothering you, were they?"

Despite the heat, the elderly man wore navy blue work trousers and heavy leather shoes. His only concession to the temperature was a dingy once-white sleeveless ribbed T-shirt. The kids called it a wifebeater. Not particularly attractive on a wizened senior citizen who had spent too many years in the sun.

" 'Course they were botherin' me," Victor grouched. "Been botherin' me since they were born again!"

Fin nodded, looking up and down the boardwalk. Like many of the town's citizens, Victor often came in the evenings to catch a breath of fresh air and watch "the moving picture show," as he liked to call it. He did not frequent the gift shops, play arcade games, or ride the now antique merry-go-round. He did not buy paper cups of fresh lemonade or plates of hot, sweet funnel cakes. He came to watch the human tourists and maybe to remember fondly what his life had once been.

"So you really let them hoodwink you into this, eh?" Lifting his chin, Victor indicated the uniform. He spread his spindly arms over the rear of the wooden slatted bench and leaned back.

Fin didn't know what to say. What was done was done. Fortunately, Victor didn't need a partner in conversation, just an audience for another one of his diatribes.

"Good-for-nothin' brother of yours. Doesn't deserve this much attention. 'E's got the whole town turned upside down tryin' to accommodate 'im." He shook his head. "I couldn't believe it when I 'eard you let Mary Kay con you into moving out of the B and B and into that crappy rental with him, just so's you could keep 'im out of trouble."

"My mother didn't *con* me into anything," Fin protested. But both of them knew Victor was right. Mary Kay Kahill was definitely a con artist and Fin had most definitely fallen for her scam. Well, not so much fallen as surrendered. It was hard for him to tell his mother no, especially when it involved Regan. She didn't deserve the worry her youngest son, by six minutes, often caused. "Mom needed the extra rooms. Business at the B and B is crazy. They're booked solid all summer."

"Lie to yourself if ye like, but don't lie to me, mate." Victor pointed to the five-and-dime. "Who's the dame with the long gams?"

Fin glanced over his shoulder in the hope of catching another glimpse of Elena, but she hadn't yet left the store. Then he realized Victor must have seen them talking. Despite his deteriorating hearing and sight, he didn't miss much.

Fin looked down at the old man and shrugged. "I don't know. Tourist."

Squinting, Victor stared hard at the store across the busy boardwalk. "Somethin' not right there. I didn't like 'er looks."

Fin frowned, checking his watch. The crowd was beginning to thin. Parents were taking their cranky children back to the hotels, rentals, and B and Bs to be bathed and tucked in after a long day in the sand and sun. His shift was over at eleven, half an hour after all the shops closed. Just a little more than two hours to go; surely he could survive another two hours. Two hours and eleven weeks. Only eleven weeks until Labor Day.

Fin glanced at Victor, who was still watching the store front. "You don't like anyone's looks, Vic. Except maybe Mary McCathal's . . . from what I hear."

The rumor around town was that Victor was keeping company with Mary, the previous postmaster's widow. Bobby had been the first victim of the beheadings two summers before. Because his head had been severed and separated from his body, he could never be reborn. His wife, not permitted to remarry by sept law, would remain a widow for all of eternity.

Victor's eyes, so pale blue with age and the salt of the sea that they were gray, darted in Fin's direction. "People in this damned town talk too much," he groused. "Haven't they got anything better to do than stick their noses in my business?"

Fin grinned. "That mean you and Mary are—"

"Means keep your nose out of my damned business, boy!" He looked up at Fin. "'Aven't you got something better to do? Catch some criminals? Make these streets safer for tax-payin' people like me?"

"Have a good evening, Victor." Fin turned to go and as he did so, he heard the wind chimes over the door of the five-and-dime. He couldn't help himself. He looked. Sure enough, Elena Ruffino sashayed out the door with those long tan legs and that gloriously slender neck of hers.

Fin walked up the boardwalk so he wasn't standing directly in front of Victor and waited for her. He was the fly drawn to the Venus flytrap. Steel shavings drawn to a magnet. He simply couldn't help himself.

"Officer Kahill." She smiled.

"Miss Ruffino."

"Please. It's Elena." She stopped, a plastic bag from Hilly's hanging from her manicured fingertips.

He met her dark-eyed gaze. In her heels, she was close to six foot tall. He liked tall women. Of course, he liked short women, too. Skinny women. Fat women. But right now, tall women were his favorite, this one in particular. "Would you like to have a drink with me after I get off work tonight, Elena?" His invitation was purely impulsive.

And her smile in response to his whim was as gratifying as any Fin had had the pleasure of experiencing in his sixteen-hundred-odd years. She made him hot just looking at him. He was just relieved he was past the point in his life where he got a boner every time a pretty woman looked at him.

She gazed at him through killer black lashes. "I'm flattered, Officer Kahill, but how do I put this delicately?" She maintained eye contact with him. "Don't you think you'd prefer to ask out a woman *closer to you in age?*"

He chuckled. Women insinuated the same thing all the time, but he liked the idea that Elena was willing to actually come out and say it. "It's Fin, and I was cursed by good genes with a baby face. I'm thirty."

Fia said his youthful appearance was one of his best attributes when investigating for the sept. Still appearing to be in their late teens or early twenties, he and Regan traveled all over the world pretending to be American college students and, thanks to their appearance, played the part quite convincingly.

"And you can't be a day over thirty," he said, guessing she was closer to forty, but unable to resist paying her the compliment.

Fortunately, she had a sense of humor and she laughed. "Well, you do know how to flatter a woman like a man who's learned some life lessons."

"Is that a yes?"

"And a flirt as well," she teased. "Actually, I can't tonight, but maybe tomorrow night. I'll give you my number." She offered her hand. "Do you have your cell?"

"Oh, yeah. Sure." He pulled it from his pocket. "You here long?"

She punched keys on his cell phone, not looking up. "A few weeks. I'm on holiday with my sister and her family."

"So you're single?"

She handed him back his phone. "Shouldn't you have asked that before you asked me out?" Again, the smile.

Sexual energy sizzled between them. She definitely liked him.

"Call me," she said.

Fin dropped his phone into his pocket, watching the way her hips and shapely buttocks swayed as she strolled away. "You bet"

So maybe this job isn't going to be so bad after all . . .

It was close to midnight by the time Fin clocked out at the station, grabbed a bag of ice from the mini-mart, because his icemaker wasn't working, and walked in the front door of his rental house. He was greeted by the sound of cartoons on the TV. Regan was lying on the couch in the same position he'd been when Fin had been preparing to leave for work. The only changes he could see were that his brother was now wearing shorts and a T-shirt and there was a box of open cereal and a bowl of milk and a spoon on the floor beside the couch.

"Hey, Krupke."

Fin frowned. "That's not funny. It wasn't funny this afternoon and it's still not funny tonight."

"But you like Krupke."

"I like the musical *West Side Story*. I like Natalie Wood. I don't like Krupke and I don't like being called that."

Regan continued to stare at the TV screen. "Bad day at the office, honey?"

Fin groaned and leaned over to pick up the bowl and the box of cereal. "You need to clean up. We'll have ants."

"Yes, Mommy."

Fin walked past the stacked cardboard liquor boxes

to the dark kitchen. He ran water in the bowl from the leaking faucet and rolled up the bag inside the cereal box and put the box away. "You lie there all evening?" he called.

"No."

"No?" Fin walked back into the living room, unbuttoning his uniform shirt. The house had no central air, only window units, and tonight they didn't seem to be doing the trick. "You empty some of these boxes? Put some stuff away?" he asked, knowing full well Regan hadn't.

"Didn't get to it."

Fin stood at the end of the couch. He glanced at the TV. A Wile E. Coyote wannabe crept across the screen. "You look for a job?"

"At night?"

Fin whipped off his shirt. "Damn it, Regan! You didn't clean up. You didn't fix the faucet that you promised you would fix two days ago. You didn't do anything about a job. What *did* you do?" He didn't intend to raise his voice, but it came out that way.

Regan jumped up off the couch, throwing down the remote. "What did I do?" he shouted back, headed for the door, barefoot. "Same thing I do every day, Fin. I disappointed you." He walked out, slamming the door behind him.

Fin tossed his sweaty shirt on a box near the end of the couch and turned to watch the coyote on the screen swallow a puppy on a leash, whole.

"Hey, what's goin' on?" He tried to play it cool, but he sneaked a glance at her. She was cute. No, better than cute. Way hot.

She shrugged suntanned shoulders. "Just out for a midnight walk. You?"

"Um . . ." He hesitated. "Roommate's got someone over." He looked down and rubbed his bare feet together, trying to brush off some of the sand. He wasn't a great liar. "I was just—you know—trying to kill some time before I went back to the apartment."

"Ah," she said. Her voice was liquidy. Sexy. She wasn't just hot. She was hot for him. "So you want to?" She nodded in the direction of the dark beach.

"Want to what?"

"Go for a walk. Maybe a swim?" She turned her head to look at him, her lips pursed. It was practically an invitation to kiss her.

Suddenly he felt like such a dork. His heart was racing. His armpits were sticky. This kind of thing didn't happen to him. Women didn't try to pick him up. His brother, yes. His friends, sure, but never him. "Sure." He stood up at the very same moment she did, and her breasts brushed against his chest. Her nipples were hard beneath the thin, tight tank top. She looked up at him and he did what she obviously wanted him to. He kissed her.

He kissed her gently first, just to be sure he hadn't misread things, but when she slipped her tongue into his mouth, he went for it.

The guys were not going to believe this . . .

They kissed twice more. She fondled his balls through his board shorts and, feeling bold, he fondled her breasts.

Holy Mother of God—he was going to get laid tonight. By a stranger he met on the boardwalk. *Unfuckingbelievable.*

"Come on," she whispered, breathy in his ear. "Let's go for that walk."

"Sure." He let her take his hand. Then he remembered he didn't have his wallet. He'd left it back at the rental. That meant he didn't have the foil-wrapped coin he would need. He hesitated, stifling a groan of frustration. How could he have left without his wallet? How could he be unprepared at a moment like this?

But his place was just a couple of blocks away. He could run to the house, run back. But what explanation would he give for the ten minutes he'd be gone? What if he was mistaken? What if she really wasn't offering to have sex with him? Then he'd look like an idiot.

"What's the matter, hon? Don't want to go for a walk with me down by the water?" She wore her long hair down and it blew in the breeze, partially obscuring her pretty face. "Where it's dark? Where we can have a little privacy?"

There was no mistaking the meaning in her voice. She definitely wanted to have sex with him.

"A condom," he heard himself say. "I . . . I left in such a hurry that I forgot my wallet."

She took his hand, directing him toward the steps that led to the beach and out of the lamplight. "Don't worry," she said, tapping the cloth bag she wore on her shoulder. "I've got everything we need right here."

He smiled as he hurried down the steps, unable to believe his luck. There was *no way* anyone was going to believe this story when he tried to tell it tomorrow.

Chapter 3

Fin heard his cell phone ring but he was slow to wake. He was having the most delicious dream; he and Elena were on a boat anchored off a Greek island. They were sunbathing in the nude on the deck, the soft sound of the Aegean lapping at the sides of the hull, amazing blue sky framing the already perfect images. She had the most exquisite breasts, firm and round with dark nipples that—

The phone rang again and Fin felt himself being pulled from the dream. The sensation was so strong that he wanted to reach out to Elena and clasp her hand, hoping she could keep him from drifting away.

And then suddenly he was back in the tiny bedroom of the rental house. The room was dark and hot and his bare legs were tangled in the bed sheets. Eyes still closed, he fumbled with his hand, in search of his phone on the nightstand. Only it wasn't beside the bed where it belonged. He lifted his head from his pillow, squinting in the early-morning darkness, trying to remember where he had plugged it in the night before to recharge.

The single outlet beside the bed didn't work, which was a pain in the ass because not only could he not recharge his phone on the nightstand, but the lamp didn't work either.

Thankfully, the phone stopped ringing. Fin let his head fall back on the pillow. It was probably Regan. Fin had never heard him return to the house last night after he'd stormed out.

Fin lay there for a minute and then opened his eyes. Regan had always called at odd times, from all over the world, usually when he was partying. What if he had gone out and scored? What if he was high? Fin was supposed to be babysitting his little brother, keeping him clean. Keeping him safe. If Regan had gotten himself into any trouble, Mary Kay was going to kill Fin.

The cell phone rang again and Fin sat up, listening to locate it. Something glowed on the far side of the room on top of a cardboard box. The phone. It continued to ring.

Scrambling to reach it before it stopped again, Fin stubbed his toe on something solid on the floor. "Ouch! Mary, Mother of *Jezus*," he cursed, hopping on his good foot. He grabbed the phone and flipped it open as he tried to unplug it from the wall charger. Still leashed to the wall, he had to lean over to speak into it. "Regan?"

"Fin? That you?" The voice was thick with a Gaelic Irish accent.

"This is Fin." He managed to finally unhook the phone from its charger and he stood upright. It wasn't Regan. Balancing on one foot, he rubbed his throbbing, injured digit. "Who's this?"

"It's yer uncle Sean. Jezus, Fin. Ye don't recognize yer own uncle's voice?"

Fin hobbled back to the bed. "Not at—" He glanced at the nightstand, trying to see what time it was, but of course he hadn't plugged his alarm clock in because of the faulty outlet. "At whatever godawful time of the morning it is." He lowered himself to the edge of the bed.

"I'm sorry to wake ye, I am," Sean went on dramatically. "But I need ye, Fin."

"You need me?"

"I can't do this again. I swear by Christ's bones, I can't," his uncle moaned, his accent so thick Fin could barely understand him. Sean's accent always got heavier when he became emotional, which seemed to happen with more frequency as he got older.

"You can't do what, Uncle Sean? What's wrong?"

"He's dead. Murdered. Don't ye see, I can't handle another murder case." The chief of police sounded near to tears. "I just haven't got it in me."

"Uncle Sean, calm down."

"Ye have to come. Ye have to help me, Fin."

Fin rose from the bed to go to the light switch by the door. Panic fluttered in his chest. Had Regan been killed? But that was impossible. Or nearly so. A person had to seriously know what he was doing to kill a vampire.

But there had been the beheadings two summers before, so it *was* possible. And Regan *had* double-crossed the Rousseau brothers in New Orleans. *They* certainly knew how to kill a vampire. "I'll help you, Uncle Sean, but you have to tell me what's happened."

Fin flipped the switch and the single overhead bulb cast a dingy light over the twin bed surrounded by boxes. He grabbed the uniform pants he'd worn the night before and stepped into them. "Who's dead, Uncle Sean?"

"Ye have to come now before people start getting up, goin' about their business. We can't have this, Fin. Not on our beach, we can't."

His uncle still wasn't making any sense, but Fin wasn't sure he was going to any time in the near future. "Who's dead?" he repeated. "Not . . . not Regan?"

"Regan? Why would Regan be dead, Fin?" Sean became temporarily sidetracked, typical behavior for him. "Is there something ye haven't been telling us? Mary Kay was just saying the other day—"

"I don't know why Regan would be dead." Fin closed his eyes and opened them, trying to clear his head. "He wouldn't," he said into the phone, grabbing a clean T-shirt from a laundry basket his mother had delivered the day before. He took the phone away from his ear for a moment so he could pull the shirt over his head. "Who's dead, damn it?"

"Ye don't have to raise yer voice, lad. We haven't identified the victim yet. A young man. Nice looking. Was." Again, emotion threatened to choke Sean's words.

"A human?" Fin asked, feeling panicky again, but for entirely different reasons. "We've got a dead tourist?"

"'Fraid we have, Fin." Sean sounded utterly defeated.

Fin dug in the laundry basket on the floor again looking for clean socks. "Where?"

"Ye can't miss it. I got my car parked right on the boardwalk."

* * *

Sure enough, Fin had no problem finding Sean's police cruiser, its blue and red lights flashing on the boardwalk in front of Sal's Pizzeria, blocking the view of the alley. Neither did a dozen other people. By the time Fin hurried south on the boardwalk on foot, the sun had risen and a crowd of locals and tourists had gathered near the chief of police's car, craning their necks, trying to get a better look at whatever was going on in the alley. Jon Kahill, one of the youngest members of the Clare Point police force, was trying to keep the crowd back, but he was having difficulty.

Fin pushed his way through the throng, recognizing about half the faces. "Back up," he grunted. "Please, have some respect." He spotted one of his mother's neighbors, Jim, who appeared to have been out walking his Irish greyhound. "Jim, can you give Jon a hand here?" Fin grabbed the dog's leash out of Jim's hand and passed it to an HF in jogging shorts. "Could you watch Sugar for a few minutes, ma'am?" Then to Jim, "I want everyone back another twenty feet."

Jim looked at Fin, then at Jon, hesitated, then turned to face the crowd, opening his arms. When he spoke, it was with a voice of authority. "If you'll just step back, ladies and gentlemen, we can let the police do their job."

Thank God you got here, Fin, Jon telepathed. *The chief's in a way.*

Just keep them back, Fin shot back. He walked around the cruiser and spotted three people walking briskly toward him from the opposite direction. *Send someone to block the south side, too,* he telepathed to Jon.

Who? We're a police force of sixteen, counting you.

I don't care. Anyone, as long as it's one of us.

Fin turned into the alley. It was darker here. Cooler. Like all Kahills, he had a keen sense of smell. The moment he turned the corner, he smelled the scent of dying human flesh. There was no smell like it on God's earth.

At the far end of the alley that ran between the pizzeria and the arcade, he spotted his uncle, a Hispanic man in an orange jumpsuit, and another one of Clare Point's finest, Pete. They stood in front of a large blue Dumpster. On the street behind it sat another police cruiser, its lights flashing.

The chief of police, in a police uniform too large for him, turned around, spotted Fin, and ran straight for him, his sagging abdominal fat jiggling. Tears dampened the middle-aged man's cheeks. "Sweet *Jezus,* you're here," he cried, his arms flung wide as if he intended to take Fin in his arms.

"Chief," Fin said aloud, then telepathed, *Uncle Sean! You've got a civilian here. A human. Get a hold of yourself.*

Sean stopped short, took a deep breath, and when he spoke again, though his voice quavered, he sounded more in control. "Officer Kahill."

"What have we got?"

"A dead kid," Sean said, stepping aside so that Fin could get a better look. He hung his head, his sagging jowls deflating. "Someone's son. Someone's brother. Dead."

Fin took a breath as he shifted his focus from his uncle to the body in front of the Dumpster. His first impression, ten feet away, was that the young man, who appeared to be in his early twenties, not only wasn't alive, but had never been so. His face was so white, it was blue. Waxen. He looked like a department store mannequin, seated casually, one knee up, his ivory hands resting on his knee. He had straight, shaggy blond hair and a couple of days of blond fuzz on his cheeks. He was wearing flowered board shorts and a T-shirt advertising a famous surf shop in Florida. He was so carelessly good looking that he could have been a surf shop dummy, posed on a surfboard.

Except for the gaping wound on his throat.

Fin took a step closer, his stomach doing a sour flip-flop. He had seen dead men before. Killed his share. But this . . . this murder was so obviously, so hideously pointless that it made him want to vomit.

"No one has touched him?" Fin questioned.

Pete moved closer. "No," he said quietly. "Manuel Rodriguez here came by to pick up the Dumpster just before dawn. Luckily, he walked around this side before he hit the hydraulic button to lift the can for dumping."

"Otherwise the body propped against the Dumpster would have fallen—"

"And the truck would have dropped the Dumpster on top of him," Pete finished for him. "He called it in from his personal cell phone at five twelve a.m."

Fin looked up. "Where's the truck now?"

"I had Manuel move it down the street so we could use my car to block the alley."

"Smart, Pete." He offered a tight smile.

Pete's gaze drifted to the ground and the discarded French fry cup at his feet. "Thanks."

"He been this way since you got here?" Fin cut his eyes at his uncle, then back at Pete.

Pete nodded. "I was the one who told him to call you. Sorry. I didn't know what else to do."

Fin took a second to get his head straight and then called to his uncle, who remained behind them. "Chief?"

With obvious reluctance, Sean Kahill moved closer to Fin, and to the dead man. "How would you like to proceed from here?" Fin asked.

Sean looked at him with the face of a lost child. His eyes clouded with tears again. "I told ye," he whispered hoarsely. "I can't do it again. It's just not in me. Not another murder case."

"Well, who *is* going to do it?" Fin snapped, keeping his voice low so their witness wouldn't hear him. "You're the chief of police. You have to organize the investigation. You have to find out who this kid is. Who did this? And you have to do it fast, sir," he said, with meaning in his voice.

After fleeing Ireland in the seventeenth century, the Kahills had survived in relative safety for the last three centuries in Clare Point, Delaware, by taking care not to draw attention to themselves. In the last sixty years or so, their small but healthy tourist industry had been what kept money in their pockets and food on their tables. It was what enabled them to do their life's work. An unsolved murder in Clare Point could mean the beginning of the end for the tourist trade in such a fickle economy, a risk they couldn't afford.

"You have to take charge of this investigation, Uncle Sean," Fin repeated.

"And I am. I am." The middle-aged man latched his thumbs through his belt buckle, extending his elbows. "I'm taking charge and I'm delegating. I'm putting you in charge." He pushed a finger into Fin's chest.

"Me?" Fin would have laughed had it been in any

other circumstances. Had he not been in the presence of a dead man. "I've been a police officer for a day. You're the chief. You . . . you've got others who've been on the force for years." He indicated Pete, who had led the witness back down the alley toward the boardwalk.

"Pete can't do this." Sean shook his head, almost in a frenzy. "You know he can't. But you could do it, Fin. You're . . . you're good at this. It's what you do. You investigate. For the sept. You investigate murderers all over the world."

Fin groaned in frustration. "This is different, Uncle Sean. I follow men. I keep track of what they do, where they go, who they see. I just report back what I see."

"So report back to me what you see here." Sean turned his teary gaze to the dead man. "Please, Fin . . ." he begged in a whisper. "Fer the boy, if not for me."

Fin drew his hand over his face, down his chin, exhaling. He could see there was no sense arguing with Sean. The chief was a good man, but not a strong man. The beheadings had taken something out of him and he just didn't seem to have regained it. The weight loss, the heavy drinking—anyone in the town could see it if they looked carefully.

Fin glanced at the dead man. "He's obviously posed," he observed aloud.

"Posed?"

"Like the body was set there, positioned after he was dead." The surfer's eyes were still open. Blue. But they were beginning to cloud. The body was already in the first stages of decomposition, although Fin didn't know yet how long it had been here. The human body started decomposing the moment the heart ceased to beat.

"Posed," Sean repeated. "Looks posed to me."

"No blood here, either," Fin observed, moving closer to the body, his hand on his uncle's so the older man couldn't walk away. "What's it mean?"

"What's it mean?" Sean repeated.

Fin hadn't meant the statement to be rhetorical. "It means the kid was killed somewhere else," he said, thinking aloud. "He bled out elsewhere and was then brought here and posed against the Dumpster."

"Right. Right. Maybe he was killed in another town," Sean offered eagerly. "In someone else's jurisdiction."

"Maybe," Fin said. But he doubted they'd get that lucky. He looked behind him, up the alley and toward the ocean, noting the bits of refuse on the ground; a paper cone from a serving of cotton candy, a crushed soda can, cigarette butts, the foil wrapper from a condom. Typical alley trash, but there could be evidence lying here anywhere. "We shouldn't be walking around without shoe coverings. We could be destroying evidence. We need disposable gloves and shoe covers and whatever evidence-gathering tools we have. Digital cameras. Paper sacks to store the evidence."

"We . . . we've got all that stuff we used two years ago," Sean offered. "In boxes in the basement back at the station. Should I send someone for it?"

"Yeah. And you already called in every officer you have on the force, right?"

Sean nodded. "Dispatcher is on it. She's calling in everyone but Johnny K. He's in Myrtle Beach with his family. Vacation."

"Call him, too." Fin walked over to the body and crouched, studying the kid carefully. "And get the witness to the station. We'll question him there. And call Doc Caldwell. We got an ambulance coming?"

Sean didn't answer.

Fin glanced over his shoulder. "Chief. You have to call the paramedics."

"I hate to be the one to say, Fin, but he can't be revived." *He's a human,* Sean telepathed.

"There're procedures. We have to have an ambulance to transport the body to the morgue." He spoke slowly, not wanting to be disrespectful. "We need to take our photos and get him out of this alley before the sun worshipers start heading for the beach." He turned back to the young man and began studying him head to toe. Nothing seemed out of place if you didn't take into account that his body appeared to have been drained of a large percentage of his blood, and he had that gaping neck wound.

But on the hem of his yellow T-shirt, Fin noticed a whitish line. A salt stain left by ocean water. He reached out to check the shirt to see if it was still damp, but caught himself before he touched it, possibly contaminating evidence. "I need gloves, Chief. Can you get me a pair of disposable gloves? There should be a box in the trunk of Pete's car."

"Gloves. Can do." Sean hiked up the back of his sagging pants as he hurried past the Dumpster, toward the police car on the street.

While he waited for the gloves, Fin stepped back from the body and took his cell phone from his pants pocket. He hit auto-dial and waited for the familiar beep. He didn't expect her to answer this early.

"Fee, it's Fin," he said, wishing she hadn't returned to Philly the night before. "I need you to call me as soon as you get this message." He hesitated, not sure of how much to say. Then he caught a glimpse of the surfer out of the corner of his eye. He was watching Fin with those sightless blue eyes, silently begging. Fin turned his back on him, afraid he wasn't up to the task of finding his murderer. "I've got a dead guy here and we need your help."

Chapter 4

"Hey."

Kaleigh looked up from where she sat squished beside Rob on a bench in front of the NASCAR arcade game. He didn't seem to notice when she got up; he was too busy gripping the fake steering wheel, trying to navigate his way around the track on the video screen in front of him. It was the fourth time in a row he'd played the stupid game, so she was relieved by the respite. "Hey," she called to Katy.

The girls had to put their heads together to hear each other above the roar of Rob's NASCAR engine and the general chaos of the arcade. Pinball machines pinged, air hockey pucks slammed against the tables' bumpers, and a mechanical voice hollered in Mandarin from the kung fu game beside them.

"You hear anything juicy about the dead HM they found this morning in the alley?" Katy questioned with morbid excitement.

"How would I hear anything? I didn't even know there *was* a dead guy until you woke me up to tell me."

Kaleigh picked at a piece of peeling skin on her shoulder where she'd gotten sunburned the other day.

"You didn't talk to your uncle? This is Fin's beat. He has to know *something*." She popped her gum.

Kaleigh frowned as she excised a nice piece of dead skin and dropped it on the cement floor. "If he's investigating a murder, don't you think he'd be a little too *busy* to talk to me right now?"

Just then, Richie Palmer walked by, jingling his apron of change. "Hey, Richie," Katy called, flirtatiously.

He turned around and walked backward so he was facing them. "Hey, Katy. Hey, Kaleigh. How's your summer going?"

Richie had graduated from their high school the year before; he'd been working at the arcade for a couple of summers. This season he'd made manager. He was pretty cute in a geeky way and nice, but Kaleigh had never hung out with him in school. His girlfriend was a total bitch and word was she'd do the nasty with anyone with a warm six-pack and a pickup truck. Richie could be doing so much better.

"You need any change or anything?" He jingled coins in his apron again.

"Nah, thanks."

"Richie! You coming or not?" some kid hollered from the next row of games. "Ninja Warrior ate my quarters again."

"Sorry. Gotta go." Richie flashed a shy grin. "See you around."

"See you around." Katy gave a little wave. As she turned back to Kaleigh, her eyes lit up. "Hey, hey, hey. Hottie at three o'clock."

Kaleigh glanced up.

"Don't look at him!" Katy grabbed her elbow and steered her across the aisle to a pinball machine featuring wizards in Harry Potter–like pointed hats. She rested her hands on the machine as if she was preparing to play and tried to look back in the guy's direction, without turning her head. "Is he looking this way?"

Kaleigh stood directly behind Katy. "How would I know if I can't look at him?" she said in a stage whisper out of the side of her mouth. "And why are you looking at other guys? HMs at that? Don't tell me you and Pete broke up again?"

"We're just having a time-out. What about now?" She whipped a tube of lip gloss from her pocket. "Is he looking at me now?"

"He's not looking at you." Kaleigh moved to the side of the pinball machine and reached around to drop three quarters into the slot.

"Are you sure?" Katy slicked on sparkly pink lip gloss as the machine lit up with flashing purple lights. "I thought he was looking at me. He definitely seemed interested." She frowned, looking down. "Why'd you waste money in this thing? I didn't want to play; I just wanted to look like I was playing."

"You better start playing for real because here he comes." Kaleigh leaned casually on the glass top.

Katy stiffened, tucking the lip gloss back into her pocket. "He's coming? This way?"

"Yup."

Katy pulled back the plunger and released it. A ball popped out from a door and rolled toward her.

"You have to hit the buttons," Kaleigh teased, punching one so a flipper shot the ball upward again.

Katy pounded the buttons on both sides.

Kaleigh watched the guy walk toward them. He was

cute enough . . . in an emo kind of way. About their age. Tall. Lanky. Pale skin and shaggy black hair cut jagged around his face. Someone had paid a lot of money for the haircut that was supposed to look like he hadn't done anything at all to it in weeks. Thick fringe obscured one eye. He was wearing black knee-length shorts and a tight black T-shirt. Black shoes.

Kaleigh wiggled her bare toes in her flip-flops. The guy looked hot to her. Not hot cute. Just hot as in elevated body core temperature. It had to be close to ninety degrees outside.

"What's goin' on, ladies?" He walked up to them to stand just behind and to Katy's left side. He gazed at the game with interest.

"Nothing going on." Katy continued to hit the pinball buttons. "Never anything going on in this boring town." She glanced at him and smiled, then looked at the game again, all casual-like. "What's goin' on with you?"

He shrugged, sliding his hands into his pockets. "Folks already drivin' me crazy and we've only been here a couple of days. Looking for something to do. Looking for some hot girls to do it with."

Kaleigh groaned inwardly.

Katy beamed, then looked down. "Ah, no!" She pounded the glass game top with her fist. "Lost another ball. I so suck at this game. You want the last two?" She pointed to the balls still in the chute waiting to be played.

He shrugged, hands still in his pockets.

Already bored with the bizarre mating habits of teens, Kaleigh let her attention drift. To her, it just didn't make sense to buck the system. Katy and Pete were destined to be married, just like her and Rob. There was no escaping the laws of the sept, so what was the point in all this strutting and stroking with other guys? Especially human guys. When was Katy going to learn? But Katy was Katy . . .

Kaleigh glanced in Rob's direction; he was still playing the stupid NASCAR game. She just didn't get it. He worked here five or six days a week. How was it that on his one day off, he still wanted to be here? On her day off, she wanted to be as far from soft serve ice cream as she could get.

"I'm Katy and this is my BFF, Kaleigh." Katy stood opposite Kaleigh and rested her elbows on the top of the pinball game, flashing the emo kid some serious cleavage. "What's your name?"

The machine lit up, pinging and ringing, as he racked up points. He glanced at Katy's boobs, then concentrated on the game again. "Beppe."

"Beppe?" Katy looked at Kaleigh, eyebrows raised as if she were impressed. "What kind of name is Beppe?"

"I don't know. What kind of name is Katy?" He flipped the pinball into a basket and the point counter spun wildly. "And what's BFF?"

"Where are *you* from?" Katy rolled her eyes. "BFFs. You know. Best friends forever."

"Yeah. Right. Right." He punched the game buttons vigorously, rocking side to side as the ball bounced from one slot to the next, the score board spinning.

"So where *are* you from?" Kaleigh studied the guy closer. "You have an accent . . . sort of."

"Italy," he said, not seeming all that eager to share.

"Italy?" Katy cut her eyes theatrically at Kaleigh. "An Italian man. I've always wanted to live in Italy."

"Or Spain, or France, or Greece," Kaleigh muttered

under her breath. She looked past Katy to see a girl she knew from school entering the arcade. Mickey was with a guy, older than they were. And he was *big*. The sept men were for the most part tall, but this guy had to be six-foot-five, maybe even six-six. Kaleigh didn't know him. Mickey lifted her chin in greeting.

Mickey was okay. A little weird. Kids at school said she was a cutter but Kaleigh didn't know if it was true. What Kaleigh did know was that she was an amazing photographer. That was where she and Kaleigh had met. In photography class at school. They'd ended up being partners a couple of times on projects.

Mickey walked over, the tall guy in tow. He was dressed like her, all in black. Her in long sleeves, always long sleeves. Him short. She was wearing bright red lipstick. He was not.

"How's your summer goin'?" Mickey asked. "Start on that project for Kinnerman?"

Kaleigh wrinkled her nose, leaving the pinball game to talk to her. Katy was still busy flirting with *Beppe the Italian guy.* "I probably won't start it until, like, the day before school starts."

"Me either." Mickey grimaced. "Oh, hey. This is my boyfriend Tomboy. He goes to Penn State."

Tomboy looked even bigger up close, with hairy tree-trunk legs and hands like hams. But maybe that was because he had to be at least a foot taller than Mickey.

"Nice to meet you." She nodded, feeling awkward. Even though it was important for the sept's teens to keep up appearances by attending a human school, it was hard to foster friendships with them. Mickey lived in the next small town north, and in an utterly different world than Kaleigh's. A world with such freedoms . . . and limitations that Kaleigh would never know.

Kaleigh was coming to grips with her world and her reality on a daily basis as her powers grew. She'd only been reborn three years ago, so she still hadn't reached her full potential, but wisdom seemed to come to her in waves now. Sometimes the truth of her situation, the whole cursed by God and turned into a V, made her sad. Sometimes for herself, other times for humans. Kaleigh would never have a boyfriend from Penn State. She'd never experience the thrill of meeting a guy she didn't know, falling in love. But Mickey would never experience eternal life. There was a cost to everything; Kaleigh was learning that, too.

"So . . . you guys just hanging out?" Kaleigh asked. She glanced in the direction of the NASCAR game. She was getting hungry. Rob had promised one more game and then they would go get fries. She didn't see him and wondered where he'd gotten to.

"I came to see the dead guy. Tomboy's living on First Street with a bunch of other guys for the summer. He called to tell me someone was dead in the alley off the boardwalk, but the cops had practically the whole beach roped off by the time I got here. So we're just hanging out. Tomboy's day off. He works at Candy Man's."

"You like saltwater taffy?" Kaleigh asked, having to tip her head back to look up at him.

"He hates it now that he has to make it all day," Mickey answered for him.

Kaleigh laughed. "I know what you mean. I work at the DQ. I used to love ice cream, but not so much any-more. I swear, I think milk oozes from my pores."

Mickey spotted Beppe. "Who's that?" she asked Kaleigh with obvious interest.

Either Tomboy hadn't heard her or didn't care if his girl ogled other guys.

Kaleigh shrugged. "Some guy Katy's tryin' to pick up. Here on vacation, I guess."

Katy must have heard Kaleigh because she blushed and then inconspicuously gave her the finger. Beppe kept playing the pinball machine. He'd won extra balls.

Mickey slowly dragged her gaze from Beppe's backside. "We're havin' a party tonight at Tomboy's." She slid her arm through her boyfriend's. "Him and his roommates. Late. Like midnight. If you wanna come"—it was Mickey's turn to shrug—"you and Katy and Rob, and your friend"—she nodded in Beppe's direction—"that'd be cool."

"I don't know what we're doin' tonight," Kaleigh said. Teens in the sept had a curfew. It was stupid. Like the adults thought the kids were going to run wild, having sex and sucking people's blood at night . . . Actually, that *did* happen once in a while . . . But the curfew was still stupid. It didn't keep them off the streets; it just made them use windows at night instead of doors. "Maybe we could make it." The real question was, would the party be worth the risk of getting caught again. She was kind of already in trouble for being out too late a couple of nights the previous week.

"We'd love to come," Katy said, apparently overhearing the conversation. "Beppe, too. Right?" She looked at him. "You in?"

Beppe didn't take his eyes off the game in front of him. "Sure. I'm in. Just have to wait until my folks go to bed."

Katy was the only one who laughed. "Where?" she asked, turning back to Mickey.

Mickey gave an address on First Street, on the block where all the human college students who worked the boardwalk stayed. "We'll be there," Katy said.

"Later." Mickey and the boyfriend walked away.

"We're not going to Tomboy's house for a party. Our parents will kill us," Kaleigh said, walking away from Katy and her new friend.

"We are, too. Come on. It'll be fun." Katy chased after her, grabbing her arm. "Beppe says he'll go," she added meaningfully.

Kaleigh pulled away. Katy could be so immature sometimes. "I'm going for fries at Sal's. You see my lame boyfriend on the NASCAR circuit, tell him where I went."

"We're going!" Katy hollered after her, above the sound of the clanging pinball machine.

Kaleigh was almost out of the arcade when she spotted Rob. He was standing in line waiting to play air hockey. She thought about just walking out, but she went over to him. "I'm hungry. Going for fries."

"I'm waiting my turn to play."

Kaleigh glanced at the air hockey table. Her uncle Regan was playing one of the Hill twins. She wasn't sure which one. Fifteen hundred years and Kaleigh still had a hard time telling them apart. Regan was the king of air hockey in Clare Point. Possibly the world. No one had ever beaten him, but all the teens tried. "There's, like, four people in line ahead of you." She gestured to the guys in line ahead of Rob.

"But it doesn't take long." He grabbed her hand. "Come on, just give me a couple of minutes and we'll go together. He's already beat three since I got in line."

"Just meet me at Sal's." She pulled her hand from his. She didn't know why she was feeling so bitchy. She'd been like this all day.

"Ka—"

She walked away, glancing around as she made her way through the maze of chiming, ringing, and flashing arcade games. The sounds of voices, human and V, washed over her like a suffocating wave. She had to get out of here. She was usually completely at home here in the arcade, but something didn't feel right. She was on edge and she didn't know why.

The dead guy.

He just popped up in her head out of nowhere.

She was upset about the dead guy. She didn't know anything about him. Not who he was or why he was dead. She'd acted like she didn't care when Katy called her to tell her about him. She had thought she *didn't* care, beyond reasonable compassion for any dead guy. But it wasn't true.

She stepped out of the arcade, out from under the awning and onto the boardwalk. Standing in the middle, she turned until the fading sun fell on her face and she closed her eyes.

A dead human on the boardwalk was bad for the tourist trade and therefore, for the sept. You didn't have to be a wisewoman to figure out that one. And anything bad for the sept was bad for Kaleigh.

Maybe that's why she was in such a bitchy mood today. Because she was learning pretty quickly that sometimes being the sept's wisewoman was a bitch.

Fin's cell rang and without looking away from the computer monitor, he picked it up. "'Lo."

"A dead guy needs me?" Fia said in his ear.

He finished his last thought on the screen—his initial notes for the investigation—and rolled his chair back, giving his aching eyeballs a break. "*I* need you, Fee. I need you to put your FBI Special Agent cap on and tell me what the hell I'm supposed to be doing here."

"I can't believe we've got a dead guy in Clare Point."

"He was just a kid."

She swore, using St. Anthony's holy name. It was completely inappropriate for a good Catholic like Fia. And completely Fia.

Fin rested his head on the back of the chair and closed his eyes, ignoring the commotion around him. Uncle Sean had called in all his officers, but no one seemed to be quietly going about their assigned tasks. There was less confusion on the New York Stock Exchange floor after a sharp drop in the Dow than there was in the police station right now. "He was murdered, Fee." Fin exhaled.

"You sure?"

"Eight to ten inch long cut in his neck. Bled out. And he was moved. Posed. Oh, we've definitely got a homicide here."

She swore again, more colorfully than before. Now St. Anthony was involved in unnatural acts . . . at least not ones becoming of a holy saint of the Catholic Church.

"And you say he was posed?"

"I can e-mail you pictures. He's posed, all right."

He could almost hear the wheels of her mind turning.

"You know who he is?" she asked.

"Not yet. He's barely more than a kid. Twenty-one, maybe twenty-two. I was hoping someone would show up saying their son, boyfriend, brother, someone was missing. Nothing all day."

"So what's Uncle Sean going to do? Identifying the body is pretty important to finding the killer."

"That's part of the problem." He opened his eyes. There was an officer sitting right next to him, trying to load a stapler. Fin got up and walked through the bullpen, out into the hall. "Uncle Sean's not doing anything." He leaned to see around the corner. The chief's office was off the bullpen, a glass wall separating him from his men. Fin could see him staring at his computer monitor, his hand moving rhythmically on his mouse. Computer solitaire. He played it by the hour while on duty, according to Pete.

Fin stood up again, speaking into his phone. "He's not doing anything. He got me out of bed at dawn. Crying, carrying on. You know how he gets himself worked up emotionally. He says he can't run another murder investigation. He says he's not up to it."

Fia was quiet on the other end of the phone and Fin knew she was feeling the pressure in her chest that he'd been feeling all day. Pain for their loved one's sorrow. Pain for the sorrow of the entire sept. The beheadings and loss of their own two years ago was still heavy on their hearts.

"So what *has* he done?"

"He's put me in charge of the investigation."

"You don't know anything about solving a murder."

He laughed but without humor. "So tell me something I don't already know, sis." He rubbed his hand across his face. He was feeling light-headed. Probably needed to eat something. That cup of coffee he had around ten a.m. just wasn't cutting it. "But who else is going to run the investigation? Pete? Tony? How about Hilly Jr.?"

"Okay, so how *are* you going to identify this poor guy?"

"I printed some photos, just a head shot. I have a couple of officers trying to discreetly show them around the boardwalk. I told them just to check with our people. Not to involve any tourists if we can help it. Maybe someone will recognize him."

"And you're sure he's a tourist?"

A dispatcher carrying two cups of coffee walked past Fin in the hall. He waited until she was out of earshot to speak. "Who else could he be? He wasn't wearing a UPS uniform. He wasn't picking up garbage. The only humans who step foot in Clare Point are the few from the outside who work here, and tourists."

"Good point. You have a good mind for this. So—"

Fin saw Pete round the corner, his face flushed. "Hang on a sec, Fee," Fin said, lowering the phone to his side.

"There you are," Pete panted, running his hand across his broad, sweaty forehead. "I was going to look in the men's room next." He stopped in front of Fin. "We've got a positive ID."

Chapter 5

"And you're sure it's a positive ID? *Absolutely sure?*" Fin stood in Sean's office with Pete, the door closed. Sweat prickled under his suffocating, tight collar. He could feel the officers and few civilians in the station watching him from beyond the glass, waiting for word on the identity of the dead man. Telepathic thoughts bounced off the walls. Eyes bored holes in his back. Fin didn't want to be there. He didn't want to be this person in this position right now.

"Sure as a man can be. *Woman,*" Pete corrected himself. He stood with his arms awkwardly at his sides; armpit stains crept downward on his light blue uniform shirt. "Liz Hillman identified him from the picture you took. Name's Colin Meding. Twenty-two years old. A Pennsylvania resident. Just graduated from the University of Delaware. Liz said Joe hired him Memorial Day weekend. Caramel popcorn boy. He was doing a fine job, according to Liz, then he didn't show up for work this morning."

"It's four o'clock in the afternoon. Why didn't she

call us this morning when she realized he was missing?" Fin demanded, slamming the back of a chair with the palm of his hand. "Why did it take us all freakin' day to show the photos around town?"

Pete stared at the floor. Sean just sat there behind his desk as if he hadn't heard a word of the exchange.

Fin took a deep breath and exhaled slowly, something he'd learned in anger management therapy. "I'm sorry, Pete. I don't mean to take this out on you. It's just that now someone has to tell his parents that their son is dead and that he's been dead for at least eleven hours and we're just getting around to contacting them." He took another breath, feeling a little more in control of himself. "You said Liz identified him from the photo?"

Pete nodded, slowly lifting his gaze. He was such a good guy. A simple man, but with one of the biggest hearts Fin had ever known. He didn't deserve to be spoken to harshly.

"I went by Lizzy's this morning," Pete started slowly. "But Liz and Joe were out. Just kids working the stand. You said you only wanted the photos shown to our own, not humans. I forgot I'd skipped the caramel stand, things being crazy and all, and then when I remembered, I went back." He lifted his chin until he was finally looking Fin in the eyes. "Liz didn't think he was *missing*. That's why she didn't call us, even after she heard about the murder. When the kid didn't show up for work and didn't call, she wasn't worried. She just figured he'd either quit and not bothered to call her, or he was sleeping off a hangover and he'd be in tomorrow, begging her not to fire him. She said it happens all the time with her summer help. She was pretty upset, Fin. Said it just hadn't occurred to her that the dead blond boy she heard about this morning could be *her* blond caramel corn boy." He looked away. "She said he was a"—Pete's voice caught in his throat—"said he was a sweet kid."

"You get an address on him?"

"Like I said, he's from P-A, but I got a local one. One of Victor's dumps on First. He was living with a bunch of guys for the summer. I was going there next, but I wanted to tell you the news in person."

"Colin Meding." Fin tasted the name. The dead kid had looked like a Colin. A college graduate. A sweet kid. His whole life ahead of him. It was such a shame. He walked to the office door and opened it for Pete. "Go to the rental house, round up whoever's there and bring them to the station. You can ask them some questions, but don't tell them anything. The parents have to be notified first." The phone rang on Sean's desk.

Sean ignored it.

It rang again. Fin glanced back. "You going to answer that?"

Sean reached for the phone. "Chief Kahill." He listened, then covered one end of the phone with his hand. "It's Doc Caldwell." He lowered his hand. "Uh-huh."

Fin returned his attention to Pete, who was walking out the door. "You need another officer to go with you?"

Pete shook his head. "I don't need to be babysat, Fin." This time he didn't hesitate to look at Fin straight-on. "Just because I'm not hero material like you doesn't mean I can't do my job. You tell me what to do and I'll do it. It's not that I'm a screwup. I'm just not you."

Hero material? Pete had to be kidding. This was yet another reason why Fin hadn't wanted to be in charge of the investigation. He was bad with people. He worked better alone. "I'm sorry," Fin said quietly. And he meant it. *You know I didn't want this job,* he telepathed, assuming Sean was too busy with his phone call to pay attention. Sean wasn't a multitasker, even on a good day. Even if he did catch a word or two, Fin didn't care. *I didn't want to be a police officer for the summer. And I certainly didn't want to lead a murder investigation. You're a good cop, Pete. Everyone knows it. And you're more a hero than I'll ever be. You keep out of the limelight. You do your job, keep your family, our family, safe better than anyone I know.*

Just doing what needs to be done for the greater good, Pete returned kindly.

The greater good, Fin repeated, still speaking telepathically.

"I'll bring the roommates in."

"Thanks, Pete." Fin closed the door behind him, turning to Sean, who had just hung up the phone. He looked pale again, his cheeks flushed, like he had earlier in the day on the boardwalk. "What did the doc have to say?" He knew very well from the look on Sean's face it wasn't good. "He have anything concrete for us?"

"He wants me to come down to the office." Sean swallowed, his Adam's apple bobbing in the flabby flesh of his throat. "Something on the body he wants me to see."

Fin was only half listening to Sean. The other half of his brain was composing the conversation he would have with Colin's family. A Pennsylvania state police officer would be sent to the home to give the parents the dreadful news, but then the family would come to Clare Point and Fin would have to answer their questions. Only right now, he didn't have any answers. "So go," he told his uncle, switching gears again. "Bring back the autopsy report if he's got it done, otherwise—"

"I can't go."

Fin stared at his uncle for a moment. He might have thought Sean's comment was unbelievable, but today had passed unbelievable hours ago. "You're the chief of police." Fin walked around the side of the massive gunmetal gray desk, wondering how they had ever gotten it in the building. The office must have been built around it. "Get out of that chair. Get in your police car. Drive to the coroner's office and see what needs to be seen." His gaze flickered to the computer monitor on the desk. *Solitaire.* He looked back at the thickset man in the office chair. "Uncle Sean, you have to."

The chief rose slowly. "If I have to go, then you have to go with me. I can't do this. I . . . I don't like dead people."

"For sweet Mary's sake, Uncle Sean. You're a vampire. You suck people's blood to survive. How can you—"

"Not human blood," he interrupted, holding up his finger as he walked from behind his desk. "I don't do that anymore."

"Let's go, Uncle Sean. We'll take your car."

"You . . . you can't drive?"

"No, Chief. I don't have a car. I'm a foot patrolman. Not a real policeman, remember?" He held the office door open for him. "I don't even have a gun."

Sean halted in the doorway, looking up earnestly at his nephew. "I could get you a gun."

"I'm not sure that would be all that wise right this minute," Fin said cynically, under his breath. If he had a gun, the question was, who would he shoot first, his uncle or himself?

The thought was moot, of course. Neither would die, no matter how many .45 caliber bullets ripped through their flesh.

Perpetual life sucked sometimes.

"Technically," Dr. Caldwell explained, "the young man died of exsanguination."

They stood in a narrow hallway outside the exam room where the ME had performed Colin Meding's autopsy. His was the first human autopsy Dr. Caldwell had done in at least a hundred years. The only bodies brought here anymore were those of sept members. With sept members in high political places, the town had been able to keep their own medical examiner, even when other small towns gave them up, and thus keep their secret. Sept members' bodies were brought here, declared legally dead, then transported to the funeral home a block down the street. Joseph Hillbert, Clare Point's only undertaker, had never embalmed a body in his life. It was another front to keep up appearances. He simply prepared vampires for their ritual wake and then their rebirth, which always came three days after their death.

"The blood loss due to the trauma to his neck, specifically to his carotid artery, is what killed him," the doctor continued. Patrick, sporting a short white beard and kind eyes, was dressed in blue scrubs and looked like a TV doctor. "I'm a little rusty on my human anatomy, but I would suspect he lost consciousness before his throat was slit and he bled out in minutes."

"He lost consciousness?" Fin asked, confused.

"Come and see the body. It'll make sense to you then."

Fin glanced at Sean. The police chief seemed more interested in the seascape hanging on the wall than what the doctor was telling them. "We haven't found a weapon so far," Fin said. "Any thoughts on what we're looking for? I'm guessing a knife, obviously, but serrated, smooth? Big? Small?"

"I've got to do some reading on the Internet, but I'd have to say small-sized blade, smooth cutting edge. There was nothing unusual about the wound except that it appeared . . ." He hesitated. "Precise."

Precise. Fin didn't like the sound of the word. It conjured up other words he disliked even more. *Experienced. Premeditated.*

"What about the rest of the body?"

"Nothing stands out." Dr. Caldwell moved toward the closed door to the autopsy room. "There was evidence that he engaged in some form of sexual activity close to the time of death."

"Some form of sexual activity?" Fin questioned, not feeling as if he had time for euphemisms.

"There was evidence of body fluids, but I can't tell you male, female, or both. I've taken samples, but there was some saltwater residue on his suit, which could compromise the samples."

Fin was trying hard to think, but his thoughts were scattered, heading in a hundred directions at once. "Had he been in the water recently?"

"No way for me to tell. No salt water on his skin, though. I'll send the evidence off to the state lab tomorrow morning, but you know how that goes. Results could take weeks or even months."

The fact that a twenty-two-year-old good-looking college graduate got laid on a hot Friday night in June at the beach didn't seem all that remarkable to Fin, but he knew that right now his job was to collect all the information he could. Later, he'd sift through it all, determining what was important and what wasn't.

"So, it doesn't sound like we have much to go on, as far as who might have done this."

"Well, there is one thing." Patrick rested his hand on the doorknob. "This is what I needed you to see." He opened the door and stepped back to let them pass. "Chief?"

Sean held up his hands, palms out. "I have complete trust in my officer, Doc. Room's small, anyway. I'll just see you in the car, Fin." He made a beeline for the waiting room door.

Patrick didn't seem surprised by the chief of police's exodus. He followed Fin into the room without comment, closing the door behind him.

The dead kid lay on a metal examining table in the center of the small room. It was the same room where Fin had been examined by Doc Caldwell as a kid and then over the years.

Colin Meding looked similar to before with his tousled good looks and pale skin. Only now he was naked, his buff chest marred by the sutured Y incision from the autopsy. Thankfully, his blue eyes were now closed.

"Here." Patrick walked to the head of the table and bent the neck of a floor lamp closer. "Look here." He touched the pallid flesh at the site of the gaping neck wound. "I almost missed it, but look closely."

Not wanting to, but knowing he must, Fin leaned over until his face was close enough to the dead man's to feel the coolness of his chilled flesh.

At first, Fin didn't know what he was supposed to be

looking at. The cut was now clean of what little dried blood had been left behind. He didn't notice anything else, except that the kid needed a shave.

"Here," Patrick instructed. "See them?"

Suddenly, it was as if the ME had drawn a red bull's-eye around the telltale wounds. Fin stood up, feeling slightly dizzy. "Two puncture marks," he murmured, falling into that pit of *beyond disbelief* again.

"Puncture marks," Patrick repeated. "Another millimeter lower and the incision would have cut them in half. The way flesh tears, even with a sharp knife, I'd never have seen them. No one would have."

"It would almost seem that the perpetrator cut him that way on purpose." Fin leaned over again, just to be sure he was seeing what he thought he was seeing. He stood again. "No possibility those could be anything but what they appear to be?" he asked, hoping against hope.

"I'm afraid not, Fin."

So that's why Colin Meding hadn't known what hit him when his throat was slit. A vampire had fed on him first, rendering him unconscious. Still stunned, Fin moved toward the door. He needed to get out of the tiny, claustrophobic room. He needed a breath of fresh air.

Two years ago, humans had come to their sleepy little town to kill vampires. It appeared that this summer, the vampires would be returning the favor.

Chapter 6

"This is a bad idea," Rob whispered from the shadows below. It was just after midnight and every window in the house was dark.

Kaleigh, hanging from the sill with both hands, wiggled her feet, dropping her flip-flops first. Then she let go and fell. She'd done it dozens of times, but tonight, of all nights, she twisted her ankle as she hit the ground. "Ouch!" She grabbed her ankle, rubbing it. "Sweet baby Jesus, that hurt. Why's it a bad idea?" She tried to stand on the injured limb and winced.

Rob retrieved her flip-flops and arranged them in the grass in front of her. "Because you're going to break a leg jumping out your second-story bedroom window one of these days."

"It's not broken." She stepped into her flip-flops and hobbled across the lawn.

"Because we're breaking curfew, *again,* and if we get caught *again,* there'll be sanctions by the General Council."

"They always say that. There never are. I'm the town's wisewoman. I've got more power in my pinkie than some of these Vs have in their entire bodies," she argued, wiggling her little finger at him. "What kind of sanctions could they invoke? I'm only seventeen," she scoffed. "They going to take away my job at the Dairy Queen?"

"You're not officially the wisewoman yet," he argued, hurrying after her. "Not until you're twenty-one. There's going to be drinking there and you know it. We're not supposed to be drinking, Kaleigh. It's not safe at our age. Uncontrolled powers—"

"You're such a worrywart." She reached the sidewalk that ran along the edge of her parents' well-manicured lawn and halted, turning to him. He was taller than she was now and his shoulders were getting broader. She clasped his cheeks between her palms and pushed, making him pucker his lips out. She lifted on her toes and kissed him hard. "Which is part of why I love you, I guess." She let go of him. "You give me balance. You're the yin to my yang. The white to the black in my black-and-white milkshake." Chuckling at her own joke, she started down the sidewalk, limping only slightly.

The neighborhood was quiet and still, the already sleepy town nearly comatose. A warm, humid breeze rustled the sycamore trees that lined the picturesque street. It was a perfect night for a summer party.

"That doesn't make any sense," he told her.

"So?" She put out her hand for him. "Come on, we're going to be late. Katy won't wait for us and I'm not sure which house it is."

*   *   *

They had no trouble finding it. It was the house on First Street pulsing with music, every window lit up, the front and back doors flung open. Teenagers and young adults spilled out of the house onto the dilapidated front porch, into the driveway, and onto the lawn. A guy had turned on the garden hose at the side of the house and was spraying down two busty teenage girls. The HFs squealed in protest, trying to block the spray with their hands, but made no attempt to escape the impromptu wet T-shirt contest.

Kaleigh glanced at Rob, who walked beside her. "You sure you still wanna go home? Looks like the kind of party where some poor, drunk girl shows everyone her titties."

He scowled, tightening his grip on her fingers as she tried to loosen them. "You know I don't care about other girls. Humans. I love you, Kaleigh. I'll never love anyone but you."

"You're loyal enough," she quipped. "I'll give you that. Now come on, smile. Have some fun." She drew her face close to his, rolling her eyes playfully. "Or at least *pretend* you're having fun."

Katy greeted them on the front porch. She sat perched on the railing, bare legs dangling over the edge, a red plastic cup in her hand. "Where you been?" she called over the heavy beat of the music. "I figured you chickened out."

Kaleigh limped up the front steps, Rob trailed behind. "Chicken out? Me? The girl who chases werewolves and lives to tell the tale?"

"Kaleigh," Rob whispered, glancing uneasily around him. "Someone will hear you."

She laughed. "No one believes in werewolves, silly. It's perfectly safe."

"Rob! Hey, man, what's goin' on?" an HM they knew from school called from the other end of the porch.

Rob looked to Kaleigh.

She gave him a gentle push. "Go on, talk to the guys. We're already stuck with each other for eternity, it's not like you don't know who I'm going home with."

"I don't want you drinking," he warned. "Not here. Not in front of humans."

"I'm not going to drink." She gazed into his eyes. She meant it. Her drinking days had ended two years ago when she'd naïvely and inadvertently led vampire slayers right into Clare Point's backyard. Kaleigh was just here tonight for a little fun. For the adventure. She knew she didn't belong among these people, but it was okay to pretend for a little while, wasn't it? Besides, it was the perfect chance to observe humans in their native habitat. The more she knew about them, the better she would fit in. Right? And if she was here, she could keep an eye on Katy. Her best friend had her a little worried these days. She just didn't seem like herself.

"I love you," Rob said

"I love you." Kaleigh gave him a quick kiss. "Now stop acting like you're my mother." She let him go. "Or my keeper."

"Then don't act like you *need* a keeper."

She stuck her tongue out at him and walked away.

"Worrywart busy worrying?" Katy was wearing her red bikini top and a pair of itsy-bitsy surf shorts.

"Of course. It's his job, right? Hard to break, these centuries-old habits."

"I'll drink to that." Katy tipped the cup to her mouth.

Before Katy could take a sip, Kaleigh snatched it away from her. "What are you drinking?" She sniffed the amber liquid.

"What do you think I'm drinking? These boys are serious. They've got a keg in the bathtub."

"No alcohol." Kaleigh turned the cup upside down over the rail and poured the beer into the bushes.

"Hey!" Katy protested. "I had to pay a five-buck cover."

"No drinking alcohol or using drugs," Kaleigh warned. "You know better."

"Sheesh. What's with you, party-pooper extraordinaire?" Katy jumped down from the railing. "Bad day in the land of the vanilla chocolate twist cones?"

"I'm just trying to look out for you." She glanced in the front door, propped open by a boogie board wedged under the knob. "Hot Italian guy here?"

"I don't know." Katy pouted. "I never made it past the keg. I was waiting for you."

"So I'm here." Kaleigh opened her arms. "Let's check it out."

Fin sat on the bench, his back to the boardwalk, and watched as the frothy waves lapped the shore in a sliver of moonlight. It was after one in the morning and the beach was deserted, the boardwalk and gated shops a ghost town. Word had gotten out that a man had been killed last night. The tourists, uneasy, had turned in early for the evening. Even the locals had stayed in tonight, or at least avoided the beach.

Fin dropped his head. He still couldn't believe what he had seen in that examining room. Could one of their own really have done such a thing? Was one of them really capable of taking a human's life that way? He didn't want to believe it. But he hadn't wanted to believe his brother had been addicted to cocaine, either.

Even vampires were not infallible creatures.

He rubbed his itchy, tired eyes. He'd gone home for a shower around eleven thirty with the intention of hitting the sack, but he hadn't been able to sleep. He'd left Regan watching TV on the couch. Neither mentioned their argument the night before. When Regan couldn't sleep, he watched old sitcoms. When Fin couldn't sleep, he was drawn to the ocean. There was something about the rhythm of the waves that he found soothing, on any shore, on any continent.

Fin couldn't get Colin Meding's face out of his mind. The empty blue eyes. His macabre pose. The gaping neck wound. What kind of person would kill an innocent young man and then arrange his body against a Dumpster in an alley? No one had said it aloud in the station, not all day, but they had all been thinking the same thing. Fin knew what kind of man would do something like this, and the thought of such a creature in his own town again made him sick to his stomach. He knew this man; every man and woman in the sept knew him because they had vowed to God to rid the earth of his kind. Colin's murder wasn't the result of a drunken bar fight or an argument over a girl. Fin knew from experience that only one kind of human killed another human and left him posed. A man who would kill again. And again. And would continue to kill until someone stopped him. But that only applied to humans, didn't it? Could a vampire be a serial killer?

"Shouldn't you be in bed, Officer?"

The female voice startled Fin so badly that he whipped around, rising off the bench.

It was Elena. He'd never even heard her approach.

He glanced up the boardwalk and down. It was devoid of human or spirit, and eerily quiet. Where the hell had she come from? How had he been so engrossed in his thoughts that he'd allowed a human to approach without being aware of her? It wasn't like him and it was dangerous.

It took him a second to find his voice, but she didn't seem to notice. She sat down on the bench. She was wearing a pair of shorts and a sweatshirt with CLARE POINT BEACH printed across it in bold graphics. And she was barefoot. Maybe that's why he hadn't heard her. But he should have sensed her approach even if he didn't hear it.

"What . . . you shouldn't be out here this time of night. Alone," he said, sitting down again.

"I couldn't sleep." She drew her knees up and rested her feet on the wooden slats of the bench. "I didn't want to wake anyone in the house with my prowling."

She sat close enough that her sleeve brushed his bare arm. He could feel the heat of her body in the cool night air. Suddenly he felt chilled and was drawn to her. "I know you know what happened here last night. You shouldn't be out here alone."

"I'm not afraid," she said softly, her voice reflecting some tragedy that made her bold or stupid, though which he wasn't sure.

"It's not about being afraid, it's about being smart."

"You're here. What makes you safe?"

The fact that I'm not human, he thought. He didn't say it, of course.

"Because you're the law?" Her voice was teasing now. "Or are you—how do you Americans say— packing heat?" She slipped her arm around his waist and felt for a weapon. In the process, she moved closer, pressing her body against his.

He turned to her to answer and found himself looking into wide, deep, dark eyes. Her full lips were pursed, moist, and begging to be kissed.

Fin knew he shouldn't, but the pull was as strong as that of the moon on the earth's tides. Suddenly he was desperate for her warmth. Literally and figuratively.

Just one kiss, he told himself as he leaned toward her. To satisfy his curiosity.

As his lips met hers, she sighed, her breath mingling with his. Her lips were soft and pliable, the scent of her perfume utterly intoxicating.

Fin couldn't stop at one. His first kiss tested the waters. On the second, he waded in. She tasted as good as she smelled and his fingertips found her slender neck as he deepened the kiss.

This time she moaned, first rising on her knees on the bench, then climbing into his lap. She wrapped her arms around his neck and curled her body around his. He kissed the side of her mouth, trying to catch his breath. His lips, of their own accord, slid downward, over her jawline to the slender length of her neck.

He felt the prickle of gooseflesh rise on sweet-scented skin and she stretched like a cat, baring more. Her pulse beat against his lips, throbbing with life and that which gave him life.

Fin was breathing hard. Harder than he should have been after a couple of relatively innocent kisses. He was rock solid beneath his gym shorts and straining against the fabric. She couldn't have not known, not the way her shapely buttocks pressed against his groin.

He tasted her skin with the tip of his tongue. It would be so easy, just a tiny nip of the skin . . . Just a taste. It had been a long time since he had sampled human blood. And he had always had an affinity for Italian blood.

He drew back, his head buzzing. He was dizzy with the ancient, cursed longing that would never be entirely satiated until he was dead. He couldn't understand why Regan needed drugs; this feeling was a better high than any chemical.

He pressed his mouth harder against her neck and she sighed again. No, it was closer to a moan.

Do it.

The voice in his head startled him and he drew back, looking down at her, cradled in his lap. He knew she had not spoken, but it had been her voice in his mind.

Hadn't it?

"What did you say?" he whispered.

She smiled, her mouth sexy, sultry. "I didn't say anything." She lifted her chin to kiss him again.

Fin resisted. He couldn't do this. Not here. Not now. Not when there was a dead man in the cooler in Dr. Caldwell's office. A dead man who was, by forfeit, Fin's responsibility. "You should go home," he said, still holding her in his arms, not meaning it, but wanting to.

She watched him for a moment and then relaxed in his lap. She didn't seem offended. A little surprised, maybe, but not angry or hurt. She reached up and brushed her thumb across the corner of his mouth. "Lipstick. Apologies."

"What?" His mind was still fuzzy, his heart still racing. He couldn't believe he had actually considered taking this woman's blood. He really *did* need some sleep. He obviously wasn't thinking clearly.

"I got some lipstick on your mouth," she said, smiling. "You're a good kisser."

He laughed. He didn't know why. Somehow her remark made him feel younger, his position in the world somehow less tragic. "You're not bad yourself." Impulsively, he kissed her cheek.

She remained on his lap but leaned back, resting her hands on his shoulders. "I'm not looking for a relationship, Fin, if that's what you're worried about. Just a little summer companionship. I'll be going back to Italy in August. I'll never see you again."

She didn't say she just wanted to have sex with him, but that's what she meant. She just wanted a sexual relationship, no promises, no commitments. It was perfect for Fin. Forbidden by the sept, obviously, but perfect. Clean. And safe. Emotionally, at least.

So why did he feel disappointed somewhere deep inside?

"I'm sharing a cottage for the summer with my brother," he told her. "Going there could get a little complicated."

"I'm sharing a house with my sister, my brother-in-law, and their three children." She smiled that beautiful smile of hers. "So that could be a little complicated, as well."

They both laughed. "Let me walk you home," he said.

She slid off his lap, brushing her fingertips over the bulge in his shorts. It was not accidental. "I don't need an escort, Fin. Whoever is out there should be afraid of me." She walked away. "We're at the Rose Cottage. You know it?"

"I know it."

Built at the turn of the eighteenth century and well maintained over the years, it was the most expensive rental in Clare Point. It was on the oceanfront block, south of the end of the boardwalk, with a phenomenal view.

"Come by tomorrow night after work," she told him as she walked away.

"I don't know how late I'll be," he called after her. "Work's become more complicated than my living arrangements."

"I'll wait."

Her words were almost lost on the ocean breeze that had kicked up. But not her meaning.

Rob wove his way through the crowded living room, circumnavigating couples dancing and a beer pong table. It was late and the party was in full swing. From the far side of the room Kaleigh watched him watch her, thinking he was kind of cute, in a geeky kind of way. She liked the way he looked at her. Like he thought she was sexy. Smart. Like he liked her.

When he reached her, he leaned down. He was taller than she was now, though he hadn't been when he'd been reborn the year before. "How's the ankle?"

"Fine," she lied. She'd been ignoring the pain all evening because she wanted to be here, but now she was tired and it was beginning to throb again.

"Done enough *research* on human teens for one night?" he asked.

She could barely hear him over the blare and throb of the Kanye West song. She ran her palm over his chest. "I guess so. I can't find Katy. I don't know if she went home or what."

"You're not her keeper. She's fine. She always is. She probably just went home."

Kaleigh glanced around. "I guess you're right."

Rob squeezed by her to head for the door, but she grabbed his arm, stopping him. "You know what's going on down there?" she asked.

"Where?" He turned back.

"The basement." She pointed to the door across the room. "Mickey's boyfriend's been manning the door all night. He's letting a few people in and a few people out. I think he's like a bouncer or something."

Rob studied Tomboy's hulking figure.

"What do you think they're doing down there?" she whispered.

Rob shrugged, not all that interested. "I don't know. Something they shouldn't be doing, I guess."

"Like what?" She glanced around the loud, semi-dark room in an exaggerated motion. "Underage drinking, gambling, making out on the dance floor. They're doing that in plain sight. What else could they be doing?"

Rob grabbed her hand and started for the door again. "Drugs, I guess. Sex. I don't know. Why do you care?"

She took one last look in the direction of the basement door as he led her onto the front porch. "I guess I don't." The air felt cooler outside and she could breathe again. "Beppe went down."

"Who?" Still holding her hand, Rob led Kaleigh down the steps.

"Beppe. That Italian guy Katy met at the arcade."

Rob halted in the driveway. Some HF girl was hunched over a bush at the corner of the house making puking sounds. Rob grimaced. "You think Katy's with him in the basement? You want me to check?"

She thought for a minute, wondering where her special powers were when she needed them. If only she could see everything and be everywhere, now that would be some cool powers. "Nah. I saw her and Pete arguing earlier. She probably just went home and didn't tell me—as usual." She exhaled. "Let's go."

"You call her?"

"She lost her cell again." Kaleigh gave a wave of dismissal, trying not to limp. "She'll be fine. Let's go."

They walked down the middle of the street, holding hands. Kaleigh could smell the ocean and she breathed deeply. Everyone else in the town still dreamed of their homeland, of Ireland, but she loved Delaware. She loved the ocean. The beach. She loved the hope this new world had brought the sept.

At the end of the street, they turned for home. The streets were empty. Quiet. It was a quaint town. It was no wonder humans liked it here. They felt comfortable here. Safe.

She wondered if Colin Meding had felt safe.

Kaleigh was just turning to Rob to ask him if he'd heard anything more about the murder at the party tonight when she felt someone approaching. Mild panic fluttered in her chest and she immediately took command of her enhanced senses. Her encounter with the werewolf last year had made her less trusting of the world, more aware of her responsibility to others. But the man approaching was not of the genus *Canis* and not *Homo sapiens*. It was one of their own.

"Shit," she muttered under her breath and took off at a hobbling run.

Chapter 7

Regan knew what was going to happen before he turned the corner off Bourbon Street onto the quieter St. Philip in the French Quarter, yet he couldn't stop himself. He couldn't turn around. It was as if he was in two places at once. He was inside his body, but also following from behind, watching, waiting, knowing the scene that would unfold.

He tipped back the beer and tasted the last of the pungent brew. Wiping his mouth with the back of his hand, he tossed the bottle onto the sidewalk and listened to the satisfying sound of splintering glass.

He was high. High and drunk and feeling pretty damned good. At least the walking Regan felt good. The following Regan, not so much.

Turn around, he wanted to shout after himself. *Turn around and run.* But of course he couldn't because this was a nightmare, one he was doomed to relive again and again.

He heard them approaching before he saw them. It was nothing more than a whistle in the wind and the feel of the change in the night air. Maybe he heard the flutter of one of those ridiculous capes they wore.

Half a block farther and he would have been safe. Even at this time of night, there was always traffic on Dauphine. But of course he hadn't reached Dauphine. He never did, no matter how many times he dreamed the dream again, knowing what would unfold if he *didn't* make it to Dauphine. But once again, Regan was alone in the alley at two a.m. and they knew it, the evil bastards.

There were three of them, brothers: Zebulun, Asher, and Gad. Which was at least two too many, even if Regan had been sober. They always came from above . . . or maybe behind. He could never really tell. The first one, the blond, always came at him head-on so Regan would see him coming. The terror factor.

Regan heard himself cry out, startled by the apparition. No matter how many times he relived it, he was still surprised to see those damned Cajuns fly out of the darkness, descending upon him. They couldn't actually fly, per se, but in his state, it always seemed like it.

Zebulun hit Regan full force in the chest, knocking him to the filthy sidewalk that reeked of rats, vermin, and human urine. His head hit the bricks with a sickening thud and bounced. He smelled his own blood oozing into his hair.

They always let him get to his feet before they knocked him down again. They always let him think there was a chance he could get away. That he might be able to avoid being trapped in the tomb. Regan half crawled, half dragged himself onto the street. The Rousseaus circled him like dogs cornering their prey.

The funny thing was, in the dream, they never said anything. The night it had happened, there had been curses and accusations made in that bizarre French-

Cajun talk of theirs. They knew he had stolen the ship-ment of cocaine. They knew he had sold some of it, lost some of it, snorted a good deal of it.

But in the dream it wasn't about the drugs. It was about the terror, about the anticipation of what he knew would come. Getting beat up wasn't so bad. It was the waking up sober, locked in the tomb with the spiders crawling over his face that really got to him.

Just as Regan lifted his head, he saw the tall one's black boot. He felt the boot connect with his chin. As his head snapped back, he heard the blood spatter on the street and on his new shirt.

One of them squealed with delight at the scent of his blood and lifted him to his feet from behind, pinning his arms against the small of his back. He smelled the sour breath of the blond as the cretin pushed back his cape and bared his pointed canines.

"No," the Regan being attacked cried out. To be forcibly fed upon by another vampire was the lowest, the most despicable form of subjugation.

"No!" the follower echoed.

"No!" Regan sobbed, thrashing in his narrow bed.

To his relief, he woke in the dark, safe in his bed in the little cottage in Clare Point, far from the streets of New Orleans.

Rob ran after her, looking over his shoulder. "Why are we running?"

Ignoring the pain that shot from her ankle, Kaleigh cut between Mary Hill's rhododendron bushes and raced through her backyard, skirting her fish pond.

"Kaleigh!"

"Go home, Rob," she told him.

"Kaleigh, what's going on? You're hurt. Why are you running? Who's chasing us?"

"He's not chasing *us*"—she jumped over a row of marigolds, landing on her good foot on the brick sidewalk that ran along the side of Mary's house—"just me. Go home, Rob."

He jogged beside her. He didn't have to run, she was moving too slowly. "Are we in trouble?"

"No." She gave him a push. "Just head for home. He'll follow me. If anyone's in trouble it's me." She came up short in front of a gate between Mary Hill and Mary Kane's side yards and gave Rob a quick kiss. "Trust me." She threw open the latch and pushed the gate open. "Go home. Now. I'll talk to you in the morning."

Once through the gate, Kaleigh hobbled off as fast as she could go. Rob hesitated in the dark.

Trust me, she telepathed.

He didn't always get her messages, as his telepathic abilities weren't all that hot yet. But after a second, he sprinted in the opposite direction.

Kaleigh almost made it into her house. She was perched on a vine trellis, just reaching for the windowsill on the second story when the window slowly lowered of its own accord and the lock on the inside spun shut.

"Crap," she muttered. Without looking down, she exhaled in exasperation and shifted her weight, as best she could, to her good foot. "So you going to levitate me down, or just leave me up here?"

"Just leave you up there," Fin said. "At least for the moment. Where've you been?"

She gripped the trellis that now groaned under her weight. "Nowhere."

"That why you were running from me?"

"I wasn't running from you." The wooden trellis shifted and wobbled a little.

"You're not supposed to be out after curfew, Kaleigh."

Kaleigh looked for a place to get a better footing. It was a long drop from here to the flowerbed, especially with one bad ankle, but she was afraid she was going to have to go for it. "Could I get a little help here before I fall and break my neck?" she snapped, clinging to the slats of the trellis.

"Let go."

Trusting Fin completely, Kaleigh let go. For an instant, she felt the same rush she experienced when an elevator dropped, only she didn't fall, she just drifted downward, the night breeze cool against her sweaty scalp. It was the greatest feeling; she wished it could have lasted longer. She touched down in a bed of purple and yellow pansies.

"Where were you, Kaleigh?" Fin sounded cross now. And tired.

She turned to him, folding her arms over her chest, slumping the way she saw human teens do when cornered by an adult. Fortunately, her stance allowed her to shift most of her weight off her injured ankle. "Why do you care?"

"Hmm. Let's see." He crossed his arms and imitated her posture perfectly. "Because you're breaking the law and hmm, I'm what? An officer of the law?"

"It's a bogus law. Passed by the town council. It would never stand up in court. And you're a bogus cop," she added.

"How about because you're my niece and it's my responsibility to keep an eye on you?"

"Only because you don't want to piss off your mom or mine."

She was disappointed he didn't take the bogus-cop bait. It would have been a good way to sidetrack the conversation.

He met her gaze. It was pitch dark, the sky moonless, but they both had keen eyesight. That came in handy when you were a vampire prowling the earth at night for victims. Or trying to sneak back into the house without your parents catching you.

"How about I care because you, Kaleigh Kahill, are the one most responsible for the safety, for the very existence, of our family? All hope of our salvation rests on your shoulders. Without you and your guidance, we would never have come to these shores, we would never have seen God's light, and our souls would truly be damned."

She threw back her head and groaned, balling her hands into fists. "Jezus," she said, imitating the Irish accent they had all once had. "You always have to pull the wisewoman card, don't you?"

He smiled sadly. "I know it's hard."

She dropped her hands to her sides. "You have no idea," she said drolly.

"So where were you?"

She stepped out of her mother's flowerbed. "Can't tell you."

"Because you're not a rat."

"I'm not a rat."

"Please tell me you're being careful."

This time she met his gaze and didn't look away. She sensed they weren't just talking about his concern for the safety of some teens sowing their wild oats a little. She tried to read his mind, but he was ready for her.

She hit a brick wall, literally. In her mind, she visualized the psychic barriers people put up differently, depending on who it was. With the good ones, it was a brick wall. Solid. Impenetrable. At least to her now, in her current teenage state.

Sometimes, when she couldn't read people's minds, she had to resort to the human way of getting information out of people. "What's up, Fin? It's the dead guy, isn't it?"

"Kaleigh, you know I'm not at liberty—"

She laughed. He was cute, her uncle. And he could be so silly. "Fin, you're talking to the woman responsible for your soul and the souls of the couple hundred of us still left. You're not at liberty? You can't pull that crap on me. What did you find out?"

He glanced at the grass between their feet. "Looks like it was one of us."

It took a moment for what he said to sink in. "Holy shit."

He looked up, pointing at her. "But you keep that to yourself, okay? I'm serious."

"Okay," she breathed, still shocked.

"Now, go to bed." He pointed to the dark window on the second story.

She looked at the window and frowned. "How do you expect me to get in?"

"Same way you got out."

"You locked the window. From the inside."

Fin turned away, but as he did, the window magically lifted.

"You're not even going to give me a boost up?" she called after him.

"Go to bed." He walked across the lawn.

"Anything I can do?" She remained where she was

standing. She felt sorry for him, him being a cop all of two days. This was bad, a Kahill killing a tourist. Bad. "I mean about the dead guy," she said. He was nothing more than a shadow now.

"Pray for our sorry souls."

"So, what have you got so far?"

Fin cradled the phone on his shoulder as he sifted through the rising stack of paperwork the Colin Meding case was producing. He hadn't meant to take over the chief's desk, or his office, it had just sort of happened. Yesterday, he'd used the office because it was the only one with a door on it and lent some sense of privacy. Here was where he had spoken to Colin's parents. Alone. Unsupported by the chief of police. Sean had never shown up for the appointment or for work. He'd had his wife call in saying he had a stomach bug. So far, he hadn't shown up today, either.

The meeting with the victim's family had been even worse than Fin had thought it would be, if that was possible. Mrs. Meding had done nothing but sob uncontrollably. Mr. Meding had been angry, bordering on violent. The older brother, a law student, was threatening lawsuits. Not that Fin could blame any of them. While talking to them, he had vacillated between wanting to cry and wanting to punch a wall. He *really* didn't want this job.

"Fin?" Fia said on the other end of the line. "Try to focus, baby brother. What have you learned about the victim's whereabouts the day he was murdered? Where did he go? Who did he see? You need to take facts to the General Council before you make accusations. You know how defensive some people get."

Fin had had men on that all day yesterday. Good investigative skills would lead to a killer, be he human or vampire. Start at the moment of the murder and work back, Fia had instructed. Somewhere in that timeline, the victim's and the perpetrator's lives had intersected. Something had happened, throwing them on course to the tragic end result. In this case, a posed dead surfer and a Dumpster.

"That didn't take any real detective work," he said, making no attempt to hide his frustration. That was one good thing about consulting with his sister on the case. He didn't have to play the tough, composed cop. "It was info easy enough to find. Everyone and their brother saw him Friday. Vs and Hs. No one acted like they had anything to hide. Colin worked an eight-hour shift at the Hillmans' caramel corn place on the board-walk. He had pizza with friends at Sal's, then went to the arcade and stayed there until it closed. Then he went home. Apparently his roommate had a girl back to the house so Colin went for a walk."

"Okay," Fia said.

"So far, we haven't been able to find anyone who saw him after he left the house on First Street around midnight."

"And no one noticed when he didn't return after his walk? Not his roommate, not the other guys living in the house?" she questioned. "What? You said there were a total of six of them in the house?"

Fin sat back in his uncle's comfy leather chair and clicked his ballpoint pen rhythmically. "Six on the lease. Come to find out, there are nine actually staying there."

"And it's one of Victor's rentals? Those places are dives and small dives at that."

"The less you pay for rent, the more you have for

beer, I guess." *Click-click.* "Everyone saw Colin leave, but no one noticed he didn't come back. Apparently, the roommates were having a Ping-Pong marathon in the backyard. When they turned in about five a.m., everyone assumed he'd come in earlier by the front door off the street and gone to bed."

"What about the guy he shared the bedroom with?" *Click-click. Click-click.* "Roommate got the munchies after sex. He and the girl went to her place, another rental, on Third. She made him pancakes and he spent the night."

"I guess it doesn't really matter," Fia said, "but I'm curious. Why didn't anyone notice when Colin didn't come out of his bedroom the next day?"

"Everyone assumed he went to work before they got up around noon." *Click-click.*

"Makes sense," Fia commiserated. "The roommates have any idea who he had sex with prior to death?"

Fin threw the pen on the desk. "The consensus was that if he got lucky the night of his death, it was his first."

"You're kidding."

"Religious family. I'm telling you, he was a good kid."

"Perfect," Fia muttered on the other end of the phone line. "I don't suppose anyone saw him hanging out with any locals?"

"Way too easy," he responded. "I've made a list of friends and acquaintances he had in Clare Point. Mostly other college students renting on the same street. Everyone he hung out with was human. So far, the only connection I can make to one of us is Liz and Joe Hillman, who he worked for." Fin hated to even suggest such a thing; Liz and Joe were some of the nicest vampires he knew.

"Not very likely killers, not with an MO like this," Fia said, thinking out loud. "Something tells me Colin Meding would not have been interested in having sex with Liz."

Unable to resist, Fin smiled at the picture Fia was painting in his mind. Liz was short for a Kahill. And round. And middle-aged. Not a hot ticket in a beach town where there were half-naked nineteen-year-old girls strutting up and down the boardwalk. "I'm thinking the sex and the murder might not be connected. Might be, but I don't automatically want to assume his killer was his sex partner. He could have had sex with a human, then bumped into our friendly vampire."

"Any evidence on the body? Hair? Fibers?"

"None." Fin lowered his head, propping it with the heel of his hand, his elbow on the desk. "ME agreed that the victim had been in the ocean prior to death. The body fluids he found on the inside of Colin's shorts were probably contaminated by the salt water. We sent them to the lab anyway. Just in case."

Fia was silent on the other end of the line.

"So what do you think?" Fin finally asked.

"Honestly?"

He sat up and leaned back in the chair. Through the glass, he could see a couple of officers milling around in the bullpen. Everyone else was out on the street, either patrolling the town or still conducting interviews on the boardwalk. The force had been amazingly cooperative and efficient so far. No one seemed to resent Fin taking over the investigation, nor did they seem surprised. "Honestly," he said. "I mean, we're coming up on seventy-two hours. I know that isn't good in a human case; it's a long time. But in V time, it's just a blink of an eye."

"I think this is going to be a tough one, Fin. When you go to the General Council meeting tomorrow night, I doubt anyone is going to stand up, raise her or his hand, and confess to the digression."

"It just doesn't make sense." He squeezed his eyes shut for a moment. "I mean, I know it happens once in a while, but why kill a tourist? Why risk our livelihood like this?"

"You know why. Human blood."

He frowned but said nothing.

"Look," she went on. "We all do foolish, dangerous things, Fin. Things we know are wrong. Sometimes we just can't help it. It's why it's called a curse."

There was something in her tone that caught him off guard. "You speaking from experience?"

"I didn't kill him," she answered, not answering his question. "Call me if anything comes up."

"That's it?" He pushed the hair out of his eyes. "I have a dead twenty-two-year-old HM and I just wait to see if anything *comes up?*"

"You keep interviewing tourists. Make sure no one saw anything that night on the boardwalk. It wasn't that late. Surely someone else was there."

"Obviously *someone* was there, otherwise Colin Meding wouldn't be dead."

She ignored his sarcasm. "Keep your ears open around town, but yeah, that's it. You just have to wait until someone confesses or something comes up."

"Like another dead body?"

"Hopefully, it won't come to that. Gotta go, bro."

Fin hung up the phone and stared at the thick file on the desk labeled *Meding, C.* He really didn't know where to go from here. All he could think of was that the kid ended up on the boardwalk. There had to be clues there.

He rose from the chair. So that was where he needed to be.

"Anyone see you?" Gazing out over her backyard to the alley behind her property, Mary held open the door for Victor.

"What do I care if anyone saw me?" he grumbled. But as he passed, he kissed her cheek. "Smells good."

Smiling to herself, she closed the door and followed him into the kitchen. Victor's bark was far greater than his bite, she was coming to learn. "Fried oysters, stewed squash, corn on the cob. All your favorites." She smoothed the flowered pink paisley apron she wore over her shorts and T-shirt. "I've missed you. I thought you were coming by Friday night. I waited for you, wore my new nightie. Didn't hear from you Saturday or yesterday, either."

"Anything I can do to help you?" he asked, though he'd already seated himself at the kitchen table she'd set for two.

She hesitated. He'd been acting a little odd lately, odd even for Victor. She considered pressing him to see why he hadn't come Friday, but decided to let it drop. She was just glad he was here now. "Supper's all set," she said. "But you could light the candles on the table."

"What's the matter, didn't pay your electric bill?" He rose from his chair and went to a drawer to get a lighter. "Back in my day, we used candles because we had to, not because they were *romantic*."

"You want the fried oysters, I want the candles." She retrieved his dinner plate from the table and began to heap it with the crispy, aromatic fritters. "You get your homemade meal, I get a romantic dinner with my beau." She began to add squash to his plate. "You don't like it, old man, you can go home to your Chef Boyardee out of a can."

Victor lit the candles on the center of the small table and sat down again. "Sure smells good."

"Thank you." She placed his plate in front of him and took her own to the stove.

Victor waited politely for Mary to serve herself. She took her time, removing her apron and hanging it on a hook on the wall before sitting down across from him. She smiled across the table. She knew a lot of people wouldn't understand her attraction to Victor, not with Bobby having only been killed two years ago. But Victor was good company for her. They liked the same foods, liked to watch the same things on TV like *Jeopardy!* and *Dancing with the Stars*. And despite his constant complaining, he was good to her. After Bobby died, Mary had felt she had died with him. Wished she had. Victor made her feel alive again.

"Would you like to say grace or shall I?" Mary asked, sliding her hand across the table to take his.

He stole a quick glance across the table, his gray eyes twinkling. "You do it, ole girl, but hurry up. Oysters are getting cold."

Chapter 8

"**T**hanks for meeting me." Fin sat across from Elena at a small high-top table at O'Malley's, a restaurant on the boardwalk. It was a private joke among sept members. The O'Malleys, a family of vampire slayers, had been the ones who had finally driven the Kahills from Ireland. Instead of wiping them out, the O'Malleys had inadvertently given them a chance to redeem themselves in the New World. The Kahills toasted to the O'Malleys regularly.

Elena wrapped her slender fingers around the pomegranate martini she had ordered. They had to lean close to be heard over the music being piped in through speakers over the bar. Classic rock and roll. "I was beginning to think you wouldn't call." Her long, dark hair framed her heart-shaped face as she studied him with big dark eyes. "I'm glad you did."

An untouched glass of Molson sat in front of him. "Like I said on the phone, can't promise I'll be great company." He met her gaze and half smiled. "But I'm glad you came."

"I understand. Preoccupied. Any leads on the murder?" She sipped the ruby red drink. "Such a handsome young man. I saw his picture in the papers." The sound of Mick Jagger's throaty voice pulsed in the air.

"I can't talk about the investigation." He sipped his beer. It was good. Light, not heavy like the ales and stouts he drank at the Hill with his own kind.

"So that would be a no." She set her martini glass on the square napkin on the table and leaned back, crossing her long, suntanned legs.

As she did so, it occurred to Fin that every movement, every gesture Elena made, no matter how small, was fluid, like a classical dancer's. Maybe she was a dancer, but he didn't think so. This went deeper than a hobby or occupation. The way she moved was about who she was, where she had come from.

"I'm sorry to hear that," she continued. "I can see you're upset. You are very devoted to your job."

"Not really. It's a summer thing. A favor. It's just that . . ." He looked down at the beer glass between his hands, and then up again. "I feel responsible. This boy was someone's brother. Someone's son."

To his surprise, Elena's eyes teared up. He was not surprised, however, that the display of vulnerability actually made her even more beautiful.

Elena averted her gaze, obviously embarrassed.

"I'm sorry." He reached across the table to take her hand. "I've said something—"

"No. It's all right." She gave a little laugh and sniffed, but did not wipe away her tears. She looked at him again. "I was just thinking how fortunate his mother is, to have a man like you so dedicated to finding her son's killer."

Fin continued to hold her hand and for a minute they

were silent, both lost in their own thoughts. With every minute that ticked by, he thought less about Colin Meding and more about Elena.

The emotional moment passed and she slid her hand out from under his to take her drink.

"So what brings you to Clare Point?" Fin asked. "You said you came with your sister and her family on holiday, but Delaware is a long way from Florence."

"How did you know I was from Florence?" She stared at him over the rim of her martini glass. He couldn't tell if she was simply surprised by his assessment or upset by it. "I didn't tell you I was from Florence."

He shrugged. "Just a guess. You sound like you're from Florence."

"My accent?" She lifted a dark brow. "Most Americans would say my English is very good."

"Oh, it is. It is. I just have this thing." He lifted one shoulder and let it fall. "For languages."

"You speak Italian?"

"*Sì sì*. I was a student there once." Only a half lie.

"So you've been to Italy. Where? Besides Florence." Her eyes sparkled again.

They talked for a few minutes about places he had visited in Italy and the architecture he admired; he had to concentrate not to reveal more information than he should. Sometimes time ran together in Fin's head. One century was much like another; he didn't want to slip and refer to a cathedral that hadn't stood for the past thousand years. Talk of Italian architecture led to a conversation of other buildings they'd both seen all over the world. He found Elena smart, observant, and sexy from the top of her dark head to the tips of her manicured toenails. The longer they conversed, the more infatuated he became. He'd asked her out with no greater aspirations than finding a willing bed partner, but Elena was clearly more.

As she sipped the last of her martini, she leaned over the table. It was so small that when he leaned toward her to be heard above the melancholy Eric Clapton, they were nose to nose. "My sister and her husband are taking the children to a late movie tonight. Ten o'clock. You should come to the cottage."

He did the math. Ten o'clock. He could make the General Council meeting at one-thirty without any trouble.

When he didn't answer immediately, she sat back. "I'm sorry. I have offended you with my forwardness." She crossed her arms beneath her small, round breasts. She was wearing a silk flowered dress that revealed hard nipples. "You American men, you like to *make the first move.*"

"No. No, not at all. I like a woman who can take control of a situation." He smiled. "Must be the Irish influence."

She tipped her glass, finished it, and slid off the bar stool. "Come if you like. I'll be there. As I said before, no strings."

Fin watched her walk out of the bar and wondered why he had the feeling he was already caught in a web.

Fin sat down on the edge of the couch, forcing Regan to move his feet to make room for him. He set his shoes on the floor. "How'd the job hunt go today?"

Regan flipped through the channels on the TV. "About as well as the killer hunt."

"That's not funny." Fin slipped one foot and then the other into his shoes.

Regan looked at him for the first time. "Where you going, all spiffed up?"

Fin glanced at his brother. Regan was wearing a pair of boxer shorts and a Mario Bros. T-shirt. "I'm not *spiffed up*. I took a shower. General Council tonight."

"Not at nine forty-five." Regan began to run through the channels again on the TV. "You've got a date, you lucky dog." It was a statement, not a question.

Fin walked to the front door. The cardboard boxes were still precisely where they had left them the day they moved in. "You fix the faucet today?"

Regan watched a cough suppressant commercial. "No, but I beat twenty-seven kids at air hockey at the arcade. Ah, cool, *Power Rangers* are coming on. Did you know they were running all the original episodes?" He turned up the volume.

"Fix the damned faucet." Fin pushed open the screen door. "Tonight. Before I get home. Or I call Ma and tell her you've relapsed."

Regan popped up on the couch. "Jezus. You wouldn't stoop that low."

Fin smiled to himself as he went out the door. Why hadn't he thought of threatening Regan with Mary Kay before? If Fin so much as hinted that his brother might be abusing drugs again, their mother would be calling twenty times a day. She'd be visiting every hour, on the hour. The woman could be relentless. "Try me," Fin dared, letting the door slap shut behind him.

*   *   *

Kaleigh spotted Katy at the Dairy Queen service window and abandoned cleaning the soft serve machine. "Hey," she said.

"Nice hat." Katy rested her elbows on the counter and leaned through the window. "Do I have to work here to get one or can anyone wear one?"

Kaleigh adjusted her white paper hat and reached for a big jar of maraschino cherries so she could start refilling containers while she talked to Katy. "At least *I* have a job."

"Right. A loser job in a loser town," Katy groaned. "God, but I hate this place. I don't understand why you don't, too."

Katy had been on this kick for months. She hated Clare Point. She wanted to live somewhere else in the world. Anywhere but here. That, of course, would never happen. "I get off soon." Kaleigh tried to sound cheerful. She tugged on the jar lid, but it wouldn't budge. "You wanna come over and watch a movie or something?"

"Can't. Got a date."

"Wait a minute." Still unable to get the lid off the jar, she turned the jar upside down and slammed it on the counter, trying to break the seal. "As of six o'clock when I came to work, you were pissed at Pete and you were never speaking to him again." The lid still wouldn't budge.

"I am and I'm not." Katy's eyes sparkled mischievously. Then she frowned. "Give me that. You're going to hurt yourself." She grabbed the maraschino cherry jar out of Kaleigh's hands and opened it with one twist.

Kaleigh looked at the lid as she took it from her. "Thanks."

"Hey, you going to order or what?" An HF stood behind Katy. Two clone children, a boy and a girl, pulled at her terry cloth cover-up, whining about chocolate ice cream and sprinkles.

Katy and Kaleigh both ignored them. Kaleigh began to scoop cherries into plastic containers using a big metal spoon.

"You're going out with someone else?" Kaleigh whispered.

"Beppe." Katy grinned.

"Katy, that's a bad idea and you know it. Flirting is one thing, but—"

"Excuse me, but if you're not going to place an order could you move so someone else could?" The HF now sounded as whiny as her children.

"Could you give me a sec?" Katy threw over her shoulder. "Or maybe go to the next window since this one says *closed,* anyway." She pointed to the cardboard sign in the window and then turned back to Kaleigh. *Jersey,* she mouthed.

The woman snatched her children by the hands and moved to the line one window over, which was growing longer by the second. The shop closed in fifteen minutes, and the last fifteen minutes of the day always seemed the busiest.

"I better help at the window." Kaleigh put the lid back on the cherry jar. "Can you wait for me?"

Katy stood, ducking out of the service window. "Can't. I have to get home so the *rents* will go to bed so I can sneak out. My mom wants to have a *family meeting.*" She rolled her eyes. "I'm hooking up with Beppe at midnight. He's got to go to some lame movie with his family, but then we're going to Tomboy's. I've got an *open invitation* to stop by any time, now."

"You shouldn't be going out with him. You shouldn't be going to humans' houses."

"You went."

"Not with a human. You're going to get into trouble." Kaleigh looked over Katy's shoulder. The line was even longer. She really needed to help the girl at the other window. "I have to get back to work. Can't you just wait?"

"Tell you all the details in the morning." Katy slapped her hand on the counter. "Well, maybe not *all* the details." She laughed and walked away.

"You better not do anything stupid," Kaleigh hollered after her.

"Do I ever?"

"All the time," Kaleigh uttered under her breath.

Either Fin walked too fast or Elena's family was running late because as he walked up the driveway to the rear, street entrance to the cottage, the door opened. A woman who could be no one but Elena's sister walked out onto the lamplit porch, speaking in Italian to someone behind her. Fin didn't really want to meet Elena's family; he was all about keeping this simple. But there was nowhere for him to go, no place to hide.

"We' il ll parla di questo quando otteniamo la casa, Beppe. Nient'altro!" The Elena look-alike strode across the porch in a dress with a pashmina thrown over her shoulders. Same amazing legs as Elena's. She was younger, but not as pretty in the face.

There was obviously a disagreement between the sister and someone. Then someone walked out onto the porch a second later. A teenage boy. An obviously disgruntled teenage boy. He was followed by two adolescent girls; one on the cusp of the teen years, the other slightly younger. A small, dark-haired man brought up the rear.

When the sister spotted Fin, she smiled. "Elena's friend, welcome to Rose Cottage." She extended her arms graciously.

Elena was the last to walk onto the porch. When she saw Fin, she lifted her arms in silence as if to say she hadn't thought they would still be there either.

He smiled back. It wouldn't hurt to meet the family. He and Elena were both unattached adults; they weren't doing anything wrong. Well, *he* was because she was human, but that wasn't the issue here, was it? He took the staircase up to the open back porch. Because the cottage was built on pilings on the beach, the porch was a full story off the street. It was breezier here. Cooler.

"Fin Kahill." When the sister offered her hand, instead of shaking it, he kissed it. A throwback from the old days. It was the right call. When he lifted his head, she and Elena were both smiling.

"My sister Celeste, her husband, Vittore," Elena introduced. "And my nieces and nephew, Lia, Alessa, and Beppe."

"Nice to meet you, Fin." The brother-in-law offered a firm, pleasant handshake.

"And you." Fin nodded to the children. The boy ignored him. The older girl offered a half-smile but then looked down at her sandals, obviously shy.

"Nice to meet you, sir," the younger daughter said.

"Stiamo andando?" Vittore gestured dramatically to his family.

"We're going, we're going!" Celeste passed Fin, headed for the steps. "My apologies for our rudeness, but we're going to be late for the movie. Enjoy your evening. *Il mio amore a voi, sorella*." She threw her sister a kiss.

Elena stood beside Fin at the railing and watched as the family hurried down the street. "I'm sorry. I thought they'd be gone by now." She lifted onto her toes and kissed one of his cheeks and then the other.

He caught her chin with his fingertips and kissed her mouth before she could draw back. "Not a problem," he murmured against her lips.

"A glass of vino?" She crossed the porch, leaving him no choice but to follow. She was still wearing the same flowered dress she had been wearing when she'd met him earlier, but she was now barefoot and her hair was windblown, as if she'd been on the beach. When he'd kissed her, he could smell the salt air on her skin.

"Sure."

"A Malbec?"

"Argentine?" He entered the kitchen area behind her. It had been years since he'd been in the cottage. The entire kitchen had been remodeled: stainless steel appliances, tile floor, granite countertops. It was a beautiful home with an open floor plan, giant windows, and a porch on the ocean side that ran the length of the house.

"You prefer Italian wine?" She took two wine tumblers from a cabinet. "I can see what else we have."

"No, no, Malbec is great. I just expected"—he chuckled—"Italian wine, I suppose."

"I get tired of Italian wine. Last winter Celeste and I went to Argentina and toured many vineyards. I returned home with an unquenchable thirst for the blood-red nectar of the Malbec grape. A French grape originally."

Fin liked the way she thought. Interesting that they both had blood on their minds . . .

She pushed a wine bottle and corkscrew into his hands and swept up the glasses. "The beach is beautiful at night. It's my favorite time. Let's sit on the porch."

The porch was dark and she flipped off the house lights behind them before stepping outside.

"Wow, what a view."

They stood side by side at the rail and looked out on the dark beach. In the distance, Fin could just make out the white froth of the waves that washed onto the sand.

"It is beautiful, isn't it?" She sat down on a chaise lounge and set the glasses on a small table.

He opened the bottle and poured each of them a healthy portion. She patted the space beside her on the cushioned chaise and he joined her there.

"Chin chin." She clinked her glass against his and raised it in a toast. *"Squisito,"* she said, taking a sip and sitting back against the lounge chair, nestled in beside him.

He slipped his arm around her and pulled her close. It was actually chilly out and she felt good against him. "You're what's *squisita,"* he told her, kissing her. And she was delicious. He tasted the cherry and oak of the wine on her lips, and the sweetness of her passion. Not just for him, but for life. It was there everywhere he looked, in the way she dressed, the way she moved, the way her eyes sparkled. *"Squisita e bella."*

She covered his lips with her fingertips. "You don't have to do that," she whispered.

"Do what?" Holding out his hand so as not to spill the wine on her, he nuzzled her neck.

She took another sip of wine and set down the glass.

"You know." She looked into his eyes. "Say things. Flatter me. I've already invited you to make love to me." She shook her head, her voice a husky whisper. "I don't need to be wooed."

"But everyone deserves to be wooed, Elena." He took another drink and put the glass on the deck beside the chair.

"Not me."

Again, he heard a hint of tragedy in her voice that he had suspected before. He sensed she did not have an easy life. There was something about the pain in her voice that made him want to hold her. Protect her.

"Come here," he whispered, pulling her closer.

Throwing her arms around his neck, she closed her eyes and kissed him. At first, their kisses were tentative. Exploring, but it didn't take long for things to heat up.

"Make love to me, Fin," she whispered passionately. "Make them stop, make them stop in my head." She kissed him again and again, hard, her kisses punctuated with words. "Just for a few minutes."

He pushed her hair off her face, trying to get her to look at him, but she wouldn't. "Make what stop?" he panted between kisses.

"Their screams."

Chapter 9

Elena raised the filmy skirt of her dress and threw one leg over his. Hands around her waist, Fin lifted her up and then settled her on his lap. As a curtain of her dark hair fell around him, he wondered if he'd found yet another woman who was not quite mentally stable. There had been others over the centuries. His family teased that he attracted them. But Elena didn't *seem* crazy; the others, he had known from the beginning.

She plunged her tongue into his mouth and he questioned if it really mattered if she was a little nutty. After all, didn't crazy people have as much right to sex as sane people? And that was what this was all about. Sex. They'd both agreed to that.

But something felt different here. Again, he felt an overwhelming sense that he knew Elena. Knew *of* her. But he couldn't put his finger on the memory. Actually, it was hard to think about anything right now, other than getting his rocks off.

His heart pounded as he slid his hand over her calf, brushing the back of her knee before moving under the skirt of her dress. Then higher. Her skin was silky smooth, her legs muscular and well shaped. For an *older woman*, she had an amazing body. She had an amazing body for a woman ten years her junior.

Elena knew the dance of lovemaking and orchestrated it well. She molded her body to his, pressing her breasts into his chest, moaning softly as his fingertips found the silk edge of her panties.

Fin had been chilly when he stepped out onto the porch, but he was pretty sure his body temperature had gone up ten degrees. He cupped the curve of her buttocks and she pushed her groin into his. He crushed her mouth with his mouth, unable to satisfy his desire to taste her. To possess her.

"Would you like to go inside?" he whispered when they came up for air.

She shook her head. "Take it off." She sat back and grabbed the hem of his T-shirt. "Everything." She pulled his shirt over his head and threw it on the deck.

He heard his wineglass tip over, but as his fingers found the waistband of his shorts, thoughts of spilt wine flew out of his head. She slid back and tugged on his shorts.

"Not so fast." He pushed her hands away. "I want to see you."

She shook her head. "No romance, Fin. Please." She slid off him and stood beside the chaise. "Take them off," she instructed.

As he hooked his thumbs into the waistband of his shorts, she reached under her dress. His heart was in his throat as he watched her lift her hands up, then pull them down. She stepped out of the silk lace panties.

He had just enough time to shed his shorts and boxers before she was climbing onto the chair with him.

"Elena," he breathed, taking her into his arms and shifting her onto her back. "We have a little time."

She laughed, her voice throaty with building need. "Time," she repeated. "If only you knew."

"They won't be back for hours," he told her. But as the words came out of his mouth, he got the impression that they weren't talking about the same thing.

Crazy women.

He always said he liked all kinds of women: skinny, fat, blond, brunette. So he liked them sane or crazy. So what?

He pushed her down into the soft cushions and straddled her, taking care to distribute his weight carefully so he didn't hurt her. She tried to pull her dress up, but he pushed it down. Elena was so hot. So soft in the right places. He didn't want to get ahead of himself.

She slid her hands over his bare shoulders, arching her neck, beckoning him.

He kissed her mouth, then her cheek, cupping a small, firm breast. It was all going so well, so humanly. Then, one second he was thinking about her dark nipple beneath his thumb, the next, her blood.

But how could he resist the desire, the way she arched her back and lengthened her neck? It was almost as if she understood his *true* need.

He pressed his mouth to the pulse of her throat and she lifted her hips to his, effectively stroking him with her mons veneris. His tongue flicked out of his mouth and he tasted her hot, salty skin.

Perspiration beaded above his upper lip.

He slid his mouth downward over the curve of her breasts where they rose and fell at the neckline of her dress. Cupping one with his hand, he closed his mouth over the fabric, feeling her hard nipple in his mouth.

But he was still thinking about her neck. About her blood pulsing just beneath the surface of her skin.

Elena ran her hands over his bare buttocks, squeezing. Kneading.

Fin's heart was pounding. His pulse racing. He couldn't catch his breath. He was utterly intoxicated by the scent of her skin, the sound of her panting breath in his ear. Behind him, he heard the waves crashing and he thought about all the times over all the centuries that he'd made love to a woman beside the ocean.

But there had never been anyone like this woman in his arms right now.

He rose up and buried his face in her silky hair, breathing in the scent of her, trying to give himself a moment.

"Enough foreplay," Elena groaned in his ear.

Beneath him, he felt her tug up the hem of her dress until they were bare skin against bare skin.

Fin wanted to make it last longer. For her. For himself. For all the lonely nights when he lay in bed wishing he could be like her. Wishing he could be human.

But when she clasped her warm fingers around his sensitive flesh, he knew delay was no longer an option. His hand on hers, she guided him inside her and she cried out when he sank deep.

Elena lay against the angled back of the chaise lounge and raised her hands over her head as if to surrender to him. He pushed hard into her but then, feeling a strange swell of tenderness, he threaded his fingers into hers. "Open your eyes," he whispered, studying her in the darkness. "Look at me."

She shook her head, biting her love-bruised lips, and turned her face away from him.

"Elena—" He brushed his fingertips across her cheek.

"Please, don't do this."

He stopped, suddenly fearing he had made a mistake. Never once in all these centuries had he ever taken a woman against her will and he wasn't about to start now. She'd made it plain she wanted sex, but had she changed her mind? He gritted his teeth. "Don't do what?" he whispered.

"Don't make me cry," she managed, her lower lip now quivering. "Because I'll never be able to stop."

Suddenly, his heart ached for her. For whatever her misfortune had been. And he felt an overwhelming sense of guilt for having even let the thought of taking her blood cross his mind.

"Just take me there," she begged, eyes still closed. "You know where. You know how. I know you do."

Fin slipped his arms around her waist and rested his head on her shoulder for a moment. He breathed in the sweet smell of her sweaty skin, her silky hair, and the ocean breeze until all the scents seemed to mingle and become one. Then he began to move inside her. If a woman asked for an orgasm, he was going to do his best to provide it.

At first, Elena just lay there, half reclining, half sitting, her arms at her sides, her face turned away from him.

He moved slowly, giving her the time she needed.

She lifted her hips beneath him, first gently, then harder. Faster. She threw her arms around his neck and sank her manicured nails into the flesh of his back.

"*Sì, sì, come quello.* Like that," she cried.

Fin kept his focus. He wanted to do this for her. He

wanted to take away the screaming in her head, no matter whose it was. Even if it was her own.

She came hard, grinding her hips against him, gasping. Moaning. *"Per favore, per favore,"* she repeated again and again, clinging to him. *Please.*

Sometimes it was the way a woman touched him that pushed him over the edge. Other times it was just the thought of her blood. This time, it was Elena's voice, begging him. For what, he didn't know.

Elena was sitting in the dark on the steps that led from the cottage's front porch onto the beach when she heard her sister call her name. Elena was half tempted not to answer. But Celeste would know where she was whether she responded or not. Celeste always knew.

"On the stairs," Elena called, in English. Though Celeste preferred speaking Italian, Elena always tried to speak the native language when in a foreign country.

She felt her sister's presence at the top of the steps, and glanced over her shoulder. "Did you enjoy the movie?"

"It was fine. I think Beppe and Vittore enjoyed it. A man movie. Lots of shooting and blowing up cars." She looked out over the sand dunes for a moment as if she could see what Elena could see. But how could she possibly? "Brrr," she murmured, drawing her pashmina tighter around her shoulders. "It's chilly tonight." She looked down at Elena. "Aren't you cold?"

"Not so cold." Elena wrapped her arms around her knees. She was cold, but she didn't mind. The cool air made her feel alive.

Elena hoped her sister would go back into the

house; she wanted to be alone, but the hope was short-lived. Behind her, she heard footfalls on the steps.

"He seems nice, the young man." Celeste settled on the riser beside Elena.

"Mmm-hmm." From where they sat, halfway down the staircase, they could see over the shadowed outline of the sand dunes, to the white beach that led to the water's edge. The tide crashed rhythmically, its sound a comfort.

Celeste put her arm around Elena's shoulders. "Not cold? You're frozen." She rubbed her hand up and down her sister's arm.

Elena said nothing.

"How long did he stay?" Celeste asked.

Elena continued to watch the outgoing tide, imagining what it would be like to ride the waves out into the great Atlantic. To drift in the swells and let them carry her where they may. "Not long."

"Does he know that you know?"

"He does not."

Her sister was quiet for a moment. "Will you see him again?"

Elena closed her eyes, trying to shut out the vision that kept flashing in her head tonight. Bodies on the piazza, their blood slick on the stone. Why did she keep seeing it so vividly? Why now? What was it about this little town that was dredging up the memories? She opened her eyes. "Perhaps I will see him again. Perhaps I will not."

"You are full of information."

"What do you want to know, Celeste?" Elena's voice was terse, but not because she was offended by the question. She was just annoyed that her sister was making too much out of her date with Fin. "Did I make love with him? I did. Will I again? Perhaps."

"I do not have to tell you, it is not a good idea to become involved with him."

"I'm not *involved*. I don't get *involved* with men. I just have sex with them. You know that." She ran her hands over her dress where it covered her knees, remembering she had left her panties on the deck. She would have to retrieve them or risk one of her nieces finding them in the morning while breakfasting. "I wish I had a cigarette," she murmured. "I miss that. A cigarette after sex. Especially the unfiltered French ones. The ones we used to buy in that little shop in Paris."

"We gave them up, remember?" Celeste's voice was gentle. Kind.

"So as not to set a bad example for the children. Yes. I remember." Elena laughed, but without mirth. The thought was tragic, really, if one gave it much thought.

Celeste drew her pashmina around Elena's shoulders, pulling her closer. "It is not that I do not want you to be happy. You know that. Of all women, you deserve a little happiness, Elena. After what you have been through—"

"Could we not talk about this?" She wanted to shrug Celeste off but stopped short of that. Her sister was only trying to be understanding. But Celeste didn't understand Elena. She couldn't. Celeste couldn't possibly comprehend the profound loneliness, the regret so heavy in Elena's heart that sometimes she feared she could not take another breath.

And yet she always did . . .

"I would never risk your family's safety. I'll be careful, Celeste. I promise. I always am."

Celeste rested her cheek on Elena's shoulder. "But this is different this time, this man. Yes?"

Elena was shocked by the moisture that welled up in her eyes. She swallowed against the lump in her throat. It *had* been different with Fin. She had tried to deny it then, was still trying to deny it now. She and Fin had made some sort of emotional connection Elena didn't understand. A disturbing connection. "I'll be careful," she repeated.

Celeste hugged her. "This isn't just about the safety of our family. I don't want to see you hurt."

As Elena wrapped one arm around her sister and returned the embrace, she watched a figure emerge from the sand dunes in front of the house and walk onto the beach. She recognized the silhouette and wondered where he was going. Celeste did not see him and Elena did not call her attention to him.

"You make too much of this. Fin is no different than any of the others, really," Elena said, still watching the boy on the beach. "You worry too much, little sister."

"I do not know why you lie to me." Celeste rose and planted a kiss on top of Elena's head. "After all these years, you should know I know you."

"Do not worry." Elena patted Celeste's hand on her shoulder and then kissed it.

"You say that, and still I worry." Drawing her pashmina around her shoulders, Celeste started up the steps. "You will be in soon?"

"Soon."

As Elena listened to Celeste's footsteps die away, she watched her nephew head north toward town and wondered where he was sneaking off to at this time of night.

* * *

Victor stirred in bed and, half awake, wondered if he should get up and go home. Mary usually made him go in the middle of the night, or at least before dawn; she still had the foolish notion they needed to keep their affair a secret. But he didn't like going home to his empty house, not when Mary was here, all warm and soft and sweet. He rolled onto his side and reached out for her. Realizing she wasn't there, he opened his eyes and glanced toward the bathroom, expecting to see light coming from under the door.

No light.

Victor rose and threw his skinny legs over the side of the bed. His bones cracked and popped and he grimaced at the pain. There were things he liked about being a senior citizen: saying whatever he wanted to say and getting away with it, the early bird specials at the diner, the wisdom that came with age. But he didn't like the way the physical body broke down. He didn't like the aches and pains. He hated Regan for what he had done to him if for no other reason than the principle of the thing, but he had to admit, he did like the promise of youth in his future.

"Mary?" He fumbled in the dark for his boxer shorts and found them on the floor. Vampires had enhanced senses, but he bet most people didn't know they, too, faded with age. "Mary? You out there?" He shuffled out of the bedroom and into the hall and saw light coming from the kitchen.

Victor ran his fingers through his thin, white hair and then scratched his belly. "Mary?"

"Here," she called.

He found her at the kitchen table, sipping a cup of tea. He was disappointed that she had put on her flowered housecoat. He liked her naked, the way she had been in bed tonight. Maybe she didn't have the perfect, high, round breasts he saw bouncing on the boardwalk, and maybe her tummy wasn't as flat as it had once been. But Victor thought she was beautiful just the way she was.

"What are you doing?" He squinted to see the clock on the wall. He had glasses, but he could never find the darned things. "Three fifteen in the morning."

She sipped tea from a flowered teacup. "Couldn't sleep. You want some?" She pointed to the tea.

He shook his head and debated whether to go back to bed or head out. If he went now, he could go back to sleep in his own house. But Mary looked troubled.

He slowly settled into the chair across the table from her. "What's keepin' you up?" He rubbed his arthritic knee. Right one was always worse than the left.

"Go back to bed, Grumpy."

"I'm not bein' grumpy," he grunted. "This is the way I talk."

She smiled at him across the table and her smile made him warm inside. "Can't help who I am," he added. "Tell me why you can't sleep."

She sighed and looked down into her cup as if she was a gypsy reading tea leaves. When she lowered her gaze, she reminded Victor of his wife. Sarah had been her name. Beautiful Sarah who had never known what happened to her husband after he disappeared; bright, quick Sarah who was now hundreds of years in her grave.

"Liam will be returning from Prague soon. He belongs here in his father's home, but"—she looked at Victor, offering a half-smile—"but I like my privacy."

Victor leaned back in the kitchen chair and grinned.

He liked the way Mary made him feel younger than he really was. "I like your privacy, too."

"I won't be comfortable having you over with my son here, Victor."

"I could get a new mattress and you could come to my house," he offered. She complained about his lumpy mattress so they had sex mostly at her house. Besides, her refrigerator was always full. He usually had a bottle of vodka and some open cans of ravioli in his.

She sighed again and he felt bad for her. It wasn't often that he saw Mary unhappy or worried.

"It's not the mattress, Victor. Liam is a grown man. He needs his own place."

"Connor's place is still empty. The boy could move in there," he said, thinking out loud. "Connor was just reborn last year, so he's back with his sister."

"That's a thought."

"Or . . . you could just move in with me."

She met his gaze across the table. "You would want me to move in with you?"

He reached across the table to cover her hand with his. "I wouldn't just like you to move in with me, Mary. We can do better than that. I think me and you, we ought to get married." Victor didn't know where that came from but the minute he uttered the words, he knew it was the right thing to say. He knew it was the right thing to do. He wanted to marry her.

"Victor, we can't marry." She pulled her hand away, her cheeks turning pink. She was embarrassed and tickled at the same time and she looked so delicious he could have eaten her.

"Why not?"

"You know why. The sept forbids it. Bobby was my

husband and when he was beheaded and taken from us, I lost my right to marriage, forever."

"The hell with the sept." He slapped his hand on the table.

"Victor, dear." She got up from her chair and came around to him. "To live with you, it would be enough." She clasped his cheeks with her hands and leaned down and kissed him. "We have to follow sept law."

"We'll see about that," he grumbled.

Chapter 10

Richie sat on the edge of the towel in the cool sand in the dark and dug his toes in. It was late. Really late. He needed to get home. His mom would wonder where he was and he didn't like to worry her, her still taking chemo and all. But he couldn't go home yet, not until he talked to Brittany. Not until he understood.

"I can't believe you cheated on me again." His voice cracked, but he was so upset, he wasn't embarrassed. He could still smell her on his hands. What kind of girl had sex with her boyfriend under the boardwalk and then broke up with him? "I mean, why didn't you just tell me you wanted to break up? I don't understand why you had to sleep with Todd."

It was dark on the deserted beach, but he could still see her. The street lamp up on the boardwalk cast pale light over them, making his hands and feet a sickly yellow color.

Brittany stood there in front of him and twirled a lock of blond hair around her finger. Her hair wasn't really blond; she bleached it.

"You're mad," she said, like it was all his fault. "See, that's why I didn't tell you. I knew you were going to be mad." She couldn't even look him in the eye.

It really is over this time, he thought.

"Damn straight I'm mad! Everyone but me knew about it. People were laughing at me behind my back." He rested his chin on his knees.

He and Brittany had just finished their first year at Del Tech and he'd gotten a great job managing the arcade here in Clare Point. They were supposed to be taking classes together again in the fall. Maybe it was just junior college, but it was a good start, what with him having to pay his own way and all. His mom just had too many medical bills to help him out. He and Brittany were going to be teachers and teach in the same elementary school some day. They loved each other so much; they'd talked about getting married. Now here she was telling him that she was going away to college in the fall and that she was breaking up with him. *And* that she had slept with his best friend.

Richie squeezed his eyes tight, fighting back tears. Brittany didn't love him. He knew that. This wasn't the first time she had cheated on him. A couple of beers at a party and if he wasn't there keeping an eye on her, she was in bed with some loser she didn't even know. She was such a slut. His mother had told him so two years ago when they started going out. His mom had been right.

So why did he still love Brittany? Why did it hurt so much?

"Look." She pushed sand around in front of him with her high-heeled sandal.

Who wears high heels at the beach?

"I'm really sorry. I didn't mean to hurt you, Richie."

"You didn't mean to hurt me?" He wiped his eyes with the back of his hand. "You slept with the guy who's been my best friend since Cub Scouts and you didn't think that would hurt me?"

She didn't say anything. She just stood there. Finally, he looked up at her. She was wearing a short gauze skirt and a skimpy tank; he knew for a fact that her panties were in her purse. She had too much sparkly blue eye shadow on. She *looked* like a slut.

"I don't want to talk about this anymore," he told her, getting up. He'd pulled the beach towel out from under the boardwalk after they were done because it was hot under there. "I gotta go. I gotta be back by ten tomorrow morning to open the arcade and Mom just had a treatment. She might need something." He stuffed his hands into the pockets of his jean cut-offs. He could feel his keys. The keys to the car and the arcade. "You, um, need a ride home?"

"No." She looked up in the direction of the boardwalk. "I called someone . . . I got a ride."

Richie turned around and looked up. He knew he shouldn't have; he should just let it go. But he couldn't help himself. He had to know. He saw the silhouette of a guy; he knew the silhouette. He lowered his gaze to his bare feet, stuck in the sand. "So you and Todd, you're together now?" He barely sounded like himself. The thought that she had just been with him and now was going to let Todd stick it to her made him sick to his stomach. He'd never loved anyone but Brittany; never made love to anyone but her.

"I wanted to tell you face-to-face. Not send you a text or an e-mail." She started to back up, headed toward the steps that led from the beach to the boardwalk. "So, see you around?"

He just stood there, head down. "Sure. See you around." Richie didn't watch her go. He didn't want to see her and Todd together. Maybe eventually he'd have to, but not tonight.

Hands still in his pockets, he dropped to the towel again and stared at the waves rolling in. It was late; the beach was empty. There was no one on the boardwalk either, just Brittany and her new boyfriend and he could hear them walking away, talking. Brittany giggling.

He was glad she was with Todd—not *with* him, but with him walking back to wherever his car was parked. They hadn't caught whoever killed the guy from the caramel popcorn place. Personally, Richie thought the authorities would eventually find out the kid was involved in a drug ring or something like that. Why else would the killer have slit his throat like that, other than to set an example for other kids who might try to rip them off? So Brittany was probably pretty safe anyway, but Richie felt better knowing Todd was there to protect her.

Tears welled in Richie's eyes unexpectedly and he rubbed them away with the heels of his hands. He felt stupid crying. He needed to get his flip-flops and get home. Hopefully, his mom was in bed, but if she woke up and discovered he wasn't there, she'd be worried.

Startled, he turned around and saw the silhouette of someone approaching. His first thought was that Brittany was coming back to apologize, to say how sorry she was for cheating on him and beg for his forgiveness. But that was crazy, of course. She wasn't sorry and she didn't want to be with him. Besides, the person was coming from under the boardwalk, which was a little weird. He knew people went under there for various reasons, like why he and Brittany had been under there half an hour ago, but he wasn't expecting a girl, not alone at this time of night.

Curious, but a little wary, he watched her. He assumed she was headed for the stairs, but she walked right up to him.

"Hi," she said, stopping in the shadows of the boardwalk that loomed above her.

He couldn't see her features very well in the dark. "Hi."

She stared at him for a moment and then gestured in the direction Brittany had just gone. "You okay?"

Richie didn't know what to say.

"I . . . Sorry, but I kinda overheard some of your conversation with that girl. I didn't mean to," she added quickly. "It's just a weird coincidence because my boyfriend just broke up with me. He . . . he wanted to go out with someone else, too."

Richie felt his cheeks grow warm with embarrassment. It hadn't occurred to him that anyone might be nearby to overhear him and Brittany. He sure hoped she hadn't been under the boardwalk earlier. That would just be too weird. But she didn't seem to be weirded out or anything.

Richie still wasn't sure what to say. Girls didn't just come up to him and start talking like this. "Sorry about your boyfriend." He stumbled over his words. "Hurts."

She sniffed and wiped her nose with her arm. "Bad."

She sounded like she'd been crying. Maybe still was. He got up and brushed the sand off his shorts. She was still standing there. He felt bad for her. Bad that her boyfriend broke up with her and she didn't have anyone better to talk to than some loser stranger on the beach.

"Hey," she said, looking at him more closely. "I know you from the arcade. You're the owner, right?"

"Just the manager. But I'm there all the time. Some old lady owns it, so I'm pretty much in charge," he explained. She obviously assumed he was older than he was. He thought maybe he recognized her. Maybe her voice. But it was hard to say in the dark.

"I . . . I'm Richie. Richie Palmer."

"Mandy." She smiled.

She *was* crying. He could see the wet on her cheeks. She was pretty. At least from what he thought he could see in the dark, which wasn't much. He wished she would step out into the light, but maybe she was embarrassed, too.

"I . . . don't exactly feel like going home yet," Mandy said.

She looked at him with big eyes, looked at him in a way that made his stomach flip-flop. Like she liked him. How old was she? He wished he could get a better look.

"You . . . you got a few minutes? You wanna go for a walk or something?" she asked.

Richie thought about his mom. He really should go home. But she was asleep for sure. Then he thought about Brittany and he was sad all over again. And angry.

This girl, Mandy. She seemed nice.

He only had to think about it for a second. "Sure, I got a few minutes."

Fin stared at the body of Richie Palmer. He knew it was Richie Palmer because the assistant manager had identified his boss right before he vomited up his Egg

McMuffin and chocolate Yoo-hoo. What Fin *didn't* know was what Richie was doing seated in the NASCAR game, hands on the steering wheel, in the closed arcade. Dead.

"What do you want me to do with the kid who found him?" Pete asked.

Fin couldn't take his eyes off the dead boy. Richie Palmer was young and nice looking like Colin Meding. His throat had been cut ear to ear, like Colin Meding's. What made Fin think that when Dr. Caldwell did the autopsy, he would find two puncture marks somewhere along the incision line? Just like Colin Meding.

"Fin?" Pete said quietly, touching his arm to get his attention.

Fin knew Pete was right there, but he still jumped.

"Sorry," Pete muttered. He nodded toward the skinny kid with the runny nose standing on the far side of the arcade, as far from Richie Palmer as he could get. "I need to get him out of here. Name is Patrick Callahan. He's been working here all of a week. Showed up for work a few minutes before ten, went to let himself in through the back with his key, found the door unlocked, and well, you know the rest."

Pete glanced at the scared young man, then back at Fin. "You want me to take him down to the station? He wanted me to talk to his parents. They're already on their way, but they're in northern New Jersey so it will be a couple of hours."

Fin looked at the live kid a second longer, then back at the dead one. Neither could have been more than twenty or twenty-one. Babies. "Yeah, sure. Take him to the station, talk to him. But don't let him use the phone again. And get his cell. I don't want him telling anyone about this until the victim's family has been reached."

"There's just a mother, apparently. No siblings. Dad abandoned them when he was little or something."

Pete spoke softly. Fin liked his demeanor. Right now, he was a hell of a lot more composed than Fin felt. Fin wanted to punch a wall, punch a person. Punch the person responsible for this atrocity. He was sick to his stomach, not just because this human life was wasted, but because of who had done it. How could a member of the sept do this, after all the sept had done to redeem themselves? It was a smear on their family's good name. On the principles they stood for.

"The state police said they would send a car over to tell the victim's mother," Pete continued. "Patrick says the woman has cancer or something."

Only child, murdered. Cancer, Fin thought. Life was so unfair for humans. "Get his statement," he said, nodding at the other boy. "You know how to handle him."

"Will do."

"Thanks, Pete." Pete started to walk away and Fin called to him again. His mind was racing in so many directions that he felt like he had ADD or something. "And when you have a minute, could you get a hold of Rob Hill? I need to talk to him. He works here. He probably has a good idea of who comes and goes."

"You want him here or in your office?"

It wasn't Fin's office. It was his uncle's, if and when he ever showed up for work again. But Fin knew this was neither the time nor the place to bring that up. "Not here," he said. He glanced at the dead kid. "At least not before . . ." He let the sentence go unfinished.

"Right. Will do."

Pete went to tend to the puking kid and Fin turned his attention back to the body driving the simulation NASCAR vehicle. The game was on. It roared with the sound of car engines. One of the other cops had wanted to unplug it to silence it, but Fin had stopped him. He wanted to get the full effect of the scene before doing so. All the other machines were quiet, so he was guessing this one had specifically been turned on. By Richie? Maybe by the killer?

Fin studied Richie's body carefully, pushing his emotion aside and allowing his logic to take over. Richie Palmer rested his hands on the steering wheel, eyes open. He looked like any college-age kid who might have wandered in off the boardwalk to play a few video games. Except for the slit throat.

How had he gotten in here? With no sign of blood anywhere, Fin had to guess that like Colin, Richie had been moved after his death. For a human that might be a big deal, but not for a vampire. Not even a female vampire.

An officer began to move around the dead kid, snapping digital photographs. Fin stood where he was, hoping to spot some detail that would lead him to the vampire who had done this. But the longer he stood there, the more he realized there would be no detail here to point toward the killer. Whoever had done this, he or she didn't want to get caught and was smart enough not to get caught.

The killer could have been anyone in the town. It could have been Fia.

With that disheartening thought, Fin stepped back. "When you're done here, I want photos of the back door that was found unlocked." He turned to another cop. "I want the perimeter of the arcade taped off. He wasn't killed here. He was brought here after he was dead, which means there ought to be blood somewhere." *Not even a greedy vampire could drink that much blood.* He looked down at the sandy cement floor, where he could make out the barest outline of drag marks.

"How far around the building you want the tape?" It was Johnny K., who'd been called back to work after the Meding murder while on vacation with his family.

"Johnny, he was killed somewhere else." Fin gestured with an open palm, his frustration building. "I need to figure out where."

"Could have been anywhere, Fin. What? We're going to rope off the whole town?"

"If we have to," Fin snapped. "And get shoe covers on. You're standing on evidence."

Johnny looked down at his shiny black shoes. "I don't have any—"

Before Fin realized what he was doing, without moving a muscle, he made a fistful of shoe covers fly out of a box left on top of a video game and showered Johnny K. with them.

"*Jezus,* Fin."

Fin looked up to see Regan walking toward him. He was wearing shorts and flip-flops and one of Fin's favorite T-shirts. "What the hell are you doing here?" Fin demanded. "You're not allowed—"

"Jezus, Mary, and Joseph," Regan swore again, seeing Richie. He stopped short in front of the video game.

"You're not supposed to be in here, Regan," Fin repeated, feeling like he had no control whatsoever over his crime scene. "Who the hell let him in here?" His last question wasn't directed toward anyone in particular. Most of the police force was there.

"He's your brother, Fin," Johnny K. muttered as he slipped a blue paper cover over his left foot. He was standing in a sea of shoe covers. Fin must have thrown half a box at him.

"Regan." Fin grabbed his brother's arm. "You can't be here. This is a crime scene."

"I'd say this is a crime, all right. Someone killed Richie. Why would anyone kill Richie?" Regan stood there and stared at the dead body. "He was, like, the nicest human on earth. And why is he playing NASCAR? He was way more a classic old-school pinball guy."

"You knew Richie?"

"Of course." Regan looked at Fin. "Anyone who hung around here knew Richie. He's been working here since he was, like, fourteen. Mary McCathal made him the manager."

"Wait a minute." Fin closed his eyes. He could feel a headache coming on. A bad one. "Mary McCathal owns the arcade? I thought it was Mary Hill."

"Mary and Bobby owned it, bro. Mary his wife, not Mary his girlfriend. You better get that one straight. What are you thinking?"

"What am I thinking?" he exploded, his eyes flying open. "I'm thinking that if we don't find out who's doing this, Regan, this could be the end of us."

"It won't be the end of us." Regan laid his hand on Fin's arm. "Worse comes to worst, we move. We've done it before. We can do it again."

Fin was surprised by his brother's physical contact and the emotional response he felt. Taken aback. It had been a long time since he had felt that kind of connection with his twin.

"It won't be the end of us because you'll figure it out, Fin," Regan said quietly. "You'll find out who's doing this."

Fin watched Regan walk away. "Where are you going?"

"You said I couldn't be here," he hollered, weaving his way between the video games, cops, and EMTs. "I'm going to Mom's to get something to eat."

"Get a job!" Fin called after him.

Without looking back, Regan gave a thumbs-up on his way out the door.

Chapter 11

"Um, you wanted to talk to me?"

Fin glanced up to see Rob Hill standing beside the video game, sunburned face apprehensive. He was a nice-looking kid, but still at that awkward age, all legs and arms. He had a quiet confidence that Fin knew in time would develop, making him one of the stronger, steadier males in the sept.

It was late afternoon. Fin had been at the arcade all day. Richie Palmer's body had been removed and eventually Fin had ordered that the garage doors that opened the arcade onto the boardwalk be lifted. He just couldn't stand the stench of the dead body and the blood still left in his body. Human blood went bad fast. Vampires didn't partake of the blood of dead humans. It repulsed them. Or at least it repulsed most vampires.

Fin had been sitting at the NASCAR game for well over an hour. Just thinking. Trying to get a vibe. He'd actually considered bringing Kaleigh in to get her impression of the murder, but he hated to drag her into the

investigation. She was still so young and the responsibility of being the sept's wisewoman lay heavy on her
youthful shoulders.

"Thanks for coming, Rob."

He stood there, gangly teen-male arms at his sides.
He stared at the game like it was some kind of apparition. "You found him here, huh?" he said softly.

"Yeah, but he wasn't killed here." Fin placed his
hands on the steering wheel. There was still dusky
print dust on it and it smudged his fingertips. "The
body was left here after he was dead."

"Makes sense."

Surprised by Rob's response, Fin glanced up. Having nothing to wipe his hands on, he wiped them on his
uniform pants. "What does?"

He shrugged. "Why he's here. I doubt Richie would
have sat down here on his own. He didn't play this
game."

Regan had suggested the same thing. Fin climbed
out of the seat. He was taller than Rob but not by
much. "What did he play?"

Rob hesitated. "He was real conscientious about
work. I swear. He didn't play much when he was on the
clock."

"Look, I'm not trying to get anyone in trouble,
Rob." His gaze strayed to the boardwalk. There was
still yellow tape keeping patrons and gawkers from entering the arcade, but they had lined up along the tape,
humans and vampires alike. A few cameras flashed and
there was a local news crew just wrapping up a piece
that would, no doubt, show on the evening news.

Fin felt like he was in a fishbowl. He turned his back
to the crowd so he was facing Rob. "Honestly, I don't

give a crap if you guys screw around all day and give free game play to every cute chick who steps through the door. I'm trying to figure out who did this."

"And you need me?" Rob sounded half incredulous, half scared.

"You worked with Richie since the beginning of the summer, right?"

Rob nodded. "Last summer, too. But not the year before." He grimaced. "I was kinda . . . too old for arcade games."

Fin offered a wry grin. Rob was referring to the fact that he had only been reborn last year. Before that, he had been a wrinkled old man. "Right. So what was Richie like? Who did he hang out with?"

"He was a good guy." Rob shrugged. "You know, for a human. He didn't steal money and he didn't let anyone else steal, either. And he was always at work on time," he added.

"Friends?"

"Umm. He was dating this girl, Brittany Patterson, but she didn't come in that much. He had this one HM friend who used to come around once in a while with the girlfriend. I think his name is . . . Todd. That was it."

Fin lowered his voice. "What about us?"

Rob looked at him in obvious confusion. "Us?"

"Who did he hang around with from Clare Point?"

"Oh, *us.* I don't know that he hung around with any of us." Rob's eyes suddenly widened. "You don't think—"

The cat would soon be out of the bag. Vampire out of the closet—however you wanted to say it. But Fin hadn't yet told anyone that a vampire had been responsible for

Colin Meding's death. Now with a second death, he would have to address the General Council again and tell them. But he didn't have to tell anyone yet. Not today and not Rob. "Come on, Rob. All our teens come here, too. See anyone flirting with him? Talking to him?"

"Everyone talked to him."

"But anyone *in particular?*" Fin fought his impatience. Rob was trying. He really was.

"Katy?" Rob finally blurted. It was a question.

Fin exhaled through his mouth.

Katy was an unlikely candidate. Everyone knew she was a big flirt. She flirted with every male between the ages of fifteen and thirty, human or vampire, but he knew her pretty well. She wasn't a killer. "What about someone . . . older?"

As he said it, a couple possibilities flitted through his head. Eva was a lesbian, but she'd been known to sleep with men and she had a mean streak in her. And then there was Tara. She'd killed that pirate back a few centuries ago just for trying to cop a feel. And it had been with a knife . . . a butcher knife she'd been carving a roast with.

"Like who?" Rob asked. He was beginning to squirm now.

"I don't know. Just think. What Kahills do you remember him being friendly with?"

"He was really just friendly with Regan."

Rob seemed hopeful *that* would be the right answer. Like he was on some quiz show. Kids today, they were *way* too influenced by television and movies.

"Regan?" Fin repeated.

Rob nodded. "They were pretty good friends, I

think. When Richie would take his dinner break, sometimes he and Regan would get fries and sit on the beach and talk."

Fin wondered why his brother hadn't brought up that fact when he'd been here, but Fin had learned long ago there was no sense racking his brain trying to figure out why Regan did anything. "Okay." Fin squeezed Rob's arm. "I need you to make a list of everyone who was in the arcade in the last day or so. I really need you to think about this, buddy."

Rob appeared to be looking beyond Fin, at someone in the crowd. "Everyone?" he asked.

"Anyone and everyone." Fin patted him on the back. "Can you do that?"

"This minute? I . . . I was supposed to meet Kaleigh."

Fin watched Rob's gaze stray past him again. "Kaleigh can wait. Find some paper and a pen in the office." He started to turn around, now as distracted as Rob. "Who are you looking at?"

"Elena. She's trying to get my attention." Rob pointed.

Fin saw her at once. She was wearing a lavender sundress and her hair was pulled back chicly in a slick ponytail. He looked at Rob again. "You know Elena?"

"Sure. She's here all the time."

Somehow, Fin didn't see her as the arcade type. "She is?"

"Yeah. Usually looking for her nephew. She knew Richie. Talked to him whenever she came in." His brow furrowed. "I think she was here yesterday. Yeah, definitely."

"Just see what you can do about that list of names." Fin patted Rob on the back and walked away.

Elena smiled when Fin made eye contact.

"Hey," he said quietly as he approached the yellow tape.

"Hey."

"You trying to get Rob's attention?" He pointed to the teen.

She laughed. "I was trying to get him to get *your* attention."

"Ah." He nodded. It was good to see her. He'd talked to her on the phone a couple of times in the last week, but they hadn't gotten together since the night at her cottage.

She tucked her hands behind her, looking utterly seductive. "So, you trying to avoid me, Officer Kahill?" She reached out and smoothed his tie.

Fin glanced around to see who was watching. He ran his hand over the tie where her hand had just been. He could feel the heat of her hand on the fabric. "No, of course not. Like I said on the phone, I've just been—"

"Busy," she finished for him. "Is that what nice American men say when they do not want to see a woman again after they have made love to her? They just say they're *busy?*" She seemed more amused than upset.

"Elena." He ducked under the tape and grabbed her hand. "I'll be back," he called to the nearest officer. Her hand in his, he led her away from the crowd.

Beyond the confining walls of the arcade, Fin was able to catch his breath. Despite the heat of the June day, the air was refreshing. Out here, he felt as if he could think more clearly. "I told you things were complicated right now." He let go of her hand. If he was going to do this, he knew it would only be a matter of time before someone saw him, but he preferred it would be later rather than sooner. Especially with another dead body lying in Dr. Caldwell's office.

"You want to grab a drink? I only have a few minutes." He gestured to a burger place two shops down from the arcade.

"I would love to." She smiled as if he had invited her to the Queen's Jubilee birthday bash.

He opened the door for her and a blast of cold air hit him.

"Ahhh," she breathed, caressing her bare neck with her fingertips. "That feels great. It is so hot out. I had forgotten how hot it could be in America."

"Iced tea?" He tried not to watch her fingers as they brushed over her skin.

"Yes, thank you."

He collected two iced teas at the lunch counter and they walked to the booth farthest from the door. The shop was narrow, only wide enough for one row of booths and a walkway, which made the back table discreet. She slid in on one of the benches and he sat across from her. He fiddled with the paper on his straw. She was still stroking her neck. It was all he could do not to lean across the table and—

"I'm sorry about the death of the young man," she said.

"You knew him?"

"No."

Fin met her gaze. There was something . . . *odd* about her tone of voice.

"Not really," she continued. "But I have spoken to him several times. My nephew loses track of the time sometimes." She hadn't touched her tea. She was no longer stroking her neck, but her manicured hand rested at the base of her throat. "He was a nice young man, Richie. Very handsome."

Fin lifted an eyebrow.

She shrugged theatrically. "What can I say, Fin? I am a woman who appreciates a handsome man."

"He was twenty years old, Elena."

"I have not tried to hide the fact that I find young men attractive. Good news for you, no?"

He took a sip of the sweet iced tea. She was a complicated woman. More complicated than he had first anticipated. He liked complicated. He liked the challenge. "Were you looking for me for a reason?"

"I assumed you would be there. Call it girlish, but I just wanted to see you."

He reached across the narrow Formica tabletop and took her hand that still rested on her throat. "It's not that I didn't want to see you."

"It is that you are busy. With the murder. Murders," she corrected herself.

"I wanted to see you. I just—"

"You just what, Fin?" She leaned against the table, capturing his hand between hers. "It is just sex between two consenting adults. I didn't ask you to marry me."

She smiled a smile so beautiful that he wanted to take her here. Now. So what if it was taboo. Sex with humans and sex on a Formica lunch table in front of half the town.

"Come tonight," she whispered.

"I . . . I don't know if I can."

Fin sensed his brother approaching before he heard the jingle of the bell above the luncheonette door. He sat back on the bench, pulling away from Elena. *Walk away,* he telepathed.

No way, his brother answered. *This is too good. Caught red-handed with an oh-so-hot HF. What are we to do with you, big brother?*

I'll kill you if you speak a word out of line, Fin warned, thinking he was probably telepathing so hard that he was grimacing.

Too bad I can't die, eh, bro? "Hello," Regan said, sliding into the booth next to Elena. He offered his hand. "Regan Kahill, black sheep of the family and brother to this white sheep."

"I see the resemblance," she teased, recovering quickly from the obvious surprise that Fin had an identical twin. "Elena Ruffino."

He shook her hand. "You have a niece and a nephew." He clicked his fingers. "Beppe and Lia, right? Hang out around the arcade."

"I have two nieces. There is also Alessa. Would you care to join us for a cool drink?"

Absolutely not, Fin telepathed.

No way I'm missing this, Regan flipped back. "I'd love to. I can grab my own. Be right back." He bounced off the bench and walked to the lunch counter.

"I should get back to the arcade," Fin said. "We still have some things to wrap up there. Can I walk you somewhere?"

"We have not been here five minutes. You need to rest. How can you solve the murder if you do not rest your mind and your body?" she plied, a calming hand over his.

Fin groaned inwardly. *No games,* he warned his brother.

No games, Regan repeated, returning to the table with a Coke.

"So, how long have you kids been dating?"

He slid in next to Elena again. Close to Elena. Too close to suit Fin. Regan had a way with women, especially humans. He could get an HF into bed faster than any vampire Fin had ever known.

"Fin can be a very secretive guy," Regan explained as he tore off the end of his straw paper and stuck the straw in his mouth. "Can't you, Fin?" He blew hard and the paper sailed off the end of the straw, striking Fin just below his Adam's apple.

I swear by all that is holy, brother, if you ruin this, I will remove your head from your shoulders, Fin threatened telepathically. *I swear by our dead brothers' graves.*

You like her?

I like her.

You? An HF? I thought you swore off them years ago after that little tart in London—

An HF, Fin interrupted firmly.

"Terrible news, isn't it," Regan said to Elena, without skipping a beat. When he was sober, he was excellent at carrying on more than one conversation at a time. He stuck his straw through the lid of his drink. "I can't believe Richie went off and got himself murdered. He was such a nice guy."

"I don't think Richie *went off and got himself murdered.*" Fin scowled. "I don't think he set out last night to die."

"Sure he did. Well, not really." Regan paused to drink. "But I mean he obviously tangled with the wrong person. A kid like him? What was he doing here so late? Stores are locked up. Beach is pretty much vacant. You can't be looking for anything but trouble here that time of night. I don't come down here that late at night. Do you, Elena?"

She didn't answer but Regan didn't seem to notice; he went on the way only Regan could. "I'm certainly not the person to tell you how to do your job, bro, but—"

"You're right, you're not."

"But you find out what no good our Too Good to be True Richie was up to and you'll find his killer. The other guy's, too, I would suspect."

Fin felt like the walls of the restaurant were closing in on him. The overwhelming smells of frying beef and fat bubbling in the French fryer were suddenly nauseating.

"I really have to get back to the arcade." Fin grabbed his cup. "I promised Mary we'd be out of there by six. Seven at the latest."

"Mary planning on opening up tonight?" Regan asked, childlike in his optimism.

"Not hardly. It's still a crime scene. She doesn't open until I give her permission to open."

"Well, Uncle Sean, technically," Regan corrected.

Fin slid out of the booth. "I can walk you as far as the arcade," he told Elena.

Regan got up to let her out. "Nice to meet you."

"Nice to meet you."

Regan slid back onto the bench. "So did my brother have enough sense to invite you to dinner at our parents' Friday night?"

Regan—

Regan ignored Fin's telepathy.

"I can see by the look on your face that he didn't." Regan reached for his drink. "Family dinner at our mom and dad's B and B, the Seahorse. You'll have no problem finding it. Ask anyone in town. Cocktails on the porch at eight, then dinner."

Elena looked to Fin.

"Well, if he didn't," Regan said, "I will. My poor brother. He's the better looking of the two of us. Certainly the most consistently clean and sober, but he's lousy at dating. Dancing, too, if you want to know the truth."

Fin exhaled. *Thanks a lot, Regan.*

My pleasure.

"Would you like to come?" Fin asked awkwardly. "It's not a big deal. Just dinner. Probably pretty boring for you." He felt as if he was sixteen again and he despised that feeling. He hated being a teenager more and more with each passing century.

"I would love to come for cocktails and dinner." She looked him directly in the eyes. Again, she touched her neck. "The question is, would you like me to come?"

Fin thought for a minute, surprised by her response. This was more than just about an invitation to dinner. She'd been the one from the beginning who had said all she wanted from him was sex. Now it seemed like she was asking him if he wanted to continue *the relationship*. Or was he reading something into it? "I would," he said. And he meant it. He had hoped that avoiding Elena this week would weaken his desire for her. If anything, it had increased. It didn't matter that seeing Elena would only make his difficult life even more difficult. He wanted her. He wanted her so badly that he almost felt as if he needed her, and that scared him.

"Then I will come." She turned to nod to Regan. "Thank you for your invitation. Will you bring a date?"

"Just out of rehab. No dating allowed."

She looked at Fin questioningly.

"No secrets in our family. No details of our lives too

painful for fellow family members not to drag across the porch, at every given opportunity. You'll see."

"I look forward to it."

Fin stepped aside, allowing her to pass. As he did, in his mind, he slid Regan's paper cup full of soda to the edge of the table. It teetered.

Regan yelped as Fin escorted Elena out the door.

Chapter 12

Fin reached for a mini corndog and glanced up at Kaleigh, who was going for the same corndog from the other side of the card table. "What are you doing here?" he asked, short-tempered.

"I was invited." Immune to his tone, she snatched up the dog on the toothpick, dipped it in a dish of honey mustard, and popped it in her mouth. "What are you doing here?"

"I live here," he defended. Having second thoughts on the wieners, he took a square of cheese. "At least I used to, before the Hannenfelds took over my room. They're staying three to four weeks. What do people do in this town for a month?" he wondered aloud.

Kaleigh shrugged and surveyed the appetizers. "How's the cheese?"

"Dry."

She nodded, crossing her arms over her chest. Like half of the teenage girls on a Friday night in June in small-town America, she was wearing a jean skirt and

tank top. But she didn't look like other teenagers. When
Fin looked into her eyes, he didn't see a girl almost
seventeen years old. He saw a woman much older and
much wiser, a vampire wisewoman coming into her
own.

"Your mom said she didn't think you were coming.
The investigation."

"I told her I was coming." Fin backed up until he
was touching the porch railing. "At least six times."

"*And* bringing a date?"

"*And* bringing a date," he conceded.

"A human date," she added with amusement.

"A human date," he repeated with serious regret.

The only reason he'd invited Elena to dinner in the
first place was because Regan put him on the spot. He
was hoping for a small sit-down meal with just his parents and siblings. What he'd found when he'd arrived
was half the town mingling on the wraparound porch
of the rambling Victorian home. Mary Kay, forever the
hostess, had really done things up. Votive candles
sparkled on the porch railings, Christmas lights twin-
kled in the trees, and she had several tables strategically placed with hors d'oeuvres. Near the front door,
his uncle James was blending margaritas.

Fin had taken one look at the three-ring circus and
almost turned around and gone home. Standing on the
sidewalk in front of his parents' place, he had cooked
up a scheme to go to the office and call his mother and
Elena from there, begging off their date with the excuse he was working on the case.

Then Mary Kay had spotted him and it was a lost
cause. The thing was, he really *should* have been working on the murder cases, because they were going
nowhere fast.

"Investigation going badly, huh?" Munching on a stalk of celery, Kaleigh circled the table to stand beside him.

"Hey, stay out of my head!"

If Fin listened, he could hear dozens of people's thoughts, but he tried to keep their voices to a soft roar. They just made him too crazy, especially in a crowd like tonight.

Kaleigh gave an innocent smile. "Oops, sorry."

"Yeah, right, oops. That might work with your mother, but not with me." He eyed her. "But if you must know, Miss Nosy, the investigation *isn't* going well." He rubbed a spot of flaking paint on the porch deck with the toe of his flip-flop. He'd changed clothes twice tonight, preparing for his dinner date with Elena. Then he'd felt like a complete fool for doing it. He was almost sixteen hundred years old, not sixteen. He'd settled on summer dress–casual: a polo, khaki shorts, and leather flip-flops. "I thought I had a piece of the puzzle, then discovered today that I jumped too fast to a conclusion."

"And that was . . . ?"

He frowned. "Kaleigh, I can't discuss—"

"Remember, I can read your mind if I want to," she interrupted.

His frown turned into a scowl. "Not without me letting you in, you can't."

She gave him a look that made him think otherwise. Most Kahills couldn't read others' minds unless permitted to do so, but there were a few of them with the ability to push through the walls put up to block such intrusions. Fin knew from the past that fully mature, Kaleigh would eventually be one of them.

Fin lowered his voice. "The first kid had had sex just

before he died. So had the second, so I was thinking somewhere along the lines of—"

"Like a black widow or something?" she asked eagerly. "She lures him into her web, has sex with him, and then . . ." She drew her finger across her throat.

"Something like that. But then I found out today after interviewing the second victim's ex-girlfriend that *they* had sex the night he died."

"He had sex with his ex?"

"Apparently they became exes *after* the sex."

"Ah." She nodded. "So you were thinking it was a woman and now it could be a guy. You know you shook up poor Rob pretty badly in your interrogation. Is he a suspect?"

"Rob is *not* a suspect and I did *not* interrogate him. I just asked him to make a list of people who had been in the arcade in the last day or so."

She scrutinized him for a moment. "There's something you're not saying." She narrowed her gaze, then gasped. "You don't think it's one of us, do you?"

"I said stay out of my head, damn it!" He exhaled, lowering his voice. "I can't talk about it and you can't either. Not before I talk to the General Council again."

Kaleigh's mouth still gaped open, her eyes still wide with surprise. "Fin, how could—"

Regan strolled over to the hors d'oeuvres table and Kaleigh halted mid-sentence. For once, his brother's interruption was welcome.

"Hey, I was looking for that shirt," Fin accused.

Regan ran his hand over the sage green polo he was wearing. "Found it in one of those boxes you haven't gotten around to putting away yet. It was kinda wrinkly, but Mom ironed it for me." He pushed half a deviled egg into his mouth. "Hey, Kaleigh."

"Hey, Regan."

"You get stood up again, bro?" Regan pretended to look around for someone.

Fin waited a beat before responding. He was not going to let Regan goad him tonight. He was not going to let him ruin his evening. "You didn't mention that Mom was having half the town to dinner before inviting my date. I thought it was just going to be us."

Regan stacked two pieces of cheese between three crackers and stuck the whole thing in his mouth. "Didn't know." His words were garbled by the food. "Cheese is dry. You guys try these hot dog thingies? They safe? There's nothing to eat in our house. I'm starved."

Kaleigh chuckled and walked away. "Just let me know if you need me, Fin," she called. "And stop picking on my boyfriend."

I wasn't picking on your boyfriend, Fin telepathed.

"What was that all about?" Regan grabbed two more deviled eggs. "You're picking on Rob?"

"Who's picking on Rob?" Fia walked around the corner of the house, carrying a red plastic cup.

"Margarita?" Regan snatched the cup from her hand and sniffed.

She watched him make a face. "Lemonade. Want some?"

Regan handed the cup back to his sister. "No thanks. I was hoping it was a margarita, just so I could smell it. This being on the wagon sucks. No recreational drugs. None of Uncle James's famous margaritas."

"Sober and clean. It does suck. So does being unemployed." She looked down at the hors d'oeuvres. "You do anything about getting a job, yet?"

"Jezus, Mary, and Joseph, now you sound like him." Regan pointed at Fin with a mini corndog.

"You didn't tell me you knew Colin Meding *and* Richie Palmer," Fin said. He still stood on the far side of the table, leaning against the porch rail.

"I did so tell you I knew Richie. Colin just came in once in a while. Hell of a hockey player." Regan reached for a napkin decorated with pink bikinis floating on a purple background. "Not as good as me, but good."

Fia walked over to the porch railing and leaned against it, beside Fin. "It's time you grew up, Regan. It's time you stopped playing games with kids, got a job, and started taking some responsibility for yourself. You've strayed from the sept's objective and you need to get back on track with the rest of us."

Regan wiped his mouth with the napkin. "Look, I'm clean. I'm doing my best, but it's not good enough for him and it's not good enough for you, either, is it?" He crumpled the napkin, tossed it into a waste basket under the table, and walked away.

Standing side by side, Fin and Fia watched him walk away.

"You think I was too hard on him?" she asked.

Fin smiled sympathetically. "Probably."

She sighed and was quiet for a moment. "So Richie had a bite wound, too, huh?"

"Yup."

She was quiet for a second, then glanced at Fin. "You think these murders could be related to him? Payback from the Rousseaus for him stealing their drugs last summer?"

Fin glanced over his shoulder, looking toward the street. Still no sign of Elena. He couldn't decide if he was relieved or disappointed. "I considered that, but it's really not their style. They'd have left their initials written in blood on the floor or something equally dramatic."

"True." She sipped her lemonade. Regan wasn't the only member of the family with dependency issues. Fia never drank any alcohol, beyond a pint of Tavia's ale at the local pub. Came from centuries of living with an alcoholic who could never forgive his children for their transgressions.

"The Rousseaus aren't the only vampires on earth who like to kill humans for fun. Any other baddies in the vicinity?"

"Not that we know of." Fin massaged his forehead; he was fighting a headache that was feeling more like a heartache with every passing day that the murders went unsolved. "No one on the radar except for some Russians working in Ocean City as store clerks and bag boys, and a couple of transplants from Devonshire trying to get in on the gambling action in Atlantic City."

"So what are you going to tell the General Council Monday night?" Fia pressed.

"The truth." He met her gaze in the porch shadows. "That it's one of us."

Fin was beginning to wonder if maybe Elena *had* stood him up. At eight forty-five, Mary Kay had announced that the buffet was ready. He was trying to extricate himself from Mary McCathal's presence to give Elena a call, but the widow hadn't taken a breath in at least five minutes.

"I don't know how soon Liam will be home, but it will be so nice to have him here again, don't you think?" People filed past them to get in the buffet line.

"Your mother says we should have a little welcome home get-together, but I don't know that he would like that. You know how Liam . . ."

Fin let Mary's voice fade in his head as he fingered his cell phone in his pocket. Mary McCathal looked pretty tonight, pretty for a woman her age, at least. Her cheeks were pink, her eyes sparkled, and she was wearing what appeared to be a new blouse. He'd thought maybe the rumors about her and Victor were just that, rumors, but Mary definitely had the glow of a widow in love, or at least a widow with a man in her bed. It was hard for Fin to imagine Victor as a gentle lover, but he knew from experience that intimate relationships didn't always make sense.

Glancing toward the empty sidewalk, Fin wondered if he should take Elena's not coming as a sign. A romance with her really was a bad idea. It would be better to end it now before it got off the ground. She'd said she wasn't looking for anything long term or emotional, but he knew women better than that. They were all looking for an emotional connection. Hell, if he was honest with himself, that's what he was looking for. Seeking but would never find.

Fin reached out to rest his hand on Mary's arm, to interrupt her mid-sentence, when he felt Elena's presence. He looked up, then turned, startled by his abrupt awareness of her. Dressed in a flowered, flowy dress and heeled sandals, she walked toward him, a bottle of wine tucked under her arm. There had to be fifty people on that end of the porch, all jockeying to get in line for the buffet, but she seemed to see no one but him.

"My apologies for being late." She leaned into him, kissing one cheek and then the other. "For your mother." She offered the bottle.

"Ah, thanks." For a second, Fin just stood there looking at her. Thankfully, Mary McCathal had found a new victim to discuss the intricacies of her son's return with. "I'm really glad you came."

She smiled, gazing around, seeming completely impervious to the crowd of exuberant Kahills. If only she knew who they were, what they were, she'd be afraid.

"Your mother?" She lifted a fine, arched eyebrow. "Would it be possible for me to meet her and thank her for her invitation?"

As Elena spoke, she rested her fingertips across the base of her throat. She had a habit of doing that. An utterly hypnotizing habit that brought a whole new meaning to the phrase *making him see red*.

"Fin? Your mother?"

He blinked. "Oh, sure. Come meet Mary Kay." He took her hand. "You're in for a treat."

"You didn't stay at Aunt Mary Kay's long." Katy held her tongue just so as she stroked the lavender nail polish on her big toe nail.

Kaleigh sat on the opposite end of Katy's bed; their bare feet were almost touching. She was going for the hot pink polish. "I just wasn't in the mood for chitchat with the old farts." She cocked her head one way and then the other. *"How old are you now, Kaleigh? Goodness, look how tall you've gotten, Kaleigh. Still no boobs, huh, Kaleigh?"* she imitated.

Katy sniggered. It was easy for her to laugh. She had been blessed with boobs. What really sucked was that every time she was reborn, there they were again. Kaleigh thought that just once, just one lifetime, she deserved some decent cleavage. But genetically it wasn't going to happen. She wondered how Rob would feel about implants. "I saw Fin there. He's pretty freaked about the murders."

"Johnny said we were mentioned on some news show the other night." Katy dipped the brush into the bottle of polish, taking care to not spill any on the bedspread. Her mom had already told them like a hundred times not to paint their nails on the bed. "It was about the decline of small towns in America. How every town is becoming a big sewer, including little ole Clare Point."

Kaleigh rolled her eyes. "The Council will love that. So much for trying to stay below the radar, huh?"

"Yeah, really." Katy leaned over her leg to paint the rest of the toenails on her left foot. "So, you think we'll have to move again?"

"Move?" Kaleigh glanced up to see Katy looking at her with kind of a weird look on her face.

Katy studied her toenails again. "You know, if the publicity over the murders gets out of hand. Will we have to pack up and disappear in the middle of the night the way we did when we left Ireland?"

Kaleigh rubbed some wet polish off the end of her toe. She didn't know why she even tried. Her toes never looked as good as Katy's. She never got the polish on evenly and then she always smudged it before it dried. "It'd be kind of hard to move again. I mean, before, we came to an uninhabited place. Well, almost uninhabited," she corrected, remembering the pirates the sept had run off the beach. "Besides, where would we go?"

"I don't know." Katy screwed the lid on the bottle of polish and stretched out her feet to observe her handiwork. "Anywhere but here. Italy maybe? Or how about somewhere in South America?"

"Maybe. But for now, we have to work with what we've got, which means we need to stay low and not draw attention to ourselves among humans. Fin's right; we need to catch this killer before the whole thing blows up in our faces," Kaleigh said, mostly just thinking out loud.

Of course she couldn't tell Katy that Fin suspected it was one of their own. But the possibility was heavy on her mind.

"Hey." Katy tapped Kaleigh's bare foot with hers. "Guess what? Beppe asked me to another party. Tomorrow night."

Kaleigh scowled at her toes. They looked like she'd dipped them in a vat of Pepto-Bismol. "You going?"

"I don't know. We only hung out for a few minutes last time he invited me. Then Pete came along and got all emotional on me." She rolled her eyes and then flopped back on her pillow. She stared up at the Guitar Hero poster taped on the ceiling above her bed. "I don't know if I really like Beppe. He's kinda weird."

"Weird how? Like he wants to stick his tongue down your throat weird?"

Katy laughed. "That's part of what's weird. He, like . . . he hasn't tried to make a single move. Like . . . not even holding my hand."

"Maybe he thinks you have BO."

Katy stuck her tongue out at Kaleigh.

Kaleigh screwed the lid back on the pink nail polish, deciding she'd better stop while she was ahead. So far, she'd only painted her nails, some of her toes, and a spot on her ankle. She knew for sure Katy's new quilt was next. "Or maybe Pete cornered him in the bathroom and threatened to bite him and suck him dry if he laid a hand on you."

"Pete!" Katy grabbed her hair like she was going to rip it out. "Don't even get me started on Petey. He's acting crazy."

"Crazy how?"

"Following me around. Calling me and texting me twenty times a day. Whining to all my friends. Yesterday he said something to my mother at the grocery store. My mother! He wants me back. He misses me. He loves me. Blah, blah, blah, blah, blah," she mimicked, opening and closing her hand as if it was a mouth.

"Well, maybe he does."

"Does what?" Katy let her hand fall on the bed.

"Love you. Miss you."

"He doesn't love me," she scoffed. "He loves my blood. He loves getting in my panties."

"Katy," Kaleigh breathed, doing a double take.

"What?" She half sat up in the bed. "Don't tell me you and Rob haven't—"

"We haven't," Kaleigh interrupted. She knew Katy and Pete were getting comfortable with each other, but she had no idea they were *doing it*. "Sex is prohibited until we're twenty-one and fully evolved again. It's dangerous."

"Dangerous?" Katy flopped back on the bed again and giggled. "I got news for you. Those old farts in Council, they've been lying to us. It's not *dangerous*. It's fun is what it is. That's why they don't want us doing it. Because it feels good."

Kaleigh got out of the bed, trying not to smudge her toenails. This was all she needed, something else to worry about. "I gotta go home. I promised my mom."

She carefully slid her feet into her flip-flops. "See you tomorrow."

Katy waited to speak until Kaleigh was at the bedroom door. "So you want to go?"

Hand on the doorknob, Kaleigh turned around. "Go where?"

"The party at Tomboy's house."

"I'm not helping you meet human guys. I wouldn't do that to Pete."

Katy popped up on the bed. "Come on. You don't want me to go alone, do you? What if Beppe is a homicidal maniac?" She raised a finger. "What if he's the one who killed those two guys on the boardwalk, huh? What if I'm next?"

Kaleigh's hand hovered over the doorknob. "That's not funny." It couldn't be true if the killer was a vampire killing humans, but Katy didn't know that.

"I hear there was some naughty V behavior there the other night," Katy sang, trying to entice her.

"What are you talking about?"

Katy hugged her knees. "It was just a rumor, I'm sure, but I heard that one of the guys got a little carried away making out with some drunk chick and had a little taste of her blood."

"Who?" Kaleigh demanded.

Katy dropped back on her pillow. "I'm not going to tell. We don't rat on each other to the elders. That's the deal. I didn't tell when you were out in the woods playing kissy-face with that psycho V slayer."

"Well, you should have," Kaleigh blurted. Then, seeing the hurt look on Katy's face, she felt guilty for saying it. There was no way Katy or anyone else could have guessed how messed up those guys were. Katy wasn't a bad person. She just liked her fun and sometimes she didn't think through the consequences of her actions.

"So you wanna go? See for yourself? Maybe it was a one-time thing, but I really think someone responsible should check it out, don't you?" Katy hesitated. "Midnight tomorrow night. I'll meet you at the corner."

Kaleigh opened the bedroom door. The General Council had enough things to worry about right now. They didn't need junior vampires running amok. "I'll be there."

Chapter 13

The evening ended better than it started. The Kahills, though curious about Fin's human date, were well behaved at dinner. Everyone could agree the match was clearly against sept rules, but they were still eager to get a closer look at her. Even after all these centuries, they still shared a certain fascination, a certain envy of humans. Not a single member of his extended family levitated, set anything on fire by spontaneous combustion, or discussed the virtues of Haitian blood in front of her. As a bonus, Mary Kay only talked one of Elena's ears off and Fin's father remained fairly sober.

The clatter of dirty dishes being washed and put away in the kitchen faded as Fin and Elena walked through the backyard, across the lawn, into the deepest shadows. Elena had been the one who suggested they take a walk around the property, but he sensed she was as eager as him to be alone. All evening a static electrical impulse had arced between them, the sexual attraction practically sizzling in the air.

The night air was heavy and humid and filled with the scents of a summer night just past the witching hour: the remnants of a backyard barbeque, wet dog, freshly cut grass, and the first roses of the season. Beneath that initial layer of scents was the deeper, darker perfume of the night; the smell of humans coexisting with vampires. Fin smelled their children. He smelled them making love. He smelled the gin on their breath and the blood that oozed from a wound, all heady scents that made him feel alive. That reminded him of his purpose in the world.

"I had a nice evening, Fin. Thank you." Elena stopped to slip out of her sandals and sink her feet into the soft, fragrant grass. Fin, who had always enjoyed the sensual feel of grass on his feet, had left his flip-flops on the porch. Catching her shoes by their straps in one hand, she took his hand with the other. For a couple of minutes they walked in silence, weaving their way around bird fountains and cultivated beds of flowers. As they walked side by side, the voices of the women in the kitchen died away, leaving them with their own thoughts and the beat of their hearts.

"I'm glad you came. Glad my brother invited you." Fin lifted her hand to his mouth and kissed it. "I really wasn't trying to avoid you. I've been thinking about you all week."

Elena stopped beside the potting shed located in the far corner of his parents' property. A tall, tangled hedgerow on two sides blocked the view to the rear alley, nestling the shed in privacy.

"It was nice to be with others." She leaned against the clapboard siding painted a pale yellow. By the glow of the moon, it seemed gold, a fitting backdrop for her dark beauty.

"I sometimes feel very . . . *isolated.*" She looked down at the soft grass and wiggled her perfectly mani-cured bare feet. "At home." She looked up at him through a veil of lashes. "It can be very lonely. We live far from others."

He moved closer to her, casually resting one hand on her hip. Here in the backyard, in the dark, he could almost forget what was going on around him, in the town, in the world. Here, he felt cradled by the sway of the trees and the softness of the grass beneath his bare feet. "Do you mind if I ask . . . are you divorced?"

Her gaze darted up to meet his, then down again. She parted her sensual lips. "Widowed."

"I'm sorry," he said quietly, enjoying the peace of the moment and the feel of her body so close, so warm.

She looked up again at him, lifting her lashes. "It was a long time ago."

"Children?"

He barely saw her lips move this time as she spoke. It was more like an exhalation.

"Dead, too."

You remember. Don't you?

The disturbing words reverberated in Fin's head. He didn't know where they came from or what they meant and he suddenly felt off balance. As if he was here, but also somewhere else. Somewhere else in time. Had the words come from Elena? It wasn't possible, of course. How could he remember what he didn't know? He looked down at her, his heart fluttering oddly in his chest. "Elena—"

"Shh," she hushed, dropping her sandals to the grass. "Let's not talk about it." She took his hand and holding his gaze, kissed his fingertips, one by one.

When she reached his index finger, she teased it with her tongue and then took it into her mouth.

It was a simple gesture, not particularly sensual as an act unto its own, but the way she touched him sent a sharp shiver of desire through him. The words that had lingered in his head a moment before were gone. Mist in the humid night air. Imagined? Perhaps.

His finger still in her mouth, he pressed his lips to hers, needing to taste her, touch her. He drew his wet finger across her cheek and threaded his fingers through the soft hairs at the nape of her neck. He thrust his tongue into her mouth and she moaned softly.

One kiss and Fin was hard. He wanted her now. Here. Had to have her.

What kind of guy was he to want to have sex standing up against his mother's potting shed in her backyard?

Elena took his hand and guided it beneath the soft fabric of her skirt, up her smooth thigh.

Whatever kind of man he was, Elena was apparently cut of similar cloth. She wore no panties and he found her already wet for him.

They kissed again and he stroked her soft, yielding flesh. Breathless, he tore his mouth from hers and he kissed along her jawline to her ear and then downward to the pulse of her throat.

Elena pressed her back against the shed, her arms stretched outward. Her small breasts rose and fell with each ragged breath. Still stroking her, he left the sweet satiny flesh of her throat to kiss the valley between her breasts. He pushed aside the filmy fabric of the dress to capture one nipple between his lips. Braless. An advantage of smaller-chested women. One Fin appreciated in this century.

Elena moaned and raised one leg, wrapping it around his hips. Her fingers found the waistband of his shorts. Before he could consider the possible consequences of having sex in his mother's backyard while she was doing dishes in the kitchen, no less, he found himself stepping out of his shorts. She shoved his boxers downward and grasped the full length of him.

For once, it was not the blood of the woman in his arms that Fin was thinking of. For once, he did not need the taste of her on his lips. Right now he needed to possess Elena. Maybe more importantly, he needed to be possessed by her.

Slipping his arm around her hips, Fin used his other hand to guide his way. She cried out as he pushed inside her and he smothered her mouth with a kiss. Mary Kay would have his head . . .

He pushed again and again she cried out, already on the precipice. For once, he didn't feel as if he needed to worry about going too fast. She was already miles ahead of him.

Slender and light, Elena was easy for Fin to hold up, pressed against the outer wall of the shed for support. She clung to him, thrusting her hips to his, moaning with pleasure.

Fin took a breath, pulled back until he heard her catch her breath, and then pushed home. Elena cried out so loudly that he slipped his hand over her mouth, afraid she might alert the women in the kitchen. She bit his finger as her muscles convulsed around him and suddenly he was lost to her silken caress. One moment he felt as if he could have held her in his arms all night and the next, his arms and legs were so weak they trembled.

Afraid he might drop her, Fin eased back, trying to

lower her bare feet to the ground as gently as possible.
Her dress fell around her, covering her nakedness and
again, like the previous time, he felt an inexplicable
tenderness wash over him. This didn't feel like *just sex*.
It felt like an emotional connection he'd not felt in a
very long time.

Her head fell forward to rest on his shoulder as she
waited to catch her breath. He held her in his arms, in-
haling deeply the sweet scent of her fresh, clean hair
that mingled with the heavier, muskier smell of their
lovemaking.

"Wow," he whispered in her ear.

To his delight, she laughed. "I am sorry. I was loud."

"Not too loud." He kissed one corner of her mouth,
then the other, stroking her rib cage. "I'm glad that I
can give you pleasure, Elena."

Smiling, her eyes now drowsy, she pushed the hair
from her face. "I should go," she said.

He kissed her exposed breast and then drew the material into place and took a step back. He wasn't quite
ready to let her go and he didn't know why.

The voice in his head came back to him. *You remember.* Did he remember? Remember what? Who
wanted him to remember? Surely not Elena. But again
he felt that strange rush of familiarity. Something was
going on here between them that he couldn't put a finger on. "Elena, have we ever met before?"

"What do you mean?" Her tone was light. She
leaned over and picked up his boxers, handing them to
him.

Fin stepped into his underwear and picked up his
shorts. "I don't know. I just keep getting this strange
feeling. Like we've met before. Do you know what I
mean?"

"You think we've met before?"

She did that a lot, he noticed. She answered his questions with questions that didn't answer him at all.

She stroked his cheek. "I should be returning to the cottage. My sister will worry."

Buttoning his shorts, he picked up her sandals from the grass. "I'll walk you home. Just let me grab my flip-flops off the porch."

"No. I prefer to walk alone." She took her shoes from him. "Good night, Fin."

Before he could argue, she walked away, cutting across the back corner of the property, toward the alley. He called after her. "If you go to the end of—"

"I can find my way," she interrupted. "Good night, Fin."

He dragged his hand over his face, still smelling her on his fingers, unsure of what to think of her. "Good night, Elena," he murmured.

The next night, Kaleigh sat on the arm of the couch watching Katy dance with Beppe to the throbbing beat of a popular hip-hop song. She'd come to the party on the pretense of scoping out which Kahill teens were here, but once she arrived, she found she was enjoying herself. She liked the music and all the activity. She liked watching the teen and young adult humans interact with each other, hoping her observations might give her a better understanding of them. And when you added pubescent Vs to the mix, it really got interesting.

Kaleigh made eye contact with Mickey, who was standing on the other side of the room, near the door to the basement. Mickey raised a red plastic cup in salute and went back to talking to her hulking boyfriend. Still

curious as to what was going on down there, Kaleigh
had been watching the basement door open and close
all night. She didn't recognize anyone that Tomboy had
allowed to pass the threshold. The local kids she knew
were staying upstairs. She considered the little bit of
drinking and hip grinding at the main party to be harm-
less, but the longer she watched, the more nervous she
became about what was going on downstairs. Maybe
they were just smoking weed down there. She thought
she'd smelled it the last time she was here. But she sensed
it was something else. Something she ought to know
about. Something potentially dangerous to the sept.

Mickey left her boyfriend's side and wove her way
across the dance floor toward Kaleigh. "Hey, you're
back." She had to lean close for Kaleigh to hear her
over the music.

"I'm back." Kaleigh raised her hands and let them
fall. "I came with Katy. She sort of came with a guy."
She nodded in their general direction.

"He's hot," Mickey observed.

Kaleigh shrugged,

"Hey, you want a beer? A smoke?"

"Nah, I'm good." Kaleigh watched Tomboy open
the basement door to allow some guy to enter. What
was it that was bugging her about that door? She looked
at Mickey perched beside her. Despite the nose ring,
tongue stud, and tattooed eyeliner, she had kind of an
earnest face. "Can I ask you something?"

"Sure. We're friends, right. Kinda," Mickey amended.

"Kinda," Kaleigh agreed. She pointed to the basement door. "This is the second time I've been here and
both times something's been going on down there. Your
boyfriend lets some people in, but some people he
doesn't let in."

"Private party." She sipped her beer.

"I get that. So what's going on down there that isn't going on up here?"

Mickey looked her in the eye. "You really want to know?"

Kaleigh nodded slowly.

"Let me talk to Tomboy. Come on." Mickey popped up off the arm of the chair.

Kaleigh followed her. As she wound her way through the couples dancing, she looked for Katy but didn't see her. She and Beppe must have stepped out on the porch to get a breath of air. It was hot in the house, despite the ceiling fans and open windows.

A couple of feet from the basement door, Mickey stopped. "Wait here a sec," she instructed. "Let me talk to Tomboy. His place. His rules."

While Mickey talked to her boyfriend, Kaleigh scanned the crowd again for Katy, but she couldn't find her. Was she in some corner making out with Beppe? It wouldn't even be that big a deal, except that now Katy and Pete were having sex and sharing blood. Once you got the taste again . . . the desire was hard to fight. Kaleigh remembered that.

What if Katy tried to pull the same thing with Beppe? She knew her friend was just sowing her wild oats, as they liked to say; she knew that eventually Katy and Pete would get back together. They'd been playing this game for centuries. But why did it have to be *this* human? She'd been watching Katy and Beppe all night and there was something about him that worried her. Something . . . absent, in his eyes.

Mickey came back to Kaleigh. "Tomboy wanted to know if we could trust you. I told him we could." She was wearing black lipstick; when she spoke, in the dark room, it made her teeth look like they were glowing. "Can we?"

"You mean am I going to go to the cops?"

"Tomboy says your uncle is a cop. The one investigating the murders."

"Fin's cool."

"So you want to?" Mickey pointed with her beer. "Go down?"

Kaleigh considered backing out of it. She should just find Katy and go home and not come back again. But something downstairs was drawing her . . . "Sure. It's not, like, dangerous or anything, is it?" She gave a little laugh, suddenly nervous. She was a little scared and she didn't know why.

Tomboy reached out with a beefy hand and opened the door.

"I don't know." Mickey handed her boyfriend her empty cup as she entered the stairwell. "Anything or anyone can be dangerous in the right circumstances." She brushed her hand over Tomboy's chest as she stepped into the dark stairwell. "Right, baby?"

He closed the door behind Kaleigh, enveloping them in total darkness.

Regan sat in the dark on the edge of his bed, his hand on his chest. His heart was pounding. His T-shirt and boxers were damp with sweat. He could feel his hair stuck to his temples.

Another damned nightmare.

It was the Rousseaus. They just wouldn't leave him alone. Not in his mind, at least.

He reached for the beer bottle on the cardboard box

beside his bed. He took a swig. It was warm and flat. He drank the rest of it anyway.

Pulse still racing, he laid down again, tucking his hand behind his head.

Why was he dreaming about the Rousseaus? Sure, maybe New Orleans last year hadn't been his best moment, but it wasn't the first time he'd gotten himself into a tight place. Not even the first time he'd gotten cornered by the Rousseaus. They were a nasty bunch of vampires. Sober, it was pretty obvious he should never have thought he could get away with stealing their shit, but what addict didn't do something stupid once in a while?

And he was clean now. Sober. Safe.

So why the bad dreams? Was someone trying to tell him something? His subconscious? The Rousseaus?

Did this have something to do with Fin's case?

A sense of dread washed over him. Could the murders be some kind of payback for what he'd done, even though his family had paid for the stolen drugs for him, supposedly settling his debt to the New Orleans vamps?

He got out of bed and walked down the dark hall to Fin's bedroom. There, he stood outside the half-open door for a moment. If Colin and Richie were dead because the Rousseaus were holding some kind of grudge against the Kahills, he wouldn't be able to live with himself.

He pushed open the door. "Hey, bro," he whispered.

Fin's bed was empty. Regan went back to his own room, unsure if he was disappointed Fin wasn't there to ask him about the Rousseaus, or relieved.

Chapter 14

"Late for you to be knocking, Victor." Peigi held her screen door open with one hand and her plaid flannel robe closed with the other.

Victor stared at his shoes. "Saw your light on," he mumbled. "Knew you were still up. 'Sides, you're still the president of the General Council, ain't you? I'd think that would mean you'd be available to your constituents day or night."

"Constituent? Is that what you are, Victor?" She sighed as she pushed open the door. "Well, come on. I suppose if I don't let you in now, you'll just be back tomorrow night."

"Suppose I will." He followed her through her dark mudroom and kitchen and into the lamplit living room. Sure enough, she had the TV on. He'd never been in Peigi's living room before. Never had any reason to come before now. The place fit her personality, practical. A plaid couch and recliner, two sturdy end tables and a coffee table. Like the clothing she wore, the furniture looked like it came out of an L.L.Bean catalog.

"I'm not offering you a cup of tea or a gin and tonic," she warned, plopping down in her recliner. She picked up the remote off the arm of the chair and turned the volume down on the TV.

"Wouldn't drink it if you offered. Not if I was dyin' of thirst," he grumbled.

"So what is it? What's so urgent that it can't wait until daylight hours?"

She tugged on the ties of her robe as if she was afraid he might be interested in taking a peek. Peigi wasn't his type, not with her short straight haircut, lumpy figure, and manly ways. He liked his women more feminine. Softer around the edges. Besides, he could never trust a woman with pyrokinetic abilities. A woman like her got pissed at you, there was no telling what she might set on fire.

"I wanted to ask—" Nervous, he folded his hands in his lap. "I wanted to get on the General Council agenda this week. I . . . I got something that needs to be addressed."

"I'm sorry. We're already jam-packed, Victor. These murders have stirred up a mess. What do you need to talk to us about?"

He fiddled with his fingers. He'd taken a shower before he'd come and even used the brush Mary had bought him to clean under his fingernails. He'd put on a clean T-shirt, and the pants were only a couple days out of the wash. It was important to him that he look respectable. Peigi had to understand how important this was to him.

He hadn't told Mary he was coming tonight because she'd have objected and then he'd have to have come anyway and then she would have been mad at him. Victor didn't like it when Mary got mad at him. "I need to talk to the Council," he repeated to Peigi stubbornly.

"Victor—"

"I want to marry Mary McCathal." The words blurted from his mouth before he could stop them.

Peigi looked at him for a second. "I see. You know, of course, that because she's Bobby's widow, she's prohibited by sept law to remarry."

"Thought it was prohibited by sept law for Regan to board my ship, suck my blood, and turn me into a vampire. Didn't stop him."

Peigi's face softened. "What Regan did was wrong. We all agreed on that centuries ago. We are eternally sorry for what he did."

"Seems to me, you all owe me an *eternal* favor," he grunted. "Least you could do."

"We can't change sept law, Victor. Mary may cohabitate with you, but she may not marry. Not you nor anyone else."

He rose. Mary had warned him this would be a waste of time. Now he would have to go back to her and tell her she was right. He would have to tell her he couldn't marry her. But it wasn't right. It wasn't her fault that some crazy human kid thought himself a vampire slayer. It wasn't Mary's fault her husband was murdered.

"I'm not asking you to change the law. Just make an exception. I deserve a favor from you all, considerin' what you done to me," he said bitterly.

"You know it's not up to me. I can't grant an exception to a law we've upheld for more than a thousand years."

"I want to speak to the Council," he repeated, thrusting out his lower lip stubbornly.

"Very well. It's within your right." She got up and stood in front of her chair as if she was standing in front of the Council, instead of in her living room in her pajamas in the middle of the night. "The agenda is filled for Monday night. I'll see you're added to the next session's agenda. You'll get an e-mail confirming the date and time."

"Don't have a computer." He headed for the door, embarrassed by the lump that had risen in his throat. One good thing happened to him after hundreds of years and these filthy bloodsucking vampires wouldn't grant him this one wish. All he wanted was to marry his Mary. All he wanted was to be happy.

"Then you'll get a call."

"Don't have an answering machine." He walked into the dark kitchen.

"Fine, then I'll have Liz type up a letter. You do have a mailbox, don't you, Victor?"

He pushed out the back door and stumbled down the steps, feeling stupid for having come at all. He hurried across the grass, ignoring Peigi's call to him. Mary said it would be a waste of time, trying to speak to the Council. She said they couldn't marry. The way he saw it, she was only right on one count.

Ordinarily, Kaleigh was comfortable in the dark. She walked around her house at night in the dark. She walked around town in the dark. She hunted in the forest when she needed to feed off the deer in the dark. Hell, she was a V. Even if she didn't sleep in a coffin like in the movies, she adored the silky darkness.

But this darkness on the stairway was different. It wasn't that it was scary, just . . . unsettling. God, she wished she could read humans' minds. She had been able to before, in some past lives, but it might be years before she developed the gift again.

"You okay?" Mickey grabbed her arm to guide her down the stairs.

"Uh-huh."

They left the hip-hop beat of Kanye West as they descended into the basement where some kind of ear-shattering Goth music was playing. A light glowed at the bottom of the steps from a single candle set on a table just outside an area that had been curtained off with heavy black drapes.

"Take one of these." Mickey had to lean close so Kaleigh could hear her above the music. She offered a black mask from a pile on the table. She took one for herself and pulled it over her face. It only covered her eyes and her nose, but it was enough to alter her appearance. Kaleigh could see how unobservant humans might be fooled by the mask, even if she wouldn't be.

Kaleigh noticed a basket of condoms on the table beside the candle. So Rob was right. They were having sex down here. And doing drugs. She could smell weed. The burning incense wasn't enough to cover its cloying sweet scent.

"No names down here. It's anonymous. You get it?" Mickey's tone was threatening.

"Sure. Yeah, I get it," Kaleigh said.

"You want one?" Mickey indicated the basket filled with condoms.

Kaleigh shook her head.

Mickey parted the black curtain.

Kaleigh started after her, then stopped. "Hey, wait."

Mickey looked back.

"Katy's not down here, is she?"

Even with the mask, Kaleigh could see the look of disdain on Mickey's face. "Katy wasn't invited. This party is by invitation only."

Kaleigh took a deep breath and followed Mickey through the curtains. They stopped just on the other side.

"Make yourself comfy," Mickey said. "Bar's over there. You can participate, or just watch. It's up to you."

Kaleigh watched her walk away, her gaze drifting. There were black curtains all around, making the basement look like a big room, even though it still smelled like a wet basement in southern Delaware. Kids in their late teens and early twenties sat in little groups or lounged on cushions on the floor. Couples in various stages of undress were making out. There were a few knots of three or four people. Naked.

Kaleigh swallowed. She could feel her face growing warm with embarrassment. A porn flick played on a TV; some guy dressed in a black cape was doing some girl on a coffin.

Sweet baby Jesus, what the hell was this?

There were votive candles everywhere and here, the smell of incense was strong. So was the smell of the marijuana. Her sense of smell keen, she sniffed the air to get a better take on things, her brain dissecting the characteristics of each scent, identifying them: alcoholic beverages, perfume, men's cologne. The scent of human perspiration and desire.

Suddenly the hair rose on the back of her neck. One distinct scent rose abruptly from the others. Human blood.

That could only mean one thing. *Shit*, Kaleigh thought. *Who's here?* she telepathed, sending the message out to anyone who had the ability to hear her. She didn't think she recognized anyone, but she wasn't looking too closely, not when people were *naked*.

No one answered her telepathic demand, but she could feel one of her own present . . . no, two.

She scanned the room, trying to look closer without really seeing what they were doing. They were all wearing the same stupid masks, of course, but she knew which ones were human. She would know which ones were not.

Two humans making out. Her pants off, his still on.

Two more humans, naked limbs entwined . . .

She looked away, wondering if such images could damage a young mind like hers. Of course, she wasn't *really* that young. She'd probably seen worse. She just couldn't remember, and didn't really want to.

Kaleigh looked at the couple again. Her fingers clenched the heavy fabric of the drapes that blocked off the staircase. Was that Johnny K. with that human blonde? It was. The mask didn't fool her. She knew the cleft in the chin. She and Johnny were second cousins . . . or was he her uncle twice removed? It got confusing sometimes.

But it was definitely Johnny, and that half-naked girl he had his arms around was definitely drunk or high and she definitely didn't know Johnny was a V. She watched as he lowered his mouth to her neck.

Johnny, what do you think you're doing? Kaleigh demanded, shooting her thoughts telepathically. *Don't you dare touch her again!*

But Johnny didn't hear her. Either he had blocked his mind or he was too lost in the feeding.

It was unlawful for Kahills to take human blood, but it happened sometimes. The nature of the beast, Peigi liked to say. And there were penalties in place when members broke the law. But when the sept said its teens were forbidden to have sex and feed on humans, they weren't kidding. If the Council found out about this, there would be *serious* repercussions.

Kaleigh wasn't sure what to do. Should she march right over to Johnny K., grab him by the earlobe, and march him up the stairs? No, she couldn't do that. It might cause suspicion among the humans. Besides, a feeding V could be dangerous. He wasn't himself. Kaleigh didn't need to get into a fight with Johnny in this basement. She wasn't even sure she *could* fight him.

"Hey." Mickey appeared beside Kaleigh, startling her.

"What the hell is this?" Kaleigh stared at her. "Some kind of orgy or something?"

She shrugged. "It is what it is. It has been since the beginning of time," she said mysteriously.

The crazy thing was, somehow what Mickey said rang true. The longer Kaleigh stood there, the more familiar the scene seemed. It was like she had been here before. Sort of. She wondered how Johnny had ended up down here. "Who . . . whose idea was this?" she asked.

"I don't know. One of the guys', I'm sure." Mickey laughed.

"I . . . I should go home." Kaleigh scanned the dark room one last time as she backed up toward the staircase. She was sure she could sense the presence of another Kahill. A female. But she didn't see her. Some of the curtains were drawn, sort of, making little cubicles. She wondered if the girl she sensed was in one of those.

"You sure you don't want to stay? It's perfectly safe."

She drew her finger along Kaleigh's shoulder blade. "No one talks about what goes on down here."

Kaleigh looked at Mickey as if she'd grown her own fangs. That had definitely been a come-on. Mickey was a lesbian? What about Tomboy? Of course, maybe she wasn't. This was obviously a room for teen *experimentation*. Experimentation Kaleigh had no intention of playing a part in. "I really do have to go," Kaleigh said, trying not to sound like she was as put-off as she was. She didn't want Mickey to think she was attracted to her sexually; on the other hand, there was always the possibility she might need Mickey for something another time. Never burn bridges. It was a good adage to keep when you lived forever. "I . . . I don't know where Katy is. She was pretty messed up last time I saw her," she lied.

Mickey pulled open the curtain behind Kaleigh, letting her out of the room.

"Thanks . . . thanks for inviting me. You know. Letting me see." Kaleigh snapped off the mask and dropped it on the table, avoiding bumping the condom basket.

"Come back any time," Mickey called after her as she hurried up the steps.

Kaleigh pushed open the door at the top of the steps and took deep breaths as she hurried across the dance floor. Luckily, she spotted Katy, and as she walked past her, she grabbed her by her T-shirt. "Come on, we're going. Later, Beppe." She practically pulled Katy out of his arms.

"What's the matter? Where are we going?"

"Home," Kaleigh said firmly. On the porch, she hurried down the steps, still dragging Katy along. "Do you know what they're doing down there?"

"Where?" Katy halted on the sidewalk, her eyes widening. "The basement?" she gasped. "You went into the basement?"

"Sex. There are people down there having sex," she whispered harshly.

"Together?" Katy wrinkled her freckled nose. "Humans having sex—eww, gross."

"Not just humans." Kaleigh marched down the sidewalk.

"Not just humans?" Katy ran to catch up. "You're kidding. Who else was down there? One of us?" she asked excitedly. "You mean one of us, don't you?"

"I'll take care of it."

"You have to tell me." Katy cut in front of her, making her stop. "Who was down there?" Her eyes widened again. "Not Pete. If Pete was having sex with a human, I swear—"

"Not Pete." Kaleigh met Katy's gaze. "But the thing is, I don't think they were *just* having sex."

Katy's jaw dropped. "Holy Mary, Mother of God—"

"Yeah." Kaleigh hurried down the sidewalk again. "That's what I was thinking."

Beppe slipped in the back door and closed it quietly behind him. He paused, waited for a moment, listening. He heard his father snoring, the *click-click* of the ceiling fan in the kitchen, but nothing out of place. Everyone was asleep. Cautiously, watching the hallway, he crouched down and set his shoes by the door. Rising, he brushed his hair out of his eyes.

On his hands, he could still smell the girl he'd been with. She smelled sour. He liked the one called Katy, but she wasn't falling for his charm the way other girls did. She might take a little more persuading.

Confident his family was asleep in their beds where they belonged, Beppe crept through the living room, down the hall. He passed his parents' room, his *zia's*. Once he was past the bathroom, he was home free. Another successful night out. Another notch in his belt. He grinned.

The bathroom door moved in front of Beppe and he took a step back, startled. His sister Lia walked out of the dark bathroom.

"Where were you?" she asked, speaking English.

"Um . . ." He pointed in the direction of the main rooms of the cottage. "Kitchen. Um. Getting a drink of water."

She looked at him. "You sleep in those?" She took a step toward him and sniffed. "Where have you been, big brother?"

Beppe pushed his hair out of his eyes. What a bitch, sneaking up on him like this. Thing was, if his sister told on him, it would be the end of his holiday fun. His parents would pack up and he'd be home in the villa before he knew what hit him. He didn't want to go home. He was sick to death of home.

"Why do you want to know? It's not your business."

"It's my business, all right." Lia took a step toward him.

She was wearing pink pajamas that made her look all sweet and innocent. That was the game she liked to play with their parents, but Beppe knew better. He knew she wasn't as sweet or as innocent as she pretended.

"You've been out, haven't you, big brother? Been out and been naughty."

He stared at her, not sure what to say. If they talked too loud, someone would hear them and he'd be caught.

"Mother wouldn't like this. Not one bit. Neither would *Zia* Elena. You know what they said. If you've done it again, there will be no more summer holidays." She sounded crazy. Not crazy maybe, but definitely crazed.

"I . . . I'm being careful."

"You going out tomorrow night?" she asked, only inches from his face now. She was so intense she was a little scary, really.

"I . . . I don't know. Probably not."

"Yes, you are." She turned around and padded barefoot down the dark hallway.

Beppe just stood there.

"You're going wherever it is that you go," Lia hissed, turning to him. "And you're taking me with you."

Chapter 15

There was dead silence, no pun intended, as Fin met the gazes of the Council members. For once, they were too stunned to speak. Peigi found her voice first. "I suppose there's no need for me to ask, because if you weren't sure, you wouldn't be standing here with that look on your face, would you?"

Fin shook his head, catching a glimpse of his reflection in the display case on the opposite wall. How many times had he stood in this room?

They met in the town's museum, built in the late sixties to encourage the town's burgeoning tourist trade. Portraying Clare Point as a pirate's den in early colonial days, the museum mixed fact with fiction, displaying many objects that had actually been on the ship the sept had traveled aboard from Ireland. When the vessel had wrecked on a reef in a storm and they were all washed ashore, they had collected the objects as well as the scrap wood from the splintered hull. They had built their first homes from those warped planks; portholes had become windows and the simple white bone china now displayed in this very case had been used on dining tables.

There had been a small colony of outlaw wreckers living in lean-tos on the beach when the Kahills washed ashore, but once the chieftain, Gair, declared that they had reached their final destination, the Kahill women had drawn their fangs, the men had raised their swords, and the pirates had moved south to Virginia to safer ground.

The glass cases in the rinky-dink museum, identified by printed signs, sometimes with humorous sketches, were filled with pieces of china, brass candlesticks, and other assorted junk, mostly brought from the ship, although some of it was bounty the wreckers had left behind in their eagerness to escape a colony of vampires. There was also a small exhibit of arrowheads and spear points from the area's earlier history when Native Americans had hunted and fished the area. Some items were displayed on the round table, now pushed to the corner, that had come from the ship's captain's cabin; the same table that was used when High Council took an *aonta* and possibly sentenced a criminal to execution.

During the museum's operating hours, a five-minute movie was shown in one corner of the room and there was a small gift shop off the hall, near the bathrooms. There, plastic swords, eye patches, fake coins, tomahawks, and other assorted souvenirs were sold. On rainy days in the summer months, the museum made a surprisingly tidy profit.

Fin shifted his gaze from his reflection in the glass display case to the Council members staring at him.

Their shock didn't last long. He was bombarded so hard that he caught himself raising his hands to cover his ears to block their voices, closing his eyes to block their thoughts.

Holy Mary, Mother of God.

"Impossible!"

"Ridiculous."

"Hail Mary, full of grace—"

Are you sure you're sure?

"It's the curse. There's no escaping the curse."

The thoughts and voices boomeranged around the museum's main room until Fin couldn't hear his own thoughts above the din.

"I said this would happen."

"You did not."

Did too.

Christ's bones, this kind of thing didn't happen when I was the law.

"I don't believe it."

Sure you do. I've been tempted to kill a tourist or two myself. Especially when they butt in line at the market. Don't say you haven't.

Council members rose from their folding chairs as they raised their voices to be heard over those around them. Someone, in his or her eagerness to one-up his neighbor, knocked over a chair. It clattered to the floor, adding to the volume of the commotion. In an effort to interrupt Mary Hall and Mary Hill's heated exchange over who had first predicted the town would self-implode in just this way, Gair spilled his cup of red punch. Rob Hail tripped over young Johnny's cane. One minute the meeting was an orderly circle of reasonable vampires, the next minute, chaos.

"Ladies! Gentlemen! Please," Peigi hollered above the racket, tapping her Bic on her clipboard.

Everyone ignored her.

"What are you going to do about this, Fin?"

We have to stop him.

Who would do such a thing? I can't imagine any one of us—

I told you this would happen.

Did not.

And blessed is the fruit—

I most certainly did. Don't you remember that day—

"I knew we should have replaced Sean sooner. I knew he'd never be able to keep the peace."

"Sean? This has nothing to do with Sean. This has to do with us. With who we are."

I knew this was going to happen. We'll have to move again. Where are we going this time? Siberia?

Fin met Peigi's gaze across the crowded room. Everyone was out of their chairs now. Sorry, he mouthed.

You should have warned me, she shot back telepathically. *I could have spiked the punch. If you ask me, they could all use a good dose of Xanax.*

Despite himself, Fin smiled. Leave it to practical Peigi to downplay a crisis.

"Ladies! Gentlemen!" Peigi tried one last time.

With no acceptable response, she tucked her clipboard under her arm and shot a ball of fire from her fingertips up through the center of the broken circle of chairs. It exploded in a belch of black powder and a shower of bright red and yellow sparks.

Everyone shut up at once. Chairs were righted; someone got napkins to clean up the red punch on the linoleum floor. One by one, the chairs were returned to the circle and the Council members took their seats. Even Fin, who *technically* still had the floor, felt compelled to sit down.

"Thank you," Peigi said, plucking her clipboard from under her arm as the last of the embers spat and popped on the old floor. The acrid smell of sulfur, charcoal, and potassium nitrate still singed Fin's nose.

"Fin, can you tell us what you know, beyond the fact that one of us is killing these young men?" Peigi picked right up where she'd left off before the spilled punch and pyrokinetics.

"Not much." He rose again, opening his arms to the Council members. "The two victims were somehow lured into the confidence of the killer—"

"They call it 'glamouring' humans," Mary Hill piped up in her gossipy tone. "I saw it on that HBO show about the vampires."

Mary Hall scooted her large bottom across her chair to speak to Mary Hill, "The girl's name's Sookie. What kind of name is that for such a pretty young thing like that?"

"Glamouring? Too bad there's no such thing," the grandfatherly Gair remarked, slurping from a cup that had been refilled. He was wearing his favorite T-shirt, the Captain Morgan rum one with the bikini-clad girl. A small dribble of punch marred her bare thigh like a trickle of blood.

"Honestly, Mary, I don't know why you watch that kind of nonsense." Maria Cane folded her arms over her chest. "Vampires *glamouring* humans. It's ridiculous."

"I don't know. I've seen Fin in action," Eva piped in.

She winked at Fin. "Those come-hither eyes, that voice. I'd let him *glamour* me anytime."

Thanks a lot, Fin shot at her. Eva grinned.

"Please, let's get back to the subject at hand," Peigi suggested. "Fin?"

He exhaled, choosing his words carefully before addressing the group again. "There's been no sign of a struggle. The killer may or may not have had sex with the victims prior to death. The victims have been fed on, but not exsanguinated. In both cases, while still unconscious from the feeding, the victims' throats were slit." He dragged his thumb from one ear to the other. "The body is then moved and posed."

"Posed?" Peigi asked. She had taken her seat; her clipboard rested on her knees.

"The body is . . . arranged. The first victim was seated, leaning against a trash Dumpster, the second was seated inside a game at the arcade. He appeared to be playing it."

Everyone was silent as they digested the information. Gazes shifted from the floor or a plate of snacks to each other.

"No suspects?" Peigi questioned.

"None. No fingerprints. No hair. No fibers. Whoever is doing it doesn't want to get caught. Obviously. So, for now, I need everyone to keep their eyes and ears open. If you hear or see anything suspicious, you need to get in touch with me."

"Victims were both young," Young Johnny, who was now pushing eighty, said thoughtfully. He tapped his cane for emphasis. "That has to mean something."

"Young and good looking," Eva chimed in.

"What about these teenagers?" Liz Hill scooted to

the end of her chair again, keeping her plate of banana bread, cookies, and two pink-frosted cupcakes balanced on her pudgy knees. "They're all so forward, this generation. They think they know everything. None of them want to follow the sept laws."

Young Johnny pointed at Liz with his cane. "No respect for their elders, that's what I say. Been saying it for centuries. It's time we did something about the—"

"I don't think this is one of our teens," Fin interrupted. He was tired. He just wanted to go home and go to bed. He needed to get out of there, away from the scrutiny of the sept, away from the failure his investigation was becoming. He had no leads. He had no idea who the killer was, except that it was a Kahill vampire, which made it all the more tragic.

"It's not one of our teens," Fin repeated more firmly.

"You said you didn't know any details." Young Johnny tapped his cane militantly. "That means you don't know it's not one of those good-for-nuthin' kids. Running all over the place, out after curfew. Experimenting with drugs, alcohol, bloodletting—"

"I'm telling you, it's not them." Fin raised his voice to be heard over the old man's. "The crime is too gruesome. Too well thought out," Fin argued, his thoughts churning. *Too . . . angry.*

An angry crime.

The words hung in Fin's head as he walked, head down, up the sidewalk. He was unsure where the insight had come from. Unsure he should trust himself. But it was the one clear thought in his head right now. The clearest thought he'd had in three weeks of nonstop investigation. These murders were not about sex, or bloodletting. It wasn't about teen vampires sowing their oats. These crimes were about anger. Jealousy. Rage.

The sound of four-pawed footsteps tapped Fin's attention and he looked up. Out of the darkness came a big black Lab. It passed him on his left side. "Hey, Arlan," he said softly.

The dog made a soft growl in its throat as it went by, on the prowl, or perhaps just keeping watch over the sleeping town.

Fin smiled to himself as he turned onto the street toward home. He had always admired Arlan's ability to shape-shift. It was such a cool gift. What could Fin do? Move packs of gum around? Regan could, at least, transport himself short distances, but Fin had never acquired that skill, either. What could Fin do for the sept? In the days when the belief in magic had been strong in humans' lives, his ability had come in handy, but these days, what did he bring to the table?

The front porch light had been left on. He flipped it off as he entered the dark house. The TV was off, for once. He sensed Regan was somewhere in the house, but he didn't go looking for him.

As he walked into the kitchen and turned on the overhead light, he loosened his uniform tie. He took a glass from the cupboard and poured himself some orange juice. As he drank, he stared out the little window over the sink, at nothing in particular. Today marked the one-week anniversary of Richie's death. Colin had been dead almost three weeks. The farther they got from the crime, the less likelihood there would be of solving it.

He drained the glass and set it in the sink, turning on the faucet to fill it with water.

"Notice I fixed the faucet?"

Fin looked up to see Regan in the doorway in a pair of Fin's boxers. "Those are mine," he accused. "Can't you get your own damned underwear?"

"You're welcome. Did laundry at Ma's and unpacked a bunch of boxes, too." He went to the refrigerator and removed the half gallon of orange juice. He didn't bother to get a glass; he drank straight from the carton.

Fin leaned against the sink, pulling off his tie. He felt like a jerk but not big enough of a jerk to apologize. "You're up late."

"Can't sleep." Regan chugged from the carton. "Nightmares."

"About what? SpongeBob SquarePants?"

"You think this could have something to do with the Rousseau brothers?" Regan wiped his mouth with his forearm. "The murders. You know, some kind of retaliation for what I did?"

Something about the tone of his brother's voice tapped Fin's attention. "What makes you say that? Have you seen one of the Rousseaus?"

Regan frowned, shoving the OJ carton back into the fridge. "Only in my dreams, bro." He drifted to the door.

Fin almost let him go. Almost. "You do anything about a job today?"

Regan caught the edge of the doorjamb with his hand, stopping himself. He didn't turn around. "You know, I could get a job if I wanted to."

"That right?" Fin exhaled. Regrouped. This animosity between them had been brewing for centuries, but it didn't mean Fin didn't love his brother. It didn't mean he didn't care. "Look, Regan. This isn't just me nagging you because I haven't got anything better to do, because I do. Your therapist said you had to get a job. You promised Mary Kay."

"And I will. When I'm ready." Regan reached back and flipped the light switch, leaving Fin in the dark.

"You going to be ready tomorrow?" Fin called after him.

He raised his hand as he went down the hallway. "I'll let you know tomorrow."

Chapter 16

The following morning, on his way to the bathroom, Fin heard a commotion in the kitchen. Wiping the sleep from his eyes, he walked down the hall barefoot in his boxers. He halted in the doorway.

Regan was on all fours on the floor, pulling pots and pans and assorted Tupperware from a lower cabinet.

"What the hell are you doing?" Fin leaned against the doorjamb. His eyes felt gritty and his mouth pasty. He had a bad case of not enough sleep and too much of the banana bread someone always brought to the General Council meetings. "It's six fifty-five in the morning."

"Don't we have a lunch box? A red one? I could have sworn Mom put a red lunch box under here." He glanced at Fin. "It was one of the squishy ones, you know, the insulated kind."

Not only was Regan dressed in a clean shirt and shorts, but they were his own.

"You tripping? Some kind of crazy flashback to . . . I don't know what."

"Guess I can use a grocery bag. I just thought a lunch box would be cool, you know, first day and all."

According to the clock, Fin had been asleep less than four hours, which meant it had only been four hours since he was in the kitchen talking to his brother. "First day of what?" he questioned.

Regan got up off the floor and grabbed a white plastic grocery bag from a pile on the counter. He stuck a sandwich in a baggie, an apple, and a bottle of Gatorade in it. "I used the last of the PB, but I'll get some more after work."

Fin felt like he had stepped into an alternate universe. He'd somehow fallen into a rabbit hole where Regan wore his own clothes, packed a peanut butter and jelly sandwich for lunch, and worked for a living. He tried a different approach. "You got a job?"

"Yup." Regan rolled up the white plastic bag.

Obviously, in this universe, information was not offered, but had to be dragged out of people. "A job? Where?"

"The arcade. I'm the new manager." Regan grinned. "I start today."

Fin ran his hand over his face. Now he really felt like a jerk. Last night he'd launched into his get-a-job speech without even asking Regan if he'd found one. But hadn't Regan told Fin he'd get one when he was ready? Didn't that indicate he *didn't* have one? "I'm so confused," Fin sighed, walking toward the refrigerator.

Regan beat him to it, opened it, and handed him the orange juice carton. Beat him to the cupboard, too. He handed Fin a clean glass. "You're confused a lot, bro." He headed for the door. "Look, I gotta go. You try to have a good day. Catch some killers, or something."

Fin followed him out of the kitchen. "Why the hell

didn't you tell me last night when I was chewing you out that you got a job at the arcade?"

"Didn't have one last night."

"You got a job in the last four hours, in the middle of the night?"

"Technically, early morning. Mary McCathal's an early riser, especially these days, when she has to get up and kick Victor's wrinkly ass out of her bed." He winked as he opened the front door. "We're not supposed to know they're doing the nasty."

"You called Mary McCathal at six in the morning and asked her for a dead guy's job?"

Regan went down the porch steps. "It's not like Pat Callahan could handle it. He's been filling in, but the place has been crazy; floors aren't swept, not enough change, no toilet paper in the bathrooms." He shook his head, seemingly appalled.

Fin stood on the steps in his boxers staring at his brother. "You got a job," he said, as if repeating it would make it any clearer in his mind. "You're managing the arcade."

"Amazing grasp of the English language and its subtleties." Regan tossed a grin over his shoulder. "See you tonight, bro. Be careful. Be safe."

"Whatcha doin'?" Katy tried to spy over Kaleigh's shoulder.

Kaleigh, seated on the railing in the shadows of the front porch of Tomboy's house, presented her shoulder to Katy, blocking her view. She'd practically become a regular at his nightly parties in the last week. To the humans, she guessed she looked like some kind of groupie, watching but not really participating; she didn't care.

Turning her face toward the moonlight, Kaleigh tucked a little notebook into her back pocket. "Nothing."

"What were you writing?"

"Nothing."

"You're a lousy liar." Katy climbed up on the rail to sit beside her. "You're obviously doing *something*. If you don't tell me, I'll just read your mind."

"You can't read my mind." Kaleigh watched two drunk human girls, arm in arm, stumble through the front door into the living room.

"Here we go again." Katy threw up her hands. "Back to the *I'm the wisewoman and I have more power than you do.*"

"I am and I do." Kaleigh glanced at her friend. "And you don't want to know what I'm doing. Trust me, it's better if you don't."

"Sure I want to know. You're obviously writing down names." Katy indicated the notebook in Kaleigh's pocket. "The question is, whose? You working for your uncle? Doing a little detective work?" She scooted closer. "You think one of the human girls here killed those guys?"

"Didn't you hear? It's not a human killing them."

Katy's mouth dropped open. "Oh my God." She crossed herself. "You're kidding!"

"You didn't hear? I can't believe it; I knew something before you did. You always hear the gossip first. I heard at the DQ this morning," she lied. "I thought everyone had heard by now. Fin made an announcement at the Council meeting the other night. A V killed those guys."

Katy gasped, genuinely shocked. "One of us?" She watched a group of human teens carrying plastic party cups of beer cross the porch and go into the house. "So you're trying to figure out which Vs are here? Someone who comes here is killing them?"

"I'm not a part of the investigation." Kaleigh eyed one of Rob's friends just inside the door. He was drinking a beer and talking to the two drunk chicks. She pulled out the notebook and pen and added his name.

"So what's with the notebook, then?" Katy still didn't act like she quite believed Kaleigh.

"We shouldn't be here. Kahill teens. At least not downstairs."

Katy watched her face as she spoke. "So what's going on downstairs?"

"You know what's going on. V kids are taking advantage of humans. I can't just ignore the situation."

"You're going to tell the Council? You can't do that."

"No, I'm not going to tell the Council," Kaleigh intoned. "Not if I don't have to."

"What *are* you going to do?"

Kaleigh smiled to herself. "I'm going to take care of it."

"Well, any way you look at it, this is bad. Maybe we need to start working on a contingency plan. You know, just in case we have to flee the country."

"We are *not* fleeing the country, Katy!"

"You hope we don't have to. But if these killings continue, you know it will have to be considered. If humans start investigating these murders, the game is over. We'll have to run."

"I don't even want to think about such a thing." Kaleigh heaved with a sigh.

"I know you don't." Katy rubbed her arm and then jumped off the rail and headed for the steps.

"Where you going?" Kaleigh asked.

"Home."

"Home?" Kaleigh turned to watch her go. "Pretty early for you. I thought you and Beppe—"

"Beppe." Katy made a face. "What a dick. What was I thinking? He's not even that hot. Probably not even really from Italy. I bet that accent is fake. I bet he's never even seen the Trevi Fountain."

Kaleigh was careful not to let Katy see how relieved she was to hear that that was apparently over. "Sorry to hear things didn't work out for you two."

"Oh, you are not. Apparently, he's got this thing for fake boobs, which I obviously do not have." Katy squeezed her ample, genuine breasts.

Kaleigh lifted her eyebrows.

"Amanda Petrie, that's where it's at, apparently," Katy said. "You know her, from our chemistry class. The one with the ginormous implants. Remember, she got them for her sixteenth birthday, instead of a new car."

Kaleigh laughed. "What's wrong with implants? I was thinking about getting them." She cupped her own small breasts. "You know, when I'm older."

"You, fake boobs? Right. Like there could ever be anything fake about you." Katy went down the sidewalk. "See you tomorrow."

Kaleigh was just plucking the notebook out of her pocket when she realized someone was watching her. She glanced up to see a girl she didn't recognize standing in the shadows of the far end of the porch. A bunch of surfboards had been left there, leaned against the wall. Kaleigh wondered how long she'd been there. Had she been listening in on her and Katy's conversation?

The girl made eye contact with Kaleigh. She was petite. Pretty, with olive skin and dark eyes. Guarded eyes.

"Hey," Kaleigh said, a little unnerved. She should have been more careful, talking to Katy. She knew better. "You, um, just get here?" she asked, racking her brain to try and figure out when the girl had walked onto the porch. Maybe she'd been with that group Kaleigh had watched pass a couple of minutes ago. God, she hoped she and Katy hadn't been speaking too loud.

"Been here awhile."

The girl approached her and Kaleigh tried to guess her age. High school? College? It was hard to say; she had a lot of make-up on. She was wearing a cute spaghetti-strap tank and her inky black hair had been flawlessly straightened.

"I came with my brother, but he ditched me," she said.

Then it hit Kaleigh. She knew why the girl looked familiar, even though she was pretty certain she'd never met her. "I don't suppose your brother is Beppe?"

The girl frowned as she leaned against the porch rail. "Please don't tell me you went out with him, too. Like half the girls in town are either in love with him or they already hate his guts." She had absolutely no Italian accent. She sounded like any other teen from the mid-Atlantic states.

Kaleigh laughed, thinking of Katy, and raised her hands. "I know him from the arcade, but that's as far as it goes."

"You're smarter than most." She folded her arms over her chest. "He's kind of a creep, if you know what I mean."

Again, Kaleigh laughed. "I'm Kaleigh."

"Lia."

"Nice to meet you, Lia. So you came all the way to Nowhere, Delaware, from Italy, why?"

It was Lia's turn to laugh. "My parents take us somewhere on holiday every summer. Last year it was Costa Rica, this year the U.S. They're parents. Who knows why they do any of the things they do."

Kaleigh hopped down off the rail. "Well, I better head home before someone gets up to go to the bathroom and realizes I'm not in my bed. Nice meeting you."

Lia smiled. "You, too."

Kaleigh went down the porch steps backward. There was something about this girl that made her seem different from other human teenage girls. Kaleigh just couldn't put her finger on it. "See you around. Maybe at the Fourth of July parade tomorrow? It's lame, but kind of a big deal around here."

"Sure." Lia pointed at her. "Just make sure you stay away from my brother."

Kaleigh was still chuckling to herself as she went down the street, the list of names safely in her pocket.

When Fin got the invitation from Elena to come to the cottage, he had considered bowing out gracefully. It had been a long, crazy day, with all the Independence Day celebrations. First there had been the annual Clare Point parade and street barricade duty, then he had cruised the crowd for hours, watching for any behavior out of the ordinary from the town locals. To his relief, everyone had gotten into the spirit of the day and had behaved themselves. Even Victor was in the spirit, sporting a red, white, and blue bandana around his straw hat, buying lemonade from a street vendor for Mary McCathal. It was the first time anyone had seen them out in public together.

Elena had called Fin, saying that even though it was after ten, the family was still all out enjoying the festivities. Fin had complained that he was tired and needed a shower and that he wouldn't be much company. She had countered by saying she needed a shower, too, and invited him to join her.

The invitation was just too good for any red-blooded vampire to resist. Elena was waiting for him on the back porch when he turned the corner on her street. She greeted him with a soft kiss. She was barefoot, wearing a soft, flowing dress.

"Still in uniform, sorry," he apologized.

"And who says I do not like a man in uniform?" She led him through the back door, into the house, pulling off his tie. "Just as well as I like a man *out* of uniform?"

Her laughter was warm and husky and when he kissed her, just inside the door, he was glad he had come. She had a way of making him forget what was going on in the town, in his life, even if it was just for a few minutes.

Her fingers found the buttons of his light blue dress shirt and a second later he heard his badge clatter as the shirt hit the floor.

"You really think we ought to be doing this in the kitchen?" he murmured against her neck. Such a beautiful neck, long and slender.

She drew back to look into his eyes. "How about a shower?"

He glanced at the door; anyone could walk in.

"We have time," she whispered, picking his shirt up off the floor and walking down the hall. "The fireworks do not even begin until eleven."

Fin had no choice but to follow her. He was under her spell, the timeless spell of . . . He pushed thoughts of her pulsing blood out of his head. *I have evolved beyond that need,* he chanted silently as he walked down the long hall. *I have evolved.*

Inside the roomy, elegant bathroom, Elena tossed his shirt on the sink and walked around the glass wall to turn on the dual showerheads. Fin added his clothing to the pile, piece by piece. By the time she had adjusted the water temperature just so and come back to him, he was naked. He reached out to her and grasping the hem of her sundress, lifted it over her head. More to the pile of discarded clothing. One kiss and he removed her bra. The next, and her thong panties were cast-offs.

For a moment they stood on the cool tile floor and embraced, the warm mist enveloping them. Cupping her breasts, Fin kissed the round curve of her shoulder. She lifted her chin, stretching, offering her neck.

How did she know what he desired most?

He kissed his way across her shoulder, taking his time, trying to slow his suddenly racing pulse. He pressed his lips to the smooth skin in the curve of her neck.

It would be so easy, he thought. *She would never know. One bite. One small bite and Elena would be rendered unconscious. She would remember nothing when she woke.*

He drew his lips upward and groaned as she reached down to stroke him. He was already prepared for her, hard and pulsing.

"Let's step into the shower," he whispered in her ear, nipping her earlobe playfully.

He was pleasantly surprised when she nipped back, catching his hard nipple between her teeth.

It was the biggest shower Fin had ever been in, bigger than the entire bathroom he and Regan shared. Elena stepped back, pressing her palms against the far wall, letting the warm water rain down on her from two different directions. She ran her hands over her head, slicking back her long, wet hair.

Fin stepped into the running water, closing his eyes as he wrapped one arm around her narrow waist. She arched her back, again presenting her neck to him.

So easy for the taking.

The water hit him in the face. Biting back a groan, he kissed her mouth. Feeling the weight of one breast in his hand, he thumbed her nipple. She sighed with pleasure, and responding to her cue, he leaned over to take it between his lips. He sucked hard, teasing it with the tip of his tongue. More sighs of feminine pleasure.

They kissed again and again and time became suspended. Nothing in the world existed but the two of them, naked, touching, the warm water cascading over them.

But time could never be suspended for long. The ache for what came next always pushed humans and vampires to the edge of the next cliff.

He stroked her gently between her thighs and she opened for him, welcoming him, already warm and wet for him.

Fin raised his head, pressing his groin against hers. She lowered both hands to his shoulders and lifted onto her toes as he pushed inside her. With the hard tile wall behind her, it was an easy fit. She rested her head on his shoulder, her lips now touching the pulse of his throat as he thrust into her.

All he could think about was the blood that pulsed just beneath the surface of her skin.

She was already close to orgasm, he could tell by the little sounds she was making. If he timed it just right, if he bit down at just the precise moment, later, she would chalk up the lost moments of memory to her exceptional climax. To his amazing lovemaking . . .

Fin felt her lips press hard against his neck and he suddenly felt unbalanced. Out of control of a situation that a moment before he had owned.

His breath was coming too quick. He was too close to that point of no return. She bit down lightly on his throat and he groaned, fighting the burgeoning sensation deep in his groin. She bit down harder and he grunted, pushing harder into her. Too late to salvage now.

Elena drew her nails down his back and cried out. Fin felt strangely light-headed, disoriented, as the familiar sensation of release shot through him. He felt himself sway as the shower walls seemed to close in around him.

One minute he was standing up, holding her in his arms against the tile wall, the next minute they were sitting on the shower floor, the warm water pooling around them. She smiled at him, a sensual, sweet look of satisfaction on her beautiful, wet face.

Fin blinked. How had he gotten down here? Obviously he hadn't fallen. Nothing hurt and Elena seemed unconcerned. But he had blacked out, he was sure of it.

He closed his eyes, letting the warm water run over

his head. He was working too hard, staying up too late, not eating enough. Mary Kay said it would eventually affect his health.

Elena rose up on her knees and picked up a bath brush from a shelf in the shower wall. She squirted soap onto it. "Let me scrub your back." She knelt in front of him.

"You don't have to do that."

"No, I do not. Turn around."

Because it was easier than arguing, drawing up his knees, he spun around on the slippery wet tile. With the water now spraying from the rear, it felt like rainwater. She dragged the slightly rough, bristled brush across his lower back and at the same time, brushed her breasts across his shoulders.

He groaned and closed his eyes. "Keep doing that and I'll be ready again in a few minutes."

She kissed a spot between his shoulder blades. "Promises, promises," she murmured.

She scrubbed his back and then his front and they made love on the floor of the shower. This time, Fin remained in complete control and was able to hold back until she'd come several times.

Finally satiated, they dried themselves with big fluffy white towels. It had been Fin's intention to go home but Elena persuaded him to come to her bedroom and lie down with her for a few minutes.

"My bed is empty and lonely," she told him in that sexy, slightly accented voice of hers that he loved.

One minute Fin was half sitting, half lying in Elena's bed, his arm around her, the bedside lamps glowing softly, the next minute, he was waking in the pitch dark.

Fin always found waking in a woman's bed to be

disorienting. A little scary, even. He liked having sex with them; he did not like *sleeping* with them. It was too intimate.

He glanced at the digital clock beside the bed. Three forty in the morning.

Crap, he thought.

Moving slowly so as not to wake Elena, nude in his arms, he slipped his arm out from under her. She sighed in her sleep as he carefully drew the sheet over her.

His eyes now adjusted to the darkness, he located his boxers in his pile of clothes on a chair near the door and stepped into them. Elena rolled over on the bed and put her arm out in her sleep as if searching for him. Fin had to get out of there before she woke.

Armed at least with underwear, he grabbed the rest of his clothes and slipped out the door. The hall was dark, but he had no problem navigating it now that his vision had adjusted. In most circumstances, the Kahills could see as well in the dark as in the daylight.

So why didn't he see her until he almost tripped over her?

Chapter 17

Elena's niece startled him far more than he apparently startled her, almost as if she routinely ran into half-naked men in her hallway in the middle of the night.

She looked up at him. Then down at his boxers. Then up. "Hello," she said.

Clutching his clothes to his chest, he stared at her. He knew she was fourteen or fifteen, but she looked younger in her white nightie and sleepy face. "Hi," he managed.

As she walked into the bathroom, he heard Elena come out of her bedroom and turned back toward her. She held a silk robe closed with one hand.

"I am *so* sorry," he whispered, nodding toward the closing bathroom door. "Your niece, I ran into her on my way out."

"Which one, Lia or Alessa?"

He hated to admit he didn't know which was which. This was supposed to be a no-strings-attached relationship. That covered family names, didn't it?

"Alessa is the younger one," Elena offered.

"Lia, then."

"Ah." She folded her arms over her chest, looking none too pleased.

Fin felt like a complete ass. After fifteen-hundred-odd years, surely he knew better than to get caught sneaking out of a woman's bed. By a kid, no less. "I never saw her until I was in the hall. I must have fallen asleep. I never even heard them come in." It wasn't like him to let his guard down that way. It was foolish and damned dangerous. "I really am sorry, Elena."

She sighed. "It's all right," she said softly.

"It's not. An innocent young girl like her—"

Elena pushed dark, silky hair from her eyes. "Lia is not as young nor as innocent as she appears, I am afraid."

Her tone was odd. Fin couldn't tell if she was angry, or just tired, or both.

"I'll go," he said.

She nodded. "You can let yourself out?"

"Yeah. Sure. Of course." Fin hurried out of the house, not stopping to dress until he was at the end of the street. As he held onto a stop sign for balance and stepped into his pants, he sensed someone watching. He glanced up to see a Doberman watching him. He knew dogs couldn't laugh, but he could have sworn he heard Arlan snicker.

Elena waited in the hallway. She had a feeling Lia was hiding from her, hoping she would just go back to bed. Elena had no intention of doing so, not without first speaking to her niece. Finally, the bathroom light went out and the door opened. Elena faced Lia in the dark.

"I'm sorry," Lia said. "I didn't mean to cause an awkward situation."

Elena crossed her arms over her chest. "I did not mean for you to meet. I try to keep my private life private."

"I won't tell Mama and Papa, if that's what you're worried about."

"I am not worried. Your parents know I see men from time to time."

"Does he know? About us, I mean?"

Elena was silent.

Lia looked down at her bare feet. She was wearing a cute baby doll nightgown. She looked like a dark-haired angel. "No need, I guess. We'll be going home in a few weeks."

"We will."

"Well, good night, Auntie Elena." The girl turned to go.

"Lia?"

She turned back.

"Do you know your brother has been going out at night?"

"No. Where is he going?"

"I do not know. That's what worries me."

"He didn't kill those boys, if that's what you're worried about," she said softly. "Beppe would never do anything like that again. He knows Papa is serious when he says he would kill him to protect the rest of us."

Lia was right; Elena knew she was right. She hadn't really suspected Beppe of murdering them. But for some reason, she was still uneasy. "It's not a good idea, you know. Him prowling about unaccompanied at night.

If I tell your parents, we will all be cutting our holiday short."

"No, please." Lia took a step toward Elena in the dark hallway. "Don't tell them," she whispered. "I'm actually making some friends here. Sort of," she added.

Elena's heart went out to the teen. She knew how hard this life was for her. She could only imagine what it was like for the children.

"Let me talk to him." Lia grabbed Elena's hand. "Please?" she begged. "Let me talk to him. Let me handle it. You know he won't listen to you but he might listen to me."

Elena looked down at Lia and patted her hand.

"Please?" Lia whispered. "I'll talk to him. I'm sure he's just walking at night. You know how restless he gets."

"You will talk to him?"

"I swear it. But it can't come from you. I . . . I'll just tell him I saw him leaving the house. You have to pretend you don't know."

Elena let go of Lia's hand, not sure her niece's plan was the best option.

"I'll tell you if there's any reason to worry. I swear it."

Elena thought for a minute, then nodded. "All right, but if you think there's any reason to be concerned, any whatsoever, you have to come to me. I don't think he's dumb enough to kill again. His desire for self-preservation is too strong, but we have to be careful, Lia. I do not have to tell you that."

"Don't worry. I'll take care of it." She stood on her tiptoes and kissed Elena on the cheek. "Good night, *Zia* Elena."

"Good night." Inside her bedroom, Elena closed the door and leaned against it, shutting her eyes. Her entire body still tingled with the feel of Fin's hands. She could still taste him on her lips.

She knew she should alert Celeste and Vittore to Beppe's nighttime prowling. It wasn't safe. Not for Beppe. Not for Clare Point. But if she told, even if Beppe was completely innocent of any wrongdoing, her sister and brother-in-law would want to return home immediately. And Elena wasn't ready for that. Not yet.

She opened her eyes, looking at the rumpled sheets of her bed. She could still smell him, his male scent lingering on the bed linens. She walked to her bed, letting the silk robe fall off her shoulders. The cool air that blew from the vents lifted goose bumps on her bare skin. Her nipples puckered, reminding her of the feel of Fin's mouth on her breasts. He was one of the finest lovers she had had since her husband's death. She would miss him when she returned home. But she wouldn't go home yet.

Kaleigh leaned against the air hockey table and sipped her orange Vitamin Water. Katy stood beside her. Grape Fanta was her poison. They were just killing time until after curfew when they would sneak into the forest. They watched as Regan moved from video game to video game, emptying the change reservoirs. He was either so entranced with his duties that he hadn't noticed them yet, or he didn't care that they were still there.

Kaleigh sipped her drink. "What'd you tell your parents?"

"That I was spending the night with you." Katy slurped her grape soda. "You?"

"That I was spending the night with you, of course." They snickered.

"Parents. You'd think they'd learn after a couple of centuries." Katy set her can down on the air hockey table. "But they never do."

"Maybe they know what we're doing, they just realize after all this time that teenagers will be teenagers."

Katy smirked. "Maybe." She studied her fingernails, drew her thumbnail over her lower teeth, and checked it out to see what damage she had done to the green glitter nail polish. "You tell Rob about your *party* tonight?"

"No. He wouldn't have liked the idea. He would have said I should just go to the Council, especially now that we know the killer's a V. He doesn't understand that the kids are *my* responsibility." She was quiet for a second. "You tell Pete?"

Katy chewed on her thumbnail. "Pete and I are not dating. I don't have to tell him where I'm going."

"You're not dating? You were making out with him at the snow cone booth the other day at the parade."

Katy whipped her head around. "Who told you?"

Kaleigh smiled. "Wisewomen have their ways."

"Oh, please," Katy groaned.

"What are you two still doing here?" Regan got down on his knees in front of the four-lane skee ball alley and used a key to open the change reservoir. "We're closed."

Katy glanced at the garage doors that led out onto the boardwalk; Regan had pulled them down and secured them twenty minutes ago. The three of them were the only ones left in the building. "I can see that."

Regan dumped the quarters into a big plastic bucket. "Which means you should be home, safely tucked in your beds. Don't you know there's a killer loose in Clare Point?"

"From what we hear, we're not the ones who have to be worried." Kaleigh finished her drink and set the bottle beside Katy's can, right next to the NO FOOD OR DRINK ALLOWED sign taped to the hockey table. "It's the humans who better be careful."

"Pretty hard to believe, isn't it?" he asked, locking the reservoir and getting to his feet. "I mean, who would jeopardize everything we've built here?"

"If I knew the answer, you think I'd be here?"

"Maybe it's someone under a witch's spell or something," Katy offered.

Kaleigh cut her eyes at her best friend.

"I'm just saying." Katy gnawed on her thumbnail. "So maybe it's someone not thinking straight. Like maybe it's someone *under the influence.*"

"Katy!" Regan looked so hurt that Kaleigh felt bad for him. He still hadn't been forgiven by the sept for turning Victor into a vampire. To many, turning a human into a V was a worse sin than just killing them.

"I would never do something like that." He stood in front of them, the bucket of change in his hand. "No matter how wasted I was."

"Didn't say you would." Katy spat a piece of nail polish on the floor. "I was just trying to make it make sense. Just like everyone else in town. I mean, she's got to have her reasons, right?"

"What makes you say it's a she?" He jingled the change in the bucket, thoughtfully. "Could be a he."

"Oh, it's a she all right. Call it women's intuition. You see those guys' pictures in the paper? They were both hot." She wrinkled her nose. "Anyone talk to Eva? She could definitely have sex with a man and then kill him."

"Eva doesn't even like men," Kaleigh argued.

"All the more reason to kill them after you have sex with them and suck their blood."

"One of them might have had sex prior to death with the killer, but not the other," Regan said.

"So? Doesn't mean anything. I'm telling you, take it from a woman. It's a woman."

Regan passed the heavy bucket into his other hand, contemplating what Katy had said. "What do you think, Kaleigh?"

Leaning against the air hockey table, she groaned and closed her eyes, tilting her head back. "I try not to think at all. I've got problems of my own. My head's already about to burst."

Regan offered a lopsided grin, then something caught his attention behind them. "Hey, get that can and bottle off the hockey table! Can't you read the sign? No food or drink."

Kaleigh snatched up her empty. "We gotta go anyway. We'll let ourselves out the back."

"Be careful walking home," he called after them.

Regan carried the bucket of change to a plastic tub he'd left on the floor near the office door. As he dumped the coins from the bucket to the tub, he watched them spill like a waterfall. As the last few hit the growing pile, he checked the clock on the wall. He was supposed to meet Fin at midnight for a beer. He'd have to hurry to finish up here or come back early tomorrow. The bathrooms still needed to be cleaned, all the trash cans emptied, and the floor swept. Plus, he needed to take a look at the Kung Fu video game. A couple of the kids had complained today that it was "eating their money."

Regan heard the back door at the end of the hall close behind the girls as they went out. He wondered if he ought to lock it. But that seemed silly. Kahills didn't lock doors. And Katy had been right. They were in no danger. It was the human tourists in town who needed to lock their doors.

He left the bucket next to the change bin and went down the hall to the closet to get the big black garbage bags and the broom. For the next forty-five minutes, he emptied trash cans and swept the floor. He piled all the bags of trash at the end of the hall next to the door that led to the alley. He'd take them to the Dumpster on his way out. He checked his cell phone for the time. He could work on the Kung Fu game tomorrow morning before things got busy, but that still left the bathrooms. He could either clean them and arrive late at the pub and piss Fin off or he could finish his work.

Fin was always pissed at him about something anyway . . .

Regan went back to the closet and grabbed the cleaning supply caddy. He'd make it quick and then he'd be outta here. Some people might get grossed out by cleaning public bathrooms, but he didn't mind. He liked busywork; it gave him time to think. And he liked feeling like he had accomplished something at the end of the day. Maybe it wasn't a position on the Kill Team, or the High Council, but it was a start to rebuilding his place in the community, wasn't it?

He opened the door to the women's room and propped it open with the caddy. As he leaned over to grab the pair of rubber gloves his mother had insisted he wear when cleaning, he got a strange feeling. The hair rose on the back of his neck and he straightened slowly, slipping one hand into a glove. He listened hard but heard nothing but the whirr of the fans in the air-conditioning unit.

He stepped out into the hall to look around the open door. Nothing. No one. Staring down the dark hall, he slid his other hand into a glove.

Something just didn't *feel* right. The girls had been gone almost an hour. Could they have come back? "Kaleigh?"

Nothing.

Regan stood there a minute longer, listening. He shook his head as he walked back into the bathroom and flipped on the lights in the single-seater. He would have said he'd been watching too many scary movies, only he didn't like scary movies. Because, well . . . he got scared.

He grabbed the toilet brush and the blue liquid stuff to clean the bowl and got down on his knees. It didn't look too bad. He squirted the cleaning stuff around the rim and scrubbed, then flushed, just the way Mary Kay had taught him. At the tail end of the flush, he thought he heard a sound behind him, but he couldn't be sure. The toilet was pretty loud.

Had it been the back door?

Regan got to his feet, walked into the hall, toilet brush still in his hand.

Something in a cape flew straight at him. Just like in the nightmares. Only this time, he was absolutely, positively sure he was not dreaming.

Chapter 18

Kaleigh and Katy hurried along the narrow, over-grown path that ran through the middle of the game preserve on the edge of town. The darkness didn't bother either of them. They'd hunted these woods for three hundred years. What did bother Kaleigh were the stupid mosquitoes.

She slapped her neck. "We should have brought bug repellent." She always used repellent in the summer when she had to hunt. Like the other members of the sept, she only needed to feed on blood once a moon cycle. The deer that lived on the state-preserved land and were cared for by the sept were enough to keep them all nourished and safe. The readily available deer here in the new world had enabled them to cease the taking of human blood.

"I don't suppose you brought mosquito repellent?" Kaleigh asked, scratching her neck. There was no breeze on the summer night air. It was hot and humid and the mosquitoes were making her itchy all over.

Katy felt around in the bag she carried slung over

her shoulder. "Nope. Got gum. Want gum? It's Triple Watermelon Blast."

"No, I don't want gum. Gum isn't going to keep these damned mosquitoes from biting," she complained irritably. "We'll be there in a minute. Once we get the fire started, I'll throw some leaves on it. The smoke will keep them away."

"It'll make my hair stink, too."

Kaleigh heard Katy unwrap a piece of gum. She smelled the Triple Watermelon Blast and her stomach did a flip-flop. Maybe this wasn't such a good idea. Rob would certainly have objected, which was exactly why she hadn't told him about the secret meeting. The question was, what was she going to do if the teens wouldn't agree to stay away from Tomboy's illicit basement parties? Would she have to go to the Council?

The two girls entered the clearing that still held bad memories from two summers before. A human had lost his life here. And it had been Kaleigh's fault. Sort of. It was his own stupid, evil fault that Fia's then-boyfriend had had to kill him. That didn't mean she didn't think that some day, when the *mallachd* was finally lifted and she died a real death and met God at the pearly gates, she wouldn't have to stand accountable for her part in the deaths of Bobby, Mahon, Shannon, and the human.

"This should only take a minute. I've got the wood ready to go." Kaleigh pulled a pack of matches out of her back pocket. "You want to grab some leaves, preferably damp?"

"Why do I always have to do the dirty jobs?" Katy grumbled, wandering off.

Kaleigh knelt to one side of the firepit. One strike of a match and a blaze leapt from the dry kindling she'd carefully stacked this morning. She sat back on her heels and watched the flames lick the edges of the wood. After all these centuries, she was still fascinated by fire and she liked the idea that something could still hold her attention this way. It made her feel more . . . human.

"Dang, girl." Katy tossed a measly handful of leaves on the fire and glanced around. The quick-spreading blaze cast a circle of soft light around them. "Looks like someone's having a party."

Kaleigh had dragged the logs once used for benches and laid them around the firepit, making a nice circle. She had to cut back some of the underbrush and haul away some fallen branches. Now the area sort of resembled the original Council fire, which had been in this very place. When they'd first arrived in the colonies, they'd come here to meet, fearful of being seen by humans. Now they met in the museum, right in plain sight. It was always the best place to hide.

"Worked your pretty tailbone off, didn't you?" Katy cracked her gum, taking in the circle of seating around the firepit appreciatively. "It looks nice. They'll want to party here with us every night."

Kaleigh looked at her and then tried to move the cooler she'd left here earlier in the day. Only it was heavy now that it was full. Realizing she couldn't pick it up, she started to drag it. "Doubtful when they hear what I have to say."

"Wow. Drinks on a hot summer night?" Spying Kaleigh struggling with the cooler, Katy scrambled over a log. "Need some help?"

"Yeah. You take one end, I'll take the other. I just want to lift it over the log."

"I'll get it." Katy leaned over, grabbed both handles and lifted it herself.

"Dang, girl." Kaleigh took a step back. "Eating your Wheaties?"

"How the heck did you get this out here?" Setting the cooler down, Katy opened the lid. "And you brought beer?"

"Get out of there. There's only enough for, like, one or two each. I carried the beer and ice separately, then loaded the cooler." Kaleigh sat down on one of the logs and scratched her shin where a mosquito bite was rising. "I borrowed one of Malachy's ATVs and hauled it out here on the back."

Ignoring Kaleigh's warning to leave the beer for the others, Katy popped open a can of Coors Light and slurped the foam off the top. "You tell him why you needed it?"

In the distance, Kaleigh heard her first *guests* approaching. By the sound of their voices, it was a bunch of the guys. Farther behind them, she heard the faint sound of feminine giggles. It had been mostly guys she spotted going down into Tomboy's basement, but not all guys. Girl Vs liked their human blood, too. "Of course not." She grabbed a stick poking out of the fire and used it to move one of the bigger pieces of wood.

"Where'd you get the beer?" Katy took another drink.

"None of your business."

Katy smirked. "You surprise me sometimes. Hard to believe that you still could, as long as we've been friends."

Kaleigh poked at the fire with her stick. "That a good thing or a bad thing?"

Katy sipped her beer thoughtfully. "A good thing," she declared with a nod.

"Just trying to keep us alive." She grinned. "Until we can die, of course."

"Of course." Katy raised her beer in a toast.

Kaleigh dropped her head suddenly and groaned. "Sweet Mary, Mother of God, what do I think I'm doing here? No one's going to listen to me. If they're getting human blood and getting away with it, why would they agree to stop just because I say they should? They're not going to listen to me." She threw up her hands. "This is a complete waste of time and an embarrassment."

"Come on, they might listen."

Kaleigh gave a doubtful glance. "Why would they?"

Katy met her gaze. When she spoke, her voice was uncharacteristically solemn. "Because they respect you in a way they respect no one else in this sept."

"Hey, hey, hey. Joe's here!" Joe Kahill burst through the trees and out of the darkness. Holding his hands up in the air, he turned to face his followers. "The party can get started now, boys."

Several guys came behind him, all laughing and shoving each other the way boys did. Eying them, Kaleigh took a deep breath. "Give me that." She reached for Katy's beer.

"Why?" Katy held the can to her breasts as if it was something precious.

"Because I think I'm going to need it more than you are."

Katy considered the thought and then handed the beer to her.

Regan didn't have time to do anything more than lower his center of gravity and raise his only weapon available, the toilet brush. He recognized the face of the man who swooped down on him. Not just from his dreams, but from his past. It was Asher, one of the Rousseau brothers who had captured him in New Orleans the summer before and locked him in the tomb. With the spiders. Regan hated spiders. He hated Asher and all his creepy brothers.

Asher hit Regan so hard in the chest that Regan fell backward to the floor. He stabbed at Asher with the toilet brush and gave him a good poke in the eye with the wet blue bristles. Asher howled, as much from indignity as pain, Regan guessed, but it gave Regan the split-second opportunity to transport himself out of the hall and into the main room of the arcade. There, at least, he'd have a chance at fighting Asher off.

Regan rematerialized beside the classic Pac-Man. The toilet brush had been teleported with him. He didn't have the ability to transport himself far, or through very dense objects, like tomb walls or bank vaults, but if he could reach the garage doors on the far side of the arcade, he thought he might have a chance at passing through the fiberglass.

Asher screeched as he hurled himself down the dark hallway, stupid cape flapping behind him. The Rousseaus were a particularly nasty nest of vampires that lived in New Orleans and ran a drug trafficking business, among other shady dealings. Their forte was the ability to launch themselves into the air and glide a short distance, appearing as if they were flying. The capes had been added for the intimidation factor.

It was pretty intimidating.

Abandoning the toilet brush, Regan threw himself down on the floor and scrambled on his belly beneath the arcade game. He could still smell the toilet bowl cleaner on the yellow rubber gloves.

Asher hit the game hard and fell back under the impact.

Regan leaped to his feet and made for the doors. Maybe he really had a chance.

The notion lasted only a step and a half. Just long enough to give Rousseau brother number two time to fly down the hall.

Gad hit Regan from the rear, knocking him face first to the cement floor. *I could use a little help here, bro,* Regan telepathed as his chin hit the cement and he tasted blood in his mouth. *Arcade, front and center, before the Rousseaus make crab bait out of me.*

I could use a little help here, bro.

Fin heard the message so clearly in his mind that Regan could have been standing beside him.

Be there in a sec, he shot back and turned and ran in the opposite direction. He was three blocks from the arcade, on his way home from work. It would take him more than a second to get there. It would take him three minutes. What if he didn't make it in time?

Fin flew down the street. At the first crosswalk, he spotted a German shepherd on the far side of the street, sniffing a paper bag that had fallen from a trash can. Fin didn't recognize the shepherd, but he knew him. It was the stroke of luck that just might save his brother.

Arlan, I need you, Fin telepathed as he sprinted across the street.

Arlan lifted his muzzle and sniffed the air. Smelled the intruders, perhaps. He growled.

The Rousseau brothers. The arcade, Fin telepathed. *Regan's in trouble.*

The shepherd shot down the street, headed straight for the boardwalk. Halfway down the next block, running hard, breathing harder, Fin lost sight of Arlan. He'd beat him there. Good thing. Vampires didn't often kill other vampires, no matter where in the world they hailed from. Sort of a *professional courtesy.* But it did happen and the Rousseau brothers were notorious for not playing by the rules. Especially when you pissed them off the way Regan had.

Gad tried to drag Regan across the floor by his ankles, but Regan was a scrappy fighter. He kicked and hollered like a madman, hurling any object he could wrap his mind around at his attackers. The toilet brush levitated off the ground and flew end over end through the air, striking Gad in the side of the head. As Regan wrapped his arms around the leg of a pinball machine, he used his telepathic powers to tip over the one trash can he hadn't emptied. It was only half full, but the crushed soda cans and Popsicle sticks made effective weapons as he hurled them through the air. Gad let go of Regan's leg as the first cans hit him in the head. One, still half full, exploded when he threw his hand up to protect himself, spewing Coke all over his nice black cape.

Crap. Regan scrambled across the floor on all fours. Now Gad was really pissed. The vampires wouldn't be satisfied with just beating him up, or beating him and then locking him up in a spider-infested supply closet. They would be out for blood. Or worse, his head. Blood

could be replaced. Heads, however, could not be reat-
tached. A vampire separated from his head was
doomed to an eternity of torturous hell, trapped in a
limbo that was neither life nor death. Definitely a sentence worse than being imprisoned in a linen closet.

Come on, bro. Need you, now, man, Regan telepathed.
Crawling out from under a pinball machine, he stumbled to his feet. He was halfway across the arcade. If
he could just get within four or five feet of the garage
doors that opened onto the boardwalk . . .

Gad flew over Regan's head and landed just in front
of him, arms crossed over his chest like he was some
kind of demented cartoon superhero.

"Come on, guys. Easy now." Regan lifted his rubber
gloved hands. "Let's talk this through." As he spoke, he
tried to see what else was available to throw at them.
The thing was, there weren't that many loose objects in
an arcade. Pinball machines were too heavy for him to
levitate or dematerialize. Maybe he could hurl a couple
of skee balls if he could manage to get them out of the
game, but it was on the far side of the room and iffy at
best. "What do you want? You got your money."

Regan could have sworn he heard a dog bark as Gad
flew into him, knocking him into Asher's waiting arms.
Asher caught Regan by the armpits and hauled him up
so Gad could take the first swing. It was a good one,
causing a bone-rattling, gut-wrenching explosion of
pain in Regan's jaw. Blood spewed from Regan's lower
lip as Gad hit him a second time and Regan slumped
against Asher.

"Is there something you want, boys? Something you
need?" Regan joked, his bloody lip making the words
come out slightly slurred.

Gad cocked his fist back. *"Fild de putain."*

Regan didn't speak Cajun, but he had a suspicion Gad was not being complimentary and as the vampire drew his fist back, Regan prepared for the next blow.

This time there was no mistaking the vicious growl as a dog exploded out of the dark hallway, its eyes glowing, its teeth bared.

"Merde!" Asher released Regan as the dog leapt through the air and sank its teeth into Asher's arm.

Gad grabbed Regan and the two of them tumbled to the cement floor. At least now it would be a fair fight, or close. Dog against vampire, vampire against vampire. Of course Regan knew who the dog was, just not how he knew to come to his rescue.

Gad pinned Regan down and began to pummel his face. Regan wasn't a bad fighter, but he was out of shape and Gad was quite a bit bigger than he was. Regan got in a good punch. Then another, but he was definitely taking the brunt of the beating.

Somewhere close by, Arlan, the German shepherd, was biting the crap out of the Cajun vampire. But Asher wasn't giving in easily. Vampire and dog rolled across the cement floor, Arlan biting and clawing, Asher throwing punches, kicking.

"Regan!"

It was Fin. "About time!" Regan hollered. That split second of redirection of his focus landed him a punch in the face.

Fin, still in his cop uniform, threw himself on top of Gad, who was on top of Regan. Fin wrestled the vampire off his brother and the two rolled under the air hockey table, exchanging punches.

Regan took a second to catch his breath before he staggered to his feet. Arlan and Asher were still going at it, but from the look of the torn clothing and bloody scratches and puncture wounds, it appeared that the dog would come out on top.

"I don't know why you two couldn't just let bygones be bygones," Regan panted as he walked over to one of the support beams and released a fire extinguisher. He wiped the blood that dripped from the corner of his mouth. "I mean, I apologized. My sister apologized, my brother apologized," he recited as he pulled the pin. "You got your money for the drugs I stole and then some, and it was over. It should have been over," he warned, walking over to Asher and Arlan. "Back up, pup."

Arlan, planted on the Cajun vampire's chest, turned his massive head and growled at Regan.

"Knock it off," Regan said, frowning. Arlan was never quite himself when he manifested as an animal. "Otherwise you'll get it, too. Now, watch out." He pulled the trigger and Arlan leapt off the vampire with a yip as the cold foam met its mark. Regan hit Asher right in the face, then sprayed his body.

Arlan growled and backed up farther. There was blood and tufts of fur all over the floor. The place smelled like wet, pissed-off dog.

"Had enough?" Regan demanded.

Asher started to get up off the floor and Regan pulled the trigger again. Asher lay back down.

"Now, that's better. Keep an eye on him, will you?" he asked the dog, turning toward Fin and Gad, who were still wrestling under the air hockey table.

"Bro, could you bring that out from under there? I don't want to ruin the table."

Fin turned his head to look up at Regan and Gad punched him in the jaw.

Regan flinched. "Sorry." He swung the fire extinguisher around. "Enough is enough, Gad. The trick here is to know when you're outnumbered and bow out gracefully. Now let him go, or you'll get it, too."

Gad drew his hand back to throw another punch. Regan pulled the trigger. Fin scrambled to get out of the way as Regan blasted Gad with the high-pressure foam. Gad coughed and choked and flailed his arms, trying to get away from the stuff pouring out of the hose.

Fin rolled and came to his feet, bloody, shirt torn, necktie over one shoulder.

"Had enough?" Regan released the trigger. He flexed his finger to pull it again. "Or more?"

"Enough," Asher grunted.

Regan slowly lowered the canister.

"What the hell is wrong with you two?" Fin demanded. "When I left New Orleans last fall, your brother Abram and I agreed the Rousseaus and the Kahills were straight. You have no right to be in Clare Point."

"Go on, get over there with your bro." Regan waved the fire extinguisher hose at Gad.

Gad half dragged himself, half crawled his way to his mauled brother.

"We wahn't gonna hur' him." Gad's accent was heavy. "Jus' havin' a li'l fun. Just passin' t'rough, I sweer we was."

Fin jerked at the knot of his tie and whipped the tie off. "Just having a little fun, you say? Just passing through? How long have you been in town?"

"Jus' passin' t'rough."

Fin raised his foot and dropped it on Gad's neck. "How long have you been here, boys?"

"An hour, is all. Sweer by our Mahter's grave."

Fin frowned. "Your mother's not dead. I've met her. She's as charming as you two. So you've only been here an hour?" He glanced at Regan. "How about before that? Say two weeks ago?"

"No."

Fin stepped back. "Two weeks before that?"

Asher sat up. "I tell you, we're jus' passin' t'rough. Haven't been here b'fore."

"Where you headed?"

Asher hesitated. Arlan growled and took a step closer.

Asher's eyes widened. "Goin' to New York. Do a li'l business for our daddy."

Fin hesitated for a moment. "Okay. So get the hell out of Clare Point and don't let me catch you here again."

Gad got to his feet and offered his hand to his brother. Regan stepped out of his way to let the men pass. They walked out of the arcade and down the hall. Regan waited to hear the heavy back door close before he looked at Fin.

"Thanks, bro." He wiped his bloody mouth with the back of his hand and glanced at the dog. "You, too, Arlan."

The dog sat back on his haunches.

Regan glanced back at his brother. "You don't think they could have had anything to do with the murders, do you?"

"Nah, they were telling the truth." Fin gingerly touched the cut over his eyebrow. The bleeding had almost stopped.

Regan grimaced and took a step toward Fin. "Looks like you could use a stitch or two there."

"I'll be all right."

Regan looked over the rest of his brother's face. His gaze caught on two puncture wounds on his neck. "Oh, damn. Did he get you?" He touched Fin's chin, turning his head so he could get a better look.

"What?" Fin brushed his neck with his fingertips.

"Right here." Regan touched the two puncture wounds. "Eww. Gad spit?"

Fin pushed Regan's hands away. He looked startled. "Get your hands off me. I don't know. I'm telling you, he didn't bite me."

Out of the corner of his eye, Regan saw Arlan morph back into a man. One second he was a dog, the next second he was standing there in shorts and T-shirt. The only sign that he'd been in a fight was his messy hair. "Look like a bite to you?" He pointed at Fin's neck.

"I gotta go. You going to be okay here?" Fin backed away, his hand on his neck, covering the marks.

"I'll stay, help him lock up," Arlan offered.

Fin took another step back, turned, and hurried down the back hall in the dark. His mouth was dry, his palms damp. What Regan was saying didn't make sense. Gad hadn't bitten him; he was positive.

Which left only one even less believable possibility.

Chapter 19

Initially, the teens seemed content to pop a beer and mill around, chatting with each other, but they all knew something was up and slowly each one took a seat on one of the log benches around the fire. One by one, they looked to Kaleigh. Conversations tapered off. Laughter died down.

"Okay, Kaleigh, out with it." Joe propped one foot up on the log he was sitting on and opened his third beer.

"Yeah, come on," Mary Hill, who they called Minnie, said, tossing her empty beer can in the fire.

In a way, Kaleigh was relieved they were forcing her into speaking up; otherwise, she would have chickened out.

"What do you want?" Joe asked. "Because obviously you wanted to talk to us, otherwise you wouldn't have called us all here."

"In the middle of the night, after curfew," Liz added.

Kaleigh poked at the fire with a stick. "You knew that's why I asked you to come?"

Billy laughed. "Do you mean did we think you were really having a party? Do we look stupid?"

Kaleigh exhaled, putting down the stick. "I don't think you're stupid," she said. Her voice grew stronger. "But it's come to my attention that some of you are doing something pretty stupid." Her gaze moved from one teen to the next, lingering on certain ones.

Joe groaned and crushed an empty against his forehead. Two more guys followed suit. Kaleigh ignored their juvenile behavior. "It has to stop."

"What has to stop?" Joe asked, feigning innocence.

A couple of the guys snickered. The same ones with beer can dents on their foreheads. Idiots.

Mary whispered to Liz, just loud enough for Kaleigh to hear. "She's just pissed because she's not getting any."

"You have to stop going to the parties at Tomboy's," Kaleigh said loudly. "At least you have to stop going downstairs into his basement."

"So we're not allowed in basements anymore?"

Kaleigh eyed Billy. "Not if you're going to take human blood."

There was more whispering. Kaleigh shut out what they were thinking; she could only deal with them on one level at a time. "It's forbidden and it's dangerous and you all know it."

"If they're stupid enough to offer their blood, why shouldn't we be stupid enough to take it?" Billy challenged.

"Because it's not good for us." She met his gaze. "Because it's not good for the sept's objectives. And they don't know what they're agreeing to. They're drunk. They're high. They're confused teenage humans."

"Christ's bones," Joe groaned. "You sound like one of the old-timers."

"Because I am one of the old-timers." She looked around at the young, attractive faces she knew so intimately. "And so are each of you. You just don't entirely remember yet."

Everyone was quiet for a minute.

"Look," Kaleigh went on. "I know the urges are hard to resist, especially right now when we're vulnerable because we've just been reborn, but you have to fight those urges. You have to try to be the best person you can be."

"You mean the best vampire," Minnie said tartly.

Kaleigh turned to her. "Absolutely. When we crossed that ocean, when we shipwrecked and dragged ourselves to shore here, we all agreed God had given us a second chance by allowing us to escape the slayers. We agreed to protect His human race, and protecting them does not involve drinking their blood."

"Even if they give it freely?"

"Even if they give it freely." Kaleigh sighed. "Because we know better, even if they don't."

"So, what? You just want us to give up partying for the summer? Become a goody two-shoes like you?" Joe finished off his beer.

"I'm asking you to draw a line. You know where the line is." She met and held Joe's gaze.

He looked away first and Kaleigh heaved a sigh of relief. She let a moment pass. The fire snapped and crackled. Thoughts flew back and forth between the teens.

I don't know why she always thinks she's in charge.
She's right, you know. You just don't want to admit it.
We were just having a little fun.

Fun, yeah, right, at some human's expense.

"This is serious business, these tourists being murdered," Kaleigh went on, blocking out everyone's thoughts again. "I don't have to tell you that."

"You don't seriously think it's one of us, do you?" Liz pushed heavy fringed bangs out of her eyes. "I mean, just because we're stealing a little human blood from some drunk guy doesn't mean we would murder him."

"No, I don't think it's one of us." And Kaleigh truly didn't. She knew these people too well. She knew none of them had it in them to murder senselessly that way. "But you know how the elders can be."

"Judgmental," someone offered.

"Exactly. And this is not the time to separate us from them." Kaleigh propped her foot on the cooler. "Don't forget, we'll be one of them in a few short years."

"Sweet Mary and Joseph, I hope not," Katy swore.

Everyone laughed.

"Fine," Joe said when the laughter died down. "So we'll lay off the blood. It wasn't all that good anyway. Chicks who are that drunk, their blood tastes nasty." He looked at Kaleigh. "So can we at least finish off the beer?"

She stepped back and opened the lid. "Drink up, and don't you dare tell your parents where you got it."

Victor lay on his back in bed, in the dark, staring at the ceiling.

Mary rolled over and put her arm around him, snuggling up against him, her naked body pressed to his. He'd been so lost in his thoughts, he hadn't realized she was awake, too. They lay in silence.

"You going to tell me, or you going to just keep stewing?" she asked after a few minutes.

He slipped his arm under her, pulling her close. He liked her soft body pressed against his. He didn't mind her saggy skin or her wrinkles one bit. Heck, she wasn't half as wrinkly as he was.

He remained silent.

"Victor, I don't know if you're the most stubborn man I've ever known, but you come close."

"I don't want to talk about it," he grumbled.

"Of course you don't. You'd rather drag around the house even more contrary than usual and not talk about it because God forbid we should talk about a problem. What if we solved the problem, then what would we have to be contrary about?"

"Can't be fixed."

She pushed up on the bed, looking down over him. The sheet slipped down, baring her breasts, and the pale light from the backyard security lamp fell over her. To Victor, she was beautiful. Maybe more beautiful than the young wife he had left behind all those years ago. The words *soul mate* came to mind, but that was crazy. Vampires didn't have soul mates, did they?

"You either tell me what's got you in a stew or you can just get up, put on your droopy drawers, and take yourself home and stay there until you can act like a man."

He looked up at her. "You'd kick me out?"

"Damn right. I'm too old to put up with your nonsense, Victor. Remember, I've got twelve hundred years on you, give or take."

He didn't want to smile, but he couldn't help himself.

"It's the Council. They made a decision on our request, didn't they?"

He turned his head, not because he couldn't look at her, but because he didn't want her to see the moisture that had suddenly gathered in the corners of his eyes. It was embarrassing. "I got the letter in the mail today. All official," he said sarcastically. "Peigi didn't even have the decency to call me and tell me."

"I thought you said you disconnected your phone again."

"Damned telemarketers."

"If you disconnected your phone and you avoided Peigi and every other member of—"

"I didn't avoid them."

"If you avoided every member of the Council for the last week," Mary finished forcefully for an old, naked broad, "then you can't expect to have gotten the news any other way. Besides, you told me Peigi told you you'd get a letter stating the Council's decision."

He frowned, still avoiding eye contact with her. "It's not right. A man ought to be able to marry the woman he, you know . . . loves." The word stuck in his throat. It was hard for him to say, but he knew he loved her and he knew if he was going to keep her, he was going to have to be willing to say it sometimes.

"A lot of things in this world aren't right," Mary said softly. She laid her hand on his cheek and turned his head until he was looking up at her. "But who cares about getting married? They can't stop us from loving each other, can they?"

"I wanted to marry you," he said quietly.

"And I wanted to marry you." She kissed him. "But some things aren't possible."

He wrapped both arms around her and pulled her down, tight against him. He kissed her temple, thinking, *you'd be surprised what's possible if a stubborn old goat puts his mind to it.*

With some concentration, Fin was able to transport himself through the locked back door of the Rose Cottage. Noiselessly, he moved through the dark house and into Elena's bedroom. Lying on her side, on top of the sheets, in a silky white nightgown, she cradled her head with her hands as she slept. With her inky hair spilling over the pillow, she looked like an angel, but an angel, he suspected, she was not.

Fin just stood there for a moment, looking down on her. How did a person start this conversation? *Excuse me, ma'am, but are you a vampire?* Unless she was, that was going to be a pretty awkward conversation. But there was no other explanation; he had convinced himself of that on the walk over. Gad had not bitten Fin and he had not been with another woman except for Elena in months. He didn't know how he'd missed the mark on his neck shaving; too busy thinking about what a mess his life was, he supposed. At any rate, impossible as it seemed, Elena was a vampire and Fin hadn't known it.

She seemed to sense Fin's presence and slowly woke, stretching her long arms and legs as she rolled onto her back. Her eyelids fluttered and she lifted her lashes, her dark eyes illuminated by the moonlight pouring through her window.

"Fin?" she whispered. She sat up suddenly. "Are you all right?"

It wasn't until then that he realized he had to be a sight. His clothes were torn and bloodstained and his nose had to be swollen, the way it was throbbing. The cut over his eye had stopped bleeding, but it was crusty and he could smell dog on his clothes.

"Who are you, Elena? More importantly, *what* are you?" he asked.

"How did you get inside? I locked the doors before going to bed."

He loomed over her bed, angry, though not sure why. Because she should have told him. But maybe *she* didn't know *he* was a vampire. Some were easy to spot, but others, not so easy. Elena had done a good job blending in with humans, he would give her that. So good that he had not seen through her ruse.

"Answer my question."

"You're upset with me." She patted the bed beside her. "Sit down. Let me see that cut. Have you been fighting bad guys again?"

"What are you, Elena?"

She looked up at him with those big dark eyes of hers. Looked at him so innocently that he considered taking it all back. Maybe the mark on his neck wasn't a bite. Maybe . . .

He turned on the light beside her bed and then leaned over, baring his neck to show her the punctures. Still, she was silent. She was going to make him say it.

"You're a vampire, aren't you?"

She was quiet for another second, then met his gaze again. "Yes."

He shrank back. She had taken him completely by surprise. Again. He had expected her to laugh, or maybe feign horror at such a suggestion. Perhaps even say he was crazy. But a simple confession? It was the last thing on earth he had anticipated.

"Why didn't you tell me?" He loomed over her.

She leaned back on her pillow. "Why didn't *you* tell *me?*"

Relief began to flood him. Then almost happiness. For once, he had fallen for a woman who was not off-limits. Elena was like him. Probably different in many ways; vampires around the world were different. But they were alike, too. More alike than different.

"How could I tell you? You had me completely fooled. I thought you were human." Fin sat down on the edge of the bed.

"Fair enough." She sat up taller, tucking her feet under her. She pushed the hair off his forehead so she could get a better look at the cut above his eye. "Tell me what happened. Who did this to you?"

"Oh, no. You're not changing the subject that fast." He grabbed her hand and held it. "Elena, you have to answer me. How did you know?"

She exhaled as if it was a silly question. "The Kahills are known all over the world, of course. Avengers of God." A half-smile. "The only vampires I know with hope," she whispered.

He didn't know what to say. Suddenly, she looked so sad. So vulnerable. "I do know you, then, don't I?" he said. "I've had this feeling since that first night we met on the boardwalk."

"Lie with me," she whispered, pulling him down.

All at once, Fin was tired. Not just from the day or the fight, but from so much pretending. He kicked off his shoes and crawled into bed beside her.

Elena turned out the light.

"How? Where?" he asked, lying back on the pillow and drawing her into his arms. "I can't believe I would forget your face."

"We didn't exactly meet." Her voice was so soft that he had to pay close attention to hear her.

"Tell me."

She was quiet for so long that he thought she would not tell him, but then she began to speak. "It was in a little palazzo in Florence." Her voice trembled. "The year of our Lord, 1421."

She didn't have to say another word. In an instant, he was transported back to Italy, back to one of the most horrendous days of his life. He heard the screams, smelled the blood, felt it slick under his boots. "The massacre."

She clutched his hand in hers. "My father was an evil man. He not only did what the Franceschi family accused him of, but he committed far greater crimes against man and God," she told him, her breath warm in his ear. "We were there with our families that day. My brothers and sisters, their spouses and children. We were going to Mass, so most of the men were unarmed. My father was feeling rather good about himself; he had an appointment that evening with a member of the Medici family."

"I remember the palazzo," Fin said, trying to remember the details of the day, of the place while blocking out the carnage that still haunted him after all these years. He hadn't intended to get into the middle of a family feud, he'd just been in the wrong place at the wrong time. "The church is still there. La Cruz."

"They came out of nowhere, the men on horseback. We were attacked from all sides. My father's men were slain within moments and then my family began to fall, one by one. My husband and two children did not survive. I lived only because my husband's fallen body protected mine."

"I'm so sorry, Elena." He kissed the top of her head. "I was unarmed, traveling as a young student. It all happened so fast." He closed his eyes, a lump rising in his throat. "I always felt guilty that I had done nothing."

"There was nothing you could have done. There were too many of them; it was over too fast." Her voice trembled. "It was better for my family this way, anyway. The quick death." She took a breath. "We fled, those of us who still lived; my father, two brothers, and one of their wives. Only Celeste and her husband and her children were unharmed because she had remained at home in confinement after a stillbirth."

Fin said nothing, almost holding his breath. He knew what would come next. It was a familiar, sad tale among vampires all over the world. *The explanation.*

"We returned home to my father's villa. They came when we slept."

He was surprised by this turn in her story. Most vampires in the world, like the Kahills, had been turned into vampires by God as punishment for their sins.

"The Franceschis sent mercenary vampires—"

"Had to be those damned Ukrainians," he guessed aloud.

"Ukrainians, to our villa in the dark of the night. They held us down"—she sobbed softly—"and made us what we are today. Unlike the Kahills, we have no life cycles; we look as we did that night." She took a breath. "And we have no hope."

"I'm so sorry, Elena," he whispered, his throat raw with emotion.

"So am I."

For a long time he held her in the inky darkness. His eyes drifted shut. He was beyond tired; he was weary. When he woke later, it was to her touch. He felt Elena's lips against his, her bare hip pressed to his. He was still fully dressed. When he reached out to take her in his arms, he found that she was naked.

Some people might think sex between vampires was rough, vicious even. Sometimes it was. But tonight, Fin's touch was nothing but gentle. His kisses, even his playful bites were tender. He shrugged out of his clothes, wanting . . . needing to feel her naked skin against his. He kissed her cheeks, her forehead, her hair. He caressed her breasts, kissing them lightly, then took a nipple in his mouth. Her soft moans filled his head and his heart. All he wanted to do was take her away from that bloody morning in Florence, even if only for a few minutes.

Fin moved unhurried, savoring the feel of skin against skin, bathing in the scent of her, in her touch. Tonight, he didn't have sex with Elena; he made love to her.

He stretched out on his side, his legs entwined with hers, and gazed into her eyes. He took his time, caressing the gentle swell of her abdomen, the curve of her hips, the long muscular length of her thighs. He kissed her navel, then the downy patch of dark hair below.

Elena moaned, running her fingers through his hair. He rested his cheek on her inner thigh and drew his fingertips over her mons veneris.

"Fin, please," Elena murmured, tugging on his shoulders. "I need you. I need you to make me feel alive."

He kissed his way back to her mouth and then gazed into her eyes again. "Elena—"

"Shh," she hushed, pressing her finger to his lips. "No talking." She parted her legs beneath him and lifted her hips. "Just this."

He dropped his head to her shoulder and pushed inside her. She gasped and sank her nails into his shoulders. At once they began to move together, first separately, then as one, and all too soon, it came to an end. Fin did not take her blood. There would be time for that later. They both found release and then he eased back onto the bed and drew Elena into his arms. He pulled the sheet over them both and held her tight as her tears fell. Fin wasn't the kind of man who cried, but that night, in his heart, he knew Elena cried for both of them.

Chapter 20

Elena adjusted her sunglasses, glancing at her niece and nephew lying on beach towels a few feet away. Celeste had just excused herself to walk up to the house to use the ladies' room and Alessa had gone with her mother. Very early this morning, Elena had heard Beppe enter the house. She had not gotten up because Fin still slept beside her, and she did not want him encountering her nephew in the hallway on the way out, as he had Lia. But in the last week Elena had come to the conclusion that she could no longer ignore her nephew's irresponsible behavior. Obviously, Lia had not been able to stop him from prowling the streets at night. It was time Elena stepped in. She sighed resolutely. And if she was going to speak with the two older children alone, she would have to make it quick.

She rose from her beach chair, taking her filmy white cover-up with her. "Beppe and Lia, let us take a stroll along the beach."

"I don't want to go for a stroll," Beppe whined. "It's hot out here. I'm going to the house."

Part of her family's curse, which Celeste often saw as a blessing, was that not only had the children never matured physically, but not emotionally either. Despite their age, more than six hundred years old, they still behaved like adolescents. "It was not an invitation, it was an order," Elena said from between clenched teeth.

Lia hopped up. Beppe followed suit.

Elena walked south along the edge of the beach, the outgoing tide lapping at her bare feet. She took long strides, forcing her niece and nephew to nearly jog to keep up. She was so angry with Beppe, she'd barely been able to keep quiet this morning, waiting for the opportunity to speak with him. "Nephew, where were you last night?" she demanded.

When he didn't answer at once, she looked at him. "No need to lie. I know you did not return until dawn. I heard you when you came in through the back door."

Lia looked at Beppe. They obviously had a secret.

"Young lady? What do you know about this? I thought you were going to speak to him?"

Lia remained silent. She was a good girl, but she had always adored her brother, always looked up to him. This would not have been the first time she had covered for him.

"You swore to me that you would tell me if he was up to no good," Elena reminded her.

"He . . . hasn't been. He's just been hanging out with humans, is all. The only reason I didn't tell you," she went on quicker than before, "was because I knew you would disapprove, even though it was nothing."

Elena studied Lia's face for a moment, then Beppe's. They continued to walk, avoiding a human mother and her red-haired infant playing at the water's edge. Red-haired baby girls always made Elena sad. Her little

Maria had had the most beautiful dark red hair. "Humans!" She shook her head. "I should go to your mother right this moment," she said.

"No!" Lia exclaimed, grasping Elena's arm.

Elena halted. The sun was bright and hot and the warm sand beneath her bare feet felt heavenly. She hated the idea that she would soon have to leave this little paradise, leave Fin. But she knew she would. Perhaps sooner would be better, before Beppe got into trouble and put them all at risk.

Lia grabbed Elena's hand. "He hasn't done anything wrong. I swear it. He's just talking to other teens. Kids like us."

"They are *not* like you," Elena said firmly. "Have you been talking with the Kahill teens, as well?"

"We haven't told them our dirty secret, if that's what you're asking," Beppe lashed out.

"That will be enough disrespect," Elena snapped back.

Lia tugged on her aunt's hand, drawing her attention away from Beppe. "Please, *Zia*, don't make us go home yet," she begged. "We only have two more weeks."

Beppe stood slightly apart from them, digging a hole in the sand with his feet. Elena looked up to see Celeste in the distance, standing at their chairs, gazing out onto the water, apparently looking for them.

"You have to stop going out at night," Elena told Beppe, her voice soft but steely. "Or I will tell your mother and we will return to Italy at once. You know that will be the decision made."

"Then she has to stop, too," he protested, pointing an accusing finger at his sister.

Elena looked at Lia with surprise.

"You heard her coming in this morning, not me."

"I followed him is all," she assured her aunt, tears gathering in the corners of her eyes. "I swear it. I was just keeping an eye on him like I promised."

"Yeah, right," Beppe muttered, crossing his arms over his pale chest.

"There you are," Celeste called, waving to them from down the beach.

"I cannot believe the two of you cannot be trusted for a few weeks," Elena admonished. Her sister was approaching. She had to make it quick.

"Promise me, Beppe. No more human blood, or you will regret it."

Beppe was silent.

"Promise me," Elena pushed.

"I promise," Beppe hissed under his breath.

"What's going on?" Reaching them, Celeste tilted her big straw hat to look at Elena. She chuckled, glancing from one to the next. "Everyone looks so serious."

"I was trying to get the scoop on *Zia* Elena's new boyfriend, Mama, but she won't say a word," Lia smiled up sweetly at her mother. "She has a date with him tonight. A real date."

"I'm going to the house. It's hot out here." Beppe eyed Elena with distaste, but his mother missed it.

Elena glanced away.

"Me, too," Lia said cheerfully. "When I come back down, I'll bring cold drinks for everyone." She took off after her brother.

"What was that all about?" Celeste asked when the children walked away.

Elena followed them with her gaze for a moment, then looked back at her sister, reaching to take her hand. They started north again, along the shoreline, toward their beach chairs. "Nothing to worry about. The water looks inviting. Shall we take a dip in the ocean?" she asked, sounding more cheerful than she felt.

Celeste smiled from beneath the rim of her straw hat. "Yes, let's."

Elena glanced once more in the direction of the children. Only two more weeks, she thought. Two more weeks with Fin. Surely they couldn't get into serious trouble in two weeks.

That evening, Fin sat back in his chair as Eva set a pub glass of Tavia's best honey stout in front of him. From across the table, Elena watched suspiciously as the barmaid set down a second glass.

"Trust me," he assured her.

"I do. I am just not sure I trust your taste in libations," she teased.

Sexy, red-haired Eva eyed Elena appreciatively, then turned back to Fin and lifted an eyebrow. *Hot,* she telepathed.

She's mine, he returned. *Find your own girl.*

Trying my best, Eva quipped. *What's she doing here? You know Tavia frowns on bringing humans into the pub.*

She won't protest this one. At least not too strongly. The proprietor, Tavia, had some sort of reverse territorial protectiveness. She didn't care all that much about the Hill per se, but she was fiercely protective of those inside it.

Eva lifted the other eyebrow. *Do tell.*

Long story. Another day.

Eva took one more long admiring look at Elena, making no attempt to conceal her lust, and then sashayed away, her tray tucked under her arm.

"Sorry," Fin said, lifting his glass. "Our resident lesbian vampire. No offense intended."

Elena raised her glass. "None taken." She touched her glass to his.

No words were necessary between them as they toasted. In the last week, Fin had grown closer to Elena than he could remember having been to a woman in centuries. He'd learned a lot about Elena and her family, but he couldn't get enough of her or her story. It was so different from his own, but in many ways, so tragically similar. He only wished his life wasn't so divided right now; he desperately wanted to spend more time with her. He didn't have more time. He still had victims' family members calling him at the station every day, demanding answers, and he still had none. It had been more than two weeks since Richie's death and with each passing day, Fin became more anxious. He couldn't help himself; he was just waiting for the next human to drop.

"So what do you think?" Fin watched Elena take another sip of the home-brewed stout. "Tavia's considered one of the finest brewers in the east. We keep telling her she ought to start bottling her stuff. She's got it all over the local brewery, Dogfish Head."

"I cannot say it is as good as the wine my father produces from our vineyards." She smiled a smile that was both sexy and warm. "But it is interesting."

"I could order wine for you, if you prefer," he said quickly. He'd have ordered a bottle of Dom Perignon right now, if that was what she wanted. Flown in from France. He was just so happy to have a female companion again. One he was allowed to be with.

"No, this is good. I like to drink whatever is native to the places we visit."

Fin was fascinated by the way her family lived and protected their secret. They were isolated most of the time in their villa in a remote area of northern Italy, but once a year, the family left the confines of their self-imposed prison and went out into the world on summer holiday. They'd been doing so since the mid-seventeenth century.

"So this is the infamous *Hill*." She glanced around.

"This is it." Fin gazed around the familiar room of the pub and sighed. It evoked so many memories, so many feelings, good and bad.

Frank Sinatra played from an old jukebox in the far corner of the public room. It had to be his uncle Sean, seated at the bar, who had dropped coins into it. Or maybe Sean's brother, Mungo. Fin had spoken to both of them when he entered the pub with Elena. Sean had greeted Fin as if they had not seen each other in weeks, as if one of them had, perhaps, been out of town, not because Sean had been parked on the bar stool for the last month. Fin wanted to ask him when he intended to return to work as the police chief, or if he had resigned and his officers were just not aware of that development. But Fin held his tongue; this was neither the time nor the place and it was not his responsibility. Sean was the General Council's problem, and he would leave him to them.

"It's been here quite a long time, hasn't it?" Elena asked.

"A long time," he echoed. "It's the second oldest continuously operated bar in the United States, right after the White Horse up in Newport. If it hadn't been for the hurricanes in the eighteenth century, it would be the oldest." He leaned toward her, across the small table, enjoying giving her the little history lesson. "The place was originally built down near the water, on top of a sand dune. Tavia and her father finally surrendered to the elements and rebuilt inland, here, on higher ground. Clare Point sprung up helter-skelter around the pub and year-round, this place is the heart of our sept."

"You mean your family?"

He nodded. "Tribe, clan, sept, different words used in different parts of the world at different times. We were a sept in Ireland when the *mallachd*, the curse, was placed on us. So we still see ourselves as a sept, even in these modern times." He glanced around the dark room, nostalgically. "No one fights, no one makes up, no one buys a new or used truck without word going around inside the Hill."

Elena studied her surroundings, taking it all in. He watched her, liking the idea of sharing this part of himself with her.

The walls of the pub were dark wood wainscoting, stained by years of spilled ale and pipe smoke. The floor was planked hardwood, once washed regularly with sand and seawater, now with something more acceptable to the state health inspectors. There were heavy wooden booths along two walls, and a few scattered tables and chairs in the middle. The bar that ran the length of one wall was built of wood from the ship that had carried the Kahills to Clare Point. Stained by salt water, years of abuse, and more than a few worm holes, the bar was as much a part of the sept as its individual patrons. The long, etched and gilded mirror reflected the faces of those Fin had known for centuries. He caught sight of Uncle Sean's reflection and returned his attention to his half glass of ale.

"Locals only," Elena said, crossing her long legs.

Tonight she was wearing shorts and sandals. He

could see her red bikini top poking out at the back of her neck and she looked so good he could have eaten her. Or at least taken a bite out of her.

"Am I welcome here?" she asked. "Have you told anyone?"

The truth was that if they were to take a vote, the Kahills would probably have preferred that Elena not be there, even if she was a vampire. Even if she was one of the living dead, she was still an outsider. But no one would dare ask Fin to ask her to leave, and for tonight, that was enough for him. He couldn't think beyond tonight. He didn't dare think about the future or what meeting Elena could mean. They hadn't broached that subject. Right now, both of them were happy just to live in the moment.

"Just Regan," he said, uncomfortably. If she asked why he hadn't told anyone else she was a vampire, he wouldn't know how to answer because he didn't know why. Maybe it was just because he wanted something or someone to himself for once. Living so communally for so long made him wish sometimes he could have something of his very own. Even if just for a little while. He also hadn't said anything because he didn't want anyone jumping to irrational conclusions; Elena and her sister were outsiders. Vampire outsiders. Someone who didn't know them might think one of them could be the killer.

"And?" she plied. "Was Regan surprised?"

"Nothing surprises him." Suddenly feeling his twin brother's presence, he glanced up just in time to see Regan walk through the door. "Speak of the devil."

Regan gave a wave but took his time, greeting other people as he made his way toward Fin and Elena's table. He said hello to Malachy, parked next to Sean on a bar stool, then Mungo stopped him to talk about the Orioles, who were on the road this week and losing, as usual. Fin knew from experience that that conversation could be lengthy.

"So what about your sister?" Elena asked, settling her dark-eyed gaze on Fin again.

He hesitated. Elena did not have the ability to read minds: not vampires', not humans', not even her own cursed family's. It was an interesting, unexplainable reality of vampires; different vampires in the world had different supernatural abilities. Some, like Elena's family, had almost none.

So Fin didn't have to tell her the truth. Of course, how long could that last in this town? With this crowd?

"You didn't tell her because you knew she wouldn't be pleased," Elena said before he could answer.

He frowned. "I thought you said you couldn't read my mind."

She chuckled. "A woman does not have to be psychic to read a man's face."

He had to smile. "You have to understand Fia. She's an FBI agent. She's . . . *overprotective*. You know, big sister and all."

Elena continued to watch him. "I understand. It is always foremost in my mind to protect Celeste and her family." She drew her fingertip around the rim of her pub glass. "What, exactly, do you think Fia will think she is protecting you from?"

He shrugged. "I don't know, Elena. Frankly, I don't care. Fia never wants advice on *her* personal life; you wouldn't believe the dickwad human she dated a while back, but she's always more than willing to offer it to me."

"What's Fia done now?" Regan walked toward their

table, grabbing a chair from another table. He spun it around and straddled it, leaning his arms on the back of the chair.

He wore shorts, a ratty surf company T-shirt, and a ball cap turned around backward. With his hair a little shaggy, and a tan, he was model-good-looking, despite the faint bruising on his face. Where Fin wore lines of worry around his mouth, Regan's face was always relaxed and smiling. Fin couldn't help but be a little jealous. Why did he always have to be the responsible twin? Why couldn't Fin be the one everyone worried about, took care of, once in a while?

Because he was who he was and Regan was who he was and would be until the end of time or whenever God smiled upon them at long last, whichever came first.

"Fia didn't do anything," Fin said. "Not at least that I'm aware of, but it's still early."

Regan twisted in his chair to call to Eva walking behind him. "A Coke when you get a chance, sweet britches?"

Eva gave him the finger as she walked by.

He turned back, grinning at Elena. "NA frowns on alcohol use as well as drugs," he explained. "It's getting to be a drag."

She smiled at him and then Fin. "I'm sorry to hear that you have had trouble. I am glad to see that you are healthy now."

"Trouble? Nah, nothing more than a hiccup. You tell her about that little trouble last week, bro?" Regan punched Fin playfully on the shoulder.

Fin frowned and rubbed his arm. If Regan stayed long, he was going to need another pint. "No."

At once, Regan turned in his chair to address Elena.

"Bunch of badass Vs from New Orleans passed through town. You know them? The Rousseaus?"

"I do not believe we are acquainted."

"Good thing. Wish I wasn't. We had a little run-in last year. Well, not last year, but anyway." Regan tugged on the brim of his ball cap, cocking the hat farther back on his head. "They were headed north on business and apparently thought they'd pay me a little *visit*. Let me tell you." He hooked his thumb in Fin's direction. "My best bro here saved me from a serious ass-whipping."

"I didn't tell her, Regan," Fin said slowly, with emphasis, "because I didn't feel the need to share."

"Sweet Jesus," she breathed, reaching across the table to take Fin's hand. "That is how you were injured that night?"

He looked at Regan. *Thanks,* he telepathed with all the sarcasm he could muster.

Welcome. Regan grinned. Then, *What, she can't hear us?*

Nope. Not in her family's bag of tricks.

What can they do? Regan asked.

Make guys who annoy their boyfriends impotent.

That what you are, now, huh? Her boyfriend?

"All right, you two." Elena drew her hand back. "I would think that would be rude in the presence of others."

"What?" Regan asked, playing innocent.

"You know perfectly well what." She stared him down for a minute and he broke into a grin.

"I like her," Regan told Fin, pointing at Elena.

Fin found himself touching the puncture marks on his neck. They were fresh from last night. "I like her, too."

Elena smiled, her fingertips finding her own neck.

Regan looked at her and then at his brother. "Jeez, you two. Could you get a room?"

"Actually, that's a little tricky," Fin said, unable to take his gaze off Elena.

"Well, I'm going over to Patrick's house to play Wii later, so the house is all yours. It's a Super Mario Bros. tournament, so I doubt I'll be home before dawn. That ought to give you two enough time to drain each other." He winked at Elena.

Fin tore his gaze from Elena's, annoyed with Regan. He was flirting with his girlfriend! Flirting with her while helping them make arrangements to get in the sack. "Patrick? Patrick who?" There were only three Patricks in the Kahill family; two were out of town, the other was pushing eighty.

"Patrick Callahan, my assistant manager."

"A human? The one who was working at the arcade when Richie was killed?"

"One and the same."

"He actually came back to work?"

"With some stipulations," Regan explained. "A raise, and an escort to and from his bicycle. I threw in a date with this cute girl who works at Hilly's."

"You got him a date?" Fin was surprised, yet really not surprised. Regan could be a pretty good guy when he wasn't intoxicated by drugs, alcohol, or love.

"She was too young for me. And human. Bad combo for a V in recovery." Regan slapped the table. "Hey, I know what I meant to ask you. Have you talked to Mary McCathal in the last couple of days?"

Fin thought for a minute and shook his head. "No."

"Seen her?"

He thought again. "I don't know. Maybe."

"I just keep getting her voice mail when I call. I

needed to talk to her about some maintenance on the air-conditioning. I left messages. Even went by her house, but she wasn't home."

"Victor's maybe?" Fin shrugged.

"Maybe." Regan glanced back toward the bar. "What's a man got to do to get a nonalcoholic beverage around here?" He got up. "So I'll see you around, Elena?"

She smiled. "I do hope so. And thank you. For being such a gentleman and allowing us some privacy in your home."

Fin could have sworn Regan blushed as he backed away from the table and retreated toward the bar.

Finishing the dregs of his ale, Fin watched his brother go. "I wouldn't blame you one bit if you got up and walked out of here with him." He pointed with the empty glass at his brother.

Elena rose from her chair, her long legs unfolding as gracefully as if to be executing a dance move. She held out her hand to him, "I would leave this place with no man but you, Fin."

He took her hand, thinking, *This has to be too good to be true.*

Chapter 21

Straddling Fin, her fingertips on the mattress, Elena arched her back. Her long, midnight hair fell away from her face. Such a beautiful face. Fin couldn't take his eyes off her, even as she thrust her hips, pushing him closer and closer to the precipice.

When Elena made love to him, the past seemed to slip away. All evidence of the years of her pain, her fears were gone. Sensual lips slightly parted, her eyes half closed, she seemed to be able to find a place with him where there was no pain. Just pleasure.

Fin slid his hands through the tangle of sheets and found her fingertips. Threading his fingers through hers, he raised his hands, taking hers with his. They pressed palms to palms and slowly she opened her eyes.

They were so deep, so dark and full of mystery.

A smile played on her lips as she lifted up and slid down on him again.

Fin groaned and closed his eyes, wanting to make this time they had together last as long as possible.

Elena gave him a moment and then flattened her body over his, still holding him deep inside her. She kissed his mouth, his razor-stubbled cheek, and drew her lips lower.

Fin stretched out his neck for her so that she could easily find the puncture wounds. She sensed how close he was and her mouth found its mark. He felt her tongue warm and wet on his flesh, but at this point, it was hard to separate the spreading heat in his groin from the heat on his neck. The anticipation was exquisite.

Fin wrapped his arms around her, moving faster beneath her, matching thrust to thrust. Then, just at the last possible instant, as his body arched, she sank her fangs into his neck.

It was excruciating pain and unfathomable ecstasy all rolled into one. Indescribable. Even among vampires.

Later, as they drifted off to sleep, satiated, naked limbs entwined, Fin wondered what it would be like to have Elena in his bed every night. Every night for all of eternity. Maybe eternal life wouldn't be so bad then.

Trey felt her lips on his, felt her tongue thrust into his mouth. She tasted like beer. He groaned and fumbled with the tie of her bikini top. God, she was so hot. He hoped he didn't come in his shorts before they ever got down to business. He was just so pumped . . . literally. He wanted her so bad. Wanted *this* so bad.

Not that this was his first time or anything; Rachel Carey, senior prom, had been his first. And his last. He'd completed his first year at Salisbury University and managed to probably be the only guy on campus not to score. But he was awkward with girls. He'd only made it with Rachel because she was more awkward than he was.

Then, just when he'd been ready to give up, ready to stop praying to God for a girlfriend and start praying for world peace again, Mandy had walked into his life. Actually, more like bumped into his life. Or maybe he was the one who had bumped into her. He wasn't really sure how it had happened, and right now he wasn't thinking clearly enough to figure it out. There just wasn't enough blood flowing to his brain.

Trey had been walking south along the beach, head down, lost in his own private miseries. She'd been walking north, toward him.

He'd practically run her over. He'd had a crappy day and had gone down to the beach to get away from his family. He'd fought with his dad over his plans to change his major from engineering to psychology. Then his mom had been angry at him for fighting with his dad. Dinner on the rental's minuscule deck had been painfully awkward; no one was speaking to him, his mother's chicken piccata had been burnt, and his little sister had talked for twenty minutes about the hermit crab she was buying tomorrow. With one day down and six to go, Trey wasn't entirely sure he could survive another family vacation at the beach.

Then Mandy had walked into his life . . . bumped. Whatever. She had laughed at their collision and started up a conversation with him. They had walked for a couple of blocks, talked. The next thing Trey knew, they were sitting in the sand, under the boardwalk, hidden in the shadows. She'd kissed him first. He would never have had the nerve. She was too beautiful. Too sophisticated.

Trey tugged at the tie of her bikini top again. He just

couldn't get the knot untied. Then he felt her hand on his. She untied it for him and her breasts spilled out of the tiny top. Trey pushed her into the sand, his mouth aching to see what it was like to taste a woman's breast. There had been no nipples with Rachel. She hadn't even taken her prom dress off.

The feel of her nipple in his mouth was the best thing he had ever experienced in his life. Hands down.

But the problem was, it was too good. He was so hard inside his swim suit that he felt like he was going to burst. If he didn't hurry, he was going to.

Trey had read things about taking your time with your lady, giving her time to warm up. Fortunately for him, Mandy seemed warm already. Before he got up the nerve to touch the waistband of her shorts, she was yanking his down.

At night, lying in bed alone in his dorm room, doin' the Han Solo, he had planned for this moment. Strategized. But all his strategy went out the window when she slid her hand into his shorts. Trey didn't know what heaven was like, but he hoped this was it.

Fin could still feel his blood pulsing in his neck when he woke. He could smell Elena's scent on his pillow, but she was gone. He opened his eyes, rolling onto his back. His bedroom was dark, but he could sense the impending dawn. He wished she had stayed. He would like to have woken with her in his arms.

Wondering what time it was, he grabbed his phone off the nightstand and opened it. Four twenty. He flipped it shut and closed his eyes. Sunday morning. He could sleep in, then go to the office and tackle the mountain of undecipherable, useless crime lab results sitting on his desk. Maybe he would even hit Mass on his way. Mary Kay would be down on her knees on the prayer bench thanking God if he showed up.

Fin opened his eyes and glanced toward the closed bedroom door. He hadn't heard anything, but he felt someone's presence. Hoping Elena might still be there, he got up, stepping into his boxers on his way to the door. By the time he opened it, he realized it was not Elena, but Regan. He could feel him in the tiny house.

Fin walked down the short hall and stuck his head around the doorway of the kitchen. He squinted in the bright fluorescent light. Regan had his head in the refrigerator.

"You just getting home?" Fin asked. He could still hear sleep in his voice. He wished now that he hadn't woken. His dream was way better than the bright light and Regan's morning breath.

"Hell of a tournament. I won."

"Great." Fin scratched his head, entering the kitchen. "You can put that on your résumé when you go back to the General Council and see what kind of job the sept will offer you."

Regan came out of the refrigerator with a pizza box, a carton of orange juice, and leftover tuna casserole Mary Kay had dropped off days ago.

Trying to avoid the casserole at all cost, Fin snatched the OJ from his brother's hand. "You didn't see Elena leaving, did you?"

"Here? No. But I saw her a couple of hours ago, kinda early actually. We were sitting on Pat's porch as she walked by. Acted like she didn't see us." Regan slid the pizza box over the sink and set the glass dish on the tiny section of battered countertop. "So no sleepovers, huh?"

"Nah." Fin grabbed two glasses. "Family issues."

"Ah, say no more." He pulled the foil off the dish, stuck a spoon into it, and stuffed a huge portion into his mouth. "Want some?" His words were garbled by egg noodles and unidentifiable sauce.

"Not if—" Fin stopped mid-sentence. His phone was ringing in his bedroom.

Regan stopped chewing.

For a second, Fin couldn't move. The call at this time of day could only mean one thing. The other shoe had dropped.

Sailing off the island of Capri. Hiking in the Peruvian mountains. Hang gliding in Brazil. Fin continued to compile his mental list of all the places he'd like to be right now. Scuba diving in Baja, sheep herding in the Grampian Mountains. Hell, digging a ditch for his parents' new septic system seemed appealing at this moment. Anything was better than this. Better than here.

Fin squatted beside the body and stared at the waxy face. This victim's eyes were still open. Pale blue. Disregarding more than one rule of crime scene etiquette, he used his gloved hand to close the boy's eyes. "Go in peace," Fin whispered and then crossed himself.

He already knew the boy's name. Trey Cline. Age eighteen. He was a nice-looking young man. Tall, maybe six-three or six-four. His parents had called the station at three-thirty a.m. to report him missing. After checking the usual party houses on First Street where most teens and young adults gravitated when they were up to no good, the two cops on duty had started a genuine search. An Irish greyhound, Sugar, had found him before the cops did. Sugar's owner, Jim, a local, had said the dog had taken off like a bat out of hell at the south end of the boardwalk. Jim hadn't seen the pooch again until he found her here between the beach and Gina's Greek Gyros, sitting under the shower with the dead kid.

Trey's parents and little sister were in the backseat of a police cruiser on their way to the station. Sugar had finally been coaxed away from the dead boy and she and Jim had continued on their walk with Jim promising to be available the rest of the day for additional questions. The police officers and EMTs were all coming and going. Photos were being snapped, paper bags were being filled with possible evidence, a gurney was being unloaded from an ambulance. It seemed as if everyone had somewhere to go, something to do . . . except Fin and Trey.

Fin stared at the dead boy for a long time, so long that eventually he got muscle cramps in his legs and had to stand up. But no matter how long he studied him, none of the facts changed. Trey was seated under the shower at the top of the stairs that led down to the beach. There were several identical showerheads placed strategically along the boardwalk; they were good for business. The showers kept sandy feet out of the shops and restaurants and kept tourists happy and sand-free, making them want to go into the shops and restaurants. Though sand-free, Trey hadn't gone shopping this morning. He hadn't made it to breakfast, either. He never would.

Not with his neck slit like that.

Fin didn't bother to take a closer look at the incision. The fang punctures were there. The MO was so identical to the last two that it was almost humorous.

Whoever the killer was, he or she was not all that creative. Like Colin Meding, Trey was posed, sitting up. He was shirtless, but wearing swim trunks. His feet were bare. No blood around him. Damn little inside him, from the color and texture of his skin.

Fin heard someone coming up the steps behind him and turned to see one of his officers.

"Found a pair of men's sandals and a T-shirt under the boardwalk, just over there." He pointed beyond the stairs. "Mother said the victim was wearing a gray Salisbury University T-shirt and new brown Rainbow sandals. Bought them yesterday at Hilly's."

Fin didn't have to ask if the sandals and shirt matched the mother's description. He crouched down again until he was eye to eye with Trey. Only Fin had his eyes open; Trey's were still closed.

"Get laid under the boardwalk, did you?" Fin asked gently. "Sweet." He nodded. "Then what?" He glanced at the victim's swimsuit. The killer had rinsed him off, which was why he wasn't sandy, but not all that well. Fin saw the telltale white stain of seawater. "Then a swim? Is that where she's doing it? She fucking you, then getting you to go into the water, skinny-dipping maybe?"

John, standing behind Fin, cleared his throat awkwardly. Maybe he didn't like the idea of his boss talking to dead humans. Not even his temporary boss.

Fin ignored him.

"Thought it was the best night of your life, didn't you, Trey? Right up until that last second when she bit you and drank your blood?" Fin thought for a moment, then stood, turning to John. He was thankful he was wearing dark glasses so his officer wouldn't see the moisture that had gathered in the corners of his eyes.

"I want everyone who is not specifically involved in getting this boy off the boardwalk on the beach. I want you looking for drag marks from the ocean to these steps." He indicated with his hand. "This kid died in the water and someone carried him or dragged him here."

"I don't know about that theory," Jim said slowly. "Beach cleaning machine came through around four-thirty this morning. I already called and checked."

"At four-thirty, Malachy was either still drunk or at the least hungover. We're always getting complaints that he's missed spots, left trash behind, or run over a garbage barrel. Check the beach, anyway. Start here and work your way north and south. It would make sense to bring him up these stairs, but that doesn't mean that's the way this played out."

John nodded and walked away, leaving Fin to gaze out over the beach to the water's edge. In his mind's eye, he knew what had happened here. He had had his suspicions. Now there was no doubt in his mind, not with the discovery of Trey's shoes and shirt. Fin didn't know why he hadn't seen it before, but he knew now why he had never found a crime scene in the previous murders. It was because they were no longer present. They had been carried out by the tide.

Chapter 22

After a quick lunch at the diner, Fin crossed the street and headed for the station. He walked with his head down, trying hard not to feel defeated. Fia had called this morning to say that she needed to talk to him and that she was coming to Clare Point tonight, or tomorrow morning at the latest. She had been cryptic and he had a bad feeling this was a professional visit, not personal. It had been only three days since Trey Cline's death, but that was just enough time for the FBI to make the decision to put their noses in where the sept would prefer they didn't. Hopefully, Fia had found a way to finagle into the case; she was, after all, considered an expert on serial killers. If Fia was running the case for the FBI, she would be able to protect the sept. Ultimately, what was best for the sept would be achieved; Fin just wished he would be the one to see it through.

There was no doubt in Fin's mind now; the killer was a vampire woman. According to the evidence and what Fin had been able to piece together, Trey had had sex with a woman just before he was bitten; then, like the others, his throat was slit. Following his hunch, Fin had had his officers comb the beach and sure enough, despite the fact that the beach cleaner had been through, they'd found a short length of drag marks. Trey was killed in the ocean, and carried most of the way to the boardwalk, but at some point, she had put him down and dragged him. Maybe because he was taller than the others and more difficult to carry. Even with phenomenal strength, a taller man would have been harder to carry in the soft sand. The killer must have picked him up again and carried him up the steps and posed him under the shower.

"Uncle Fin?"

It took him a second to realize someone had spoken his name. He looked up.

"You better watch where you're going or you're going to get hit by a car or something." It was Kaleigh. She must have walked right past him.

"Lost in my thoughts, I guess." Getting a good look at her, he smirked. "Nice hat."

She snatched the white paper hat off her head. "I have *got* to get a better job."

"Speaking of good jobs, things have been quieter on First Street this past week. I want you to know it hasn't gone unnoticed."

"First Street?"

She was cute. Especially when she was trying to lie; she had never done a good job of it. "The partying. Our teens have been lying low. Keeping a little more to themselves, staying clear of the humans."

"Why are you thanking me?"

"I'm a cop, Kaleigh. Acting chief of police, apparently. It's my business to know what's going on in Clare Point."

"Who told you?"

"No one told me. Power of deduction." He tapped his temple. Then he grew more serious. "Hey, I'm glad I ran into you. I need to ask you something. I hate to, but I'm trying to cover all the angles."

"So ask."

"This is probably going to sound crazy." He scratched his head. "But do you think anyone attending those parties, one of our girls, could . . . would, kill?"

"One of the teens?" She looked shocked. "Sweet baby Jesus, no."

"I think these boys are being seduced, Kaleigh."

"Seduced?"

"The killer had sex with the young men," he said frankly. "Then she killed them."

"Wow," she murmured. "Wow." She thought for a moment. "But whoever did it had to carry Richie all the way to the arcade without leaving any evidence. The first one was left in the alley. She'd have to be incredibly strong. It couldn't be a teenager. Our strength doesn't come until the end of the maturation cycle."

"I know. I just wanted to make sure I wasn't being naïve." He thought for a minute. "And you don't think anyone could have developed their strength and you just didn't know it?" He gestured. "I mean, powers come and go, at first. We didn't know last year that you were having visions."

"Anything's possible, I guess," she said slowly. Suddenly, she looked off into space.

He tried to listen to what she was thinking, but her mind was well guarded. He got nothing. "Kaleigh?"

"Yeah?"

"Something you're not telling me?"

"No." She fiddled with her hat. "No, I just remembered something I forgot to do. My mom's gonna kill me." She looked up at him. "What about the other Vs, the family from Italy? Couldn't one of them have done it? Didn't they arrive around the same time that first guy was killed?"

Old Mrs. Cahall, the clerk at the Lighthouse Hotel, went by in her VW bug and tooted her horn. Fin and Kaleigh both smiled and waved.

Fin looked back at Kaleigh. "Regan has a big mouth. The family preferred no one know."

"He was happy for you, that's the only reason he said anything. You know, happy that you'd found someone."

"Elena did not do this."

"I didn't say she did. But you know people are going to have questions. About her, and about her sister. I mean, you have to admit, they fit the profile and it would be a lot easier to think an outsider is killing, instead of one of us."

"Except that they don't fit the profile. They're not like us. They have no *gifts*."

"So she says. I don't know how you prove something like that, but . . ." She opened her hands. "Look, I'm not trying to be a jerk about this, Uncle Fin. It's just that people in this town are starting to get scared. Can't you feel it? They're afraid that if humans find out about us, we'll be without a country again, without a home."

"Humans are *not* going to find out about us. We're going to take care of this ourselves."

"I hope you're right, because Katy thinks we ought

to flee to Bolivia." She looked away again, then pulled her cell phone out of her bag and checked the screen. "Shoot. I gotta go or I'll be late." She headed in the opposite direction he was going. "Catch you later."

Fin turned to continue on his way, then, remembering something, he turned back. "Hey, Kaleigh."

"Yeah?" She turned and walked backward, still moving away.

"On a completely different subject, have you seen Victor in the last couple of days?"

"We haven't been anywhere near his house," she defended, lifting her hands, palms out. "Or his stupid boat. I swear it. Why, what's he say we did now?"

"He hasn't said anything. I was just wondering if you'd seen him."

She shook her head.

"How about Mary McCathal?"

"Nope."

"Neither has anyone else," he mused.

"Maybe they're holed up in his house, or hers. Love shack, baby, love shack," she sang, doing a little shimmy.

Fin grimaced.

She stopped dancing. "I know." She chuckled. "Gross to even think about. Gotta go."

Kaleigh hurried down the next block, tucking her hat under her arm. What Fin had said about the killer possibly being one of the teens had her scared.

What if it *was* Katy?

Katy was sexually active. She liked human males. She also was hell-bent on the idea of the sept moving to another place in the world. And what about that day she had opened the jar of cherries? The night she had moved the cooler? Had her strength improved and Kaleigh didn't know it?

Kaleigh wasn't sure what to do. Did she just confront her best friend and ask her if she was a serial killer? Ask her if she was the one risking the safety of every member of the sept? Of course, if it was Katy, she wouldn't be dumb enough to admit it, would she?

Maybe the thing to do was just keep an eye on her. A close eye. See if she was acting strangely, doing anything strange. At least if Kaleigh kept her close, she couldn't kill again, right?

Kaleigh pulled her cell out of her bag and hit the speed dial.

"Hey," Katy answered. "I thought you were at work."

Kaleigh looked both ways and crossed the street. There was a long line at the DQ and only one window was open. "Just walking in. Hey, you want to come over and spend the night?"

"Um, sure. I guess so."

Kaleigh hurried around the side of the building. "Okay, see you tonight, right after I get off work."

"You okay?" Katy asked, sounding concerned.

"Sure. Can't a person invite her best friend over to spend the night?"

"Yeah," Katy said. "But she can't act weird."

"I'm not acting weird." She hurried through the back door. "Gotta go." She dropped her phone into her bag and put her stupid paper hat on her head. "Sorry I'm late, guys."

"That wisewoman gig taking up too much of your time?" Tom, one of the assistant managers, asked.

Kaleigh tossed her bag under a counter and hurried

toward the front to open another service window. "Yeah, something like that."

That night, Fin met Elena on his front stoop.

"Were you waiting for me?" she said, coming up the steps.

"I missed you today." He kissed her hard on the mouth.

She gazed into his eyes as she kissed him back. "What's happened? What's wrong?"

"Regan's still at my parents' house." He took her hand and pulled her inside, locking the door behind her. He pushed her up against the door and crushed her mouth with his.

"Mio tesoro," she murmured, stroking his cheek and then wrapping her arms around his neck.

Fin thrust his tongue into her mouth, caressing a breast through the fabric of her dress. She wore no bra and he felt her nipple harden under his fingertips.

"You *are* eager," she breathed, kissing him again

He pushed down the shoulder of her wrap dress, freeing her bare breast, and leaned down. Elena pressed the palms of her hands against the door and tilted her head back, closing her eyes. Fin caught her nipple between his teeth and tugged gently, then sucked.

Elena whispered words of encouragement in her native language. It wouldn't have mattered whether Fin knew Italian or not, he knew what she wanted. Still teasing her breast with the tip of his tongue, he drew his hand up her thigh. She moaned.

Fin kissed his way to the pulse of her neck, moving his hand upward. He cupped her soft mound, then slid his fingers beneath the elastic of her lacy thong.

She bared her neck, encouraging him.

Fin caressed the soft, damp folds with one hand. With the other, he stroked her neck, feeling the puncture wounds he had left on her two nights before. It was less painful to have blood taken from an old wound, but not as pleasurable for the one drinking. He licked the punctures and she parted her legs farther, grinding against his hand.

Bloodletting was not usually part of foreplay; most vampires liked to save it for the *main event*. Fin didn't know what had gotten into him tonight. He was angry. He was sad. He was frustrated. He needed release. He needed to taste her blood.

"Yes?" he whispered huskily, stroking her faster, pressing kisses to her neck. Nibbling. It was always polite to ask, even if you were certain that a woman was offering her blood.

She elongated her neck even farther. "Yes," she moaned.

Fin looked into her face. Her eyes were closed, her lips parted as she breathed heavily. A thin sheen of perspiration shimmered above her upper lip. He was overcome by his fierce, throbbing need for her. He thrust his fingers into her, and at the same time, sank his teeth into her flesh.

Elena jerked in his arms, crying out with pleasure and pain, writhing against him.

Her hot blood gushed into his mouth.

She whimpered, trembling all over.

Fin supported her against the door as her knees buckled. He took one last sip and then swept her up into his arms. He carried her, half conscious, down the hall to his bedroom and laid her gently on his bed. Throwing his clothes off hurriedly, he slipped off her sandals, tossed them on the floor, and lay down beside her. He pushed up the hem of her dress and caressed her thighs.

Elena nuzzled his neck and he kissed her. She thrust her tongue into his mouth, tasting her own blood. Fin slipped her panties off and tossed them to the floor. He stroked her until she came again and only then did he climb on top of her. He thrust again and again and she lifted her hips to meet him. It went too quickly then, though he would have liked to have prolonged her pleasure. They cried out in ecstasy as one and at last he was satiated. He rolled off her and held her against him, kissing her damp temple.

For a long time they lay in the dark in his single bed. Slowly their breath came more evenly. His heart began to beat in a normal rhythm and he felt his body temperature drift downward. He kissed her on the cheek. "I'm sorry if I—"

She pressed her fingertips to his lips. "It's all right," she whispered. "I understand. We all lose control sometimes. It's good for us."

"I didn't hurt you, did I?"

"Certainly not." She lifted her head to look down on him and her hair fell across his cheek. She searched his gaze, in the darkness. "Now tell me what's wrong."

"Victor?" Mary called from the bed. She was already in her nightgown, under the sheets with the light out. They'd found a nice hotel off the interstate that offered a senior discount *and* a buffet breakfast. "Are you coming?"

The bathroom door opened and light spilled into the room. "I'm coming. Hold your horses."

She heard the water run in the sink, then turn off. He shuffled out of the bathroom in a pair of boxers, shutting off the light behind him. "Wouldn't go in there just yet, if I was you."

She chuckled and lifted the sheet for him. "I lived with a man for fifteen hundred years. I know better."

He slid into bed beside her. "Not sure how far we'll go tomorrow. I was thinking we might stop at one of them peach farms, get some fresh Georgia peaches." He looked at her in the dark. "Want some peaches, Peaches?"

Her eyes glistened. "Are you sure we're not making a mistake?"

"You think you're makin' a mistake, comin' with me?" he asked stiffly. He stared up at the ceiling.

"That's not what I meant and you know it." She rolled onto her side and rested her head on his shoulder.

He slid his arm around her.

"I mean, just running away from our problems like this. Like two kids. People will be worried about us."

"People will be worried about themselves," he grunted. "Afraid we might do something crazy and put them at risk."

She ran her hand over his bony chest. "We did do something crazy."

He chuckled and she knew he was smiling.

"That we did," he agreed. "I still can't believe you came with me. Can't believe my luck."

She kissed his cheek. "You're my luck."

He squeezed her in a hug. "Don't worry your pretty head. We get settled, we'll go to one of those fancy Internet cafés and you can e-mail Regan about the arcade. E-mail that bunch of biddies in your book club and tell them yer pickin' the next book. Hell, if fishin' is good, I might buy you a laptop for Christmas and you can e-mail right from the boat."

She felt her cheeks grow warm with a mixture of embarrassment and pride. "I'm too old for a laptop, Victor."

"Never too old for nothin'." He kissed her temple. "Now shut your trap, woman. Can't you see I'm trying to get some sleep?"

"I love you, Victor Simpson, you cantankerous old fart."

"I love you," he whispered softly.

Chapter 23

Elena sat up and pushed her dress down over her thighs. She had no idea where her panties were; she didn't care. She was barely listening to what Fin said as his first words sank in.

The detail that has not been published in the papers or been on the TV news is that the killer is a vampire.

The moment he said it, she knew who it was and she was overcome with a horrible sense of guilt. How could she have been so stupid, so naïve?

"So I guess what I'm saying," Fin went on, "is that you need to be prepared for questions. Just tell them the truth, if anyone asks. You and your family are not suspects. You don't have the powers we do. It would have taken phenomenal strength to carry the bodies of those men into the arcade and the alley."

"I have to go," she said, getting out of bed.

"Elena, please, I don't think you had anything to do with this." He put his hand out to her and when she stepped out of his reach, he slid across the bed and sat up.

Elena found one sandal and, standing on one foot, she slid it on the other foot. She searched through his clothes on the floor, looking for the second sandal. Her hair kept falling in her eyes, but she didn't pull it out of the way. She didn't want him to see her face.

"Please don't be upset with me," he said. "I'm in a bad place, here."

"I'm not upset with you. Of course I understand." She found the silver sandal, at last, and stood on one foot to put it on. "This is a terrible responsibility placed on your shoulders."

"I wish you wouldn't go." He grabbed her wrist.

She stepped in front of him and he stood up. With him barefoot and her in heels, they were exactly the same height. She gazed into his eyes, thinking this might be the last time she ever saw him. "I told you I could only come for a short time," she said evenly.

"You're sure you're not angry with me?"

"I am not angry with you." She pressed her lips to his, closing her eyes, savoring the feel of his lips. Tears welled up in her eyes. "I could love you, Fin Kahill."

She walked out of his bedroom, down the hall, and out the front door. He did not follow, for which she was thankful.

Hurrying back to the cottage in the dark, Elena wished she had some of the psychic powers the Kahills were blessed with. She wished she could teleport her body to Rose Cottage this instant. She wished she could communicate with her sister and warn her to prepare herself. She wished she had powers that did not exist except in God. She wished she had the power to change what she knew would take place next.

The moment Elena walked into the bright, airy living room, her sister knew something was wrong. Celeste, curled up in a chair reading a book, glanced up. Beppe and Lia were playing a video game on the large flat-screen TV.

"Where is Vittore?" Elena asked.

"Taking a shower." Celeste set down her book, her brow creasing with concern. "Elena, what's wrong?"

"Get Vittore. Now." She walked to the front windows of the living room that looked out on the beach and began to close the blinds. "Shut that off, Lia. Shut it off, now."

Celeste hurried into the back. "Vittore!" she cried, her voice high pitched.

"What's wrong, *Zia?*" Lia turned the TV off.

"Wait for your parents." Elena continued to close the blinds. She sounded calm, but inside, she was shaking.

Celeste returned, leading Vittore. His hair was still dripping wet and he wore a terry bathrobe. Alessa hurried behind them.

"We're all here, now tell us what's wrong," Celeste said.

Elena closed the last blind. She was probably being paranoid; surely they had time. But her fear lessened her reason. "Sit down. All of you."

They stared at her, but did as she said. Celeste, Vittore, and Alessa sat on one of the leather couches, Lia and Beppe on the other, across from them.

"I have just come from Fin's," she said. There was no way to ease into a conversation like this. There was no time. Decisions had to be made at once.

Celeste took Vittore's hand. She knew it was bad.

"What we have read in the newspapers, what the locals are saying about the murders here in Clare Point," Elena said, looking from one family member to the next, "is not the entire story. What the general public does not know, what we did not know"—she met Celeste's gaze—"is that the killings that began the week we arrived were committed by a vampire." She shifted her gaze, looking directly at Beppe.

Everyone else turned to look at him.

Elena held her breath.

"What?" Beppe demanded, coming to his feet. He was wearing black jeans, a tight black T-shirt. His damp hair was slicked back. He looked young, handsome, and innocent.

Elena knew for a fact that he was not.

"You're accusing me?" Beppe shouted, thumping his chest with his fingertips. "You bitch."

Vittore flew off the couch. He was a small man, but he was quick. In an instant, he stood in front of his son. He raised his hand and slapped him across the face. "How dare you speak to your aunt that way."

Tears filled Beppe's eyes; his father had hit him hard. "How dare she accuse me of killing those insignificant humans."

"*She* does not have to accuse you. *I* accuse you," Vittore spat, furiously. "You swore to me, you swore, Beppe, after Rome, that it was an accident. That this would never happen again."

Celeste cried softly into her hands. Alessa slid over next to her mother, trying to comfort her.

Lia sat perfectly still on the couch, knees pressed together, watching the family drama unfold.

"You think I did it?" Beppe said through clenched teeth.

"I gave you a chance," Elena reminded him. "How could you be so stupid? How could you think you would get away with it? I knew you were sneaking out at night."

"You knew and you didn't stop him?" Celeste cried.

Beppe looked back at his father, who still stood directly in front of him. "I didn't do it," he said quietly.

"What?" Vittore boomed, reaching out to grab a handful of his son's T-shirt.

"Vittore, no!" Celeste rose off the couch. "Don't!"

Beppe looked into his father's eyes with a fury that matched the elder man's. "Are you sure I did it? Absolutely sure? Because what her lover left out, apparently, is that the killer usually has sex with the victim first. The killer is female." He turned slowly until his gaze was fixed on Lia.

Elena stared at her nephew. "You're lying."

"Call him and ask him," Beppe challenged.

The look on Beppe's face told Elena her nephew was not lying.

"Why don't you ask my dear little sister about the dead humans?" Beppe taunted. "The dead male humans who were first seduced and then sucked dry."

It had never occurred to Elena until that instant that the killer could possibly be anyone but Beppe, and now she felt guilty for having not gotten all the facts. Her attachment to Lia had clouded her reason. Stunned, Elena sank onto the couch beside her sister, still staring at her niece. What Beppe said was true; she could see the guilt on Lia's face.

Vittore stared at his eldest daughter. His voice cracked when he spoke. "Tell me it is not true. Tell me you did not kill those men."

Lia's face was impassive. She bit down on her lower lip. "Would you believe me if I told you it wasn't me?"

Her tone was shocking. It was not filled with fear or regret. It was angry. Resentful, and full of sarcasm. It was the voice of a woman guilty of murder.

For a moment, no one said anything. Vittore stood frozen in front of his son. As awful as it was, he could believe Beppe could have killed innocent humans. But Lia, his sweet daughter Lia . . .

"Is it true?" Vittore asked weakly.

"It's true, all right," Beppe sneered.

"You knew?" Celeste shouted at her son, tears streaming down her face. "And you didn't stop her?"

He slid his hands into his pockets, slouching. "She never admitted it to me, but I suspected. And I warned her. Do the deed. Pay the price, if you get caught. Right?" He shot a glare in Lia's direction.

"Why, Lia? Why?" Celeste sobbed, her hands together as if she were in prayer.

The pretty girl stared at her mother for a moment, then smiled sweetly. "I don't know. I didn't mean to do it the first time, but when I found out I could"—she shrugged—"I did it again. And I liked it. So I did it again. They made it so easy. I liked being in charge. I've never been in charge of anything before."

Vittore sat down on the far end of the couch where Lia sat and looked down at the floor. Only Beppe stood, smirking, as if he took some delight in the family tragedy.

"What are we going to do?" Vittore murmured, still in shock. He stared straight ahead, but his gaze was unfocused. "She has broken the rules. After the incident in Rome, after we were all nearly caught by the vampire slayers, we agreed it would not be permitted again."

"We can make an exception," Celeste said quickly. She wrapped one arm around Alessa, who was crying softly in her mother's lap. "We ... we can go home tonight. The Kahills don't know where we live. No one will ever know."

Elena stared sadly at Lia for a moment. "No," she said. "We cannot make an exception. Fin will figure out eventually that it was one of us. He will tell his Council."

"But you could ask him not to." Celeste reached for her sister's hand. "You ... you said he was fond of you. You could—"

"We cannot make enemies out of the Kahills, Celeste," Vittore said, his voice hollow with pain. "They are too powerful a family. Too large. We have others to think of, back in Italy. Others whose lives we are responsible for."

"What about our daughter's life? Are we not responsible for that?" Celeste sobbed.

"We have obviously failed in our responsibility to her." He met his wife's gaze. "But Beppe is right. She knew the consequences."

"Vittore," Celeste whispered. "My daughter . . ."

Vittore hung his head. "I am sorry, my love."

Elena squeezed her sister's hand. "As I see it, we can judge her now, here . . . and carry out the sentence—"

For the first time, Lia looked as if she cared. "Mother! You wouldn't let them . . . You wouldn't—" She tried to get up, reaching for her mother, but her father pushed her back onto the couch with his small, broad hand.

"Silence," he ordered his daughter. "You have broken your mother's heart. You have put all our lives at risk."

"What about Beppe? What about the man he killed in Rome?"

"It was an accident. It was not premeditated." Vittore stared at his daughter. "And it was not *three* men," he managed bitterly.

"You would kill me?" Lia screamed. She looked to Celeste, sliding to the edge of the couch. "Mother, you would let them cut off my head?"

Celeste bent over, sobbing into her hands.

With one arm around her sister, Elena looked up at Vittore through teary eyes. "The other option is to turn her over to the Kahills. They do things differently than we do. Perhaps their justice—"

Lia leaped to her feet. "No," she screamed, tears of fury running down her face. "No, you can't! You're my family! You can't—"

Suddenly, Lia bolted, headed for the door. Elena flew off the couch. Vittore sprang up. But Beppe was faster than them both. He caught his sister before she got through the door onto the porch.

Lia scratched at her brother's face, screeching like a wild animal. She was incredibly strong; what Elena had told Fin was that they had no psychic powers. He had misunderstood, thinking their family had *no* powers.

Fortunately, as a male, Beppe was stronger than his sister and he was able to drag her back into the house. Elena slammed the door behind them as Beppe forced Lia to the floor and held her down.

"You want me to lock her up in her bedroom?" Beppe asked, wiping at his mouth with the back of his hand. Lia had given him a bloody lip.

"Let me go," Lia whimpered, no longer fighting her brother. "You can't turn me over to them. They'll kill me. You can't do it. You're my family."

Elena pushed her hair out of her eyes. "Should I call Fin?" she asked Vittore.

He was standing near the couch, holding Celeste in his arms, supporting her weight.

"No," Celeste sobbed, burying her face in his robe.

Vittore met Elena's gaze, his eyes glistening with a profound sadness. "I cannot sentence my own daughter to death. I should be able to," he said, his voice breaking. "But I cannot. Call Fin Kahill. He will know what to do with her."

Kaleigh glanced at her cell phone on the nightstand and wondered who was calling her this late. It was after midnight. She'd talked to Rob an hour ago and said good night. Besides, it wasn't his ring tone, the theme song from Spiderman. And Katy was here with her. Kaleigh had tried to talk to her a little, tried to poke around in her head, but she hadn't gotten anything about the murders out of her. If Katy knew anything about them, she was doing a good job of keeping it hidden.

Katy rolled over on the bed. They had been watching TV, a movie from the rental store. "Who's that?"

"I don't know." Kaleigh picked up the phone. Startled by the caller ID, she sat up in bed and hit the green key. "Peigi?"

"Sorry to bother you," Peigi said crisply. "We have a *situation*. Gair has requested that you meet us at the museum."

"Now?" Kaleigh asked, incredulously.

"Now."

"What . . . what's going on, Peigi?"

"We need our wisewoman. We believe we have our killer."

"Sweet baby Jesus," Kaleigh whispered, crossing herself.

"What's going on?" Katy whispered, her eyes round with excitement.

"We'll expect you in fifteen minutes," Peigi continued. "We would prefer no one know."

"My parents?"

"We would prefer no one know," Peigi repeated.

"How am I supposed to get out of the house? It's after midnight."

"The same way you usually get out after curfew, I suppose," Peigi said curtly. "We'll be waiting for you." She hung up.

Kaleigh slowly lowered the cell phone to her lap.

"What's happening?" Katy demanded.

"I'm not sure," Kaleigh murmured. She could feel her heart pounding in her chest. All she could think was *thank God it wasn't Katy*. If they did, indeed, have the killer in custody. "Peigi says Gair has requested my presence at the museum."

"Now?"

"Now."

"Is it a High Council meeting?" Katy asked excitedly. "Have you been called to the High Council? Wow, that's so cool."

Kaleigh got out of bed and grabbed a pair of shorts off the floor. She dropped the boxers she slept in and pulled on the shorts. She grabbed a bra off her dresser. "I'm not supposed to say anything." She felt shaky. Scared. But relieved, too. They caught the killer; the sept would be safe.

"Oh my God, they caught the killer!" Katy scrambled off the bed.

"Stay out of my head," Kaleigh snapped. That didn't

happen often anymore. She'd gotten good at keeping up her guard, but when she was stressed, or emotional, the wall wasn't all that strong.

Katy began to dress.

"Katy, you can't come."

"Oh, I'm coming." She shimmied into a pair of jeans she'd picked up off the floor. They were Kaleigh's. "There's no way you're leaving me here."

"Peigi said no one was to know. I'm not supposed to tell anyone, not even my parents."

"You're not telling me." Katy opened her arms. "I already know. Now you have to take me for my own good. To make sure I keep my mouth shut."

Kaleigh exhaled.

"Come on," Katy whispered. "I'll walk you there, at least. I know they're not going to let me inside." She hesitated. "You know, it's not easy being the wise-woman's sidekick. No one ever notices that I can be of help to the sept, too, sometimes. Please?"

Kaleigh glanced across the bed at her best friend. She knew she should say no, but Katy looked so sad. And it probably was hard to be Kaleigh's friend; she'd just never thought about it that way. "We'll have to go out the window," she warned. "You can either climb down or let me try to transport you to the ground."

"Am I going to end up on a raft on Hilly's ceiling?"

Kaleigh threw a flip-flop at her.

Chapter 24

"**B**ut why?" Fin asked in frustration. His heart was breaking for Elena, for her family. "That's what I don't understand. Why would you risk your life, the lives of those you love to do something like this?"

He stood on one side of the bars with Elena; Lia stood on the other. They were in a small room in the bowels of the museum. The room was soundproof, with reinforced walls and windowless. It had been built for emergencies such as this, when the sept did not want a prisoner in the holding cells in the police department's basement.

Lia grasped one of the bars and glared. She looked like a kid in her tank top and shorts, not a cold-blooded killer. "You don't understand what it's like, living year after year, decade after decade, century after century where nothing changes. I am forever Celeste and Vittore's *little girl*." Her eyes shone with angry tears. "You understand what that means, *Zia* Elena? My mother still tells me what time to go to bed. After five hundred years!" She looked down at the floor. "This was one thing I could do on my own."

Elena made a sound in her throat, something akin to a sob. Fin put his arm around her.

"You killed those boys because you were angry?" Elena asked, in disbelief. "Because you were disappointed by how your life turned out? They are not to blame for what happened to you."

"Who *was* I going to kill? Grandfather?" Lia demanded. "Don't think that hasn't occurred to me." Her bravado was fast fading. "Probably to all of us."

"But those humans had nothing to do with us or with your grandfather's sins!"

"Neither did I."

Elena looked up at Fin and he wished desperately that he could do something for her, somehow ease her pain.

She looked back at her niece. "When you killed those innocents, you became nothing better than the men who did this to us."

"So now you're going to kill me." Lia stepped back from the bars, crossing her arms over her chest. "You're going to cut off my head and hurl my soul into everlasting, burning purgatory."

"It's not up to me. Fin says you will have a hearing before their Highest Council. They will judge you."

"How convenient. This way, you can walk away without my blood on your hands and tell yourself you're better than the men and women who will judge me."

Elena pulled away from Fin and grasped the bars, looking in on her niece. "How could you do this to your mother?" she admonished, fighting another wave of tears. "How could you break her heart this way?"

Lia's gaze met Elena's and for the briefest moment, Fin thought he saw a glimmer of remorse in the girl.

Lia turned away and walked over to the narrow bunk built out of the wall. She laid down and closed her eyes.

Elena stood at the bars for a moment, looking in on her niece, dabbing at her eyes with a Kleenex. He pulled her into his arms and hugged her, his chest tight with emotion. He was intensely relieved that the killer had been caught and aching for Elena at the same time. Of course, had it been one of the sept members, as he had suspected, would he have been any less heartbroken? He loved every man and woman in this town, just as Elena loved her family.

There was a tap at the door and then it opened. It was Kaleigh. She looked pale. "Gair needs to speak to you," she said, not yet looking at Lia. "Both of you."

Fin glanced at the cell. "One of us must remain with the prisoner at all times."

"I'll stay," Kaleigh murmured. "You talk to Gair."

As Elena and Fin walked past her, the two women met each other's gazes.

"I'm sorry," Kaleigh whispered. "I'm so sorry, Elena. We all are."

"Thank you." Elena squeezed Kaleigh's hand. "That means a lot to me."

Kaleigh waited until the heavy door swung shut behind Fin and Elena and then walked over and got a chair from a small desk in the corner of the antechamber. She carried it over to the bars and sat down in it. For a minute she just sat there. If Lia knew she was there, she gave no indication.

Kaleigh had spoken with Peigi and Gair and they told her what was going on. Kaleigh was shocked that the girl could have done such a thing, but relieved that the sept would be safe again. No more tourists would die in their quiet little town.

Kaleigh had been summoned by Peigi and Gair because they needed her to agree they were right to hold the accused prisoner, a practice that was always followed. Peigi reminded Kaleigh of the procedure in cases such as these. Kaleigh did not have to participate in the hearing that would follow to determine Lia's fate. Peigi said it wasn't even necessary for Kaleigh to see the doomed teenager, only give her approval for the incarceration and hearing. But Kaleigh had to see Lia. She knew they weren't friends or anything; they had just talked that night on the porch at Tomboy's. Still, she needed to see her.

"Why are you here?" Lia asked after a minute or two of complete silence. Below ground and well fortified, the room was like a tomb. "It's not like I can escape."

"I came to see if there was anything I could do for you," Kaleigh said gently.

Kaleigh expected more sarcasm, more flippant words out of Lia. The tiny sob took her completely by surprise.

"What have I done?" Lia whispered. "How could I have killed those boys?" Still lying on the bunk, she raised her hands, staring at them. "How could I have ever thought I had the right to take a life? How could it have made sense to me?"

Kaleigh wiped at her own tears. She couldn't help thinking that Katy might have been on the other side of these bars. Or any one of the other teens in Clare Point.

Even herself, maybe. It was so hard being young. She couldn't imagine what it would be like to be this age forever, like Lia. It was only by the grace of God and the love of their families that Kaleigh and her friends did not act on impulse and do something so irreparable as what Lia had done.

Lia sat up, wiping at her eyes. She glanced at Kaleigh. "Your uncle said you were the wisewoman of your family. That's pretty amazing the way it works with you guys. You get to be young *and* old."

Kaleigh didn't know what to say; she just listened.

"I think it would be cool to be the wisewoman."

"It is sometimes," Kaleigh agreed. "But it's hard, too. Especially now when I'm still young. I'm so conflicted so much of the time. Sort of an adult, a real adult. Sort of just a kid still."

Lia walked over to the bars. "Tell me about it," she joked.

"I wish there was something I could do to help you." Kaleigh stood up and gripped one of the bars.

"It's okay. I understand. You can't have vampires running all over the earth, killing the humans. If people like me killed all the humans, how would vampires like you redeem yourselves?"

"You knew about us?"

"Every vampire in the world knows about the famous Kahills." Lia smiled sadly. "I always wanted to be in your family. Imagined what it would be like, flying all over the earth, saving people."

"That sounds more exciting than it is. Most of the time it's just scary."

"I guess." Lia lifted a slender shoulder and let it fall. "So how long do I have?"

"A few days. The General Council will meet and

make the recommendation that your case be submitted to the High Council. One of our elders will represent you. The High Council will hear your case and then vote."

"And carry out the sentence," Lia added, her voice sounding far away now.

Kaleigh stared at the pretty girl on the other side of the titanium bars. "And carry out the sentence."

"How soon after the verdict?"

Kaleigh didn't want to answer, but she felt like she owed it to Lia to be completely honest. "Immediately."

"And my family?"

"They'll be permitted to leave as long as it's determined they didn't play a part in what happened."

"They had nothing to do with it!" Lia grasped the bars, her hands touching Kaleigh's. "They knew nothing about it. You have to let them go back to Italy."

"I'll do what I can to make sure that's clear."

The door opened behind Kaleigh and she saw Fin.

Kaleigh looked back at Lia. "I have to go, but I'll come back tomorrow." She started to move away and Lia laid her hand on Kaleigh's.

"Please come back." Lia's voice trembled. "Promise me?"

"I promise."

Kaleigh left her chair where it was. As she went through the door, she grabbed Fin's sleeve. She looked into his eyes. Kind, sad eyes. *Isn't there anything we can do? She's just a kid. I really don't think she realized what she was doing,* she telepathed.

She killed three innocent young men and put our sept in danger. We have rules. She won't be treated any differently than one of our own.

But she isn't like us, she countered. *She never had the benefit of having an adult mind, adult emotions.*

I'm sorry, Kaleigh. There's nothing that can be done.

Kaleigh glanced back at Lia, who still stood at the bars. "You'll make sure she's not mistreated?" Kaleigh asked aloud.

"I promise." He offered a grim smile and kissed her on her forehead. "Go home, get some sleep." He winked. "And be careful getting back in that window."

"You wanna play air hockey?" Rob asked. He and Kaleigh were standing under the arcade's awning, next to the photo booth.

"Nah," she said glumly.

"I'll let you win."

She cut her eyes at her boyfriend. "You don't have to *let me win*. I can beat you on my own. I just don't want to."

"Skee ball?"

She gazed out at the boardwalk, watching people walk by. Nothing had changed since last night, as far as the human tourists knew. But every vampire in town knew that the killer had been apprehended and the humans were now safe. Peigi had contacted all the Council members early that morning and the good news had spread. The sobering good news. Everyone was relieved the killer had been caught, but no one was looking forward to the hearing or the inevitable finale.

Kaleigh watched a mother with a baby in a stroller go by. "I don't feel like playing any games."

"You didn't want to go down on the beach. You didn't want to watch a movie." Rob exhaled. "I'm outta ideas, Kaleigh. I'm sorry you're upset about your friend, but—"

"She wasn't my friend."

He stepped in front of her and looked into her eyes. "I don't understand why you're so upset, K. This wasn't your fault." He touched her cheek.

She closed her eyes. "I know. But I still feel bad for her. It's not like she's an awful person. She just . . . she got lost somewhere along the way."

"There have to be rules. There have to be consequences."

"I know that." Kaleigh opened her eyes and rested her foot against the photo booth. "But all I can think about is, what if she was one of us? Wouldn't we try to help her? What if it was me? What if I'd been held accountable for the deaths of Bobby, Mahon, and Shannon?"

"Entirely different circumstances. You didn't *kill* them."

"What if everyone hadn't seen it that way? What if I'd been accused? Wouldn't you have done anything you could to save me?"

"Of course," Rob agreed. "But I don't think there is any way to help her. She confessed her guilt."

"You're probably right." She leaned back, her foot still resting on the photo booth. "Why don't you go play some air hockey? I'm sure you can find someone to play with."

"I can hang here with you." He slipped his hands into his pockets. "I don't mind."

"Here comes Katy." She motioned with her chin. "She can commiserate with me. Go on. I'll be fine."

"All right, I'll be back in a few." Rob gave her a quick kiss and walked away.

Kaleigh watched Katy walk toward her, carrying an

enormous tub of fresh boardwalk fries. She could smell the vinegar.

"Hey," Katy called.

"Hey," Kaleigh answered without much enthusiasm.

"Want a fry?" Katy held up one of the hand-cut fries.

"Not hungry."

"Jeez, mopey." Katy leaned against the photo booth beside her and ate the fry. "I don't know what you're so miserable about. I'm the one who ought to be miserable. My BFF in the whole world thought I might be a serial killer."

"I didn't *think* it was you. I knew it wasn't. I just . . ." Kaleigh halted, then started again. "You have to admit, you were acting kind of weird, talking about wanting to move. And you were able to open that jar and move that cooler, only you didn't say anything about the increase in your strength."

"Sorry I didn't tell you about that. I just felt uncomfortable about it. You know, like being the only girl in gym class with boobs. It hasn't happened to most of the guys yet. I didn't want to be the only one bench-pressing three hundred pounds."

Kaleigh chuckled. "You worry about the damnedest things."

"Which is why you love me." Katy pushed a fry into her mouth.

"Which is why I love you," Kaleigh agreed.

"So, you going to the Council meeting tonight?"

"I don't have to."

"I'd go if I was allowed. Peigi said no one but Council members, though." Katy frowned. "Said she didn't want a *three-ring circus*."

"I might go." Because of her position, Kaleigh had a right to sit in on General or High Council meetings, though she did not yet have a vote. "I know Lia's going to be scared. None of her family is allowed to go. I guess I could go and sit with her."

Katy studied a fry before popping it in her mouth. "That would be nice of you."

"What's Kaleigh doing nice?" Regan came around the photo machine. "Get your feet off, ladies."

Both girls lowered their feet and stood up.

"Kaleigh might go to the Council meeting and sit with the doomed."

He looked at Kaleigh. "That *would* be nice of you."

"I feel bad for her. What she did was wrong, but if there was some way she could have a second chance, I really think . . ."

"You think what?" he asked.

"I think she could do great things," Kaleigh finished with a nod. "It's just this feeling I have about her."

"Too bad they're going to lop off her head." Katy pushed her container of fries into Kaleigh's hands. "BRB. Potty break." She walked away, licking her fingertips.

Regan continued to stand there, looking kind of thoughtful. At least for Regan.

Kaleigh waited.

He took one of Katy's fries.

"I know this isn't my place to say, me being the resident drug addict and all."

"Recovering drug addict," she corrected.

"Recovering," he agreed with a nod. "But did anyone consider any alternative to dealing with this kid?"

"Alternative?"

He stroked his scruffy beard. "I keep thinking somewhere in the back of my mind, something like this happened once before."

"With us? Not any time in the last fifty years. Not since the laws were rewritten and penalties became stiffer."

"No, it wasn't us. It was another family. Sixteenth century, maybe."

"Who?" she demanded.

"I'm trying to remember. Jeez, give me a break. You know I must have killed some brain cells somewhere along the way."

Kaleigh waited, bouncing up and down on the balls of her feet, the fry bucket tucked under her arm. "Come on, Regan. I really need you to remember this."

"I'm thinking it was the Thomases." He pointed his finger at her. "Lizzy Thomas told me about it."

"The Thomases?"

"You know them. Well, you did. You will. English. Decent Vs for the most part. Most of the women are redheads. Hot. Even the old ones." He took another fry.

"You've always had a thing for redheads. Can you remember anything else?"

He squinted as if digging mentally into the recesses of his mind. "There was this boy from, I can't remember, Germany, Yugoslavia . . . or was it Poland? No, I think it was Germany. Somewhere where they make good sausage."

"Anyway." Kaleigh pushed the container of fries into his hands.

"Anyway, the kid got caught up in a bad crowd. Was involved with a bunch of zombies from Istanbul and some ugly murders they committed. The Thomases captured him with the zombies, put the zombies to death, but they didn't have the heart to behead the kid."

"Then what did they do with him?" Kaleigh grabbed his arm. This was the first time she felt a glimmer of hope for Lia. Everyone had been so sure the girl's fate was already sealed.

Regan munched on another fry. "I think . . . I think Liz said they adopted him."

"Adopted him?"

"There was this crazy ritual they had to go through that involved blood draining and blood donations." He waved a French fry in the air. "It was pretty intense. They had to, like, kill him and bring him back in this ceremony."

Kaleigh planted herself in front of him. "How can I find out what actually happened? I mean, if I can find a precedent . . ."

"He wasn't a Kahill, Kaleigh."

"But we've followed other families' precedents before," she said quickly.

"When?"

She thought for a second and couldn't for the life of her remember. But she *knew* they had. "I don't know," she groaned. "I'm telling you we have. Can you track her down?"

"Who?"

"The redhead. Lizzy."

"Don't you think you should talk to someone about this before you get your hopes up? Peigi? Gair, maybe?"

"No. I don't want to give them the opportunity to stop me. It might be a waste of time, anyway. I just want to find out more about this adoption thing. Can you find Lizzy Thomas?"

"Now?"

"Sure."

He grimaced. "No way. I haven't seen her since, like, the eighteen nineties. It's not like I have her phone number."

Kaleigh made her hands into fists. "There has to be a way. Can't you . . . I don't know. Go to England? Find her?"

"I'm grounded, remember?"

She groaned in frustration. "What about the books?"

"Books?"

"Our records. All those books and piles of papers in the library in the museum basement. All that stuff about vampires." Before leaving Ireland, the Kahills had buried what they couldn't take with them, planning to return for it at a later date. Thankfully, they had left all their written records. Otherwise, they would have been lost in the shipwreck. Over the years since then, the books and records, along with other artifacts, had been dug up and brought to Clare Point. "Don't we keep records of what happens in other families?"

"Some, I guess. I'm not exactly a big reader."

"This is an unusual case. Surely someone wrote the information down." She gazed at him anxiously. "Victor would know. He's the current librarian."

"He might. Problem is, apparently, he and Mary McCathal are AWOL."

"AWOL?"

"Absent without leave. No one's seen them in more than a week. No one knows where they went."

Kaleigh's eyes got big. "You think they ran away?"

Regan shrugged and ate another fry. "Possible. Victor was pretty pissed that the Council denied his request to marry Mary." He grinned. "I like the sound of that, marry Mary."

"He wanted to marry her?" Kaleigh rested one hand on her hip. "Where was I during all this?"

"Apparently, you were partying with a bunch of humans."

"I was not *partying* with them." Suddenly the fries smelled good and she was starving. She hadn't eaten all day. "Give me one of those." She nabbed a fry. "Technically, I'm supposed to get permission from the librarian to look through the records."

"*And* you have to get the key from him."

"And the key," she concurred. "But Victor is AWOK."

"*AWOL,*" Regan corrected.

She made a face. "Whatever. Anyway, I need to get into the library. How do I do that if Victor's not here?"

"You could ask the Council's permission."

She shook her head, reaching for another fry. "No time. They're only meeting tonight to vote on sending Lia's case to the High Council. I would have to wait until the next meeting to get permission. By then, she could be dead. I need to get in there now. Tonight."

He thought for a minute. "You steal the key?"

She rolled her eyes. "You ever been in Victor's house? It would take a century to find a key in all that junk." She took the bucket of fries from him. "Can you pick a lock? One on a library door?"

"I could try." Regan licked his fingers. "Or I could just open the door from the inside."

Her eyes lit up. "You could materialize on the other side of the door." She looked at him. "You'd do that? For me?"

"Give me the rest of those fries"—he pointed—"and I will."

She pushed the container into his hands. "Can we go now?"

"Sorry. My trusty second in command got his wisdom teeth out the other day and he's laid up. I have to stay here until I close."

"You can't sneak away for a few minutes?" she begged.

"With Mary gone, I feel like I need to do this right. You know, protect her interests."

Kaleigh sighed, knowing he was right. It probably made more sense not to be breaking in in the middle of the day anyway. "Okay, tonight. But as soon as you close the arcade. I'll meet you there."

"Council will be meeting at midnight. Going to get a little crowded. You want to go to the meeting and then meet me after?"

She thought for a minute. If she did get into the library, she had no idea how long it would take her to find what she was looking for. Hours for sure, possibly days. And Lia didn't have that kind of time. "I'll meet you after you close. I'll just skip the Council meeting. No one was expecting me."

Katy approached them, wiping her hands on her shorts. "Out of paper towels in the bathroom, Regan."

Kaleigh grabbed her hand. "You wanna go with me to talk to Lia?"

Katy's mouth fell open. "The condemned?"

"Not if I can help it." Kaleigh led Katy out of the arcade. "Later, alligator," she told Regan.

"Hey, he's got my fries," Katy protested as Kaleigh pulled her past him.

"You don't need them. Loads of saturated fat." Kaleigh led her down the boardwalk, through the throngs of people. "It goes straight to your butt."

Katy glanced over her shoulder. "You think my butt is getting big?"

Chapter 25

"Come on," Kaleigh whispered, looking at the library door and then down the dark hallway. The guards watching over Lia had just changed shifts down the hall and Pete Hill had come on. Upstairs, the General Council members were filing in.

"Regan?" Kaleigh whispered, pressing her palms against the library door. She hoped he hadn't rematerialized in the bathroom down the hall or something. He said that sometimes happened to him if he *got his wires crossed*. Whatever that meant. Kaleigh didn't know anything about teletransporting herself yet; she was still working on gum packets and ants.

"I'm sure she won't give you any trouble," Kaleigh heard Fin saying to Pete. He must have been visiting Lia; she could have no visitors from her family.

"Regan," Kaleigh breathed, rattling the doorknob. "Where the hell did you go?"

Just as Kaleigh heard the door open down the hall and Fin's voice louder, the lock on the library door clicked. Kaleigh turned the knob and rushed in, closing the door behind her. "You okay?"

"Yeah," Regan said from the dark. "I'm just a little rusty is all. Landed on top of a bookshelf."

Even though she could see pretty well in the dark, Kaleigh felt for a light switch and flipped it on. The room filled with eerie fluorescent light. There were no windows in the library, so as long as she kept quiet and kept her mind closed to intruders, no one would know she was there. The library was rarely used so there was little chance anyone would come for some light reading, especially with Victor missing. She turned around to look at the floor-to-ceiling bookshelves. The room smelled like paper and stale air. "All this stuff is about vampires?"

"Not just vampires." Regan ran his finger down the spine of an old, ratty book. "Zombies, werewolves, yetis, you name it."

"There's such a thing as yetis?" she asked with amazement.

"Look, I'm going to go. I need to be home when Fin gets there. Otherwise he gets crazy and starts to worry about me. Then he calls Mary Kay and all mother-hell breaks loose."

"No problem." Kaleigh was already pulling down books, reading titles, and pushing the books back into place. Her plan was to start on one side of the room and work her way along the shelves. "This could take, like, a hundred years to read through all this stuff," she said, trying not to feel too depressed. "But the High Council is not going to take my word, or yours or even Lizzy Thomas's, if we could find her. I have to find evidence to support the idea of adopting Lia into our sept and sparing her life."

"I'd offer to help you, but I'm not good at this kind of thing."

"Don't worry about it. I'm probably wasting my time. The High Council isn't going to listen to me, anyway."

"You never know." He rested his hand on the doorknob. "Put something across the bottom so no one sees the light coming from under the door in the dark hallway."

"You're good." She followed him.

He offered a lazy grin. "Good luck."

She smiled grimly. "Thanks."

"And Kaleigh?"

"Uh-huh?" She didn't look in his direction; she was reading book titles.

"Even if you don't find anything. Even if you can't pull this off . . ." He hesitated.

"Uh-huh?" She glanced at him.

"It doesn't mean you failed her." He sounded so serious. "You can't take the weight of the world entirely on your own shoulders."

"I know. 'Night, Regan. And thanks again."

" 'Night."

Kaleigh let him out the door and then used a small throw rug to block any light that might seep under. Satisfied with her handiwork, she turned to gaze at the rows of books and manuscripts in front of her.

There wasn't a chance in hell she was going to find anything here to help Lia. But when she stood witness to the girl's beheading, at least she would know she had tried.

* * *

Fin waited with Elena in the dark parking lot of the museum, perched on the front bumper of his police cruiser. The air was warm and humid and filled with the sounds of a July night: chirping insects, the hum of the building's heat pumps, the rustle of a mouse poking in the grass beneath a flowering cherry tree. Fin breathed deeply, separating the scents of the night: Elena's skin, freshly cut grass, asphalt still warm from the day's sun.

He held Elena's hand. They didn't talk. What was there to say? He had suggested there was no need for her to be here tonight. She wouldn't be permitted to attend the meeting, and they already knew what would take place. At this point, this was all a mere formality; Lia had confessed to the murder of all three young men and had been able to offer no suitable justification. The Council would pass Lia's case on to the High Council.

But Elena had told her sister she would be here to confirm the decision and so Fin waited with her.

He turned her hand in his, savoring the feel of her soft skin, her slender bone structure. He lifted her hand and pressed his lips to her knuckles.

"I left Celeste with the task of packing up the house," she said, her tone distant. "She needed something to keep her occupied."

Fin didn't know what to say, didn't know that anything was required of him, so he just listened.

"She asked me"—her voice broke—"what we should do with Lia's clothing. I thought, perhaps, it could be donated locally." She looked at him. "Would that be possible?"

"Sure. Um, I know someone who volunteers at a shelter for battered women in the county. They always have teens passing through."

"You could take care of that for me?"

The pain in her voice was palpable and her pain was becoming his. "Not a problem," he managed.

She was quiet again for a minute, but he could tell she wanted to say something. He wished he could read her mind. Occasionally, over the last weeks, he realized now, he had heard her in his head, but he couldn't control it. Neither could she, apparently. It was more like the psychic connection he felt occasionally with certain humans.

"Fin," she said, taking the time to choose her words carefully. "I do not want you to feel in any way responsible for this."

"If I had caught her after the first—"

"She would have already been guilty of murdering an innocent man," Elena finished for him.

She was right. He knew she was right, but facts didn't ease the feelings. He still felt guilty. He still wished there was some way he could have spared those boys' lives, spared Elena and her family from this heartbreak.

Fin heard the rear door of the museum open and shadows of people appeared. The meeting was over. It was done. He held Elena's hand tightly. "Would you like to come home with me? Maybe just for a little while?" he asked.

"Would I like to? Yes. Can I? No. I need to return to the cottage and be with my sister." She pulled his hand into her lap and leaned over, pressing her cheek to their entwined hands.

He felt the dampness of her silent tears.

"I wish that we could make love again," she whispered.

"Maybe—"

"Maybe," she interrupted.

But both knew they would not. The High Council would meet tomorrow at midnight. The smartest thing for Elena and her family to do would be to return to Italy tomorrow. They would not be permitted to attend the High Council meeting. There would be no need to attend the beheading, even if the Council would make an exception and permit it.

"My work takes me to Italy sometimes," Fin said. He watched several Council members cross the parking lot. They walked silently, somberly. "Maybe I could—"

"We do not permit outsiders to enter the villa."

"Elena?" He studied her face. He couldn't believe he was losing her so soon after finding her. "Don't want to see me again?"

She held his gaze. "It's not that I don't want to see you, Fin. But it would be better if I just go. You knew from the beginning that this would only last a short time. I warned you. I must return to the villa. You have your job, your family, your hope."

Fin wanted to tell her she was being unreasonable. That the present circumstances were keeping her from thinking clearly. But who was he to tell her how to feel? He knew the pain that accompanied the loss of a loved one; it could not be weighed or measured. Every man, every woman had to deal with it in his or her own way.

"I wish that we could take her body home, bury her in the family churchyard," she said, watching the quiet figures fan out into the darkness.

"I'm sorry, but that's not possible. Too difficult to get the body through customs," he said, hoping he would not have to elaborate.

"I understand."

Spotting his mother's next door neighbor, Fin got up. "I'll be right back." He walked up to Joe. "High Council?"

Joe scuffed the toe of his sneaker in the loose gravel of the parking lot. "Tomorrow night." He didn't meet Fin's gaze.

"Thanks." Fin squeezed his arm and walked back to where Elena waited. "It's done," he said. He stood in front of her.

She still sat on the front bumper of the police car. She was wearing a summer dress and a thin white cardigan over it. She fiddled with the hem of the sweater. "I should go."

"You want me to give you a ride?"

She rose, smoothing the fabric of her dress. "I think I need to walk."

"I could walk with you."

Her eyes glistened with tears, but somehow she managed a smile. She stroked his cheek. "I prefer to walk alone." Then she kissed him, her soft lips lingering over his.

Fin watched her walk away, and wondered if this was the last time he would ever see her.

Kaleigh woke to the feel of her cell phone vibrating in her shorts pocket. She lifted her head off the table and wiped a spot of drool off the page of a book. She wondered how long she had been asleep; there was no way to tell in the windowless room. The last time she had checked, it had been four-thirty in the morning.

The phone continued to vibrate and she fished it out of her pocket. It was Katy. "Hey."

"You have to call your mom in, like, the next five minutes or we are *so* busted. This is the second time I called you. Are you still at the library?"

Still not entirely awake, Kaleigh drew the back of her hand across her mouth. It was sticky from the gummy bears she had eaten in the middle of the night when she got hungry. Now she was thirsty. Crazy thirsty.

"I'm still here."

"Find anything?"

"If I found anything, would I still be here?" Kaleigh asked, exasperated. She got up to walk out her stiff legs. "Sorry."

"It's okay," Katy said gently. "But you gotta call your mom. I told her you were in the shower."

Kaleigh yawned and dragged her finger along a bookshelf as she read book spines. She'd made a mess of the library. She'd checked every title of every book here and then she'd started leafing through diaries and notes. They weren't well organized. Sometimes they were filed by date, other times region. Other times, there seemed to be no reason whatsoever for what she found where.

"I'll call her," Kaleigh said.

"You want to meet at the diner? Have some breakfast?"

"What I want is to pee." Kaleigh exhaled. "Maybe some breakfast would be good. Then I'll come back."

"How you going to get back in?"

"Leave the door unlocked. Who's going to check it? Then I'll sneak back in."

"I could come with you," Katy offered. "We could tell our moms we're going to the beach, then I could help you."

"I don't know," Kaleigh hemmed. She pulled down a big cardboard box off one of the shelves and carried it to the table. "I don't want you to get into trouble."

"It's not like you have a lot of time," Katy reasoned. "High Council meets tonight."

Kaleigh plopped down in the chair and pushed her hair out of her eyes. "I better call my mom. See you at the diner."

"I'll pack snacks," Katy said excitedly. "See you in a few."

It was a good thing Kaleigh let Katy join her because it was Katy, in the end, who found what they were looking for.

By six that evening, Kaleigh had been ready to give up. She'd checked so many books, pored over so many documents that her back hurt from lugging the books and boxes and her eyes hurt from trying to make out the faded ink of old tomes.

Kaleigh had just sunk onto the floor and declared there was no record of a German vampire being adopted by the Thomas family when Katy came upon something called "field notes" written by Robert Kahill in 1674. Kaleigh's Rob. The recorded location was London, England.

"Listen to this," Katy said excitedly. "There's something here about helping some Vs catch some zombies who were killing citizens. The writing is crazy. Fancy English, but—"

"It's no use, Katy. It's not here."

"Are you listening?" Katy shouted.

Kaleigh glanced at the door. "Maybe keep it down?"

"Johnny's on duty. He brought a TV. He's watching *Jeopardy!*, so unless you know the nickname for the West African beet bug, he's not going to hear you." Katy leaned over the table that was piled with books and loose papers. "Now get your cute little patootie over here and look at this."

"My patootie is tired is what it is and it's not here. The information isn't here. It might not have even happened." But Kaleigh got up and dragged herself over to the table, anyway.

"Right here," Katy said.

Kaleigh stared at the paper bound in a small leather notebook for a minute, then brushed her fingertips gently over the page. "It's Rob's handwriting," she murmured.

"It is?" Katy looked and then made a face. "Doesn't look like his handwriting. Of course, it's his name inside the cover."

"Not now." Kaleigh studied the page. "A long time ago," she said dreamily. She was so tired that her thoughts were in a jumble. She vaguely remembered those years, but the memory seemed more like a recollection of something she had seen on TV rather than experienced herself. Rob *had* been briefly assigned to London and something had happened involving zombies. She had just forgotten, until this very moment.

Kaleigh read a page, then the next, then skimmed the next few. It was slow going. The handwriting was faded and it *was* in fancy English. But what Rob had written was quite clear. He'd been meticulous in recording the account of what had happened to a boy by the name of George Baecker. Kaleigh looked up at Katy. "Sweet baby Jesus," she whispered. "This might be all we need."

"This is it? Really?" Katy jumped up and down and clapped her hands. "You're kidding. Rob wrote it down? Rob knows about it?"

"I doubt he remembers." Kaleigh closed the book. "I'll ask him, of course, but don't you see? It doesn't matter if he remembers. He wrote it down." She hugged the book to her chest. "That's why we write these things down. So we don't have to remember." She headed for the door.

Katy grabbed her backpack off the chair. "Where are we going?"

"First to see Rob, then Fin. Fin will know what to do with this."

Katy glanced at the mess they had made of the library as she walked out the door. "Shouldn't we clean this up?"

"No time. The sentence must be carried out at once. If we can convince the High Council that this is a better option than a beheading, we have to be ready to do it."

Katy hurried down the hall after Kaleigh, past the room where Lia was being kept. "Ready to do it? Do what?"

"You'll never believe it. It's too crazy to—"

A door opened behind the girls and Johnny Hill stuck his head out. The sound of the *Jeopardy!* game show spilled out of the room. "Hey! What are you two doing down here?" He looked down the hall in the opposite direction, spotted the library door open, and looked back at them. "Hey!"

"We'll clean it up later, Johnny," Kaleigh hollered. Then the girls made a run for the stairs.

* * *

Fin left the teenagers in his office taking turns spinning in his chair while they drank Cokes and ate cheese crackers he'd retrieved from the break room. He was shocked by what they had found in the library, but he didn't have time to dwell on it; he had to take action.

He'd stepped out of the room to call Dr. Caldwell and make the necessary arrangements, should they be able to convince the High Council of the justice in the solution offered in Rob's diary. Unfortunately, Rob did not remember the incident. He didn't even remember that life cycle, but Fin was confident that Kaleigh was right. It didn't matter that Rob couldn't tell the tale; he had done so in the diary.

Before Fin made the call to Dr. Caldwell, he dialed another number. He prayed she would pick up.

The phone rang once, twice, three times. In a minute, the answering system would take over. Fin's heart took a tumble. "Elena," he whispered.

"Hello?"

Fin was startled by the sound of her voice. He was afraid she had already gone. "Elena! It's Fin."

"I can't talk, Fin. The van has arrived to take us to the airport."

"No! No, you can't go." He gripped the phone. "You and your family need to stay tonight. You need to be here."

"We had agreed there was no need for us to be here. We've already said our good-byes to Lia," she said sadly.

"No, you don't understand." He glanced in the direction of his office. Kaleigh was watching him. He held up his finger to tell her he'd be with her in a moment. "Elena, you have to stay," Fin said. "Because Kaleigh may have figured out a way to save Lia's life."

For a moment there was silence on the other end of the phone. Fin was afraid she might have hung up. "Elena?"

"You could save her?" Elena managed, emotionally.

"It's complicated. She could never go home."

"We don't care," Elena said desperately. "Anything would be better than this. My sister, she would—" Her voice broke and she couldn't finish her thought.

"Listen, I have a lot to do and not a lot of time. The hearing will take place in the churchyard. You know where the church is, right?"

"Yes."

"Be there with your family at midnight. Come on foot. Draw no attention to yourself and no flashlights or anything, of course."

"Of course."

"And come prepared to say good-bye"—he held his breath—"no matter what."

"Thank you, Fin," Elena breathed. "I . . . my family can never thank you enough."

His gaze settled on a bulletin board on the wall across from him. Pinned across the top were the photos of Lia's three victims. The young men were all smiling. "Not having to tell another family that their loved one is dead will be thanks enough."

Chapter 26

Fin walked slower than he would have ordinarily, but Lia's legs were short, as was her stride. Pete Hill had suggested leg irons, but Fin had put his foot down. The girl wouldn't attempt to escape, escorted by two male vampires. Fin wasn't entirely sure she even wanted to. In the last two days, despite her words when she was first incarcerated, she seemed to have had a change of heart. He saw remorse in the face where he had seen anger that first night. She hadn't begged for her life. She seemed to accept her fate with a dignity that surprised him. Maybe Kaleigh was right; maybe her soul could be redeemed.

Lia walked down the dark street between Fin and Pete. She didn't look at her surroundings, or at them, she just walked, head down. She was sure this was the end.

When the time had come to take Lia from her cell and escort her to the waiting members of the High Council, Fin had considered telling her that her life might yet be spared, but he thought better of it. It was not his place, he told himself. But he wondered if the real reason he hadn't told her was that he feared giving her false hope.

"How much farther?" Lia asked. It was the first time she had spoken in hours.

"Not much farther."

Ordinarily, High Council meetings were held in the museum. For practical reasons, considering the impending beheading, however, the meeting had been moved to the cemetery behind the old brick church, St. Patrick's. Kaleigh had warned Gair that she would be offering an alternative to the death sentence and had asked for special permission to allow the Ruffino family to attend. Somehow, she'd gotten him to agree to her request. Fin wasn't entirely sure having them here was a good idea, but he was glad he would see Elena one last time.

Fin and Pete led the prisoner, who more resembled a scared teenager than a cold-blooded killer, down the brick sidewalk toward the dark, silent church. Here, at St. Patrick's, the Kahills had worshiped since they built it in the late sixteen hundreds. At the rear of the church, under a canopy of pin oaks and silver maples, was an iron gate which they passed through.

The gate opened into a cemetery, but no ordinary cemetery. Here, Kahills were not buried, but brought back to life in teenage bodies. The elaborate marble tombstones marked fake graves, with the exception of a couple, including the three sept members killed two years ago. The old and new tombstones were there to make humans who might pass through think it was an ordinary, quaint cemetery like many that dotted the area.

"This is creepy," Lia whispered, moving closer to

Fin. She looked like a little girl. Sounded like one. It was hard to believe she had had sex with three young men and then murdered them. Actually, she'd only had sex with two. It hadn't been necessary with Richie, she had explained during her confession the night Fin was called to Rose Cottage.

"It's so dark," Lia whispered. "I know it sounds silly, but I've never liked the dark."

Her comment re-emphasized Kaleigh's argument that even if the girl was five hundred years old, she was still a child in many ways and could not be tried as an adult.

"It's okay," Fin whispered, surprised by the compassion he felt for her. "Your parents will be here."

Her voice quavered. "Kaleigh?"

"She'll be here, too."

"She was nice to me," she commented softly.

Fin led the girl deeper into the cemetery that bordered the forest reserve, soft, fragrant grass under their feet.

Lia gasped when the High Council members came into view and she froze. They had already gathered in a circle around the aboveground tomb that served as a platform for the bodies of those in transformation. The members wore long, black ceremonial cloaks with hoods pulled up to conceal their faces. Fin knew every man and woman on the Council; Fia was among them.

"You need to stand over here," Fin said, gently pushing her forward. *Thanks, Pete. I can take over from here*, he telepathed.

Pete took a few steps back.

"Right here." Fin directed Lia to stand near the tombstone of Mary O'Malley. It was an inside joke. There were no O'Malleys buried in the churchyard, but

they had all known a Mary O'Malley once upon a time.
Her sons were the vampire slayers who had ultimately
driven the Kahills out of Ireland and inadvertently offered them the potential of salvation.

"Do I have to stand?" Lia asked shakily.

"You can sit if you want. They'll tell you when to
stand."

The girl glanced over her shoulder at the tombstone,
but realizing she had no choice, she sat on the grassy
grave.

Kaleigh entered the graveyard with Patrick Caldwell,
the town's only doctor. He carried a duffel bag. Behind
them walked the Ruffino family, dressed in somber
clothing, heads bent as if already in mourning.

"Stay put, Lia," Fin warned. He passed Kaleigh as
he walked toward Elena. *Ready?* he telepathed.

I think I'm gonna throw up, she returned.

Fin almost smiled.

At the sight of her family, Lia made a sobbing
sound, but she did not get up and her family knew
enough to stay back. Fin nodded to Celeste and her
husband and grabbed Elena by the hand and pulled her
away from the group.

"What did you tell them?" he whispered. There was
no need to continue to hold her hand, but he did anyway.

"I just told them that the High Council demanded
their presence."

"They expect her to die?"

She looked into his eyes, her own dark eyes were
moist with tears. "I thought it better."

"You're probably right," he agreed grimly.

Movement in the trees beyond the graveyard caught

Fin's eye. At that moment, Gair saw it, too. One figure after another appeared from the forest and gathered at the top of the small rise at the edge of the churchyard. Fin recognized the teenagers. It was Kaleigh's *gang:* Rob, Katy, her boyfriend, Pete, and others all about the same age.

Gair turned to Kaleigh. He didn't speak.

"Please," Kaleigh murmured to the old man. She laid her hand on his arm, something few in the sept would dare do when Gair was wearing the black robe.

"If the High Council agrees to my proposal, we'll need them," she said, taking care to keep her tone reverent.

Fin couldn't see Gair's facial expression, but he could tell it softened. He'd always had a special place in his heart for Kaleigh. He was also the type of leader who knew when to give his people a little latitude.

"They may not be a part of these proceedings."

"I know. They know." She glanced up at them.

The teens remained in the tree line.

The chieftain stepped back from Kaleigh and lifted his arms skyward. *"Caraidean."*

The teens had been quiet before, but now they were utterly silent. Ghosts in the darkness. The only sounds were those of the wind gently rustling the trees overhead and the night song of the birds and insects.

"It's time to start." Fin held Elena's gaze. "You are observers. You may not participate in any way. You may not speak unless the chieftain orders it. And no matter what, you all must remain here on the sidewalk, you understand?" he asked.

Elena nodded. She understood. She understood that even if Kaleigh could not convince the Council to spare Lia's life, even if Lia was sentenced to death and the sentence was carried out, the Ruffino family could not interfere.

"Is there anything I can do?" Elena whispered as he walked her back to her huddled family.

"Pray," he answered. Then he squeezed her hand and let go, moving to stand behind Lia, among the gravestones.

"Caraidean," Gair repeated, seeing that he now had everyone's attention. "We gather tonight in solemn accordance with the laws established by this sept . . ."

The chieftain uttered the words of the sacred ritual. As always, he spoke in the old tongue, their native Gaelic, his gravelly voice crackling in the night air. With each ancient word, the lives of those who gathered seemed to grow more tightly woven until the energy in the graveyard crackled and a faint blue light arced between the twelve cloaked Council members.

In the same manner that each High Council meeting began, Gair chronicled, by rote, the establishment of the sept in the fifth century of recorded time. Those were the days when Rome was in decay and the great tribes of Ireland and Scotland struggled with old and new ways, battling for their faith. Christianity was on the ascent, but not without violence. It was a time when the sept developed a taste for power and for blood.

Then came the *mallachd*.

They were all damned by God for their refusal to reject their pagan gods, for their refusal to accept St. Patrick's message of the new faith. They were cursed for the blood of mankind they spilled.

With all the skill of a trained Shakespearean actor, the chieftain continued his time-honored speech. He reminded the Council members of their vow taken three centuries ago. He warned them of the magnitude of the decision the High Council would make tonight, and of the reason such difficult judgments had to be made. He reminded them of their ultimate goal; to ease the pain and suffering of humans and to ultimately gain God's absolution for the sins they committed so many centuries ago.

Without further introduction, Gair switched to English and asked Fin to give the facts of the case. Fin tried to close off his feelings. He knew his words were sentencing Lia to death as he provided the details that everyone in the cemetery already knew. He finished by speaking the names of the three dead men, his voice ringing ominously: "Colin Meding, Richie Palmer, Trey Cline."

Gair turned to Lia, who still sat on Mary O'Malley's fake grave, and signaled for her to stand.

As Fin stepped back, he fought the urge to help the girl to her feet.

Lia was shaking all over.

"You have heard the charges," Gair declared, his tone grave. He took no pleasure in proceedings like these. "How do you plead?"

The silence of the dark graveyard was almost overwhelming at that moment. The High Council members waited. The teens waited. Lia's family waited. They all knew the answer. Yet they waited.

"Guilty," Lia declared, her voice surprisingly clear.

Somewhere, an owl hooted.

"Guilty," Gair repeated. Then he raised his hands again. "Before the sentence is handed down, does anyone wish to speak on this woman's behalf?"

Fin caught Elena's eye and shook his head. The invitation was meant for Kahills only.

Lia lowered her hands to her sides. Her mother had
sent her clean clothes to change into tonight. She wore
a pale yellow sundress. Fin wondered if this would be
her death shroud.

Fin looked to Kaleigh, realizing she had not yet spoken. *Go on,* he telepathed. *We're listening. This is your
chance.*

Kaleigh stepped forward. "Me. I'd like to speak for
the accused."

There was a twitter of sound from the teenagers on
the fringes of the graveyard. Their thoughts bounced
around, mixing with the thoughts of the Council members.

You go, girl.
I heard she was going to speak.
This is why these hearings should be closed.
If this works, do we have to be friends with her?
*Holy Mother of God, what does she possibly think
she could say in the girl's defense? The Italian con-
fessed!*

"Kaleigh." Gair's voice seemed to soften. "You wish
to defend this woman who has freely admitted her
guilt?"

"I do not wish to challenge the verdict." Kaleigh's
voice trembled as she left Dr. Caldwell's side and
moved to stand in front of the tomb where the cloaked
Council members stood. "It . . . it's the sentence I wish
to challenge." She paused. Swallowed. "According to a
basic interpretation of our laws, this girl should be beheaded for the crimes against humans that she has committed. But I would suggest that this vampire cannot be
held accountable in the same way that we hold each
other accountable."

There was more whispering. Fin blocked the thoughts

still bouncing around. They made it too hard for him to concentrate on what Kaleigh was saying.

"Lia Ruffino Deluce's curse is not our curse. Her entire family and the families of her village were made vampires because of the sins committed by her grandfather. Since the fifteenth century, she has been locked in this child's body, worse, in this child's mind."

She looks like a child, doesn't she?

My little Maria had the same sweet smile.

Man, you really think she didn't understand what she was doing?

Child? I don't care what she looks like. She fucked them and then she slit their throats.

Fin hoped that Kaleigh was smart enough not to be listening to what everyone was thinking, even her friends. He made eye contact with her and she went on faster than before as if she feared the Council members might grow impatient and cut off Lia's head before Kaleigh had finished stating her case. "The Ruffino family's *mallachd* does not include life cycles. This girl, although she is five hundred years old, is still a fourteen-year-old, emotionally. Around the age we're all reborn."

Kaleigh paused, looking from one cloaked figure to the next. "Would you condemn one of us to the same fate, the day we were reborn?" She hesitated. "What I'm saying is that our laws are intended for those with old souls. Lia is not an old soul."

"Even if what you say is true, there must be punishment," Gair said. "She cannot be permitted to move about the earth killing humans because she *knows no better*. It's our duty to protect God's humans from vampires like her."

There must be punishment. The voices pressed the edges of Fin's mind.

There must be punishment.

"Yes," Kaleigh agreed. "There must be punishment, but I have an account of a punishment handed down by another family that might be more appropriate in this case. It's recorded in Rob Kahill's own handwriting in the seventeenth century."

"But it was not handed down by our family?" Gair questioned.

"No." Kaleigh put out her hand and Dr. Caldwell handed her a small leather book. "But at previous hearings, we've used other councils' precedents." She clutched the book to her chest. "I'm sure that you remember that time we accepted the ruling by the Chin family in Singapore? And . . . and what about the Red Mark incident with the Coyote Clan of the Comanche?"

Gair nodded and Fin could have sworn he detected a note of pride in the old man's voice. "Your memories are returning. You're beginning to learn how to use them. That's good, Kaleigh, good for all of us," he said, raising his voice. "So what punishment do you suggest?"

Kaleigh glanced at Fin. *They're listening,* she telepathed.

Told you they might, he answered.

"I thought you should hear it from him."

Kaleigh put out her hand, and Rob moved in from the shadows, down the little hill to stand beside her. She handed him the book, open to the specific page. When Rob started to read, his voice was shaky, but as he continued, it grew stronger. He recounted the frightening tale of a young German vampire taken in by zombies and the crimes the boy committed, at their instruction, on the streets of London. The Thomas family of vampires apprehended the boy and found him guilty of the crimes, but not entirely responsible for his actions. Rob then related the process by which the Thomases killed the boy and brought him back from the dead, making him one of their own.

Every vampire in the graveyard listened with rapt attention to the words as Rob read them. When he was done, he closed the book and looked up at the chieftain.

"Is this what you propose we do?" Gair asked Kaleigh.

"Yes." She met his gaze. "I suggest we drain Lia's blood and fill her body with our blood. I suggest we make her a Kahill."

Chapter 27

There was less resistance to Kaleigh's idea than Fin expected. Gair allowed High Council members to question her and Dr. Caldwell on the mechanics of the adoption ritual which Rob had carefully recorded more than three hundred years ago. Once the members' questions had been answered and a vote was taken, Gair asked Lia to step forward.

Fin glanced in Elena's direction as the young girl inched closer to the authoritative figure in the hooded cloak. Celeste gripped her sister's arm as if she might wrench it off.

"Unusual circumstances here," Gair said to Lia. He pushed his hood back, surprising them all by revealing his grandfatherly face. "You have been found guilty based on your confession, but our High Council has decided you will be given the choice of your sentence. You may be beheaded, or you may accept the punishment as outlined by the text that was just read."

Lia turned her head to look at her parents.

Celeste attempted to take a stumbling step toward

her, but Vittore and Elena held her back. Beppe stood beside his younger sister, watching without particular interest.

"I . . . I could never go home?" Lia asked, sounding confused as to exactly what was entailed in the alternative punishment that Kaleigh had proposed.

"You could never return to Italy, at least not as a Ruffino. Clare Point would become your home," Gair explained. "*We* would become your family."

Lia glanced over again at her own family. "I wouldn't . . . I wouldn't remember my mother?"

"It would be better that way, really, don't you think?" Kaleigh whispered.

Lia kept staring at her sobbing mother, her voice disconnected. "I . . . I don't know. I can't imagine never going home again."

"Take life," Celeste cried. Elena had to hold her back.

Gair glanced warningly in Fin's direction and Fin moved toward the Ruffinos.

"You must decide, child," Gair urged.

"If not for yourself," Kaleigh whispered, "do it to spare your family."

Lia's gaze drifted to Kaleigh. "You really think this is better than just . . . dying?"

Kaleigh took Lia's hands in hers. "If you become a Kahill, I'm not positive, but I think you'll take on our life-cycles."

"I would get to grow up?"

"I can't swear it, but I think so." Kaleigh gripped the girl's hands tightly. "But what's more important is that you'll have a chance to save your soul. Beheading isn't really dying, you know."

"We must have an answer," Gair announced.

Lia looked back once more at her family and then pulled her hands from Kaleigh's and turned to face the chieftain. "Yes," she said in a very small voice. "I will accept the sentence of being made a Kahill."

The teens in the woods broke into chatter at once. Celeste cried out with joy, maybe anguish, probably both, Fin thought.

"Can I say good-bye?" Lia asked.

"You've already said good-bye," Gair responded, waving Dr. Caldwell to approach. "We must begin the rite at once."

"Please?" Lia begged, putting her hands together. "Just let me walk over there. It'll only take a second. I swear."

Gair hesitated, then signaled with his wrinkled hand. "Quickly." He turned to Dr. Caldwell. "You've brought the necessary instruments?"

"Yes, sir."

Lia flew the short distance over the graves and threw herself into her mother's arms. "Forgive me," she cried.

Fin stepped back to allow the family one last moment with the girl. When Elena hugged her, he had to look away. The acting chief of police couldn't cry in front of the High Council.

"We forgive you," Celeste wailed, hugging her daughter tightly. "Of course we forgive you."

Lia pulled herself out of her mother's arms and hugged her father and her little sister. Then she looked at Beppe, and turned away. "I'm ready," she announced, walking back toward the High Council members, wiping away the tears on her face.

"Let us begin, then." Gair took a step back from the raised tomb and the other cloaked figures followed suit.

"We will need donors," Dr. Caldwell explained.

For a moment there was silence. Just the wind again and the soft sobs of a woman who would lose her child.

The sept's physician looked up. "We must have donations from our own sept. The more the better. If I'm reading Rob's explanation right, she will take on the memories of those who give their blood." He waited.

Another second skipped by.

"Me," Kaleigh said, raising her hand. "I'll donate." She looked at the Council members, a trace of anger in her voice. "Please. You only have to give half a pint."

Fin stared at the Council members, surprised by their reluctance. If they had agreed on behalf of the sept to adopt the girl, why wouldn't they be willing to offer their blood? Were they afraid of taking on the responsibility of another life? "Me," he said, making no attempt to share his annoyance. He glanced at the robed figure he knew was his sister.

"Half a pint is nothing," Fia said from under her hood, stepping forward. "Who will join me?"

"Me." Rob, who had returned to the cluster of teenagers, came down the hill, entering the cemetery again.

"Me." Katy hurried after him.

"Me."

"Sure, why not?"

"Wait for me!"

Fin watched the teens descend into the graveyard, one by one, and he felt a swell of pride.

"You have to lie here," Kaleigh told Lia, leading her up to the stone tomb.

The girl looked petrified, but she seemed to trust Kaleigh. She climbed up on the cold granite bier and lay down. Dr. Caldwell grasped her wrist and straightened out her arm. "Sorry, this is going to hurt," he warned gently. "But you won't feel anything after this."

"What . . . what will happen?" she murmured.

"You'll just go to sleep."

"Don't be afraid." Kaleigh moved to the other side of the tomb to look down on Lia.

"Wouldn't you be?" the girl asked.

"Pee-in-my-pants scared." The two teens shared a smile.

Kaleigh clasped her hand. "I'll be right here."

Gair cleared his throat. "Are you ready, Dr. Caldwell?"

"I am."

Even in the dark, Fin could see that he held a scalpel. The light from a rising moon glinted off its blade.

Gair nodded and the physician brought the instrument down her arm vertically, hitting the radial artery. Lia gasped.

Celeste strangled a sob.

Blood poured from Lia and the vampires gathered around her fought instinctual responses. Someone grunted. Others moved closer. One of the teens giggled childishly.

As the Italian girl's blood dripped down onto the soft earth, its scent rose thick and hot in the humid night air.

Kaleigh held Lia's hand tightly. The girl closed her eyes as her heart continued to pump her life's blood onto Kahill soil. Dr. Caldwell wiped at the incision with a towel and pumped her bicep, probably to keep her blood from coagulating and slowing down the process.

Celeste, clinging to her husband, continued to cry softly, but Fin saw that Elena's tears had dried. When he met her gaze, he had to remind himself that she could not communicate telepathically with him. All the same, her eyes seemed to be telling him *And now it's done*.

A woman Lia's weight probably had seven pints of blood in her. It amazed Fin how quickly seven pints of blood could flow out of a body. Only a few minutes seemed to go by before the doctor placed Lia's arm beside her and stepped back to go into his duffel bag. Fin noted that the girl's chest no longer rose and fell. There were details he still didn't understand about the physical life and death of vampires, but he knew that Lia was as close to death as possible, without being dead.

"I'll go first," Kaleigh said bravely.

The other teens fell into line behind her and Fin guessed that the adults' blood would not be needed. There had to be close to twenty kids in line; Caldwell wouldn't even need all of them.

Fin looked back and caught Elena's eye. She beckoned him. "How long until we know if it worked?" she whispered in his ear when he drew close.

"I don't know. We've never done this before. Not long, I would think."

They watched as Dr. Caldwell bandaged Lia's wound and then hooked a simple blood transfusion device to her opposite arm. One by one, starting with Kaleigh, the teens donated approximately half a pint of blood.

"What if it doesn't work?" Elena whispered after what seemed like an eternity. Dr. Caldwell had just given Lia her thirteenth donation of blood.

Fin didn't want to tell Elena that if it didn't work, their only choice would be to behead Lia after all. "It'll work," he assured her, slipping his arm around her waist.

The first time Fin thought he saw Lia move, he feared

it was his imagination. He was afraid that he wanted it so badly for Elena and for her family that he was seeing things. But others saw it, too.

"It's working," Kaleigh murmured, throwing her arms around Rob's neck. "It's working!"

Dr. Caldwell leaned over his patient and placed his stethoscope over her heart.

Everyone in the cemetery seemed to hold his or her breath, Fin noted.

. . . Except Lia.

Her chest rose. Then fell, and slowly rose and fell again.

Dr. Caldwell lowered his stethoscope and nodded to Gair. "It worked, I think," he said.

Elena buried her face in Fin's shoulder. "She is alive."

Fin kissed her head, breathing in deeply the tantalizing smell of her hair.

Gair slowly approached the girl lying on the monument and leaned over and whispered to her in Gaelic. Fin couldn't quite hear what he said, but his purpose was obvious. The Ruffinos did not speak Gaelic.

Fin heard a distinct female reply. It was Lia's voice, the same . . . yet different. In Gaelic.

Gair lifted his head and looked out at his people gathered in the dark cemetery. "The punishment has been carried out. Lia Kahill's transformation is complete."

All the teens began to talk at once. The girls hugged each other.

"Thank you all. Now go home," Gair ordered. He spoke privately to Dr. Caldwell again, presumably about taking Lia back to the doctor's office where she could be monitored, as planned.

The High Council members dispersed first, followed by the teens. Celeste, Vittore, and their two remaining children retreated silently back down the brick path that would lead them through the gate and around the church.

"You should go, too, Elena." Fin didn't want to say good-bye, but he knew it was time. He pressed his lips to her temple. "Dr. Caldwell will see that Lia is taken care of."

"But who will take her in?"

"That will have to be decided, but it won't be an issue," he explained. "Many of us have been adopted over the years. My mother has taken several teens without parents." He rubbed her arm. "We should go."

She nodded, her voice thick with emotion. "We have rented a car. We go directly to the airport."

His arm around her, he ushered her toward the gate. "I suppose that's best. I'll walk you out."

Near the gate, they passed Pete Hill, who stood off the moonlit path. It wasn't until Fin had walked by him that he halted. "Could you wait a second?" he asked, releasing her.

He walked back to Pete, and standing in front of the cop he admired so much, he removed the gold badge from his uniform. As Pete stared at him in confusion, Fin took Pete's hand and pressed the badge into it.

"What are you doing?" Pete asked.

"Resigning from the police force."

"You can't do that."

"Sure I can." On impulse, Fin removed his tie and handed that to Pete, too. "And I'm recommending to the General Council that *you* be made the new police chief. Sean obviously no longer wants the job and you're the best man to take it."

Pete stared at the badge in his hand. "I can't—"

"You *can* be the chief. You have to, Pete. I'm not cut out for this, never was. But you are. You deserve this position and I'm going to do everything in my power to see that you get it."

"Thanks, Fin," was all Pete could manage, still staring at the badge.

"You're welcome."

Fin walked back to Elena, put his arm around her, and escorted her out front to the waiting car.

"I can't thank you enough for this, Fin." Elena brought his hand to her lips and kissed it. "My family will never forget the kindness you have bestowed." At the car, she turned to face him. "We will be forever indebted to the Kahills."

"We never wanted your indebtedness. We only wanted to do what was right."

"Kiss me good-bye," she whispered.

Fin didn't want to kiss her good-bye. He wanted to continue the disagreement, only so that he could delay this moment.

"Fin—"

"I don't understand why this has to be good-bye. Why can't we—"

"I think this is better, at least for now. It will only pain my sister, any contact between our families," she explained.

"For now?" Fin felt a flutter of hope.

"For now, at least," she repeated.

He kissed her hard, fighting the feelings welling up inside him. Weren't vampires supposed to be cold-hearted? What he wouldn't have given, at this moment, to have been just a little more coldhearted.

"Good-bye." Elena pulled away from him and before he could speak again, she got into the car and closed the door.

As the car pulled away from the curb, he wished he had told her he loved her.

Fin was surprised to find Regan waiting for him, in the dark, on the front porch of their rental house.

"It work?" Regan asked.

Fin walked slowly up the sidewalk toward his brother, feeling like each of his feet weighed a ton. He wondered how long it had been since he slept, really slept. "It worked."

Regan grinned. "That Kaleigh of ours, she's pretty bright."

"That she is," Fin agreed, taking the steps one leaden foot at a time.

"Elena gone?" Regan scooted over on the top step, making room.

"Yup."

"Sorry, bro."

"Thanks." As Fin went to turn to sit down, he noticed envelopes sticking up out of the mailbox attached to the wall near the door. "When was the last time you checked the mail?"

"I don't know." Regan shrugged. "A couple of days, probably."

Fin grabbed a handful of envelopes, sales fliers, and assorted junk mail and sat down on the top step. As he dropped the mail into his lap, he noticed a beer bottle between them. "Please tell me—"

Regan snatched up the bottle and pushed it into Fin's hand. "Please. It's for you." He reached to his side and came up with an open Coke can. "I figured either way things went, you'd need it when you got home."

Fin twisted the top off and took a long drink. It tasted as good as any beer had ever tasted.

Regan looked at him more closely. "Lose your badge?"

"Yup." Fin took another drink, thinking he might need another beer. Maybe two more. "Lost my tie, too."

"I never trust a man wearing a tie, anyway." Regan grabbed the mail off Fin's lap, placed it in his own, and began to thumb through it. "So, you looking for a job?"

"Possibly." Fin closed his eyes and leaned his head against the rusty stair rail.

"I might be hiring at the arcade."

Fin chuckled.

The mail rustling stopped. "Well, I'll be damned."

"What?" Fin opened his eyes.

"He did it."

"Who did what?"

"Victor. He always said he wanted a little houseboat in the Keys." He handed Fin a postcard.

On one side was a collage of pictures depicting a sunny, tropical paradise: palm trees, clear blue waters, sandy beaches. Across it were printed the words *Weather is here, wish you were beautiful . . .*

Fin flipped the card over. It was addressed to Regan. No return address. In pretty, feminine script it instructed, *Don't close the arcade until Labor Day.*

Fin looked at Regan. Regan looked at Fin, and they both broke out in laughter. They laughed until tears ran down Fin's cheeks: tears of joy, of sadness. He cried for what he had lost, but mostly for what he knew he still had.

Welcome to the quiet coastal town of Clare Point, Delaware, where the Kahill vampire clan has made its home for centuries . . . and where one vampire's love for a human woman could put their entire world at risk . . .

RAVENOUS

As a member of his clan's kill team, Liam McCathal helps rid the world of undesirables. It's the perfect job for a vampire of his talents—except that lately, Liam is getting a little *too* good at it. Which is why he's back home to "cool off," when Mai walks into his antique store and changes everything.

Liam's not in the habit of making friends—least of all with beautiful, exotic human females. But something about Mai ignites a spark he hasn't felt in over a century. When Mai's uncle is killed and her father threatened, Liam takes on a ruthless crime boss and puts every vampire in Clare Point in danger of discovery. Because Mai's father has secrets too, and Liam is edging ever closer to losing his reputation, his clan, and the woman he would do anything to protect . . .

Please turn the page for an exciting sneak peek of RAVENOUS,
the latest Clare Point novel
available at bookstores everywhere!

L iam smelled the perversity on their hands even before he flew over the wall into the courtyard of the *palais* in the *Marais* district of Paris. He knew what the Gaudet brothers were, what they had done, what they had gotten away with for two decades, but he had not expected such a stench.

Liam landed on the stone wall and gazed down into the courtyard, slowly flapping the wings of the raven he had become. Black, beady eyes focused on the iron bars in the windows he would have to slip through. Even among shape-shifters, Liam was an oddity. Not only could he shift from his human form to an animal form of his choice, but he could shift from one animal to another, as easily as a human shrugged off a coat.

Night after night, Liam relived the nightmare and it always began here: the stink of the Gaudet brothers' sins, the soft beat of his own wings, the reflection of pale moonlight on the old glass.

What happened next in the nightmare varied. Sometimes Liam felt his body rise and glide into the night air, wings spread. Sometimes he relived slipping easily through the bars in the window, a quiet gray mouse. But always the blood came. Always black and putrid, oozing from the stone walls. From their eyes. And the screams of the children. It was always the cries of the children that brought him out of a dead sleep.

Liam startled, his eyes flying open as he gripped the thin sheet with stiff, cold fingers, his body bathed in perspiration. Darkness enveloped him; the sheet had become a death shroud and he threw it off. Had he screamed out loud again? Or was it just the screams of the tortured children in his head?

Trembling, he pushed up and off the narrow cot and stumbled, nude, to the bathroom. With a shaky hand, he pulled the string on the light overhead and the single, bare bulb threw pale, ugly light on the mirror. He leaned forward on the stained porcelain sink and gazed at his face: the face of a killer.

Yesterday at the local diner while he'd stood in line for his tuna on wheat, no pickle, he'd heard one of the old bats talking about him. They gossiped as if he wasn't there, standing behind them at the cash register. She said he'd been sent home to Clare Point in shame. She said that she'd heard the General Council was going to pull him off the Kill Team for good this time.

A cooling-off period. That's what he'd been told it was when they'd come for him in the dingy walk-up in Montmartre. Then they'd had the nerve to *escort* him all the way home to Clare Point, as if he would have disobeyed orders and gone into hiding if they hadn't. Which, of course, he would have.

Liam brushed his fingertips over the crucifix he wore around his neck, then spun the antique faucet handle and splashed cold water on his face. Then he washed his hands. As if he could ever wash the blood off. . . .

He had disobeyed a direct order the night he had flown into the Gaudet courtyard. He'd broken multiple rules in the ancient book.

. . . Even before he had broken their bones.

Liam shut off the faucet and ran his hand through his dark hair, glancing into the mirror again. Black, heartless eyes looked back at him, the raven's eyes. He turned away. What if they really did pull him off the Kill Team? A hundred years, the penalty for his disobedience if it came down to punishment, was a hell of a long *cooling-off* period. What would he do then? He couldn't imagine living here in this silly little town with its silly little problems. Not after lifetimes of travel. Not after the things he had seen. The things he had done. He had the highest kill count of any man or woman in the sept; he was good at what he did and they knew it. The Council wouldn't really pull him off the Kill Team, would they?

The sweat on his body had dried and suddenly he was cold. Shivering, he went back to the small, bare room, pulled on a pair of sweatpants, a T-shirt, and a hoodie, then slipped on his running shoes. Just as the sun rose over the lip of the ocean, he burst into the cold morning air and ran, ran for his life, for his salvation. It never worked, of course, but you couldn't blame a vampire for trying.

After a five-mile run along the beach, Liam showered, ate a piece of cold pizza from a box on the counter, and went down to the antiques shop below his apartment. He'd been a *purveyor of antiquities* for more than two hundred years, although nowadays he was an *antiques dealer*. When he wasn't stalking serial killers and pedophiles. It was easy enough work, a good cover when he was forced to return home, and it allowed him to pay his bills and travel at his own expense rather than the sept's.

Liam bought things all over the world—some new, some already antiques—and shipped them home. He acquired items that struck his fancy: clocks, paintings, sculptures. He'd bought three Model T trucks in 1925 for $281 each. He had sold the last one only the previous year for so much money that he was almost too embarrassed to accept the cashier's check. Almost.

He sold the items out of the little antiques shop when he was in town; otherwise, he advertised them and had someone in Clare Point make the actual sale. Internet sales were his latest venture. It had been three years since the last time Liam had been home, but he continually sent items back to the States so the place was stacked tall with shipping boxes, most never opened.

When Liam had returned to the *loving bosom* of the vampire nest, he'd been warned by the General Council leader that he'd be in Clare Point for at least a few weeks. He was to be interviewed and his case investigated. While imprisoned in the sleepy seaside town, he thought he might as well make use of his time and dig through some of the mess. He had a warehouse, too, but right now, he couldn't imagine even walking into it.

Thinking he'd start small, this morning he'd just picked a pile of boxes and begun to open them. They were pretty old boxes. Inside, he found all sorts of kitchen gadgets, which he organized on shelves along one wall of the shop. It was dusty, boring work, but he didn't mind; he liked the solitude. His reward for his diligence throughout the morning was the box he'd just opened. Inside was a brand, spanking new 1936 KitchenAid stand-up mixer. Still in its original packing. If memory served, he had three more somewhere.

Pleased with his find, Liam was searching for an electric outlet behind the impossibly piled-up counter when he heard the little bell over the front door ring. Surprised by the melodic sound, he turned. He must have left it unlocked when he returned from his run this morning. "We're closed," he called. "Read the sign."

"Sign says open." A gorgeous Asian woman turned the dusty sign around so that it now read OPEN on the back of the door.

Liam frowned. It must have flipped when he slammed the door. "I'm still closed," he told her, trying not to stare.

Liam didn't like HFs. *Human females.* Well, actually, he liked them a lot. Which was exactly why he stayed away from them. This one was stunning: late twenties, early thirties, tiny, with long, dark hair, brown eyes, and a rich skin tone. Her face was oval with sensual lips. Cherry ChapStick. He could smell it from here. He loved the taste of cherry ChapStick on a woman. She looked delicate. Fragile. But there was a fire in her eyes, fire and a definite hint of amusement.

"You know, I've been coming here for the last five years hoping to catch you open."

"Too bad you caught me closed again," Liam deadpanned. He stood where he was, not trusting himself to walk toward her. If he did, he might reach out to touch the silky black hair that had pulled loose from her ponytail and fell to frame her exquisite face. There was an equal chance he'd bite her in the neck. Then he'd have to erase her memory, deposit her on the curb, and hope no one saw him. He was already in enough trouble as it was. They were a messy business, humans, which was, again, why he stayed away from them.

"That a '36 KitchenAid? Wow." She walked toward him with little or no sense of self-preservation. Of course, she didn't know he was a vampire; they rarely did. "Brand new? You've got to be kidding me. You know, this was the first year they downsized them, making them practical for homes." She drew her small fingers over the white enamel and Liam found himself wondering what it would be like to feel her fingertips caress his bare skin.

She was pretending to look at the mixer, but he knew she was looking at him. He had that effect on women. All vampires did, on some level, even the old guys and gals. There was something about vampires that tragically drew humans to them, even though they never recognized them for what they were. Vampires accepted this age-old truth but never quite understood it.

He blinked, clearing his head. "You an expert on the history of the KitchenAid mixer?"

"Not an expert. But I love kitchen appliances. Kitchen gadgets, too: glass fruit reamers, oyster servers, ice cream knives. I sell antiques in a shop in Lewes." She looked at the electric plug he still held in his hand. "So, does it work?"

"I . . . I don't know."

"You going to plug it in and see?"

He was just about to give a smart-ass reply when a car horn beeped loudly out in the street. Through the filmy storefront window, he spotted a minivan. It honked again. Louder.

"That you?"

"That's me." She glanced at the window, then back at him. "Actually, it's not me. It's my dad. We're late for lunch."

"It's eleven-thirty."

"Senior citizen. What can I say?"

She opened her arms and he imagined the feel of them around him. He didn't know what was going on here. He wasn't usually like this. He was *never* like this. Not with an HF. But she kept looking at him and he couldn't keep himself from looking back.

Again the horn.

"I better go," she said.

He hesitated, then pushed the plug into the outlet and switched the mixer on. The motor purred.

She turned back to him, smiling. Her face lit up the room in a way that made his black heart ache.

"It works!"

"It works," he said, stifling his own enthusiasm. There was no need to be too nice. Nice got you in trouble.

She glanced around as she walked toward the door. "You *sure* you're closed? You have some amazing things here. Oh, my God! Is that a Neuchâtel clock Le Castel?"

"Where?" He followed her to the door, trying not to get too close to her. It was the smell of HFs that he loved. Not just their blood, but their skin, their hair, their sweet body scents; it was everything about them. The smell of their shampoo, their hand cream, even nail polish. Liam knew right then he should walk away. Play it safe. He wasn't good at safe.

"There!" She pointed to a pile of junk. "Inside that nasty birdcage."

He glanced in the direction she pointed. The place was so stacked up with crap, furniture covered in canvas drapes, wooden crates of mysterious stuff from far-off places, and cardboard boxes turned over, spilling their contents, that it took him a second to make out the outline of the clock behind the bars of a birdcage. "I think so."

"You *think* so?" She arched a dark eyebrow. "You know how much that's worth? You don't even have bars on your windows." She glanced at the dirty, old-fashioned storefront window. "No alarm system. You're lucky no one has robbed you blind."

"We don't see a lot of robberies in Clare Point." He opened the door for her and the bell rang over their heads, strangely melodic to his ears. The truth was, they had *no* robberies. The vampires of the Kahill sept owned all the property in the town and patrolled their own streets. The occasional burglar who tried to break into a house or store was escorted out of town by one of its citizens, and though his memory was erased, he never lost the feeling that something had scared the crap out of him in Clare Point. Scared him badly enough that he didn't return.

"I wish you were open," the woman said longingly, looking back over her shoulder one last time at the piles of treasures.

The old man in the front passenger seat of the van laid on the horn again.

"Enough, *Babbo!*" she shouted.

"You're *Italian?*" It was his turn to lift an eyebrow incredulously. She didn't *look* Italian.

"Sicilian and Vietnamese. I look like my mom. You speak Italian?"

"A little," Liam answered.

Again the old man blew the car horn. And against all reason, Liam found himself being drawn in to their sweet, mortal humanity and actually chuckling. Even more surprising, he heard himself say, "Maybe another day. When things aren't such a mess. I just got back into the country."

"I don't mind coming another time. When you're open." She studied his face. "But you're not planning on opening, are you? You're just blowing me off."

"No. I'm not." And he meant it.

"So how about if I give you a few days and then I call you? You got a business card?"

"Somewhere in this mess, probably." He looked around, then back at her.

"How about just a number?" She pulled a pen out of the bag slung over her shoulder and dug deeper. "Why can I never find a piece of—"

Her father hit the horn, long and hard, drowning out her voice. "I'm going to kill him," she said when Liam could hear her again. "But I guess that's illegal in this state."

"Most states," he suggested.

She poised the pen over her hand. "Give me your number and I'll get that public nuisance off the street."

He gave her his cell number, already having second thoughts. But then he realized there was no harm in giving her the number. He didn't answer his phone half the time anyway.

"Thanks." She started to back out the door, then took a step toward him, offering her hand. "I never introduced myself. I'm Mai, Mai Ricci. My dad is Corrato. The old coot in the backseat"—she leaned so she could get a better look at the van—"*that's* his *older* brother, Donato."

Liam held her hand a second longer than he should have. Her handshake was firm, her touch warm. This close, he could smell the fragrance of her shampoo and he found himself breathing deeply. "Liam McCathal," he said.

"Nice to meet you, Liam." She pulled her hand from his and raised the other, showing him the number written in black marker. "I'll call. Maybe we can do some business. I'd at least like to have a look at that clock."

Liam closed the door behind her, making sure he locked it this time. *I'll never see her again,* he thought to himself. Just as well. She didn't smell just of herbal shampoo; she smelled of danger.

"So exactly *what* is the purpose of this stakeout?" Katy stirred her mug with a spoon until it was a whirlpool of creamy white marshmallow and chocolate.

Kaleigh glanced out the window of the coffee shop that was situated diagonally across the street from Alice's Antiques. The lights were out. The sign on the door said CLOSED but she knew Liam was in there. She could feel his presence. She looked back at her best friend and sipped her iced tea. It was early October; it would be cold soon enough. She wasn't ready to switch to wintertime drinks. "It's not a stakeout."

"Feels like a stakeout."

Kaleigh's gaze drifted to the storefront window again. She hadn't seen Liam since she'd been reborn. This was always awkward, seeing people again through this young girl's eyes.

"You know, I heard he had to come home because he ate some bad guys."

Kaleigh cut her eyes at Katy. "*Ate* them?"

"You know, cannibalized them. Killed them, put them on a spit, and roasted their juiciest parts. Then he ate them."

"You need to stop listening to the gossip gaggle at the diner, Katy. Your brain is turning into rice pudding."

"I'm just saying, that's what they said."

"That's gross. Liam did not eat anyone. Can you imagine how nasty a serial killer would taste?"

Katy made a face and sipped her hot chocolate. "It does sound kind of disgusting. Even for Liam. The weirdo. He's way too dark and gloomy for me." She licked her finger, wiped it on the empty plate to catch any stray cookie crumbs, and popped it in her mouth. "Oh, I brought the book for you."

"I told you, I'm not going to read it. It's stupid."

"It's not stupid." Katy dug into the backpack at her feet and pulled out a hardcover book. "It's the best series that's ever been written." She slid it across the table. "You're the only person I know who hasn't read it, or seen the movies."

"I don't understand how you can like it. You said they got a lot of things wrong about vampires. And Bella makes out with a werewolf?" Kaleigh made a face of disgust. "I've met a werewolf, Katy. They slobber. They're disgusting. There's no way you'd give a werewolf tongue."

"Please? Just read it. You should know what everyone is talking about, at least."

Kaleigh reluctantly accepted the book and crammed it in her backpack.

"And then we can watch the movies together. I have all the DVDs!"

"I'm not watching the movies with you," Kaleigh warned.

Katy exhaled. "Change of subject. You taking the SATs tomorrow?"

"My mom paid the money, but I don't know." She started picking her schoolbooks up off the floor and sticking them into her backpack.

"You don't know *what?*"

"I don't know if I'm taking them."

"You don't know if you're taking your SATs? Kaleigh, this is our last chance! College applications have to be in soon. You can't go to college if you don't take your SATs."

Her books packed, Kaleigh worked the zipper of her backpack. The stupid thing stuck all the time.

Katy watched her. "You're not really considering not going to college, are you? We finally all get permission to leave town for college and you don't want to go? Are you out of your cotton-pickin' "—she glanced around the mostly empty shop to make sure she saw no humans "bloodsucking mind? Me, I'm going. I'm going as far as I can get from here. Stanford's at the top of my list."

"Stanford isn't on the list. We can only go to colleges approved by the General Council. It has to be a place where they think we'll be safe, where there's one of them close enough to get there if we get into trouble."

Katy sat back in her chair, crossing her arms over her chest. "Guess they better add Stanford to the list, because I just might get in. And if I do, I'm going, and those old farts on the Council aren't going to stop me."

"Weren't you one of those old farts a couple of years ago before you were reborn?"

"We're not talking about me. We're talking about you, Kaleigh." She leaned forward, elbows on the table. "Why wouldn't you go to college?" she asked, softening her tone.

"I have responsibilities here. The world's changing. It's getting harder and harder to keep our cover and the humans seem to be cranking out more psychos every year. It's more dangerous when we're spread thin, all over the world. I think my place is here."

"Bullshit, Miss Wisewoman. If you're going to help us keep our cover, you need to be a part of the world. You need to know what we're facing."

Kaleigh knew Katy made a good point; she just didn't know if it was good enough. "Mom already paid, so I guess maybe I'll go."

"Great. Can you drive? We have to be at Cape Henelopen High School by seven forty-five."

"You grounded *again?*" Kaleigh laughed, finishing her iced tea. "What'd you do now?"

"Total misunderstanding." Katy got up, taking her backpack off.

"I can borrow Arlan's truck. He and Fia went somewhere for the weekend."

"Cool. See you in the morning." She pulled a couple of wrinkled bills out of the pocket of her jeans and left them on the table. "My turn. You pay next time."

Kaleigh took her time getting her stuff together. As she pulled her sweatshirt over her head, she watched the window across the street. She could still feel

Liam's presence. It was hard to miss. He wasn't a weirdo like Katy said, but he was one of the darkest souls she knew. She respected him a great deal. She even liked him, but he scared her sometimes.

She didn't believe the nonsense about him eating those guys in Paris. But she had questions. And sooner or later, whether either of them liked it or not, she was going to have to walk through the door of the antiques shop and he was going to have to start talking.